"Ever let an[...] [o]n the other side of the door.

"What do *you* think?"

"I think I'll pull out one of your fingernails," Nikki said thoughtfully. "No, two."

"*That* seems rather rude. . . ."

"I know, I know. Usually I let *him* do all the work—some of the stuff he does, I can't stand even being in the same room. But for you, sweetheart, I'll make an exception."

"And who is he supposed to be? Your big bad pimp, charging in to save you in his shining Cadillac?"

"No. He's in the same business you are."

"What?"

"He kills people. Slowly."

"*Sure* he does—"

There was a crackle of electricity, followed by something heavy hitting the door. It swung open slowly, revealing her partner with a stun gun in his hand, and her captor unconscious at his feet.

Nikki lit a cigarette. "This is the Closer, you poor bastard. I almost pity you."

She kicked him in the head, hard.

"*Almost,*" she snarled.

THE CLOSER

DONN CORTEZ

POCKET STAR BOOKS
New York   London   Toronto   Sydney

An *Original* Publication of POCKET BOOKS

 A Pocket Star Book published by
POCKET BOOKS, a division of Simon & Schuster, Inc.
1230 Avenue of the Americas, New York, NY 10020

ISBN: 0-7434-7698-0

First Pocket Books printing October 2004

10 9 8 7 6 5 4 3 2 1

POCKET STAR BOOKS and colophon are registered
trademarks of Simon & Schuster, Inc.

Cover design by Carlos Beltran

Manufactured in the United States of America

For information regarding special discounts for bulk purchases,
please contact Simon & Schuster Special Sales at 1-800-456-6798
or business@simonandschuster.com.

For Juliet, who taught me
about the tears of Mermaids

ACKNOWLEDGMENTS

I'd like to thank the following: my agent, Lucienne Diver, for her tireless work on my behalf; my editor, Kevin Smith; Chris and Nikki, for tent-trailer assistance; the Vancouver Freaks group for various kinds of support, technical and otherwise; the Templeton Café and Bon's Off Broadway, for providing atmosphere, dazzling waitresses and lots of coffee; and all the people who believed in me, stuck by me and treated me as fairly as I treated them.

A special thanks goes out to Coyote—one storyteller to another.

PART ONE:

Inspiration

Our torments also may in length of time
Become our elements.

—Milton, *Paradise Lost*

CHAPTER ONE

It was a slow night on the Stroll, and Susanna grinned when the late-model Taurus with the rental plates pulled over. Rental plates meant an out-of-town businessman with an itchy credit card and a lonely hotel room; it meant a quick hundred dollars, maybe one-twenty with tip. It meant she could kick off her damn shoes for a few minutes, and go someplace where the wind wasn't turning her nipples into raw pencil erasers.

She leaned over and stuck her head into the passenger-side window. The guy driving was a surprise—younger than she'd expected, with a shaved head, scruffy goatee and chrome rings piercing his eyebrows and lower lip.

Street instincts sized him up in the time it took her to smile. Once, anybody looking like him was sure to be trouble; these days, everyone under the age of thirty seemed to have something pierced. Susanna herself had a ring through her belly button.

What the fuck. Maybe he's got some coke.

"Hey," she said. "Wanna date?"

"Nah," he said, matching her grin. "I just pulled over for a few fashion tips."

She laughed despite herself. The outfit she was wearing—black latex minidress with four-inch matching heels—was brand new. She knew it showed off both her long legs and her waist-length black hair, but she didn't expect a john to appreciate it as any more than a candy wrapper.

"Well," she said, "I know what'd look good on *you*."

"What's that?"

"Me."

He chuckled and nodded, his piercings glinting chrome green in the glow of the dash. "Okay. I'm in."

"Not yet," she said sweetly, "but you will be."

She got in on the passenger's side. He pulled smoothly away from the curb.

"I'm Todd," the driver said.

"Susanna."

"For a second, I thought you were going to tell me to get lost," Todd said. "What, I don't look like I have a Gold Card?"

"Just checking you out. A girl can't be too careful, you know?"

"Sure, I understand. Lotta freaks out there . . ."

Afterward, he lay in the hotel bed, smoking.

Man, that was sweet. Not as good as the real thing, of course, but pretty good all the same.

He put his arms behind his head and stretched out luxuriously. *And the stupid bitch never suspected a thing. Thought I was Mr. Normal. Hah.*

The bathroom door opened and Susanna stepped out, wearing the minidress but barefoot. She bent down and grabbed her stiletto heels from the floor.

"That was great, Todd," she said. "I'm gonna go wait for my cab downstairs, okay?"

"Sure," Todd said with a lazy grin. "Hey, I'm going to be in town for a few days—you got a number I can reach you at?"

"I left my business card beside the sink. It's got my pager number," she said, wincing as she put on her shoes. "Call me any time you feel like a party."

She was halfway out the door when he said, "Hey, wait a sec!"

She turned back. He motioned toward the table beside the door. "At least finish your drink. . . ."

She grabbed the scotch and water he'd mixed for her and downed the last half of it. "Thanks," she said. "That'll keep me going."

"And everybody else coming," he said, grinning.

As the door swung shut he called out, "And hey— be careful! Lotta freaks out there!"

Click.

He got out of bed naked and padded over to the door. He took a tissue from the box on the table and used it, very carefully, to pick up the glass Susanna had used.

He held it up to the lamp on the nightstand and squinted at it. He could see several usable fingerprints already.

"Oh yeah," he murmured. "Whole lotta freaks out there . . ."

• • •

The hooker's name was Nikki. She was in her early thirties, pretty, her hair currently long and blond. Makeup hid the lines in her face. She got her tan from a UV booth and her smile from years of practice; her eyes were as sharp and blue as a pissed-off Siamese cat's. Skintight white pants and a black halter top showed off her flat belly—she had the hard physique of someone who treated her body the same way a soldier treated his gun.

Her feet sported a pair of stylish white sneakers with four-inch soles. A thick chain bracelet, heavy with charms, was her only jewelry. She chewed gum constantly, and blew big pink bubbles from lips exactly the same shade.

Nikki had been on the street circuit since she was seventeen; she knew how it functioned. The first thing she'd done when she'd gotten into town was find the all-night coffee shop where the working girls hung— there was always a place near the Stroll—and get a quick feel for the scene. She'd worked Seattle before, but things shifted; it was always a good idea to check out the flow first. She didn't want any territory hassles.

A black car pulled up. Nikki bent down to talk into the open passenger-side window, then got in. The car pulled away.

A second later, a white van rolled out of the alley. It swung in behind the black car and followed it at a discreet distance.

Nikki turned in the seat to face the driver and studied him coolly. He was middle-aged, white, balding. Typical. His suit was wrinkled and badly out of style, and the car smelled of old tobacco. "So, Stanley," she said. "What do you like?"

"I, uh—nothing unusual, really. And call me Stan."

"Okay, Stan—so what's *usual?*"

"Uh, well—I'm sorry, but I really don't want to get into any trouble. You're not—you're not a policewoman, are you? I've heard they sometimes disguise themselves—"

"Oh, is that the problem? Okay."

She leaned over and slid a hand into his crotch. He gasped, but she left her hand there.

"If I was a cop, think I'd do this?"

"N—no, I guess not."

He gave her an embarrassed smile. She smiled back and blew a big pink bubble.

Ah, Todd thought as he dropped his duffel bag on the floor. *It's good to be home.*

Not that "home" was much. A studio apartment with a pull-out bed, a desk and a dresser, a tiny kitchenette that could hold two people at a time. He hadn't bothered to put anything on the bare white walls, and the small space reserved for a dining table was occupied by a mountain bike. He usually ate out, or over the sink.

The apartment was really only a place to sleep—and to keep his most prized posession, which he headed straight for. It was his lifeline, his doorway into the Real World.

As soon as he sat down and logged in he began to relax. He stretched, yawning. It had been a long flight—but hey, you did what you had to. Besides, it wasn't like the job didn't have its perks. He thought about the hooker's legs wrapped around his waist, and grinned.

He dived into the datastream of the web with the same fierce joy a snowboarder would show the Matterhorn. Graphics blurred past as he jumped from website to website, checking out postings, gossip, rumors. The websites had names like Serial Killer Hall of Fame, True Gore, and Monsters of the 20th Century; they were as familiar to him as the local mall, and about as tame.

Time for the real deal.

The chat room was called the Stalking Ground. It was his own system, a dedicated server accessible only through an intricate system of encryption and rerouted messages. He logged on with his name—not Todd, which was about as genuine as the name the hooker had given him—but his real name, the one he'd taken for himself: Djinn-X.

The screen split into three horizontal bands of color: black, red, and white. At the very top of the screen was the word *Discussion* in elegant script. Djinn-X's name appeared in the right-hand corner of the top band, which was black. There was a picture of a blindfolded woman screaming on the far left margin; when he typed, her mouth moved and his words appeared in a dripping, blood-red font.

DJINN-X: Hey, fellow hunters . . . looks like we'll have a new member of The Pack pretty soon!

The second band on the screen was a swirling red, and the name in the right-hand corner was The Gourmet. His icon to the left of the screen was an animated meat cleaver, which split a skull and released a little gray brain, over and over. When he typed, the thick black letters slowly coalesced as if appearing out of a scarlet mist.

GOURMET: He's passed the initiation?

DJINN-X: Not yet, but the sheep is on the altar—
sent her stats last night.

The third band on the screen was a crisp, clean white. The name in the corner was Road Rage, in elegant script. The font used was the same, verging on calligraphy but simple and easy to read.

ROAD RAGE: Did anyone see the Patron's latest posting?

Djinn-X grinned. "All right! The master of disaster returns. . . ."

GOURMET: Not yet. Body count?

ROAD RAGE: Only five.

DJINN-X: When you're talking about the Patron, numbers don't matter and you know it. It's *how* he did them. Hang on, I gotta go check it out.

He jumped to another area of the site. The expression on Djinn-X's face went from intense interest to shock to outright awe as he scanned the screen. "Fuck *me*. . . ." he whispered in admiration. He scrolled down greedily, then returned to the discussion page.

DJINN-X: Can you believe that? "Drowned in the youngest child's blood." God*damn*.

GOURMET: He's a genius.

ROAD RAGE: He's a monster. Even by our standards.

Djinn-X shook his head and leaned back. "He's both, boys," he said softly. "He's both."

Stan's house was two stories high with the first built flush to the ground, and looked exactly like every other house in the suburban cul-de-sac: painted white with red tile roofing, a white iron-railing fence with stone pillars every few feet and cheesy plaster lions on top of them.

The automatic garage door opened as the car approached. The van pulled over a block away.

Nikki followed Stan from the garage through a connecting door to the kitchen. Beige linoleum on the floor, appliances in Harvest Gold. Formica countertops in a sunshine yellow that didn't quite match the fridge or stove. A sink piled with dirty dishes, but otherwise clean. Her wet sneakers squeaked on the linoleum.

"The bedroom's this way," Stan said. He seemed more relaxed now. They always did, once they were on their home turf. She followed him down a short hallway.

The bedroom itself was about what she expected: nondescript, unmade double bed, pile of dirty clothes on a chair by the window. Heavy drapes on the window, drawn shut. A musky odor was evident, a mix of unwashed sheets and stale air.

"Would you mind, um, washing your hands?" said Stan. "Before we start? The bathroom's right through there."

He pointed. The bathroom door was just off the bedroom, and opened inward.

"Sure. Why don't you make yourself comfortable?"

He circled the house silently. All the doors were locked, but he found a sliding glass door off the sundeck. He pulled a glass cutter from the pack slung over his shoulder. It took him less than a minute to etch a circle in the glass, pop that out and reach inside to unlock the door.

He pocketed the glass cutter and pulled out something the size and shape of an electric razor. He tested it; a blue spark leapt from electrode to electrode where the rotating heads would have been. Holding the stun gun at the ready, he stepped across the threshold.

Nikki entered the bathroom, keeping the door open.

The bathroom was narrow and claustrophobic, done completely in white tile. There was no towel rack, no towels, no mirror and no window. A recessed light was set into the ceiling, and an inset fan above the toilet. There was a bathtub that had a shower head, but no shower curtain. There were no toiletries of any kind except for an almost empty roll of toilet paper hanging on the wall.

The sink was against the far wall, forcing Nikki to go all the way into the room to wash her hands. She wrinkled her nose; the place smelled like the basement of a parking garage.

She entered warily and turned on the faucet in the sink. No water came out.

"Hey, your sink's busted—"

The door slammed shut. The other side of the door had a poster of a kitten hanging from a branch, with the words *Just hang in there!* printed on it.

"Stan?"

She tried the door. Locked. She looked around, then pulled a cell phone out of her purse and hit a button. The phone gave her a *No Carrier* message.

There was a loud thump from the other room. Nikki put her cell phone back in her purse—and pulled out a .38 instead.

"I've got a gun, *Stanley*. Unlock the door or I'll blow the fucking doorknob off."

A voice crackled from the other side of the door. It sounded like someone whispering into a bullhorn, with the volume cranked way up.

"Stanley isn't available at the moment. He's . . . *busy*."

Nikki fired. The doorknob was some kind of heavy-duty industrial model; the bullet ricocheted off it and shattered a tile beside the shower head.

"Go ahead, shoot the door," the voice whispered. "How many bullets do you have?"

Nikki hesitated, then rapped the butt of the gun against the door. It rang like metal. She traced her fingers over dents in the metal, recently painted over, and nodded slowly.

"Look behind the poster," the voice whispered.

She peeled the poster away. There were six photographs taped to the door behind it; three were obviously from a black-and-white video feed, taken from a POV above the bathroom door. They showed three different women, all obviously prostitutes, all with long blond hair. The first woman was looking at a cell phone in her hand with a confused expression; the second woman was angrily pounding on the door with a gun in her hand; the third was naked and pleading, hands clasped together and tears ruining her mascara.

The next three were color Polaroids. They showed the same women with their throats cut.

She looked up. Now that she knew it was there, she spotted the pinhole camera above the door immediately. She took the gum from her mouth and blocked it.

There was a hissing sound as gas began to come in via the shower head.

"What type are you?" the voice whispered.

"I'll tell you if you shut off the gas," she said coolly.

"A bargainer. Good. I prefer those, I really do. I don't like the bitchy ones. Unblock the camera and you have a deal."

She did. The gas shut off, leaving an acrid smell hanging in the air. She tried to keep her breathing shallow, but it still burned the inside of her nose.

"See? I'm a reasonable man. Go ahead."

"Go ahead and what?"

"Offer me something."

"I guess you wouldn't just settle for a blow job, huh?"

Laughter, crackling with static. "You'll have to do better than that. I've had women offer to be my slave, to fuck dogs, to eat their own shit. One even offered her best friend in her place."

"What about the ones that don't offer you anything?"

"Oh, the *threateners*. They always say the same things—my boyfriend's in the Mafia, I'm really a cop, I have AIDS. I had one put a voodoo curse on me, though—that was entertaining. But sooner or later, the threateners always turn into the pleaders."

"Ever let anyone go?" Nikki asked.

"What do you think?"

"I think I'll pull out one of your fingernails," Nikki said thoughtfully. "No, two."

"That seems rather rude . . ."

"I know, I know. Usually I let *him* do all the work—some of the shit he does, I can't stand even being in the same room. But for you, sweetheart—I'll make an exception."

"And who's *he* supposed to be? Your big bad pimp, charging in to save you in his shining Cadillac?"

"Fuck, no. He's in the same business you are—
Stanley."

"What?"

"He kills people. Slowly."

"*Sure* he does—"

There was a sudden crackle of static from the
speaker, followed by something heavy slamming into
the other side of the bathroom door.

"That would be him, now . . ." Nikki said. She
fished a pack of cigarettes out of her purse.

The door swung slowly open. Her partner stood in
the doorway, stun gun in one hand. Stanley, unconscious, lay at his feet.

Nikki lit her cigarette and looked down at Stanley.
She shook her head.

"This is the *Closer,* you poor bastard. I almost pity
you."

She kicked him in the head, hard.

"*Almost,*" she snarled.

Stanley woke to find he was bound, naked, to a chair
in his own kitchen. There was a rubber sheet under
the chair. His wrists were tied together in front of him,
and lashed to his knees. Duct tape sealed his mouth.

The Closer entered with a black bag, which he set
down on a chair and opened. He was around thirty,
with mid-length brown hair that hadn't seen a comb
in a while, and wore a black leather trenchcoat. He
began to empty the bag of its contents, which he carefully arranged on the table.

A box of surgical gloves.

A small vise, a hatchet and a pair of pliers.

A pair of pruning shears.

A hacksaw and a ball-peen hammer.

A packet of razor blades, a clear Baggie full of fish-hooks, and a box of table salt.

A container of lighter fluid, a can of Drano, and a large hypodermic needle.

An electric knife.

A propane torch.

The last items he pulled out were a small tape recorder and half a dozen cassette tapes.

"Now, then," he said calmly as he pulled on a pair of surgical gloves. He put a tape into the cassette deck and hit *Record*.

"Let's go back to the beginning. . . ."

He reached out and ripped the duct tape off Stanley's mouth with one hand.

With the other, he picked up the hacksaw.

She found them in a shoebox in the closet, eight white linen napkins folded into neat triangles and sealed in Ziploc bags. In the center of each napkin was the scarlet imprint of a pair of lips, a kiss captured on cloth.

Nikki studied them. Each bag had a letter stenciled on the back in Magic Marker. She found one with a G on it, and inhaled sharply.

"Gee . . . Genevieve? Is that you?"

She sat down on the bed and pulled off the blond wig, tossing it to the side. She stared at the napkin through the clear plastic of the Baggie, studying the lips and tracing their outline with a fingertip. She suddenly felt immensely weary, like her body weighed a thousand pounds.

"Oh, Genny. I hope you're in a better place, sweetie. I hope this helps."

A muffled but agonized scream came from the kitchen.

Nikki butted her cigarette out in a large, empty ash-tray beside the bed. She let the baggy fall to the floor and put her head down, covering her face with her hands.

"I know you're lying."

"No! No! I swear to God!"

"You're as predictable as your victims. First you'll deny you were really going to do anything, that it was all just a game. Then you'll act tough, say I have no proof, threaten to sue me. When that doesn't work you'll try bribery, and finally pleading."

"I'm telling the truth, please, oh Christ—"

"And then we arrive at this point." The Closer reached down, selected a razor blade. He leaned forward intently. "This is when you lie. You tell me something that I'll have to go check, because stalling is the only option you have left."

He crammed a rag in Stanley's mouth to stifle his screams, and worked in quick, precise strokes. The flesh peeled back easily. He used fishhooks to pin the flaps to the tops of Stanley's ears.

"We're past that point now. Now you're going to start telling the truth."

Stanley nodded, tears leaking from his eyes, then gave a muffled yelp as the salty drops slid across the raw, exposed meat of his cheeks.

"Consider that a preview," the Closer said. He picked up the box of salt.

He reached down for Stanley's gag, then stopped. The two flaps of skin stretched to either side, with their tracery of red and blue veins, had their own grotesque beauty; they looked like the wings of a flesh butterfly, with Stanley's nose the body.

The Closer shook his head, and removed the gag.

"Look in the freezer," Stanley gasped. "Look in the freezer, I did it for the initiation. I'll tell you everything I know about them, just *please don't kill me....*"

And Stanley began to tell him some very interesting things.

Seven hours later.

The Closer raised a bloody, rubber-gloved hand and opened the bedroom curtains a crack, letting in a ray of early morning sun. Outside, a kid delivered a newspaper. In a house across the street, a mother kissed her husband good-bye as he got ready to drive his kids to school. The Closer stared at them, regret on his face.

In the kitchen, Nikki sat in a chair next to the table. Various bloody implements were scattered over the table's surface.

"Know what she liked to do on her days off?" Nikki asked Stanley. "Dress in baggy clothes, baseball cap, no makeup, and try to meet guys. Seriously. She wouldn't go to a bar, but anywhere else was fair game: the park, the library, the fucking corner store. Wanted to meet someone who didn't just want to fuck, she said. I told her, *all* guys just want to fuck—only difference between 'em is that some are willing to pay for it. Lucky for us." She paused, fumbling for a cigarette.

"Except then a prick like you comes along, Stanley, and all the luck turns shitty." She lit the cigarette, her hands trembling.

"I rehearsed what I was going to say a million times, you son of a bitch. What I was going to say when I finally caught you. Now it feels like it doesn't make any fucking difference." She shook her head and gave a grim little laugh.

"But there's a few things I want you to know. Her real name was Janet, not Genevieve, and—and people *liked* her. She was a good person. She liked cheesy disco music and going to malls, and old cars from the fifties and drinking beer and she wasn't a goddamn *trophy* to stick in a shoebox after you *killed* her, you sick *fuck!*"

One of Stanley's eyes hung from the socket. It swung grotesquely against his face as he twitched.

"Kill me . . ." Stanley whispered.

"Is that all? *No fucking problem.*"

She grabbed the hatchet and raised it over her head.

Before she could bring it down, the Closer seized it from behind.

"No."

Nikki whirled to face him, furious. She didn't let go of the hatchet.

"Why the fuck *not?* You said you were finished with him!"

"I am. But I can't let you kill him."

Tears of rage and sorrow spilled down Nikki's face. "He killed my *friend,* goddammit!"

"I know. But we made a deal when we agreed to work together. You take one kind of risk, I take another."

She glared at him, then let go of the hatchet.

"You don't want blood on your hands, Nikki. Not even his."

"Okay, okay." She locked eyes with the Closer. "But this time—I want to *watch.*"

The Closer met her eyes levelly, his face unreadable. "All right."

He turned without warning and swung the hatchet at Stanley's skull.

Dymund and Fimby arrived at Stanley's house at 3:15 P.M. Three police cars, the coroner's wagon and a newsvan were crowded into the end of the cul-de-sac. Neighbors gathered in a small, nervous clump across the street.

Dymund was the senior detective. He was close to retirement, tall and bulky, with thin white hair he kept slicked back.

Fimby was the junior. He had a pear-shaped body and a pear-shaped face, with a salt-and-pepper handlebar mustache riding on top of fleshy jowls. Both of them wore tan trenchcoats and fedoras—not so much for style as to fend off Seattle's ever-present rain.

"It's gotta be him," Dymund said as they walked in the front door, flashing their badges at the patrolman who guarded it.

"It's not him," replied Fimby.

"*Gotta* be him."

"*Can't* be him."

They entered the kitchen and saw the body for the first time. They both stopped dead and stared for a second.

"Okay," said Fimby. "It's him."

"Oh, yeah."

Dymund leaned in to take a closer look at the body as Fimby snapped on a pair of rubber gloves.

"It's the Closer, all right," Dymund sighed. Fimby picked up one of the five cassette tapes lying in a neat stack on the table.

"Four tapes," said Fimby. "Ninety minutes each. Six hours."

"Whatever else he is, he's thorough."

Another patrolman entered the kitchen. His face was pale, and he carefully avoided looking directly at what was left of Stanley.

"Detective? We've found a second body."

They followed him to a back room where a police photographer was taking a picture of an open freezer. Dymund and Fimby peered inside.

The body was young, nude and female. Her throat had been cut.

"Right hand missing," Fimby said.

"Doesn't sound like the Closer's style, does it? Probably done by the guy in the kitchen—guess we'll know once we listen to those tapes."

"Detective?" the patrolman asked. He was young, with acne scars on his cheeks and a bristling blond crew cut."Why do you call him the Closer?"

"Don't you read the tabloids?" Dymund asked.

SERIAL KILLER STALKER STRIKES AGAIN!

WEEKLY WORLD NEWS, June 4, 1999—Seattle, Washington.

The vigilante known as the Closer—so called because he closes unsolved murder cases—struck again this week, ending the murderous rampage of yet another maniac: Stanley Dupreiss, whom the police have confirmed as the killer of at least eight local prostitutes. No details of Dupreiss's death have been released, but rumor has it he was found in the same mutilated condition as the Closer's other victims.

This brings to four the number of serial killers the Closer has introduced to his own brand of grim justice, leaving police on both sides of the U.S./Canada border no nearer to his identity—or are they?

Some say the police aren't trying very hard to find the Closer. "Hell, why should we?" says a police officer who asked not to be identified. "He's doing our job for us. Why should we waste the public's money on a task force to stop this guy, when he's doing what most of us wish *we* could do? Instead of millions being spent on these creeps to catch, prosecute and incarcerate them, one guy is making sure they get what they deserve."

The question is, how is he doing it? Are the police, with all the resources at their disposal, so incompetent that a single determined man can outperform them not once, but four times? Or is the truth darker—that the Closer is one of their own, a renegade cop who's decided to take the law into his own hands?

Some say this explains not only the reluctance of the police to pursue the Closer more actively, but also the vigilante's uncanny ability to find his victims. If he has access to police files, then he has a shopping list of suspects to pick from.

So far, the only people the Closer has killed have been reprehensible murderers themselves. But even the police make mistakes—what happens if the Closer does?

You can only hope you're not on his list.

• • •

Charlie Holloway leaned back in his chair and yawned; it had been a long day. His eyes fell on his own portrait hanging on the wall across from his desk, and he wondered how long it would be before his real face no longer resembled the one captured in oils. He'd always have the big, potato-sized nose, of course, but his hair, full and black in the painting, was already mostly gone and hardly black. His face had gotten fuller as middle age had added pounds along with the years, and his blue eyes—always his best feature, his mother had told him—were usually hidden behind glasses these days.

Ah, if only I had Dorian Gray as a client, Charlie thought ruefully. *Still, that painting's going to be worth a mint one day—*

The phone rang, interrupting his reverie.

"Hello, Charlie Holloway."

"Charlie."

"Jack? Hey, I was just thinking about you." Charlie's voice softened from friendly to concerned. "How are you?"

"I—I don't know. I'm all right, I guess."

"It's been a while since I've heard from you. Been keeping busy?"

"Yeah. Yeah, I have."

"Working, I hope."

"Not exactly."

"Oh. That's too bad," Charlie said, shaking his head. "You know I don't want to push you, Jack, but—"

"But it's been three years. I should move on."

Charlie sighed, and rubbed the bridge of his nose. "No, no, that's not what I mean. What happened was horrible, Jack, and it didn't just happen to *them,* it happened to *you,* too. I'm not trying to trivialize it, or give you some New Age bullshit about inner peace—"

His assistant, Falmi, came in with a clipboard. Falmi was a Goth, skeletally thin with spiky jet black hair and skin the color of vanilla ice cream. He wore black eyeliner and had Celtic tattoos curling up the side of his neck; Charlie had never seen him wear anything that wasn't black or chrome. Today it was black jeans, a black T-shirt and studded leather gauntlets. "Charlie?" he said. His voice was high and nasal.

"Just a sec, Jack. What is it?"

"I need your signature on this manifest."

Charlie grunted, took the clipboard and signed it. Falmi was amazingly anal for a Goth, but he had a meticulous attention to detail that Charlie appreciated. He handed the clipboard back and Falmi left.

"Sorry, Jack. What I am trying to say is that the kind of pain you're carrying around is—well, it's a real thing. It has weight, it has depth, and it's *toxic.* If you don't find a way to let it out, it'll eat you alive."

"You should have been a writer, Charlie."

Charlie grinned. "I'll leave the creativity to the artists like you, thanks. I'm happy to flog your stuff and take my cut."

"Guess you're not too happy, then. Not much of my stuff to flog, is there?"

"Look, I didn't mean it like that—I just think you'd be happier if you were working, that's all. Don't even worry about doing anything commercial. Do it for yourself."

"Art as therapy."

"Why not? Just give it a chance."

"Thanks, Charlie—but I'm already in therapy. Kind of a radical approach, but it seems to be working."

"Oh? Well, as long as it works, I guess. That's the important thing."

"I thought I might come for a visit."

"That'd be great, Jack. Anytime at all."

"My schedule's a little . . . murky, at the moment. I'll call you when things firm up a bit."

"You do that."

"I'll talk to you later, Charlie."

"Not too much later, I hope."

Jack hung up. Charlie put the phone down and glanced back up at the portrait Jack had done of him. He frowned.

"Ready to go?" Nikki asked.

"Yeah," the Closer said, putting down the phone. "I'm ready."

Art as therapy. That wasn't the problem.

It was therapy as art. . . .

INTERLUDE

Dear Diary:

I, Fiona Stedman, have come to a conclusion: I'm in love with my uncle Rick.

Okay, maybe not in love—but a major-league crush, anyway. He's twenty-four, ten years older than me, but my dad is ten years older than my mom, so it's not that much. And nobody else understands me the way he does.

Actually, nobody even tries. Dad's always working late, and Mom's so stressed over her charity work she's in a permanent bad mood. And I can forget about any of my so-called friends; they already tease me about "wanting to jump my uncle's bones"—I'd never hear the end of it if they knew how I really felt.

So the only shoulder I have to cry on is an electronic one with a dumb name: Dear Diary. No offense, but that's just way too cheesy sitcom for me—mind if I call you something else?

Hmmm. How about Electra? Yeah? Okay, let's start over. . . .

Dear Electra: Today sucked. I asked my mom if I could go to the Undulating Fools concert and she said no way. I told her a bunch of my friends were going and that seemed to make it worse, like I was in some kind of gang or something.

By the way, Electra, did you know you have my uncle Rick to thank for your existence? I mean, my parents did pay for you, but it was Uncle Rick who *actually unpacked you and helped get you up and running. Without him, you'd probably still be in your box.*

Sigh. Uncle Rick. It is so not fair that we're related. Electra, he is so good-looking. Tall, dark wavy hair, big brown eyes, a gorgeous smile . . . and a really nice body, too. Last summer he went to the beach with us, and I had to try really hard not to stare. I mean, he's not a bodybuilder or anything, but he has muscles—and he isn't all hairy either, just a little curly patch in the middle of his chest.

God, is there something wrong with me? I mean, I haven't even kissed a boy yet and I'm thinking about my uncle like he was my boyfriend or something. This is seriously weird, Electra.

Did I mention he rides a motorcycle? He lets me ride behind him sometimes, and I put my arms around his waist and my face close to his neck. He smells like leather and cigarettes and something sweet.

It's just not fair.

He surfed through the Stalking Ground's various areas. The website was set up on a give-and-take basis; the menus and subheadings were all readily accessible, but if he wanted more detailed information he was expected to contribute some of his own.

He clicked on a heading that read Territory. A map of North America popped up, and then an inset block of text.

It read: *Okay, so you want to know who hunts where. Fair enough. Don't worry too much if your Hunting Ground overlaps somebody else's; as you'll see, that's pretty common. Plenty of prey to go around, right? The important thing is to respect the other Hunters. If you're planning on moving into somebody else's territory, it's to your advantage to let them know—after all, they know the terrain better than you do, and can let you know about any possible problems. Remember: it's Us against Everybody Else. The Pack Hunts Together.*

Below the text was a button labeled *Mark Territory.* He clicked on it, and the cursor transformed into an icon of a little wolf with an evil grin on its face. When he moved it around, it raised its hind leg and left a yellow line behind it.

He started to mark off the area around Seattle, then expanded it to a zone that went as far north as Vancouver, Canada. He hit *Done* when he was finished.

A crazy-quilt of colors and patterns superimposed itself over the map, each a territory claimed by a killer. Jack clicked on Nevada. It belonged to someone called the Gourmet, with eleven kills. Jack clicked on the Link button, and a text bar informed him that he would have to fill in his own profile before he could link to the others.

He spent the next hour doing so, making up most of it. He didn't use the victims Stanley had told him about, except where Dupreiss's files showed he'd already mentioned a particular kill; he wanted to distance Deathkiss's identity as far as possible from the corpse he'd left for the police. The website actually encouraged this, warning him against using details that might reveal his true identity but asking for specifics concerning the location of bodies.

Remember the Clifford Olsen case in Canada? a prompt asked. *He traded the location of bodies for a hundred grand in cash for his family. Knowledge is power. If you're arrested, you can use this knowledge to your advantage.*

It works like this: use the locations of bodies as a bargaining chip. Trade them for a reduced sentence, or extradition to a state that doesn't have the death penalty. Then, don't give the cops the location of your kills—give them someone else's. Claim you did them. Not only does this confuse the hell out of the cops, but if you can later provide an alibi that contradicts your original statement, you might even get off!

He clicked on a button marked *Gravesites*. The form that appeared was configured to look like a baseball card, with empty spaces for a photo and statistics on the victim. The logo at the top of the card read *Collect 'em All!*

Trading cards.

Jack just stared at the screen for a few moments, clenching and unclenching his fists. "You sick fuck," he murmured. "You're the one. The one that designed this website. The one that brought all the others into the fold."

He reached out and pressed his hand against the screen, as if he could reach through it and wrap his fingers around the throat of its creator.

Stanley had given him his name.

Djinn-X.

"You're the one," the Closer said softly, "I'm going to kill *first.*"

"Advertising execs or stockbrokers," Djinn-X said. "I'm really not sure which one I hate more."

Djinn-X sat on a skateboard with his knees drawn up. The man he was speaking to was bound to a lawn chair with cheap packing twine and gagged with a strip of white duct tape. The chair was in the middle of a corridor that ran a hundred feet in either direction. The floor was rough plywood, the walls on either side stacked cages of wooden slats, three tiers of ten-by-ten storage lockers. Industrial fluorescents thirty feet above buzzed like a prison full of bees. It was just after three A.M.

Djinn-X tightened the laces on both inline skates of his captive, then started winding white duct tape around one of the ankles. "Both of them are parasites. Leeches. The advertising exec finds different ways to lie to people so they'll buy his client's product, and the stockbroker finds different ways to move around little pieces of paper so that the rich get richer and the poor get poorer. Neither one produces anything of value, but both suck big honking wads of cash out of the economy."

His captive blinked sweat out of his eyes. He was in his forties, handsome, with a jogger's lean body and neatly trimmed black hair. His name was Michael Fitzpatrick. Besides the skates, Djinn-X had dressed him in a white paper coverall, the kind used by painters.

"Of course, being an advertising exec, you're probably biased," said Djinn-X. The laces of both skates were now sealed under a thick layer of white tape that reached from the prisoner's ankles to halfway up his shins.

Djinn-X stood up and kicked his skateboard to the side. The board was decorated with logos of bands Fitzpatrick had never heard of. His captor wore a black T-shirt with a green skull on it, ripped jeans and scuffed army boots.

"But you know what? I think you guys are actually worse. I mean, the money-shufflers built this toilet that passes for a society, but you're the ones that keep it filled with shit. It just keeps pouring out, TV and radio and magazines and billboards, twenty-four-seven. I went to take a whiz the other day and there was a fucking Gap ad over the urinal. Even when I got my dick in my hand, you're pissing in my eyes."

He reached down and picked up his gun. He'd taped a machine pistol to the barrel of a shotgun and strapped a palmcorder to the top of that; the weapon looked like it belonged in a science fiction movie.

Djinn-X stuck the shotgun barrel between his prisoner's legs, chuckling at Fitzpatrick's sharp inhalation—then pulled a utility knife from his pocket and cut through the twine binding Fitzpatrick's legs and arms to the chair.

He stepped back and let the man pull the tape off his mouth himself.

"What do you want?" Fitzpatrick asked. His voice trembled.

"Know what I really hate? Video games. Not playing them; fuck no, I love that. It's the idea *behind* them. Doom, Quake—they're like *drugs,* man. You put a gun in a kid's hand and turn him loose, tell him to blow away as many people as he can—then you're surprised when he shows up at school with his dad's hunting rifle and an itchy trigger finger. But *you're* not responsible, right? You're just giving the people what they want."

"My firm doesn't have anything to do with video games," Fitzpatrick said carefully. "We promote retail chains—"

"Shut up," Djinn-X said cheerfully. "This isn't a debate. People like you created people like me, my whole generation—now I'm gonna show you what we've learned."

He flipped open the viewscreen of the palmcorder, a square videoscreen that jutted off to the side like an open page. He tapped the power button and it blinked to life.

"Get up."

Fitzpatrick did. His legs were shaking so bad he lost his balance on the skates immediately and crashed to the ground.

"Try it again. Carefully."

Fitzpatrick managed to get to his feet.

"Turn around."

The walls of the corridor behind him had been lined with black plastic to a height of about eight feet, on both sides. "That's the start of the maze," Djinn-X said. "You're going to blade your way through it. I'm going to chase you on my board. You stay ahead of me, you live. You fall down—you die. Pretty simple, huh?"

"You can't be serious—"

"Serious as a pit bull on crack," Djinn-X said. He nudged his board into position with his foot and raised his gun to his shoulder, using the videocam as a sight. "Now get rolling."

Fitzpatrick turned and started off, awkwardly. There was a small glimmer of hope beneath the panic in his gut; it came from the fact that he rollerbladed every weekend, was in fact damn good at it. Once he was around the first corner, he planned to put on a burst of speed that would leave his pursuer far behind.

Djinn-X let him get about fifty feet away before he shot him.

Three sharp *pops*. Three separate impacts slammed into Fitzpatrick's back. A wave of fear so great he couldn't even scream exploded up from his stomach. He crashed to the floor, the smell of plywood filling his nostrils as his face smacked into the rough wood.

He lay there, twitching—but somehow, he was still alive.

"I'm gonna give you the first one for free," Djinn-X called out as he pushed off on his board. The polyurethane wheels thrummed on the wood. "See, this fancy machine pistol I have here isn't a MAC-10 or even an Uzi; it's a paintball gun. Shoots little plastic balls filled with dye. They make a real nice red splash on your white suit, but they won't give you more than a bruise."

There was another *pop* and another stinging impact.

"Better get going, adman," Djinn-X said. "The shotgun part of the package is for real. And don't try to fool me with that I-don't-know-how-to-rollerblade shit. I've been watching you for a while."

Fitzpatrick scrambled to his feet and took off. This time, he went all out.

With a whoop of joy, Djinn-X gave chase.

Later.

Djinn-X was playing with the digital footage he'd downloaded from the videocam to his laptop, and bragging about it online at the same time via his regular computer.

Wait 'til you see the new level, he typed. Major mayhem. Here's a little preview.

He uploaded the image he'd been working on: Fitzpatrick bombing away from him down the corridor. Djinn-X had digitally painted the black walls, making it now appear that Fitzpatrick was racing down the narrow streets of a city. Wisps of vapor streamed off the ugly red blotches on his coveralls.

Nice, was the reply a few moments later. How'd you add that vapor effect?

Chemistry. I doctored a few of the paint pellets with a syringe and some epoxy. I thought a little hydrochloric acid might make things more interesting.

Bet he really "felt the burn," huh?

Djinn-X grinned.

No, I saved *that* pellet for last.

What pellet would that be?

The kerosene-filled one. With the phosphorus core.

Beautiful! Who needs special effects when
you've got the real thing?

That's what this whole trip is about, man. The Real
Thing—and I *don't* mean fucking Coca-Cola.

I hear you.

I know you do. Just like I know you're for real, and
you know I am. Just like everyone else in The Pack
is. The Initiation, it's not just some bullshit ritual. I
pick out a sheep, ask you to kill it and mail me a
hand for proof—there's no way that can be faked.
That's why every member of The Pack goes
through it. It establishes trust.

Does it?

Djinn-X frowned, then tapped out,

What do you mean?

You know I'm a killer. How do I know you are?

You have any doubts, visit one of my dump sites.
Don't forget to bring a shovel.

Any graverobber can plant bodies.

Djinn-X leaned back and studied the screen, his
eyes narrowed. A smile slowly surfaced on his face.

Okay, then—pick somebody else's dump site.

They're all over the country. Even if I'm some kind
of online wannabe, you don't think I'd be able to
fake them all, do you?

It seems unlikely. But that doesn't prove
you're a killer. It proves the other members of
The Pack are.

Unless they're a bunch of grave-robbing wannabes,
too. I know they aren't, because I have a freezer full
of severed hands that say otherwise—but you only
have my word for that.

Yes.

There is one thing you know for sure. I picked out a sheep and told you to kill it. You did. In the eyes of the law, that makes me as guilty of murder as you.

Except you didn't get blood on your hands.

The law is meaningless—you should know that.

"You're really starting to piss me off," Djinn-X muttered.

All right. I'll give you the same deal you gave me. Pick a hooker, lift her prints and tell me when and where. I'll send you a little present.

I've got a better idea. Crisscross.

Explain.

The most ironic part of being who we are is this: you can never kill anyone you know.

Anonymity is our biggest asset.

But *I* could kill someone *you* know—and vice versa.

"You sly devil, you," Djinn-X murmured.

Who's the sheep?

A real-estate agent. Don't bother sending me anything—I'll know when she's dead.

You got it. All I need is a name, a city and a phone number.

Djinn-X grabbed a pen and jotted down the information that appeared on the screen. "Looks like I'm going back to Seattle," he sighed. "Airplanes and rain. Fuck."

You're going to owe me, Deathkiss.

Don't worry. I always pay my debts.

• • •

"You've been glued to that thing for twelve hours now," Nikki said. "Learn anything, or you just surfing for porn?"

"This isn't what I'd call pornographic," Jack said. "Obscene is a better word."

He leaned back and stretched. The kinks in his neck sent a sharp bolt of pain into the base of his skull. "Ah! Goddammit," he said, wincing.

Nikki came over and put her hands on his shoulders. She dug into his trapezius muscles with her thumbs. "You need to loosen up," she said. "You've got knots the size of golf balls."

Jack closed his eyes, tried to relax. Images from the website kept flashing through his mind: dismembered bodies, a row of severed heads, graphic descriptions of rape and mutilation. He shook his head and opened his eyes.

"Can't. There are still a few areas of the website I haven't reviewed yet."

Nikki let her hands drop from his shoulders. "And you still have to eat. Come on, I'm sick of takeout. Let's hit a real restaurant."

"I'm not hungry."

"Well, I am. And I hate eating alone."

He finally gave in because arguing didn't seem worth the trouble. Nothing mundane did, anymore; he wouldn't bother to shower or shave if Nikki didn't remind him. Food was fuel, sleep simply the absence of consciousness. He sometimes forgot to urinate until his bladder began to ache.

Nikki picked a restaurant called Chantarelles, a French bistro in Seattle's Capitol Hill district. She insisted they take a cab instead of the van.

The restaurant was small, quiet, elegant. Somehow, it didn't seem quite real to Jack; he kept glancing behind him, as if he could catch the truth behind the illusion.

"Cut it out, Jack. You're making me nervous."

Nikki asked for a table with some privacy; the maître d' gave them one in the far corner. There were only two other couples in the place, both of them seated by the window near the entrance.

Jack sat with his back to the wall.

A busboy came and filled their water glasses. He was young, eighteen or so, Asian. Jack wondered if he played video games.

The menu was short and expensive. "Don't worry about the prices," Nikki said. "My treat."

"Sure." Jack didn't think much about finances anymore, either. He'd been living off insurance money for the last three years; he had no idea how much was left. He supposed he'd find out when his bank card stopped working.

"Hmm, I think I'll have a Caesar salad," mused Nikki. "I wonder if they make it right at the table? Ever had that?"

"No."

"It's really good. They make the dressing, too—crush the anchovies, whip the egg right in front of you. Can't get any fresher than that."

Crush. Whip.

Jack said nothing.

When the waiter arrived, Nikki asked for a glass of the house red. Jack just shook his head. For him, drinking to loosen up was like trying to put out a fire with gasoline.

"Our special tonight is pork medallions with an apricot—"

"I'll have that."

Nikki glared at him, then said, "I'll have a Caesar salad and the lobster."

"Very good."

They sat in awkward silence after the waiter left. They'd been together every day for the past two years, had shared a kind of intimacy and passion most couples never even imagined—but they had never so much as kissed. They were bound together by hatred and loneliness, not love.

"So, isn't this better than Burger King?" Nikki finally asked.

"Sure."

"I—" She fumbled for something to say. "I went shopping today. Found some nice shoes."

He looked at her blankly.

She looked back, a kind of pleading in her eyes. It was that look that finally reached him.

"Oh. That's . . . good. That's *good.*"

"Yeah. Yeah, they were a real bargain."

A long pause.

"What *kind* were they?" Jack asked carefully.

"What? Oh, they were pumps. Red-and-black pumps, with little bows."

"I see." He tried to smile. "I'm sure they'll be useful."

"Yeah." Her voice hardened. "Yeah, I'm sure they'll be just the thing to grab the attention of the next psycho we torture to death."

"That's not what I meant."

"Oh, just forget it," she snapped. "I mean, what the hell was I thinking? Trying to pretend I had a *normal* life for a few hours—what a load of *bullshit.* I'm a thirty-five-year-old whore with a serial killer for a partner, and what's the only nonpsychotic thing we can find to talk about over dinner? Shoes. Fucking *shoes.*"

"Pumps," he said. "With little bows."

She stared at him for a second, then started laughing. He tried to join in, but the best he could manage was a wry smile.

Nikki laughed until her eyes watered. She dabbed at them with her napkin, trying not to smear her makeup and failing miserably.

Then she glanced down, and saw that she'd managed to get lipstick on the napkin, too.

She began to sob. She threw the napkin away convulsively, and it fluttered like a wounded bird to another table and settled over a water glass. She bolted for the restroom.

Jack just sat there.

After Deathkiss had sent him a few more details, Djinn-X realized his trip wasn't going to be the chore he'd first thought. Quite the opposite, in fact.

He ran through the details in his head during the flight, trying to keep his mind off the fact that he was in an airplane. What he hated about flying wasn't the danger of a crash; it was the unpredictability of turbulence. You'd be in a nice comfortable seat surrounded by other people, maybe watching a movie, sipping a little wine out of a plastic cup, not so different from being in a theater; and then *Wham!* the whole building suddenly drops fifty feet straight down.

After that, you were *fucked.*

You couldn't relax and watch the movie; you didn't know if you should gulp down that wine and ask for another, or stop drinking altogether 'cause you might wind up spewing all over the stewardess. It felt like a betrayal—like eating a nice dinner at home, everything quiet and peaceful, and suddenly someone punches you in the face for no reason.

It felt a lot like living with his father.

He closed his eyes and forced himself to concentrate. The trip was going to be worth it, for two reasons; one of them was the sheep herself. From the description Deathkiss had sent, she was quite the hottie. She was forty-two but could pass for thirty-five, and she was a real-estate agent. A *salesperson.*

He loathed salespeople. They were the real predators of twenty-first century civilization, roaming through the economic jungle with their always-hungry bank accounts, armed with demographic studies and contracts filed to points. Many were baby boomers, flower children who had traded in their ideals for cynicism and greed. They hadn't just betrayed themselves, they'd betrayed their own children—Generation Xers like himself, not only locked out of a decent job by the population glut of their parents, but ruthlessly targeted by marketing agencies eager to shove products down the throats of their own offspring. Aging parasites consuming their young.

Doing her would be a real pleasure, but it wasn't the main reason he was going. No, he would have gone even if she'd turned out to be an eighty-five-year-old widow in a wheelchair, and the reason was simple.

Trust.

It was, as far as Djinn-X could tell, the most valuable and fragile of all emotions. All it took was one lie to destroy it—and yet, once established, it could prove to be the strongest emotion of them all, bearing the entire weight of a relationship. It was the sinew that bound together all the higher feelings: friendship, honor, duty, love.

Djinn-X had few of those feelings in his life. His family certainly hadn't provided them, and his father's constant transfers from one army base to another hadn't let him make any lasting friends, either. The birth of the internet had provided a solution, of sorts; it didn't matter where you were in the world if your relationships were all in cyberspace.

But that had proved to be a betrayal, too. He'd reached out to what seemed to be a kindred spirit, a seventeen-year-old girl named Kelly who liked Japanese animation, ska music and Clive Barker. They'd carried on a torrid electronic romance, him in California and her in Idaho, exchanging the most pornographic emails and masturbating together online.

He thought he was in love. But when he finally caught a Greyhound to meet her, Kelly turned out to be a forty-three-year-old transvestite named Kevin. He claimed he was just as much in love.

He was a salesperson, of course. And Djinn-X's first kill.

After that betrayal, he'd decided he would always be alone. Killing Kevin had placed him in a different subset of humanity: *homo homicidus*. He'd felt no remorse over the murder, only a deep satisfaction. It was what he'd been born to do, and he plunged into his new career with a sense of purpose he'd never felt before. His day job let him spy on the very people he intended to murder while staying virtually invisible; no one noticed a bike courier except as an obstacle in traffic.

For a while, it had been enough. But there was an old saying, often repeated on the net: *Information wants to be free.* One night, after a particularly satisfying kill—an advertising executive who claimed he was responsible for the Mentos commercials—he found himself bragging about his murderous exploits online.

No one believed him, of course. And why should they? You could claim to be anyone or anything online; he knew that better than anyone.

But it gnawed at him. The internet had the power to bring together people with similar interests, people who might never meet otherwise. It offered almost instantaneous communication and complete anonymity. More than one underground subculture had discovered it was perfect for distributing information with little chance of reprisal: anarchists, kiddie-porn rings, music and video pirates.

Why not serial killers?

Alienated from the culture around him, Djinn-X had decided to create his own. It had taken time, patience, and a winnowing-out process, but he had finally refined his technique to the point where he could guarantee one thing: the person he was communicating with was a killer, just like him. That knowledge, powerful and secret, was the fire that trust was forged in. Djinn-X did not take it lightly.

Deathkiss was a member of The Pack, now. Djinn-X trusted him, and Deathkiss had to know—*deserved* to know—he could trust Djinn-X in return.

It was, after all, the foundation their community was based on.

Djinn-X took a bus from the airport to the downtown core, then found a pawn shop and paid cash for a used mountain bike. He'd resell it on the way out of town; taking a loss of twenty bucks or so was worth it for the independence it afforded him. Cruising through strange city streets, jumping curbs and dodging traffic, powered by his own muscle; it was the closest he could come to the feeling he got surfing the net. He checked the map Deathkiss had sent him, and headed toward the warehouse district.

A sheep that was a real-estate agent was sweet, but the fact that she specialized in industrial properties was pure candy. His map had several buildings she represented marked, all big and empty. All he had to do was pick one and make an appointment; she'd show up, probably wearing one of those stupid orange blazers, and unlock the door for him. "Right this way, Mr. Todd. Here's a great big empty space with no place for me to hide. I bet you could get some really terrific echoes once I start to scream. Don't worry about the noise; this entire district is deserted after dark. You can do whatever you want . . . and look! A gigantic industrial sink!"

There were three possibles, all within a few blocks of each other. The first one had windows lining the entire first floor, and was on a fairly major street. The second was okay, but there was an all-night diner just down the block, a little too close for comfort.

The third one was an old meat-packing plant, on a dead-end street flanked by an auto parts warehouse and a vacant lot. There were no windows on the first floor but plenty on the second, most of them broken. He found a rickety fire escape, climbed up and peeked into one of them. Nothing but empty space, embroidered with dust and cobwebs. Perfect.

He climbed down, got on his bike and rode until he found a pay phone. He punched in the number Deathkiss had given him.

"Hello, Davis Properties."

"Hi. I'm interested in one of your warehouses."

"Which one?"

He gave her the address.

"Oh, yes, the Waterman property. It's been empty for quite a while, but it's a prime site."

"I'd like to take a look at the inside."

"Sure. What time is convenient?"

"I'm only in town overnight, and I'm in the middle of a business meeting right now. Can you meet me there at, say—nine o'clock?"

"I think I can manage that. My name is Julie Saunders, by the way."

"Hi, Julie. I'm Todd Simkack."

"Okay, Mr. Simkack—do you have any other questions, or would you like to discuss this further tonight?"

"Tonight would be fine."

"I'll see you then."

He took out his piercings and changed into a suit at the motel, then took a cab to a corner six blocks away from the warehouse. He walked the rest of the way, enjoying the late summer evening. The air smelled of diesel fumes and hot asphalt, but that was always a smell he'd liked; it reminded him of playing basketball on tarmac as a kid, on one of the many army bases his father had been stationed on.

The sheep was waiting for him outside. She was just as Deathkiss had described her, tall and blond and gorgeous, wearing a miniskirt that didn't leave much to the imagination. He had a sudden, powerful flash of her on her knees, begging for her life. The smile on his face as he approached her was genuine.

"Hi, you must be Mr. Simkack."

"Call me Todd."

"All right, Todd. Right this way—oh, dear. It looks like someone's broken in. I'm afraid we have problems with squatters sometimes—"

"That's all right. They're not dangerous, are they?"

"Oh, no, it's usually just runaways with no place to stay, but be careful where you step. There might be needles."

"I'll keep my eyes open. Boy, it sure is dark in here. Is the electricity still on?"

"Shut up, you piece of shit."

". . . What?"

The world suddenly jumped like a bad video edit. Somehow, he was on his back, staring up at a bright light while his muscles twitched uncontrollably. A man's voice said, "Don't move. Nikki, get his weapon."

Strong, impersonal hands found the knife tucked in the small of his back, under his shirt. The voice behind the flashlight said, "Do you recognize this moment?"

"What the fuck are you talking about?" he gasped. "Look, if you want to rob me—"

"This is the moment of control. The pivot that your relationship with the victim turns on, when everything changes. Except this time, you're on the other side."

"Deathkiss?" he whispered.

"No. I'm the one who killed him."

A familiar feeling settled slowly in Djinn-X's gut. Betrayal.

"And now you're gonna kill me, right?"

"No. I'm not going to kill you. I just want to talk to you . . . ."

ROAD RAGE: I think we have a situation that needs our attention: The Closer.

GOURMET: I agree. He's a threat that should be dealt with. We're fortunate he hasn't caught any of us yet.

ROAD RAGE: What if he does? He could learn all our secrets.

PATRON: Then we'll just have to catch him first. . . .

INTERLUDE

Dear Electra:

I invited Sarah over to watch some scary movies with me and Simone and Jessica. I didn't know if she even watched movies, but she does—she just turns on the captioning on the DVD player, which made me feel stupid because it's so obvious. And besides, she's really good at lip-reading.

We rented a couple of slasher flicks and watched them in the basement with the lights off. We spent more time laughing than being scared—some of these movies are just so dumb! I mean, you'd think that if a psychopath was going around killing people, you wouldn't hang out in the graveyard or the deserted house or wherever—you'd leave, and you'd take your friends with you. You wouldn't go wandering off alone, and you sure wouldn't go exploring any dark basements where you heard a weird noise.

We all agreed it was pretty insulting; I mean, it's always teenagers they show doing these incredibly moronic things.

Jessica pointed out that it wasn't just teenagers—it was horny *teenagers. Anybody making out might as well paint a bull's-eye on their naked butt.*

"Yeah," Sarah said. "What are they trying to tell us about sex?"

"Don't have it unless you want to die," Simone said.

"Or use protection," said Jessica. "Like, heavily-armed protection."

"Kids!" I said, doing a fake-announcer voice. "Are you having unsafe sex? Are you doing it in deserted summer camps and abandoned factories? Use our special psycho-resistant condoms! Personally approved by Freddy, Jason and Chucky!"

"Yeah!" Sarah said, laughing. "With a little hockey mask for the head!"

"And the Freddy one could be made of, like, burned flesh," Jessica said.

"Eeww, GROSS!" I'm not sure who said that—I think it was everyone.

Well, Electra, the discussion got pretty weird after that. By the time we were done we'd designed a whole line of slasher-movie sex supplies, including: the Chucky blow-up doll decoy, good for a temporary diversion while you escape (made of special slash-resistant rubber); the Freddy vibrator, in orange-and-green stripes; and Jason sex cream (keeps you coming back for more—even if you died in the last movie!).

I'm really glad Jessica and Simone like Sarah. It would bite if they decided she wasn't cool enough to hang with—I mean, not that any of us are that cool either, but sometimes Jessica can be funny. We used to hang around with Jenny Birch all the time, and then she and Jessica got into a fight. Jessica started saying all these bad things about her, and then Simone was, and I guess I did too. I don't know why; I don't even remember what the fight was about. We don't hang around with Jenny anymore.

Anyway, I'm glad Sarah fits in with us. If you don't have a group to hang with at school, it can suck—I remember when I first moved here, it was *really hard to make friends. I wound up joining Girl Guides, which is where I met Jessica and Simone.*

Sometimes I look around at the different groups at school, and I imagine they're all from different planets; the Jocks, the Brains, the Druggies, the Goths. I wonder what it's like on their worlds, and what it would be like to go there. Weird, huh, Electra?

Some people don't have their own planet, though. The girl that's really fat, the guy that's really dumb, anyone too ugly or clueless to make friends. I see them in the halls and they make me feel sad and angry at the same time. Sad because they'll probably always be alone, and angry because no one even tries to be nice to them.

Including me.

Maybe Uncle Rick was wrong. I shouldn't be a writer, I should be Ruler of The World; then I could fix everything and everyone would be happy.

Right.

Maybe that's why people become writers in the first place—World Ruler isn't really an option, so they make up a world they can rule instead. A place they can fix all the mistakes they can't fix in real life.

Hmm. I don't know if that's cool or pathetic. What do you think, Electra?

I THINK YOU ARE A BRILLIANT AND TALENTED HUMAN BEING.

Why, thank you, Electra. You're too kind.

FURTHERMORE, EVEN THOUGH I AM ONLY AN ELECTRONIC FIGMENT OF YOUR IMAGINATION, I AM IN AWE AT THE BEAUTY OF YOUR PHYSICAL FORM. CLEARLY YOU ARE A SUPERIOR

EXAMPLE OF HUMANITY AND ANY MALE WOULD BE PROUD TO GROVEL AT YOUR FEET.

Sigh. Now, if only Uncle Rick were as easy to convince.

HOWEVER, YOUR FEET *DO* SMELL.

Oh, shut up.

CHAPTER THREE

The first thing Djinn-X saw when the bag was removed from his head was a bright light shining directly into his eyes. He squinted past the glare and said, "Kind of a cliché, don't you think?"

"I prefer to think of it as traditional," the Closer answered.

"Yeah, like dumping me in your van and hauling me out here," Djinn-X sneered. "Where are we, your basement?" He glanced from side to side, but all he could see beyond the glare was darkness. "You should have kept me at the warehouse, you know—empty, deserted, no connection to you unless you're even dumber than you seem. Now you have to worry about traces: fibers, blood, my whole fucking body. Maybe even witnesses. You're a bigger idiot than Jeffrey fucking Dahmer was."

"I caught *you*, didn't I?"

"Only because I trusted you, you traitorous motherfucker. Killing sluts wasn't enough, huh? You had to come after one of your *own*."

He heard steps as his captor moved through the darkness. A rectangle of softer, colored light blinked into existence beyond the harsh brightness. He recognized it immediately: a computer screen.

"The first reason you're here is because I needed a phone line," the Closer said. "To access your website. You're going to give me the passwords that will let me into your system files."

"Not a chance in hell, asshole."

"The second reason you're here is because I knew it would take some time to get those passwords from you. I needed a place I could work without being disturbed."

Djinn-X felt his stomach twist the way it did when he was flying and the plane hit an air pocket.

The light was suddenly moved. He blinked spots out of his eyes, trying to readjust his vision. When he could see clearly again, he wished he couldn't.

The instruments gleamed, laid out in neat rows on a plastic sheet draped over a table. The walls of the room were hung with sheets of black plastic, eerily like the plastic-lined corridors of Djinn-X's self-created video game. They reflected the light like dark, wet flesh.

"Okay," Djinn-X said. "You're a cop. You caught Deathkiss, and he gave me up. You think this voodoo inquisition bullshit is gonna make me roll over, too? You're bluffing. *Fuck* you."

"I'm not a cop," the Closer said. He picked up a small butane torch, not much larger than a cigarette lighter, and lit it with a wooden match. It hissed to life with a flickering tongue of blue flame. "The papers keep saying I must be, but I'm not. I'm just someone who closes cases."

"The Closer, huh?" Djinn-X knew the name, of course—he'd just never believed the Closer actually existed. It was a boogeyman, created by the police to scare the ones they were hunting. He figured the corpses were either suicides mutilated by the cops or actual suspects they just executed because they didn't have the evidence to prosecute them. But the idea of a lone man, able to actually track and catch *real* predators like himself? It was ludicrous. . . .

"I can see you don't believe me," the Closer said. "Maybe I can change your mind." He set the torch down on the table. Its hissing glow was hypnotic; Djinn-X's eyes kept returning to it.

"The real reason they call me the Closer hasn't been reported in the papers. I do more than kill killers; I get them to confess. The bodies I leave behind haven't been mutilated, as the press claims—they've been *coerced*. Persuaded, over the course of many hours, to give up the secrets of their owners."

"That how you get *your* kicks? A little psychotic revenge?" Djinn-X asked. "Let me guess: one of us killed your innocent little sister, who wasn't *really* a whore like everybody said."

"This isn't about revenge," the Closer said calmly. "Not as much as you might think, anyway. It's about holes. That's what serial killers leave: great big holes in people's lives. I can't fix the big ones, the ones left by a daughter or a sister or a wife. But I *can* fix the smaller ones. The holes left by unanswered questions: Is my child alive or dead? Where is her body buried? What lie did that man say to make my son trust him?"

The Closer picked up a pair of needle-nose pliers.

He held them over the tip of the torch, watching the ends turn a glowing orange.

"What I provide . . . is *closure*. The only kind the families of your victims are likely to get. You see, nothing in life is free; everybody pays, sometime, somehow. The answers you're going to give me are simply payment for what you owe."

Djinn-X couldn't take his eyes off the pliers. The tips were white-hot now. "You—you don't have to do that. I'll give you answers."

"That's only half of what you owe. How I get the *right* answers—that's the other half."

The Closer removed the pliers from the flame. He grabbed Djinn-X by the hair with his other hand. "It works best if you have to watch what's being done to you. . . ."

The pliers were suddenly right there, so close he could hardly focus on them. He could feel the heat coming off them. He could smell the scorched metal.

"Please," Djinn-X whispered.

"I don't want you closing your eyes. So I'll just make sure you can't."

Jack snapped off the surgical gloves. It used to feel like shedding armor, getting rid of a bloodstained layer of protection; but lately if felt more like stripping away a second skin, throwing away some essential part of himself. His hands felt naked and exposed, trembling slightly as he placed them on the keyboard. For an instant he thought he'd gotten blood on the keys, but it was just the crimson light from the screen.

"Spell it," Jack said.

"Ragnarok. R—A—G—N—A—R—O—K," Djinn-X gasped. "I swear."

Jack studied the laptop in front of him, angled so that Djinn-X couldn't see it. There was a rectangular gray window imposed in the center of the screen over a constantly shifting background, blinking a single request over and over.

Password.
Password.
Password.

Jack found the shifting images in the background hypnotic. Grotesque in content, they were arranged in a graceful ballet of colors and shapes. Photos of victims' faces were layered row upon row so that only their wide staring eyes were visible, a mosaic of pleading and terror that morphed into a collection of body parts dancing a jig with gleaming scalpels and chromed handguns.

It was well done, Jack decided, but would be more effective if the audio was integrated as well. Screams set to something bouncy, perhaps . . .

He tapped a few keys. "Hmm. I guess I should have expected that," he said. "The screen just went blank."

Djinn-X made a huge, bubbling sigh.

"Some kind of universal delete, right?" Jack said. "I wonder how many you programmed in."

"One is all it takes, motherfucker. You lose."

Jack turned the laptop so that Djinn-X could see it. The gray rectangle was still onscreen. "I guess I would have—if I'd actually entered that code."

He stretched on a fresh pair of gloves, then picked up the can of lighter fluid and a syringe. "I guess we'll just have to start all over again. . . ."

• • •

"You're stronger than I thought."

"Huh. Huh. Huh."

"Give me the password."

"F-fuck you."

"Why do you care what happens to them? They don't care about you."

"You're wrong. Wrong."

"They're sociopaths. Murderers. The only thing that matters to them is the taking of life."

"Us."

"What?"

Djinn-X grinned up at him with bloody teeth. "Us. The only thing that matters to *us* is the taking of life."

"Give me the password."

"Why? You already *have* access. You want names, dates, places? It's all there, right on the website—you don't have to torture anybody. That's what the Stalking Ground is *about*, the exchange of information. The other hunters are more than happy to brag about their kills."

"My method is more reliable."

"No. Your method is more *fun*—AAAAAAAAAHH! *Fuck, don't do that!*"

"Give me the password."

"It won't do you any good. I don't know the real identity of *any* of them."

"I don't believe you."

"That's not what you're after at all, is it? You just want to get into the system so you can pose as *me*—so you can hide behind my name and betray them, one by one. No. No way. I'll never let you do that."

"Why?"

"Fuck you—NNNO! NO! OH *CHRIST!*"

"Tell me why."

"THEY'RE MY FAMILY!" Djinn-X screamed.

The Closer stopped what he was doing.

"They're my *family*," Djinn-X sobbed. "Don't you get it? None of us ever belonged, not *anywhere*. But in The Pack, *all of us belong*. We're not *alone* anymore. . . ."

The Closer stared at Djinn-X for a long moment.

Then he turned and left the room.

After two years with Jack, Nikki had evolved a routine. She slept until noon, then got up and went to a local gym. She spent at least three hours there, working out and taking a sauna if they had one. Then she'd grab some takeout food and bring it back to Jack. For the first part of the evening, they'd work on strategy: studying Dangerous John lists, newspaper and police reports. Most serial killers targeted a specific type of victim—Ted Bundy had preferred girls with long, straight brown hair. They'd try to figure out where and when a given killer might strike, and what type he preferred. Nikki had gotten proficient enough with wigs, contact lenses, and makeup to portray anyone from a blond amazon to a black transsexual.

Around nine, they'd go to work. She'd walk the streets, and Jack would shadow her. She had a spycam and a transmitter in her purse—the same device Stanley Dupreiss had used to block her cell phone had also messed with the bug, letting Jack know something was wrong.

Usually all he got to eavesdrop on was her trading blow jobs and quickies for cash—but five times now, they'd caught something else.

When that happened, she left Jack alone. If Jack did the interrogation on-site, she'd stay in another room—if they'd lured the killer to where they were staying, she'd go out. They'd moved from the airport motel to a small house in a low-rent part of town so Jack would have the privacy to question Djinn-X; he'd set up an interrogation chamber in the basement.

Today she'd decided to go shopping, but her heart just wasn't in it. She wandered from mall to mall aimlessly, unable to find anything she wanted. She didn't see clothes anymore; she saw disguises.

And somehow, she found herself outside a church.

Before she knew it, she was inside. Nikki had been raised Catholic, but she'd shaken off all the rites and thou-shalt-nots when puberty hit. She hadn't been back since—but it was impossible to do what she was doing without thinking about life and death, good and evil. Justice and retribution.

The church was beautiful, in the way only a Catholic church could be: a high, vaulted ceiling, long rows of solemn pews, a central aisle that led, inevitably, to the burnished wooden pulpit with its ornate golden cross. The whole thing lit by elaborate stained-glass windows, sunlight filtering through saints in frozen tableaus of pain.

She walked down the aisle. There were two old women lighting votive candles up at the front; she walked around them and to the side. To where the confessionals were.

She opened the door hesitantly, then swallowed and stepped inside.

She believed in what they were doing, believed in the rightness and necessity of it, but there was a big difference between her role and Jack's. When they first started their partnership, she thought she was taking all the risks and Jack was getting all the satisfaction—but that stopped the very first time she spied on him while he was working.

She was just risking her body. Jack was risking much more.

She sat down. The panel separating her from the priest slid aside, leaving a wooden screen between them. How did the ritual go again? "Bless me Father, for I have sinned. It's been . . . a long time since my last confession."

She stopped, unsure what to say next. When she'd seen what Jack was capable of, she'd felt an overpowering mix of emotion: shock, disgust, fear—and yes, satisfaction. She was glad his victim was dead, glad that he'd suffered; but she'd never have been able to do the things Jack had done to him.

But this last time, with Stanley Dupreiss—she hadn't been nearly as sickened when Jack had killed him in front of her. A part of her had felt more than satisfaction; it had felt *hungry*.

What did Jack feel, after all *he* had done?

The shadowy figure on the other side of the confessional screen prompted her. "Yes?" His voice was low, soothing. Gentle.

"There's someone I work with. A man. I'm worried about him."

"Why are you worried?"

"It's his job. He's forced to do . . . unpleasant things. I'm afraid of what it's turning him into."

"What kinds of things is he forced to do?"

"He has to . . . hurt people."

"Is he a criminal?"

"Not like you think. He doesn't hurt people for money."

"Are other people making him do it?"

"No. It's his own choice."

"If he can choose to start, he can choose to stop. God will always be waiting to forgive him—"

"It's not that simple. He has very good reasons for what he does. But—" She stopped, trying to put her thoughts into words. "What he does, I think it *needs* to be done. But every time he hurts someone, it hurts *him,* too. I know there's a good man in there somewhere—he's just buried under all this pain. And he keeps adding more and more."

"He sounds like he considers himself a martyr. One who suffers for the sins of others."

"Yeah. Yeah, I guess so."

"Martyrs usually believe they deserve to be punished. Could your friend be taking on all this pain because of something in his past?"

Nikki thought about Jack's family. About the story he had told her, and the deadness in his voice when he did so.

"You hit the nail on the head, Father. I used to think if he could just . . . *resolve* that one thing, it might be enough to make him stop. Problem is, he's been trying for the last couple of years, and it's starting to look like that might not be possible. He needs to find a particular person—and they seem to be real good at not being found."

"Sometimes it's not possible to face the one you blame, or the one you've wronged—except in your heart. The important thing is for him to forgive *him-*

self, first. Until he does so, he will continue to punish himself for this incident in his past."

She thought about that. Tried to imagine Jack accepting the loss of his family, moving on. Leading a normal life. Abandoning all those victims in unmarked graves, and those headed for them . . .

She couldn't.

"I think the problem might run a little deeper than that, Father," she said slowly. "What he does, it's sort of taken on a life of its own. It's not just about the past anymore. It's about the future—making sure some people are in it, and others aren't."

"I don't understand."

"Never mind." She stood abruptly. "Thanks for the talk, Father. I don't know what I thought it could solve, but I do feel better. Things are a little clearer in my head. I guess confession *is* good for the soul."

"Just a minute, my child—"

She left without looking back.

"I've been doing some thinking," the Closer said.

"Good for you," spat Djinn-X. He seemed to have gotten his second wind; he glared at his tormentor with eyes that could no longer blink. "Figure out what a poor, deluded shithead you are yet?"

"I want to know how you did it."

"Is that all? Shit, it was easy. Stupid goddamn yuppies will open the door in a second if you say you're collecting for Jerry's Kids—"

"Not that. I want to know how you found the other members of The Pack."

"Put an ad in the Yellow Pages. Call 1-800-PSYCHOKILLER."

The Closer picked up the electric knife. "I'll make you a deal. I know about the initiation—what I don't know is how you screened out all the posers and wannabes before that. Tell me, and I'll let you die with your reputation intact. I won't pose as you in the Stalking Ground."

"Why? What do you care *how* I did it?"

"Prevention. If I can duplicate what you did, I can catch killers earlier."

"So you want me to betray *potential* members as opposed to *current* ones. Right."

"Don't think of it as betrayal," the Closer said. He turned the electric knife on, brought it closer to Djinn-X's chest. Let it hover, humming, over his right nipple.

"Think of it as a *trade*. First in a series, collect 'em all. . . ."

Jack knew Djinn-X would talk, and he knew why. He'd found his fracture point.

Everybody had one. It wasn't the same as a breaking point, where you simply overloaded the body with so much pain and the mind with so much horror that the personality disintegrated. That could take days, even weeks, and you risked sending your victim into a catatonic state where no amount of punishment could reach him.

A fracture point was a flaw in someone's personality that reached into the very core of who they were, what was most important to them. If you could find that point and apply pressure to it, you could punch right through a person's defenses, lay bare their soul. When he'd first taken up his quest, Jack had thought fracture points would be based on fear—he had found, to his surprise, that just as often they could be rooted in pride, sorrow, or longing.

Djinn-X's fracture point was loneliness. He'd felt alone all his life, and he blamed an entire generation for that isolation. That blame had turned to murder, which isolated him even further.

Creating the Stalking Ground had finally given him the emotional validation he craved. He had built his own tribe, his own country. It was the single thing he was most proud of in his life.

And he couldn't tell anyone.

Like all serial killers, he was an anonymous celebrity. He got the respect and approval of the rest of The Pack, of course, but they were just words on a screen. No one ever looked him in the eye with anything except vague disdain or blind terror, and he knew they never would.

What he really wanted to do was howl his rage at the world, let everybody know who he was and what he'd done. It was a flaw many serial killers shared—and the reason most of them got caught.

So Jack gave him a way to get what he wanted.

"I'm going to distribute your methods on the web," Jack said. "How you did it. What programs you used. Profiles you targeted. And I'll tell everyone who was responsible."

"You're—you're lying," Djinn-X gasped. "Doesn't make any sense . . ."

"Sure it does. No matter how clever you were, there'll be ten thousand people on the web who'll tear your ideas apart and design ways to beat them. Within a month of its release, your method will be useless. But look at the bright side," Jack said. "Everyone will remember your name. . . ."

And after a long, silent pause, Djinn-X had whispered, "All right."

"Good. Let's go back to the beginning. . . ."

The first step had been research. A website called the Serial Killer Tracking Bureau listed states where serial killers were known to be operating; those areas of the country got flagged on Djinn-X's computer. Next, he compiled a list of webpages of possible interest to killers: anarchists detailing ways to make bombs, purveyors of hardcore S&M, freelance mercenary ezines with descriptions of assassinations and torture, archives devoted to mass murderers and killers throughout history. He used a search engine and fed it words that ranged from "Auschwitz" to "zealot."

Next, he used a program called Remora, which attached itself to those websites and kept track of email signatures that visited at least two of the sites and originated in one of the areas that might hold a serial killer. Since there were thirty-five to fifty killers operating at any given time in the United States and they often moved around, this didn't narrow the possibilities down much.

Next came his own webpage. He called it "Serial Killer Update," and used a program called ChainLink to automatically link all the other sites on his list to his own; anyone scanning those webpages could jump to his with the click of a button.

Serial Killer Update was only a stepping-stone, though. He designed it to be as grotesque as possible, knowing it would weed out the casual cybersurfer. Graphic depictions of dismembered corpses and text that mocked the victims would drive away the merely curious.

The webpage had several sections, and only after you had visited every one would a link button pop up, inviting you to check out another webpage: The Gauntlet.

The Gauntlet was exactly that—a test. It had one hundred questions, culled from several studies of serial killers plus Djinn-X's own perspective, and you had to generate a score of eighty percent or higher to graduate to the next level. Some of the questions required research—what was the name of Son of Sam's third victim?—and some were designed to be infuriating, asking for intimate and embarrassing details of the subject's life; the angrier the response, the higher the score generated. Djinn-X offered no incentive to complete the test, just a promise of complete anonymity through an elaborate email rerouting system.

Even so, he still got hundreds of replies. He compared these replies to the results of his Remora program, seeing which respondents fit the profile he'd worked up. He pored over the results, and struck up an email relationship with those that showed promise. He freely admitted to his own murders, and asked his correspondents if they'd ever done the same.

Most of them said yes.

He knew some were telling the truth—but how could he bridge that final, fatal gap?

He already knew how to verify the real killers' bona

fides; the initiation was the first thing he'd designed. But none of them would go through with it until he had proved himself to them, first. They had no more reason to trust him than he had to trust them; they were wolves, slowly circling each other and growling. There had to be a test, something that couldn't be faked, something that all of them could verify. A public sacrifice, performed by Djinn-X to christen the birth of his creation.

They discussed it among themselves. They decided on a school bus.

Djinn-X agreed. Pipe bombs were easy to make.

The morning after the horrific crash—twelve dead, twenty-two injured—half the discussion group vanished. Djinn-X immediately took down his webpage; he knew he was entering the most delicate and dangerous part of the process. He contacted the remaining members and told them about the private website he was setting up, one they could connect to but no one else could—and if they wanted to join, they would have to go through an initiation of their own. Most said yes, but only a few followed through. One sent an obviously embalmed hand whose fingerprints didn't match.

The ones who passed became members of The Pack. There were only four of them at first, but that was enough.

Enough to make a family.

DEATHKISS: I've been having trouble accessing your page.
PATRON: I apologize for that. I prefer to give a guided

tour to new members—after that, you're free to look at it anytime you wish. This allows us to get to know each other on a more personal level.

DEATHKISS: The other members spoke highly of you. They refused to give details.

PATRON: I do have something of a reputation, though I'm afraid it's limited to the Pack. The world at large is still unaware of my existence—I vary both my methods and my quarry to such an extent that no one has connected my various endeavors.

DEATHKISS: I see you also claim the entire country as your territory.

PATRON: Not in any proprietary way, I assure you; I simply travel a great deal.

DEATHKISS: I'd be interested in seeing some of your work.

PATRON: Certainly. I'm sending you a file I call "Swaying Madonna." Let me know if you have any trouble decompressing it.

A dead woman appeared on Jack's screen, dangling from a hangman's noose. It was a video clip, not a still photo, and the body was moving slowly to one side. The camera's focus widened and Jack saw that the body was hung from a crude mobile, like the kind hung over cribs to amuse infants. Instead of Fisher-Price plastic, this one was made of rope and two-by-fours.

It was counterbalanced by two children.

DEATHKISS: Memorable.

PATRON: Thank you. A young family in St. Paul. Very little blood, actually—note the pristine whiteness of the ropes.

DEATHKISS: Were they dead when you hung them up?

PATRON: Oh, no—that was half the fun. Strangulation takes a few minutes, you know; each of them was very aware of the others.

DEATHKISS: I can see you appreciate the psychological element. So do I.

PATRON: But of course. The actual act of killing is no more complex than turning off a switch. But the emotional landscape to be explored, before and after the fact—that's what's fascinating. Study the look on the mother's face. What is she feeling? Terror at the imminent loss of her life? Horror at watching her children die? Guilt over the knowledge that it is *her own weight* keeping her offspring's feet kicking in the air—or rage because it is *their* weight doing the same to her?

DEATHKISS: An interesting question. I prefer to ask such questions more directly.

PATRON: How so?

DEATHKISS: By punishing the wrong answers.

PATRON: Ah, torture. It's always seemed a bit crude to me.

DEATHKISS: Maybe if done for its own sake. But pain is the key to unlocking many doors. You can learn just as much by which lies your subject chooses to tell as you can by his honesty.

PATRON: "His"? I didn't think your tastes ran that way.

Jack's fingers froze on the keyboard. All Death-kiss's previous kills had been women. The Patron had sharp eyes. . . .

DEATHKISS: Seeing the work of the rest of

The Pack has changed my perspective. As a matter of fact, my first male target is also my current work in progress.

PATRON: You mean he's still alive?

DEATHKISS: For the moment.

PATRON: Well, this is a first for The Pack—an online kill. Would you mind sharing?

DEATHKISS: I was planning on it.

He tapped a key. Djinn-X had a digital camera with him when they'd captured him, and Jack had taken some pictures of its owner with it. It had been easy to transfer those pictures to the laptop.

It took several minutes before the Patron's reply came back.

PATRON: I apologize for my earlier disparaging comment. You have quite an artistic touch.

DEATHKISS: That's not my intention. I'm simply interested in communication.

PATRON: All art is about communication. Art should either raise a question or attempt to answer one, don't you think?

"Yes," Jack found himself whispering.

DEATHKISS: Which one do you prefer?

PATRON: The question, of course. Answers are endings. Questions can lead anywhere.

DEATHKISS: Isn't what we do about endings?

PATRON: What you do, perhaps. What I do is about beginnings.

DEATHKISS: I don't understand.

PATRON: And you want an answer, hmmm? Well, I have those, too—not answers of my own, but the answers of others to questions I have posed.

An icon flashed, telling Jack that the Patron was

sending him a file. He waited until it had finished downloading, then opened it.

The image that filled his screen was an oil painting. A man, barely recognizable as such, was huddled in a heap on the ground. Above him, angels with twisted, demonic faces hovered, holding lances tipped with bloody hearts. An immense, white-bearded face dominated the top half of the painting, leering cruelly. His teeth were sharpened fangs—God as a cannibal.

Jack studied the painting, eyes narrowed. There was something familiar about the style. . . .

PATRON: And here's what inspired this reinterpretation of faith.

Another file. This one showed him horror: an elderly woman, naked except for a flowery hat, crucified in a doorway. Her wrists had been nailed to either side of the frame.

Jack's eyes widened. "Finally," he whispered.

With nothing more than that single, grotesque image and the feeling in his gut, he knew.

He'd found his family's killer.

CHAPTER FOUR

Three years ago.

A white Christmas in Vancouver was so rare that a local jeweler had promised to refund the full price of any wedding or engagement ring he sold in December if it snowed on the twenty-fifth. He'd made the promise in previous years as well, and so far his money had gone unclaimed.

He must be awfully nervous right about now, Jack thought as he lay in bed, still not quite awake. *If I weren't already married, I'd be doing some ring shopping myself.* It had snowed on the twenty-second and twenty-third, and not the slushy drizzle the West Coast usually got; every once in a while it would snow in Vancouver the way it rained, a steady barrage that went on and on and on. It came down in clumps like cottonwood fluff, big, heavy, white flakes that drifted earthward in a thick, sound-deadening curtain. Jack hadn't gotten much work done on the twenty-second; he'd spent the whole day staring out the window of his East Side studio, just watching it fall.

By the twenty-third his opinion had changed to match most Vancouverites: snow *sucked*. Beautiful as it was, the city wasn't equipped to cope—it didn't have enough plows, and the majority of the population wasn't used to the driving conditions. The city's light-rail transit system, Skytrain, didn't like it either; elevated, exposed, and electric, it shut down and sulked. City buses ran an hour to three hours behind schedule. Cab companies refused to take any fares that weren't emergencies.

On the twenty-fourth, Jack did what most citizens did—he gave up, and stayed at home.

"Ja—ack," called Janine's voice from downstairs. "Come on, sleepyhead. Your folks are going to be here in an hour."

Jack groaned, and burrowed underneath the comforter. He'd almost drifted off again when the covers were pulled away from his head.

"Argh! Lemme sleep," he growled, diving face-first under a pillow.

His wife sighed, and sat down on the bed beside him. "All right. I'll tell them you decided to hibernate for the winter."

"Mmmph."

"And they can give your presents to charity."

He slid an arm out from under the comforter and around her waist. "You won't tell 'em anything, because you're going into hibernation *with* me. Gotta have something to keep me warm—and I hear long women with short hair give off a lot of heat."

Janine laughed. She always kept her hair short, and currently had no more than an inch of blond fuzz covering her skull. "Oh, really? And what about Sam? Who's going to take care of him?"

"He's smart. He can learn to forage for nuts and berries."

She yanked the pillow away and hit him with it. "I can't believe you'd say that about your own son," she said, pretending to be indignant.

"*I* can't believe I married someone who's coherent before nine A.M."

"I bet you weren't like this when you were a kid," she said, lying down beside him. He eased an arm under her head.

"Not at Christmas, anyway," he chuckled. "I was a lot more like Sam—couldn't sleep the night before, up at five-thirty Christmas morning. So hyper I swear I *vibrated.*"

"So what happened?"

"I discovered masturbation. Calmed me down a lot."

"Well, Sam's only six—I think he's got a few hyper years left." Janine sat up and swung her legs off the bed. "Come on. I've got coffee made."

"Caffeine? Why didn't you say so . . ."

He got up and had a quick shower, whistling an old Devo song while he shampooed. He threw on some black sweat pants and a white T-shirt when he was done and padded downstairs in his bare feet.

"Dad! Just one more sleep!" his son announced from the living room. Sam had his mother's narrow face and upturned nose, but his father's wavy brown hair. He'd made a point of counting down the days for the last two weeks.

"You got it, Sam," Jack said as he headed for the

kitchen. His son followed him, waving a comic book in one hand.

"Look! Marshall gave me a *Spawn* number one for Christmas! Know why?"

"Uh—because he bought seven copies when it came out?" Jack poured coffee into a black mug with a green alien head emblazoned on it.

"*No*," Sam said in exaggerated exasperation. "It's 'cause I'm his *best friend.*"

"I thought I was your best friend, buddy," he said, getting cream from the fridge. The fridge was covered with magnets Janine had collected from tourist traps. The one that caught his eye every day when he grabbed the door handle was from a ghost town in Arizona: a skull wearing a cowboy hat grinned at him, with "Yahoo, Buckeroo!" printed underneath.

"Yahoo," Jack said, pointing a finger and cocked thumb at the skull and firing an imaginary shot.

"Dad?"

"Yeah, buddy?" He pulled a chair away from the kitchen table and sat down.

"How come you're always shooting the fridge?"

Jack laughed. "It's just a thing I do when I'm in a good mood. A ritual, I guess."

"What's a rich-yule?"

"It's what you're gonna have, once Grandma and Grandpa get here."

"Oh. Okay." He grinned in that completely accepting little-boy way he had, and ran back into the living room. Jack shook his head and grinned himself; he couldn't remember a time when he'd had that kind of complete confidence in his father. It was heartwarming and a little scary, all at once.

Janine came into the kitchen and sat down at the table with him. "Well, the guest room is ready. All we need now is your folks."

A double honk sounded from outside, the greeting Jack's father always gave when he arrived. "And there they are," Jack said.

Mr. and Mrs. Salter walked through the front door with their arms full of packages. "Merry Christmas!" his mother shouted. She was a tall woman, with curly hair dyed aggressively red. "Look what Santa dropped off at our house by mistake!"

"Wow!" Sam said, running up and hugging his grandma around the waist. "Are there some for me?"

"Oh, I think there might be a few in there," Jack's father said. He was a short, bullish man, with a square jaw and gray hair he kept cropped short. "Hey, there's my twin!" he said with a laugh, getting a hug from Janine.

"Merry Christmas," Jack said, accepting an armload of packages while Janine got their coats. "Oof. You buy out Toys-R-Us again this year?"

"Ixnay on the Oystay," his father said. "Antasay, got me?"

"Huh?" Sam said.

"Never mind," Jack said. "Your grandfather slips into an old Swedish dialect now and then."

Jack ushered them into the living room. An eight-foot Douglas fir dominated one corner, decorated in a lavish and somewhat eclectic manner: action figures from Sam's collection waged war in the tree's branches over the fate of baby Jesus in a manger, illuminated by glowing chili peppers—patio lanterns strung up in lieu of Christmas lights—the tableau made even more surreal by Jack's handcrafted ornaments. They were all composed of found objects, often silverware; Jack had discovered you could make a quite serviceable angel out of two forks, a spoon and a bit of wire, especially if you spread the tines out for the wings.

"Good Lord," his father said, examining the fir. "Well, at least the tree is real."

"I thought you'd be late," Jack said, depositing the presents under the tree. "Considering the roads."

"Oh, you know your father," his mother said, dropping into an armchair. "Made us leave an hour early, just in case."

"Good thing I did, too," Mr. Salter said. "The main routes are all right, but we almost got stuck a few times on side streets. Slow going, I can tell you."

"Well, they say it's supposed to warm up by tomorrow," Janine said.

"Yes, and then we'll have to deal with the slush," Mr. Salter grumbled.

"Anybody want a drink?" Jack asked.

"I wouldn't mind a hot chocolate," Mrs. Salter said. "Take the chill out of my bones."

"How about you, Dad?"

"Sounds good to me."

"Me, too!" Sam piped up from under the tree. He was rooting through the boxes, looking for his name and saying, "Yes!" every time he found it.

"I'll make some for everyone," Janine said.

DEATHKISS: I recognize this.
PATRON: I assume you mean the painting and not the photo.

DEATHKISS: Yes. By an artist named
Salvatore Torigno, isn't it?
PATRON: Very good. Yes, Torigno is one of my
successes.
DEATHKISS: I didn't know he was dead.
PATRON: He isn't. His dear mother, though—as
you can see by the photo—has attended her last
Easter Mass.

It was late afternoon when Jack got the call. Janine
and his mom were in the kitchen fixing dinner and his
dad was in the middle of a serious debate with his
grandson: "No, Sammy, I don't think Batman could
beat Spiderman in a fight. Not a fair one, anyway . . ."

Jack picked up the cordless on the second ring.
"Hello?"

"Jack?" The voice had a German accent as thick
and heavy as a Black Forest cake. Jack recognized it
immediately.

"Mr. Liebenstraum—merry Christmas," Jack said.

"Jah, Jah, merry Christmas to you, too. I am sorry to
be bothering you at home, Jack, but it seems I will not
be returning after the holidays, not for some time. I
have pressing business concerns."

"I'm sorry to hear that." Liebenstraum was a
wealthy German art collector who'd bought one of
Jack's pieces through an intermediary. He'd apparently been impressed enough to contact Jack about a
European exhibit, maybe even a tour; it was the kind
of opportunity that could make an artist's career.

Jack had never met the man in person. The German
had been in town for the past two weeks, but so far

had been forced to cancel appointments twice because of business. The last time, he'd said he'd be busy until he left on Christmas Eve— but that he'd be back in town shortly after New Year's.

"I am so sorry, Jack," Liebenstraum said regretfully. "I wanted so much to see your studio, your pieces. Now that I finally have a few spare moments, it is too late."

A few spare moments. "What time does your flight leave?"

"Not until ten."

"Well, if you wanted, we could still get together," Jack said. "It'd take me about an hour to get to my studio. As long as the cabs are running again, you could meet me there."

"Are you sure? I don't mind, I have nothing to do but drink schnapps in the airport bar, but you—you must be home with your family, *nicht wahr?*"

"It's okay. They'll understand."

"Well, then—I would like that very much. And this time I will be there, I promise."

"Great!" Jack gave him the address, thanked him, and hung up.

Now all he had to do was tell everybody else. . . .

DEATHKISS: I don't understand your definition of "success."
PATRON: My objective was not to kill Torigno. It was to find the person he loved the most, and destroy that person in the way that would resonate most deeply in his soul. Torigno is a devout Catholic; I chose the religious symbology

carefully. The Easter bonnet was a nice touch, don't
you think?
DEATHKISS: Yes.

The sun was already starting to set when Jack set out
for his studio. Under normal driving conditions he
would have been able to get there in half an hour;
now, he knew it would take him at least twice as long.

He drove through a surreal landscape. Almost three
feet of snow had fallen within forty-eight hours, turning his neighborhood into alien terrain: vehicles that
had been parked for the last two days were completely
encased, white bulges lining the street like the foothills
of a glacier. Hedges, bushes and trees were coated so
thickly they were only shapes, globes and ridges and
cones of sparkling white. It felt like staring at a blank
page and seeing half-formed ideas pushing their way
up through the paper.

As Jack had expected, Janine and his mother had
been supportive, while his father had grumbled. The
senior Salter had never been crazy about his son's chosen field; he had tried to convince Jack more than once
to pick something "with a little more stability in it."
Jack had long ago learned to simply change the subject, rather than defending his point of view. Art
wasn't something Jack had chosen; it had chosen him.
That was the closest thing to an explanation he could
give his father, and Jack knew his father didn't understand.

Despite that, they had come to a kind of truce, a
treaty unknowingly written by Sam. He had seen
them get into an argument once, started crying and re-

fused to stop until Jack and his father had hugged each other. After that there were no more loud disagreements, not when Sam was around.

In the end, his father had insisted Jack take their car. "It's got snow tires on it, and you won't have to dig it out. Just don't leave the radio on that junk you listen to."

Jack lived in Burnaby, while his studio was on the east side of Vancouver, just off Main and Terminal. He took Hastings Street, but even that was moving at a crawl; there'd been some sort of chain-reaction accident on the long downslope just past Boundary Road. At least three tow trucks and five police cars blocked the road, turning the snow into a strobing rainbow of yellow, blue, and red.

By the time he got to his studio it was just past six, and full dark. Liebenstraum wasn't there yet, so he unlocked the door and went inside. He puttered around for a few minutes, pulling out a few pieces he had in storage and arranging them nervously. Jack worked primarily in mixed media, combining elements of painting, sculpture, and text; his stuff tended toward pop culture and the three-dimensional, like the bust of Madonna he'd made out of condom wrappers, Styrofoam, and white glue.

Fifteen minutes passed, then half an hour. No Liebenstraum. Jack wondered if he'd been able to get a cab. He thought about making some calls, seeing if taxis were available, but there were too many cab companies in Vancouver—besides, what if Liebenstraum were trying to call him?

Finally, there was a knock at the door. It wasn't Liebenstraum, though; it was a cop. "We got a call about a prowler," she said. She was in her twenties, with short dark hair and brown eyes. She was amazingly cheerful for someone working on Christmas Eve.

Jack showed her some ID, told her what he was doing there. She wished him a merry Christmas and left.

He waited for another half hour, then called home.

No answer. He got voice mail after four rings, and hung up on the sound of his own voice. He tried again and got the same thing. Weird; he chalked it up to the snowstorm and the fact it was Christmas Eve. Overloaded lines, probably.

He waited another thirty minutes before he accepted the fact that Liebenstraum wasn't coming. Either he couldn't get a cab or he'd just been jerking Jack around the whole time; Jack didn't know whether to be pissed off or disappointed.

Neither, he decided as he got into the car for the long ride home. It was Christmas Eve, goddammit, and he was going to spend what was left of it with his family, drinking eggnog and listening to his father's bad jokes and having a good time. Poor Liebenstraum would be stuck thirty thousand feet in the air, eating rubber chicken and watching *Home Alone 4* while a stranger snored on his shoulder.

He turned on the radio, found a local station that was playing "Rockin' Around the Christmas Tree," and started singing along. He made excellent time on the way back, and by the time he pulled into the driveway at home he was in a pretty good mood.

The front door was slightly ajar.

• • •

PATRON: What creates great art?
DEATHKISS: Great artists.
PATRON: Precisely. But what creates great artists?
DEATHKISS: Training. Perseverance. Talent.
PATRON: Sadly, no. There are many artists with all of the above qualities who produce merely *good* art. Something more is needed to make that leap from the competent to the sublime, from the ordinary to the inspired. If you don't know what it is, I'm sure your prisoner does.
DEATHKISS: Pain.

Jack knew, even before he stepped inside.

He had that kind of paranoid flash everyone gets from time to time, especially when hearing about a car accident or plane crash in the news; the utter conviction that a friend, a lover, a parent is now dead. It strikes the brain like lightning—and then rationality takes over, soothing the nerves, taming the fear.

Jack went through this entire process in an instant, but this time the fear would not be tamed; it snarled and leapt and devoured logic whole.

Hand trembling, he pushed the door open slowly. He could hear Bing Crosby crooning "I'm Dreaming of a White Christmas," inside.

His mother was the first thing he saw. She hung from the stairwell that led to the second floor, suspended by a string of Christmas lights that wound around her neck and lashed her wrists to her ankles. The lights blinked off and on, turning his mother's bulging eyes and protruding tongue blue, green, red, yellow. She turned slowly in the breeze from the open door.

PATRON: Pain. Exactly. Such a simple word to
encompass an infinity of variations. On a biological
level, it's nothing more than a warning system—but
when we consider the emotional realm, it becomes
something else entirely. Emotional anguish is a fuel,
one that can power many engines: fear, lust, rage,
ambition.
　　Creativity.

He ran forward blindly, down the short hallway, past
the living room and into the kitchen. When questioned by the police later, he couldn't tell them why
he went into the kitchen first, or how he'd gone right
past the living room without noticing what was in it.
　　His father was sprawled on his back on the kitchen
table. He'd been dressed in a Santa Claus suit, the
front left unbuttoned to expose his disemboweling.
Blood dripped off the fake white beard and the ropy
loops of intestine hanging over the edge of the table.
Jack could smell blood, shit, and roast turkey.

DEATHKISS: You've mentioned Easter twice.
Is that when you killed her?
PATRON: Yes. The photo doesn't show it, but there's
a pot of milk chocolate bubbling on the stove. Smell
is such an important component of memory; I
wanted to fix the *experience* of Easter morning firmly
in Salvatore's mind. He will never see the crucifix
again without seeing his mother's corpse, nor will he
take a bite of chocolate. I have entwined the two
events together in the very depths of his being. . . .

• • •

Jack was in shock. He moved through a world he did not understand, could not comprehend.

There seemed to be no urgency, just a disjointed kind of momentum that kept him moving forward.

Janine was in the living room. She'd been used to decorate the tree.

Jack was starting to see everything in tightly focused snapshots, single details in frozen bits of time. A severed finger, balanced on the halo of one of his silverware angels. A bare foot, still wearing the red nail polish he'd applied himself, hanging near the base. Her heart, wrapped in bloody tinsel, resting on a branch.

Her head, impaled on the very top where the star was supposed to go.

Everything suddenly went very far away, without moving at all. It was the strangest feeling.

DEATHKISS: What, no Easter Bunny?
PATRON: One can only take a metaphor so far.
DEATHKISS: You said Torigno was a success. Why?
PATRON: Because he survived. I have struck twenty-one times, each time choosing someone I believed had potential and destroying the person or persons nearest to him. Of the twenty-one candidates I selected for this process, five have committed suicide, three are alcoholics, one is addicted to heroin, four are in psychiatric hospitals and two are in prison. Five have channeled their pain into their art, with varying degrees of success; one of them won a Turner Prize two years ago.

Many members of The Pack claim that what they do is art. I do not create art.

I create artists.

He came back to himself slowly, by degrees. He was sitting slumped in the hallway, his arms around his knees, staring at the wall in front of him. He couldn't remember how he got there. He could hear Mel Torme singing about chestnuts on an open fire.

There was something he had to do, something that nagged at him. Something he dreaded.

He had to go upstairs.

In the end, it was hope that made him edge past the slowly twisting body of his mother and up the stairs. Hope that maybe the killer had spared Sam. That maybe Sam's body wasn't waiting for him up there, that somehow his son had gotten away or even been kidnapped. It was a very small, fragile hope.

It didn't last.

His son's bedroom had been turned into a nativity scene. Life-size cardboard cutouts of the wise men, Joseph, and Mary were grouped around Sam's bed, which had a small wooden manger placed on top of it.

Sam was inside. His arms and legs had been amputated to make him fit. They were never found.

DEATHKISS: Your list only totals twenty.
PATRON: One is still undecided. Of them all, I thought he had the greatest potential; while many of my subjects lack focus in the beginning, he never did. With him, it was simply a matter of redirection.

> **DEATHKISS:** But he's turned out to be a disappointment?
> **PATRON:** I'm still not sure. He may yet live up to my expectations.
> **DEATHKISS:** Careful. Expectations are dangerous.

A neighbor finally came over to check on the wide-open door. She took one look inside and screamed.

The police found Jack inside, kneeling beside his son's bed. He didn't resist when they took him away in handcuffs; he didn't say anything at all until they asked him to give a statement. Then he told them what had happened in an emotionless monotone and exacting detail.

The same neighbor that called the police, Mrs. Krendall, had received an odd phone call at just after seven o'clock. A man claiming to be Jack's brother had asked her to come over to the Salters' house right away; when she'd knocked on the door, there had been no answer.

Another neighbor, out shoveling his walk, had seen Janine wave good-bye to Jack from the front door at five. Jack had talked to the female officer at his studio at around six-thirty, and the coroner put his family's time of death between seven and eight P.M. There was no way Jack could have committed the murders; he was released.

No hard evidence to support the existence of "Mr. Liebenstraum" was ever discovered.

> **DEATHKISS:** With such a distinctive style, I'm surprised the police haven't linked any of your crimes together.

PATRON: Art is not something the constabulary appreciates—thus, my motives are invisible to them. My kills are spread across the country, done with a different technique every time, and my victims are of every gender, race and age. While I have a certain fondness for holidays—the rituals are so firmly ingrained in our society that they continue to resonate year after year in my artists' minds—I do not always go after the candidate's immediate family. I have killed lovers, best friends, teachers, and students. I have killed aunts, uncles, cousins, and even a long-lost twin.

    The police see only who might benefit from a murder; no one notices the bereaved artist in the background.

DEATHKISS: I'd like to see what else your candidates have produced.

PATRON: Certainly. Here's a piece by the Turner Prize–winner I mentioned—and then you can share what you're doing to your captive, hmm?

The Patron tapped a key, sending a file of a painting he found especially moving. It depicted a child lying in a meadow, head pillowed on his arms, staring up at a blue sky alive with his daydreams; knights on winged horses jousted, while cartoon monsters played baseball in the clouds.

Below his smiling face, the child's body was vivisected: bones and muscles and organs clearly visible, hungry insects already burrowing into the exposed flesh.

Yes, the Patron thought. *The Closer should appreciate this.* . . .

Dear Electra:

I need your advice. Let's say a certain hypothetical boy asked out a certain hypothetical girl. Not on a date, exactly, but not on not-a-date, either, if you know what I mean. Am I making any sense here?

Oh, screw this, Electra—if I can't be honest with you, who can I be honest with?

Bobby Bleeker asked me out. Kind of.

I guess I should tell you about Bobby. He's my age, has short blond hair, and blue eyes with really long lashes. He's got a nice smile, and he's tall. He's sort of cute.

Okay, he's really cute. And he asked me if I was going to the mall later, because his friends were going to do a pizza and he wanted me to come because he knows I like pineapple and so does he but his friends never let him order it because they think pineapple is gross, so he wanted me there to vote for pineapple.

That's a date, right? Electra?

MORE DATA REQUIRED.

Okay, so I asked Jessica to ask Belmont (that's Bobby's friend) if he thought Bobby liked me, and Belmont said he didn't know, but Jessica thought he was covering up.

INSUFFICIENT INFORMATION.

No kidding. Anyway, I didn't say yes or no, and now I don't know what to do. Or what it means if I *do go, or if I don't. I don't anything, Electra. Help me out.*

PLEASE DEPOSIT ANOTHER FIFTY CENTS FOR THE NEXT THREE MINUTES.

Oh, I get it. You don't know any more about this than I do, do you? Don't know why I thought you would—you're just a bunch of electronics.

AND YOU'RE JUST A BUNCH OF HOR-MONES.

What? Electra, I'm shocked. That's not very polite.

YOU KNOW IT'S TRUE.

Well . . . maybe. I have to admit, I did think about what it would be like to kiss Bobby.

AND?

Halfway through the kiss, he turned into Uncle Rick.

DANGER! DANGER! RED ALERT!

I know, I know . . . I just couldn't help it. And now I feel guilty, and I'm not even sure why—is it because I thought about kissing Uncle Rick, or because I'm thinking about going out with Bobby? This is all messed up, Electra.

I HAVE A POSSIBLE SOLUTION.

I'm all ears. And hormones.

TRANSPLANT UNCLE RICK'S BRAIN INTO BOBBY'S BODY.

Hmm. That way, I'd get Uncle Rick's personality, but I could still date Bobby's body without gett-ting into trouble. Electra, you're brilliant!

Of course, it would have to be our secret. I'd be the only one who'd know. I'd have to help Uncle Rick adjust to being a teenager all over again, and

tell him which clothes he could wear without look-
ing dorky, and teach him about music and stuff—
though most of the stuff he listens to now is pretty
cool. Except the jazz.

There's only one problem, Electra—aside from
the obvious one of finding a brain surgeon willing to
work cheap. I don't know how to say it, but . . .

I still want Uncle Rick's body.

**WARNING! WARNING! POSSIBLE IN-
FORMATION OVERLOAD!**

I can't help it, Electra—maybe it's wrong, but
that's how I feel.

**I BELIEVE THE TECHNICAL TERM FOR
WHAT YOU ARE FEELING IS: EXTREME
STUPIDITY.**

I know, I know . . . God, what am I going to do?
This is driving me crazy, Electra, it really is.

I went down to Uncle Rick's studio yesterday. He
promised to show me the new piece he was working
on, even though he never shows anybody a piece
until it's finished.

His studio is in a loft in a cruddy part of town,
but I guess the rent is cheap. I took the bus to get
there, after school.

I really like his loft. It's in an old warehouse with
bare wooden walls and all these huge rusty pipes
and oak beams running across the ceiling, which is
about twenty feet high. There's a row of dusty win-
dows all the way around the top of the loft that
probably haven't been cleaned in about fifty years. I
offered to wipe them down once, but Uncle Rick
wouldn't let me—he says he likes the quality of
light they let in.

So I knock on the door, which is this big slidy metal thing that Uncle Rick really has to yank on to get open. He's wearing ripped jeans and a dirty white T-shirt, he's covered in sweat, and he's got grease marks on his arms and face. Disgusting, right?

God, he looked sexy.

I swear, my brain just seized up. He told me to come in and I didn't say a word, just stumbled inside. It was a really sunny day, and it took a moment for my eyes to adjust—at first I couldn't see a thing. I just stood there, trying not to breathe too hard. I could smell hot metal and freshly cut wood. And him.

When my vision cleared I saw this form in the middle of the room. It was a sculpture of a bald woman leaning over a bowl she held in her lap, her head down. It was made out of metal—aluminum, I think. Her skin was like scratchy chrome.

"Just a sec, I'll turn it on," Uncle Rick said.

When he did, water started to gush from the woman's head. All of a sudden, she had this beautiful liquid hair. And it didn't just fall straight down, either—there were some glass parts sticking up that I didn't notice at first, that made the water kind of swirl as it fell.

It didn't flow into the bowl; it funneled into glass pipes on either side of her chest, wound around each other so the water flowing through them looked like shimmery braids. The pipes connected to the bottom of the bowl, which slowly filled up with water.

I got closer and saw that the woman was studying her own reflection in the bowl of water. He'd painted the bottom of the bowl silver, turning it into a curved mirror.

"It's fantastic," I said. Maybe it was just my imagination, Electra—but I think the woman looked a little like me.

Uncle Rick shook his head and lit a cigarette, and I could see sunlight sparking off little metal shavings stuck in his hair.

"Nope, not yet," he said. "There's something missing."

I know just what he means.

CHAPTER FIVE

Two and a half years ago.

"Can I ask you a few questions?"

Nikki looked over the man at the next booth, carefully. He was around thirty, with unkempt brown hair, a stubbly beard, and eyes that looked like they hadn't seen sleep in a week. He was dressed too well to be homeless, but he didn't have the vibe of a customer. She made him for a cop, but that didn't bother her; she dealt with cops every day, they were as much a part of hooking as the johns.

"I'm not working, honey," she said. "Coffee break, you know? Get back to me in twenty minutes or so."

"I'd rather not cut into your profits," the man said. "I'm a journalist. I'm doing a story about the Stroll and I'd like your take on it."

She smiled at him. A smile was her automatic reaction to dealing with anyone, regardless of how she felt—it lowered people's defenses while giving her a second to raise her own. Every working girl she knew had one unbreakable rule about dealing with johns, and Nikki applied that rule universally: go with your gut. And her gut said . . .

Danger?

Sorrow.

"Okay," she said abruptly. "Have a seat."

Later, she analyzed that moment over and over, trying to figure out why she had agreed to talk to him. There was something not quite right about the guy, something damaged and hurt—she'd never have gotten in a car with him. And yet, the overwhelming impression she got wasn't rage, but a deep sadness.

He picked up his coffee cup and slid into the booth across from her. "My name is Jack."

"Wendy." It was the name she used on the street.

Jack pulled out a notepad and pen. "How long have you been doing this?"

"Since I was seventeen—fifteen years, give or take."

"How'd you get started?"

"Same reason everyone does—drugs. I got hooked on the worst one of all."

"Crack?"

"No—money." She pulled out a pack of cigarettes. "See, the money to be made can be *amazing.* When you're young and dumb, it almost seems like they're giving it away. So you spend it. Life becomes one long party. Next thing you know, you're addicted to something expensive, and now you don't have a choice anymore. You can't just quit and go work as a waitress, because minimum wage plus tips won't support your habit, and besides, you're not qualified to do anything else."

"You don't look like a junkie."

She lit her cigarette with a small butane lighter.

"That's because I'm not one. Wrong part of town." She waved one red-nailed hand, indicating the diner they sat in. It was called the Templeton, and it was funky but not run-down; a row of booths lined one wall and an old-fashioned counter with chrome stools the other. It was decorated in a retro-chic fifties' style, with a sign over the servers' pick-up window that read *Specials* in glowing neon script. Each of the booths had its own chrome mini-jukebox mounted next to it, the kind where you flipped through the selections by turning pages mounted behind glass. A few other working girls sat at another booth, and a young man with a goatee tapped away at a laptop at the counter.

"See, every city has two Strolls: the downtown and skid row. Skid row is where the crackheads and junkies work. They work cheap because all they want is enough for that next fix. The downtown is different—young, pretty and upscale. We cater to businessmen, mainly. You took a poll of the girls downtown, you'd get mostly single moms and college students."

"Which one are you?"

"Neither. I'm an old-timer, been doing it my whole life. I'm used to the money and don't really know how to do anything else."

"You could always go back to school."

"And do what? Become an accountant? I could just see me at the staff Christmas party—'Hey, everyone! Wendy's giving blow jobs under the mistletoe!' "

Jack winced, almost imperceptibly.

"Yes, the Christmas season," he said. "Brisker business during the holidays?"

"No, men are pretty much horny all year round."

"What about bad johns? Any increase at particular times of the year?"

It was an odd question. She thought about it, then said, "Maybe in the summer. Hot weather, hot tempers. But the really bad ones—well, they're bad all the time. All that stuff about the full moon bringing out the crazies is bullshit. You're just as likely to get a creep on a sunny afternoon in July as midnight on Halloween."

"Ever had it happen to you?"

"Sure. Not in a long time, though—my instincts are pretty sharp."

"How about friends of yours?"

"Everybody gets a bad trick sooner or later. If you're lucky, you'll only get robbed."

"Ever known someone who was unlucky?"

She glanced at him sharply. He met her stare eye to eye. After a second, she answered.

"If you're talking about *dead whores,* yes. Yes, I've known several *dead whores.* Would you like *details?*" She threw the words at him like broken glass.

His reaction wasn't what she expected. He simply looked thoughtful and said, "I don't care how they made a living. Were they your friends?"

She glared at him, not sure what to think. "Some were. Others probably deserved what they got and more."

"That might be true. But how do you know?"

"I trust my gut. Some people are just shit—the planet would be better off without them."

"I wish my gut was as reliable as yours."

"What, don't journalists have instincts?"

"No," he said. "Just questions . . ."

• • •

And he'd asked her a few more and then gone away. She saw him a few more times over the next week, talking to other girls, and from what they said he'd asked them pretty much the same things he'd asked her.

But Nikki was the only one he interviewed twice.

He came back to the same restaurant about ten days later. She was sitting by herself, and nodded when Jack asked if he could sit down. Outside, a gray rain was drizzling down.

They stared at each other for a moment without talking. They never spoke about that moment afterward, but Nikki knew exactly what had happened. They had *recognized* each other, had understood on some deep level they were alike. It had taken an effort to smile.

"So," she said. "How's your story going?"

"I'm not a journalist."

"Big surprise. Cop?"

"No."

"What do you want?" she asked flatly. "I don't work for pimps."

"I'm not a pimp. Why don't you have a partner?"

That stopped her for a second, but she pretended not to know what he meant. "Because *I'm* not a cop either, I'm a hooker—"

"Most girls use a buddy system. One gets in a car, the other one writes down the licence plate."

"I can take care of myself."

"So I hear."

"What's that supposed to mean?"

A waitress hurried by. Jack waited until she was out

of earshot before replying. "Most hookers don't carry weapons or drugs because they're more likely to be busted for that than soliciting. You not only carry weapons, you're not afraid to use them. Frankly, the other girls are terrified of you."

"Fuck 'em."

"And what about Sally? Fuck her, too?"

Her smile faltered, but only for an instant. "You knew her?"

"No. But I know what happened to her."

"Only one person knows that," she said calmly. Her hand crept toward the purse beside her on the booth seat.

"I didn't kill her," Jack said. "But I know how she probably died."

Her hand slipped inside the purse.

"She was picked up on the night of July nineteenth, in a white car stolen an hour before. Nobody saw the driver's face, including you. She was probably raped, strangled and dismembered, but the body still hasn't been found."

Her hand found the pebbled roughness of the handgrip and tightened around it. She thumbed the safety off.

"Three girls in the last eight months," Jack said. "All of them with dark hair in curls. Sally was the only working girl, and the only one whose body—or body parts—haven't been found."

Her finger wrapped around the trigger, ever so carefully. "Why?" she asked.

"I don't know. But if you'll help me, maybe we can ask him in person. . . ."

And after a second, she'd thumbed the safety back on.

• • •

He told her, calmly and rationally, exactly what he planned to do. He explained the risks, and what he expected of her. He told her she could walk away at any point.

She told him she'd have to think about it. He gave her a week.

She'd taken the rest of the night off and gone home—no way was she going to be able to work with Jack's offer on her mind. She lived in an apartment in Yaletown, just off the downtown core, overlooking False Creek to the south. It cost her a good chunk of money every month, but she wouldn't scrimp on living space; though she never stayed in one city for too long, she always made sure she was comfortable. She didn't do drugs, hadn't had a boyfriend in years—designer furniture and an address with a view were relatively harmless vices in comparison.

She changed out of her working clothes and slipped into a pair of sweats and a T-shirt, then curled up on her white leather couch with a glass of scotch. She took a sip and looked around her home: plasma-screen television, CD jukebox, DVD collection, computer and computer games. Toys, distractions. Something to do when she wasn't working or working out. The same went for the Rollerblades, the mountain bike, the snowboard. She'd get rid of them the next time she relocated, and buy brand-new stuff in another city.

Her eye fell on the bookshelf. The books were the only thing that traveled with her from place to place, even though they were heavy and a pain to transport. Travel books mostly, big hardcovers with lots of pictures. Spain, Tahiti, France, Greenland—she liked variety. She had maps, too, and a big hollow globe in the corner that doubled as a bar. There were also recipe books from all over, even though she never cooked—they were something she'd gotten into the habit of picking up when she traveled. Some people collected spoons, some collected ceramic figurines, she collected cookbooks. Go figure.

Travel was her true addiction. She'd save up every year and go someplace for a month or two, taking a vacation not just from her work but from herself. She'd travel under a different name, dye her hair, experiment with different kinds of clothes, food, even the TV shows she watched. At first she'd regarded it as a kind of game, a harmless hobby like all her others, but eventually she realized she was doing the same thing she did for her clients—playing a role. The difference was she was doing it for her own pleasure, not somebody else's, which made it masturbation as opposed to prostitution.

What the fuck. Considering how many hand jobs she'd given in her life, she deserved a little self-satisfaction.

But was it enough?

Maybe that wasn't even the right question. Maybe she should be asking herself if Jack was crazy, or if she was. So why wasn't she?

Because she already knew the answer.

What she found herself thinking about instead was Sally. And Janet. And Billie and Yolanda and Joyce and CC and Veronique . . . the list went on and on, girls she'd known that had turned up dead or just disappeared. Nikki hoped some of them had made it out of the life; had gotten married or moved or just plain quit.

Maybe some of them had. But not many.

The phone rang. She frowned, got up and checked the call display. Private Caller, no number. She didn't pick up. She'd been having problems with a client the last couple of days, an Asian guy who had been hanging around the Stroll. Unlike Jack, this guy was definitely creepy—he'd picked up Nikki, then tried to talk her into a freebie by claiming he was a pimp scouting talent. She hadn't fallen for it, but apparently he'd pulled the same thing on several other girls who weren't as bright; one of them—probably Teresa, that bitch—had given him Nikki's phone number, and now he kept calling. The guy had dressed well and talked a good game, but no way he was a pimp—too short, too round, too ugly. She might have believed he was some kind of Chinese gangster, but those guys tended to travel in packs and their girls usually worked out of massage parlors.

The phone had stopped, but now it rang again. Same ID. "Fuck," she said, and picked it up.

"Hello, Wendy?" It was him.

"Yeah?"

"I'd like to see you again."

"Look, Richard, I told you—I'm not interested."

"Why not? I've asked around, you don't have a manager."

"And that's just how I like it."

"Really? You're not considering someone else?"

"I'm a solo act, Richard. I don't like to share."

"Then who was that guy in the coffee shop—the one you were talking to for so long?"

Her eyes narrowed. "You've been spying on me?"

"No, no. I was just down on the Stroll and saw you, that's all. Who is he, your boyfriend?"

"No," Nikki snapped. "He's someone I trade favors with now and then. I fuck him, he fucks somebody else—like some jerk that won't take no for an answer."

"That supposed to worry me?"

"Thing is, he uses a badge and a gun. He fucks you, you *stay* fucked."

Richard laughed. "Sure. I'll be in touch." He hung up.

She growled, and slammed the phone down. She'd have to change her phone number . . .

Or she could change everything else.

"Fuck it," she said.

Jack hadn't left a number; she'd had to wait for him to get in touch with her. It was a long, strange week—she found herself looking at every one of her tricks with new eyes. She'd always been cautious, but now she found herself turning down even regular customers. There was a tightness in her belly that at first she thought was fear . . . but after a while she realized it was simply anticipation. She wound up spending most of her time in the diner where they'd first met, waiting.

Finally, seven days later, he walked in and sat down. She told him she accepted.

And the training began.

She'd thought at first that he'd be the one in charge, a drill sergeant putting her through her paces.

What actually evolved was more balanced: Jack trained her mind, while she trained his body. Nikki held a master-level belt in Akido, a martial art that relied primarily on submission holds, and worked out with weights three times a week; Jack had two years' worth of art school. When they started, he was soft and out-of-shape—six months later, he could bench-press three-eighty and run a mile in four and a half minutes.

Jack's academic background proved more useful than Nikki would have guessed. He knew how to research, how to learn and how to teach—both himself and Nikki. His apartment was crammed with psychology textbooks, criminology papers, magazines that specialized in everything from surveillance equipment to mercenary services.

Most of all, he had *focus*.

Nikki had never met anyone as single-minded as Jack. He was a knife, a human blade sharpening himself every day against a whetstone of pain, honing away feeling and distraction and weakness until only an edge was left. An edge sharp as death itself.

And somehow, just as exhilarating. One night, lying on the foldout bed in Jack's apartment that she now slept on, she realized she hadn't turned on a TV set or gone to a movie in weeks. She spent every day working out, reading, and discussing strategy with Jack. Before, she could make a thousand dollars on a good night; now, she was living on savings. She was on a path that would almost inevitably lead to either prison or the morgue . . . and there was a place inside her, a place that had been empty for so long she'd almost forgotten it was there, that was starting to fill up.

She had traded one drug for another. She wondered if this was why people joined cults.

She learned a lot. She learned about the difference between an organized serial killer and a disorganized one. She learned about methods of body disposal, which chemicals were often used and what they smelled like. She and Jack worked out a list of questions that might push a serial killer's buttons, and she studied books on body language so she could interpret reactions.

Jack learned, too. Nikki taught him Akido, and whatever she could about the street—how to talk to cops, how to spot a hustler, scams to look out for.

And then there were the subjects Jack studied on his own.

Every night, he retired to his room for several hours to do "research." She'd seen some of the books on his bedroom shelf: Histories of the Inquisition. Studies of Nazi atrocities and psychological warfare. Books on brainwashing, interrogation, torture. He never discussed any of them with Nikki, but she understood what they were for.

"You've never done it before, have you?" she asked him once. They'd just finished a workout in the old garage Jack rented as a bare-bones gym; it had a cracked concrete floor, a punching dummy in one corner and a weight bench. They were sprawled out on the tumbling mats they used to practice takedowns.

"Killed someone?"

"No. Tortured them."

"No."

"Think you can do it?"

He'd looked at her for a long moment before answering. "I'll make myself," he said.

He hadn't sounded angry.

Just sad.

After six months, Jack thought they were ready—and he thought he knew where to start.

The killer who had murdered Sally had struck twice more, though the police seemed unaware of the fact. Two working girls with curly black hair had vanished from the street, and Nikki's contacts had no idea where they'd gone.

"Stupid *bitches!*" Nikki raged, throwing her cell phone across the room. It hit the couch, bounced off and slid under the dining-room table. "Don't they read their fucking bad john list? I *warned* them, for Christ's sake!"

"Nikki." Jack walked across the room, stood unflinching in the face of her anger. "No more."

"Don't tell me that! I—I just wanna *break* something—"

"No. I mean no more waiting. No more training."

She blinked back furious tears, met his steady gaze.

"No more dead friends," Jack said. "It's time to go to work."

There were only two of them. They had no experience, limited finances and few resources. They had no access to police records, manpower or equipment. Their one advantage was that they were criminals themselves—but it was a crucial one.

"Killers that target prostitutes don't always kill them," Jack said. He was working on retrofitting the cargo space of the white Econoline van he'd bought secondhand. "Sometimes they just have sex with them."

Nikki handed him a pair of vice-grips. "Yeah, and sometimes they have sex with them and *then* kill them. Or vice versa."

Jack took the vice-grips and used them to tighten the nut on the ring-bolt he'd attached to the floor. "Once he knows you're not a cop, he might get overconfident. Drop hints about what he could do to you, or what he's done to others. Can you handle that?"

"Don't worry about me losing my nerve," Nikki said. "I could blow the Devil himself with a smile on my face."

"Good. You may have to. . . ."

Nikki wore a dark, curly wig. Jack shadowed her on tricks, eavesdropping via a tiny bug in her purse and never more than a moment away. They soon settled into a routine: every night from nine P.M. to three A.M., they would hit the street and Nikki would trade fake intimacy for real dollars while Jack stood guard in the background.

Three months passed.

Jack listened to her give a hundred blow jobs. He listened to her have sex in hotel rooms, in cars, in alleys. The number of bad johns she encountered jumped, because now she actively sought them out; and if a john was acting strangely, she did everything she could to push him further. More than once, Jack was poised to intervene—but it always proved to be a false alarm, a trick that didn't want to pay or liked things just a little too rough. She went home with bruises sometimes, but none of her customers tried to strangle her. She kept an eye out for Richard, the wannabe pimp, but apparently he'd taken the hint; nobody on the street had seen him for months.

And then, one night in late March, she met Luis.

He pulled up in a station wagon, a family vehicle that still had a *Baby On Board* sticker in the rear window. The driver was a man in his mid-thirties, balding and portly with an olive complexion and a thick, black mustache. He beamed at her in delight.

"Hola, beautiful one! How are you tonight?"

"Lonely and short on cash," she said, beaming right back.

"Ah, then I think I can help. Would you care for a ride in my chariot? I would gladly pay you a hundred dollars for such a privilege."

"I'm thinking more of two."

"Ah, rides are getting more expensive. But you look like you would be worth it, yes?"

"Only one way to find out . . ."

He grinned and nodded. She slid into the passenger seat, glancing into the back as she did so. No child seat, no toys, no mess or clutter of any kind.

The *Baby On Board* sign still had a price sticker on the back.

"Careful on those yellow lights," she said as the car pulled away. "We don't want to get stopped, do we?"

The word *yellow* was a warning signal. When Jack heard the trick ask if it was okay if they went back to his place rather than a hotel room, Jack knew they had a possible. He tailed the car, but stayed well out of sight—the GPS unit Nikki had in her purse would let him track her to within ten feet.

He followed them across the Georgia viaduct, then around and under the overpass itself. This was largely undeveloped industrial land, sandwiched between Chinatown and the shores of False Creek. The Vancouver Indy race wound its way through here every summer, but right now the steel bleachers and concrete barricades stood row after lonely row in razor-wire-fenced lots.

Somehow, Jack wasn't surprised when the station wagon stopped.

He pulled over himself a block away, and covered the rest of the way on foot. He moved quietly and efficiently through the dark, preparing himself.

"He's unlocking the gate to a storage lot," Nikki's voice said in his ear. "Says he has a key to a trailer inside. I'm going to let him lock it behind us—should make him feel all safe and secure."

Jack froze.

He'd left the bolt cutters in the van.

No way to tell Nikki, no way to change the plan. He sprinted back the way he came.

By the time Jack grabbed the bolt cutters, the john had relocked the gate. Jack stopped worrying about stealth and ran.

"Okay, Luis, hope you're ready to party," Jack heard Nikki say. The reception from the bug was so clear she could have been standing right next to him. He could hear the door of the trailer open, almost see her and Luis stepping inside—

He hadn't run in the dark like this since he was a child, tearing full-tilt through the wide-open spaces of a playground on a summer night. It was almost dreamlike . . . and then Jack's foot hit something in midstride.

There was a single, airborne moment of flailing through the dark, then an explosion of pain as he smashed face-first into a wall. Everything went red, then gray.

". . . I don't know, Luis." Nikki's voice. It brought him back, cut through the haze of pain in his skull. "I don't like making it with bi-boys, y'know? You might give me something."

She was taunting him, pushing his buttons. Counting on Jack to back her up.

He was lying in a puddle of cold water. How long had he been out? His right hand was submerged, so cold it was numb. The bolt cutters were gone, lost somewhere in the shadows.

"Oh, *chiquita*, I'm not like that." Luis's voice. He didn't sound angry at all. He sounded happy and confident. That was bad, very bad.

No, no, it was good. It was what they'd been looking for, working so hard for. As long as Jack could just stand up . . .

He made it to his feet, but the world was on a strange angle and he fell down again. His head was spinning like it was full of tequila. He threw up, trying not to make any noise.

"You have lovely hair," Luis said.

Suddenly, Jack's head was clear.

He got to his feet carefully, got his bearings. The gate was that way. He walked quickly toward the nearest source of illumination, sodium-vapor brightness glaring from the top of a streetlamp, a lone steel palm generating its own island of orange-tinted light.

"But I don't care too much for your attitude," Luis said.

On the far edge of the island of light was a chain link fence. Jack sprinted toward it, tearing off his trenchcoat as he ran.

"I don't much give a fuck," Nikki said. "And I mean that literally. You give before I fuck."

Jack reached the fence. It was topped by coils of razor wire. He took his coat in his teeth and began to climb.

"Oh, I have plenty to give, *puta*. I have more to give than you can take. . . ."

At the top of the fence, Jack tossed his coat over the jagged barbs. It shielded his hands from the worst of it, but he still took painful gashes on both forearms and one calf. He dropped to the ground on the other side, leaving his coat tangled and impaled.

In his ear, the sounds of a scuffle. A dull thud.

And then nothing.

The trailer was fifty yards away, a white rectangle on its own atoll of light. Jack pounded toward it, straining to hear any sound from his earpiece. It felt like he was running on a treadmill, the trailer getting bigger but not any closer. Just as he reached the door he realized he'd left most of his equipment and weapons in the pockets of his trenchcoat.

He wrenched at the door, but it was locked. "NIKKI!" he yelled. He slammed into the door with his shoulder, but only wound up bouncing off it and losing his footing. He landed on his butt in the mud.

The door unlocked. It swung open.

"Jesus," Nikki said. "Try knocking first, huh?"

•   •   •

Inside, under a flickering fluorescent light, Luis lay facedown on a small cot. He was unconscious, a small trickle of blood behind his right ear.

"Had to smack him with this," Nikki said, holding up a heavy glass ashtray. "Would have used the stun gun, but he went for something in that drawer real quick."

Jack looked around. The only decoration on the cheap wood-paneled walls was a tattered calendar, and the air smelled of mildew and old sweat. Beside the cot, a card table held a coffeemaker and three stained cups, and a small desk stood in the corner with its top drawer open. Jack reached inside, pulled out a bottle of whiskey, a pair of handcuffs and a short electric cord. "Looks like he was planning on having a real party."

"Yeah. Hope I didn't kill him."

"He's still breathing," Jack said. "Get him ready. I'll bring the van around."

They took him to the garage they worked out in. Jack had soundproofed the room as best he could, lining the ceiling and walls with egg cartons sandwiched between acoustic tiles. The floor was concrete, with a drain in one corner.

Nikki helped get Luis out of the van and into the garage. Jack tied him to a kitchen chair with rope, making sure both his arms and legs were immobilized.

Jack stared at the unconscious man, unblinking. "Go," he said quietly.

Nikki left.

Jack took out a pair of large scissors. He used them

to cut all the clothes off Luis's body, and put the scraps in a white trash bag when he was done. He laid out his equipment. He lit a large candle, and turned out the rest of the lights.

Then he got out a bottle of smelling salts and waved it under his captive's nose.

Luis's head jerked, and his eyes fluttered open. He moaned.

"Do you know where you are?" Jack asked him.

"What? No, no . . . what's going on? Who are you?"

"Who I am is not important, Luis. It's who I'm not."

"You're crazy!"

"No, Luis. I'm not a lunatic. I'm not a police officer. I'm not a thief, or a kidnapper. I'm not a practical joker hired by your friends. And the one thing, Luis, that I most definitely am not, the one negative that defines me the most, is this: I am not someone who believes you are an innocent man."

"What—what do you want from me?"

"The truth. But first, you have to become somebody else."

"Who?" Luis whispered.

"Someone who would never, ever lie to me." Jack picked up a small tape recorder, hit the Record button. "Now. Let's go back to the beginning. . . ."

Six hours later, he gave up.

"I can't do this, I can't do this," Jack said to himself. He was sitting in the alley beside the garage, staring at his hands. There was no blood on them, but they wouldn't stop shaking.

Luis wouldn't confess. He had begged and pleaded

and cried, but he wouldn't admit to anything beyond soliciting a hooker. He had talked about his children, and his pregnant wife. He had apologized for every bad thing he had ever done in his life, and asked God to forgive him.

Jack had done terrible things to him. He'd had to leave twice to throw up, the last time producing nothing but ten minutes of painful dry heaves—but he'd forced himself to return and continue.

After four hours, Luis changed his tune.

He was guilty, he sobbed. He'd done it all, everything Jack had accused him of. He would sign anything, say anything—but when Jack pressed him for details, Luis had none to give.

"Am I wrong?" Jack asked himself softly. "Am I wrong?"

The sun was starting to come up, a gray hazy glow in the east. The alley stank of garbage, but the wet, fresh scent of rain was there, too. A swirl of pink dots blew past him, early cherry blossoms from a backyard tree.

Jack thought about his son. He thought about being a father, and what a father does. And then he stood up and went back inside.

Luis. Or whatever your name is. No wallet, no registration papers in the car, no ID at all.

"I told you, I explained that. In case I got arrested, I didn't want my family to find out."

Smart. You have a little boy, right? Roberto.

"Yes, yes. He's a good boy, he loves his father—"

Why? What do you do together?

"We, we do many things together. We go to movies, we go to the park and play soccer—"

Ah. He likes soccer. He must play on a team then, at school.

"Yes. I take him to practice, every Saturday—"

Never his mother. Only you.

"Always me. I love to see him play—"

Tell me about his first game. Against another team.

"What?"

How old was he? As a father, I'm sure you remember.

"Of course. He looked so handsome in his little uniform . . . oh, God . . ."

Go on.

"They lost. Four to one. He played so hard."

I'm sure he did. How old was he?

"Seven."

And the weather that day?

"Raining. Vancouver, it rains so much."

Yes. And what was the name of his team?

". . . I don't remember."

That's all right. I'll help you.

"No! No, it was—the Wolves. The Wolf cubs, all the parents called them that."

No.

"Wh—what?"

No. They didn't. The school league for seven-year-olds in Vancouver names their teams after the schools. There are no Wolves.

"I'm mistaken. What I meant—"

There is no Roberto. There is no Luis. There is only a stolen station wagon, a plausible cover story, and a *Baby on Board* sticker bought at a dollar store for color.

"No, no please, I swear to you—"

I know you now.

There is only one thing you will learn about me: I will not stop. When it gets bad, when it becomes so terrible that you pray for death, remember that one, simple fact: *I will never, ever stop.*

Until I know everything . . .

It took three days.

VANCOUVER POLICE TRANSCRIPT #332179, "Roberto Luis Chavez," Tape 7. The other voice on the tape is identified simply as "Unknown."

CHAVEZ: She was my sixth. I did her about halfway through February, it was my birthday and I was feeling all mixed-up, I thought I deserved something special—

UNKNOWN: Slow down. We're very close now.

CHAVEZ: I know, I know, I just—okay, okay.

UNKNOWN: Just breathe.

CHAVEZ: Her name was Bonnie. I picked her up on Seymour Street on a Friday. She was wearing a red leather miniskirt. I drove her down to the trailer and had sex with her before I killed her. I strangled her with an extension cord.

UNKNOWN: And the body?

CHAVEZ: I dumped it with the last two, that's where it is, I swear.

UNKNOWN: Yes. I checked it out. She's still there.

CHAVEZ: Oh, good. Good.

—pause—

UNKNOWN: What were her last words?

CHAVEZ: She—she said, "Michael."

UNKNOWN: Michael?

CHAVEZ: Yes. Oh God, oh God, please. Now?

UNKNOWN: Yes. Now.

—unidentifiable sound—

Tape ends.

They dumped the body at the same site Luis had left his kills, in the woods off the Sea-to-Sky highway. Jack duct-taped a Tupperware container holding seven ninety-minute tapes to his chest.

Nikki made the anonymous call to the police. Five minutes later they were on their way out of town.

They hit Des Moines next, where it took them just under a year to catch Duncan Shields. Jack stripped away his secrets in just under forty-eight hours; Shields gave up the location of nine bodies.

Back into Canada. In Calgary, Alberta, a cowboy-and-oil city that reminded Jack of Dallas, they snared Helmut Lansgaarden, a German immigrant with a taste for redheads and meat cleavers. They nailed him in seven months and Jack broke him in a day; they were getting better. For the first time, the Canadian and American authorities compared notes and realized what was going on. Someone found the story too good to keep to themselves, and the media got involved. By the time Nikki and Jack set up shop in Seattle, he had been officially christened.

The Closer was born.

INTERLUDE

Dear Electra:

This is too good not to write down. Today Uncle Rick took me shopping—clothes shopping. Whoohoo!

Okay, okay, not really clothes—more like stuff to make clothes—but still, in the ballpark, right?

We went to this fabric store in Little India, and looked at material to make me a costume. Most of my friends are all like, "No way I'm dressing up for Halloween, that's for kids," but I don't care what they say. Dressing up was always the best part, way better than free candy. You got to be someone else for a night, you know? Someone with superpowers, or magic friends, or just somebody everyone loves. You put on a costume and you don't have to worry about homework or Anna Johnson calling you fatface or your mom showing up at the PTA meeting drunk.

So, anyway, we looked at about a thousand different kinds of material. Indian women (from India, not First Nations—you should know better, Electra) use them to make these long dresses called saris, and they're beautiful! Blue and gold and crimson and silver and green and turqoise and pink! Every pattern you can think of, all swirly and intricate, on fabric as wispy as silk or heavy and smooth as leather. And you wouldn't believe what some of them cost, either.

So, what, you may ask, is my costume going to be this year? Well, let's take a look at some of our previous entries—what's that, Electra? A Top Ten List? Sure, why the heck not?

Fiona's Top Ten Halloween Costumes (Worn by Her)

10. *Luke Skywalker.* It was a cheap store-bought costume, but I got to run around and whack people with a lightsaber.

9. *A Horse.* This one beats out Luke because I made it myself—okay, I had a lot of help from my teacher, but still—and because it was pathetic. I was going through my Ohmigawd-I-LOVE-Horses phase, and I somehow thought I could capture all the beauty and grace of Black Beauty in a costume. It looked ridiculous, I could hardly see, and all my friends laughed at me. So I kicked them.

8. *The Terminator.* I didn't really pick this one and I was only two at the time, but I've seen pictures. My parents put me in this little leather jacket and shades and gave me a really butch haircut. I looked *dangerous.* According to my dad, it was also a pretty good description of what I was like at that age.

7. *Calvin.* I got a *Calvin and Hobbes* book when I was six, and I was hooked. I was so angry when I found out the newspaper

strip was going to end that year. Calvin
was the same age I was, and he was my
hero. Uncle Rick made a full-size Hobbes
for me to drag around, too.

6.   *Buffy the Vampire Slayer.* I was eight years
     old, and Buffy was the coolest girl alive.
     Also, I just wanted to dress like her.

5.   *American Maid.* Uncle Rick told me about
     this cartoon called The Tick, which I
     thought was the funniest thing I'd ever
     seen—even though all my friends thought
     it was dumb. American Maid is a superhero
     who throws high-heels at bad guys. I beaned
     a lot of people that year.

4.   *Arwen.* Lord of the Rings was my favorite
     movie at the time, and Liv Tyler was so
     gorgeous as the Elf Princess. I got my
     hair done the same way and made the
     dress myself. Uncle Rick said I looked
     beautiful.

3.   *Dead Elvis.* Okay, *I* thought it was funny. I
     got to be a rock star (kind of) and a zombie
     at the same time. Plus, I could say things
     like, "Can I eat your brains? Thank you.
     Thank you verra much."

2.   *The Bunny Princess.* My first real costume,
     which I made when I was four. All I can
     really remember is that I was convinced

that rabbits had magical powers, and I wanted to be a princess because everybody did what they said. The costume itself was some kind of tutu and a hat with bunny ears on it. There was also a magic carrot, which eventually transformed itself into a shriveled, rubbery stick with mold growing on it when I slept with it under my pillow for two months.

1. And Fiona's number one costume of all time (so far): *Joan of Arc*. Which I did last year and most of my friends thought was lame, mainly because they didn't know who she was. Well, she was an amazing woman who led whole armies and defied the church and was burned alive for her beliefs.

   And Uncle Rick helped me make the costume.

It was great, Electra. It was knight's armor made out of actual metal, and then we charred half of it and made little cellophane flames sticking up from the edges. My sword looked like it was on fire, too. Way better than a lightsaber.

This year, though, is going to be different. This year, instead of just copying someone else, I'm going to try and make something original. Something that says something about me. It's not just going to be a costume, it's going to be art. Well, maybe not ART, or even "Art," but at least art.

Uncle Rick says art should reveal something about the artist. "Art is an outer surface showing an inner truth," is the way he put it. If that's true, then Uncle Rick is a pretty complicated guy.

What's that, Electra? I've stalled long enough? All right, all right.

I'm going to be a moon goddess.

Oh, quit laughing. A moon goddess is mysterious, beautiful and enchanting. She's feminine and powerful. And I found this terrific material to make it from, all black and gauzy with little stars and moons on it like the night sky. And this year, Uncle Rick is going to take me to the Parade of Lost Souls, the big Day of the Dead festival that happens down on Commercial Drive. There's lanterns and shrines and drum circles and fire performers on stilts—I'm so excited! I can't believe Mom and Dad are actually letting me go—they're a little afraid of me going to "that part of town," like I'm going to get mugged or something. It's okay, though—Uncle Rick convinced them I'm old enough, and he won't let me out of his sight. Like I'd even want to be . . .

He wouldn't tell me what costume he was going to wear, though. Poophead.

PART TWO:

Execution

Impaling worms
to torture fish.

—George Colman the Younger,
Lady of the Wreck

CHAPTER SIX

Now.

"The Patron killed my family," Jack said.

Nikki stared at him. Jack sat in the living room of the crappy little bungalow they'd rented, on a thrift-store couch that had come with the place; Nikki sat cross-legged on the floor. She'd just woken up and was dressed only in a T-shirt. An upended cardboard box between them served as a coffee table, the only light in the room coming from the screen of the laptop it held.

"You sure?" Nikki asked. From the tone of Jack's voice, he could have been discussing something he saw on television.

"Yes. He kills those close to artists, and he likes to strike on holidays. He even made reference to me as one of his failures."

Nikki shook her head. She still wasn't fully awake, and this was a lot to absorb. "Jack—that's great, isn't it? I mean, this is the guy you really want, right? This is the guy you've been hunting for—"

"He doesn't kill prostitutes," Jack said.

"What? Hey, I don't give a shit about that, I'll still help you get him—"

"That's not what I mean. I mean, until now we've been hunting prostitute-killers because those are the ones we can catch. The monster who killed my family . . . I never thought we could get him. I thought he was beyond my reach." Jack stared at the screen of the laptop without blinking.

Nikki looked around, grabbed her cigarettes from the arm of the couch. "You still want to go after him, right?"

He turned his head to look at her. She met his eyes, then quickly looked away.

"I have to be very careful," Jack said. "I have to be *perfect.*"

"You can do it," she said softly. "*We* can do it."

"I have to plan. We can't just go after him first," Jack said. "I'll have to gain his trust—not as a new member of The Pack, but as their leader. I'll have to convince him I'm Djinn-X."

She shook out a smoke, put it in her mouth. Lit it, took a long drag and exhaled slowly. "Think you can pull it off?"

"Yes," Jack said. "I've broken him. Passwords, encryption codes—Djinn-X gave it all up. He *wants* to help me—I'm the last person on earth he's going to talk to, and he knows it.

"The Stalking Ground belongs to *me* now. . . ."

Djinn-X Rant One Million and Twenty-Three: Irony? Yeah, sure.

Irony has ruined everything. And if I hear that fucking Alanis Morrisette song one more time, I'm going to hunt the bitch down and kill her with a curling iron. Wouldn't *that* be fucking ironic.

There's nothing pure anymore, nothing that's just *itself.* Everything is just a riff on something that's already been done. Every goddamn sitcom, pop song, buddy-cop movie video-game action-figure Saturday-morning cartoon spinoff is just a clone of an idea that's been recycled a hundred times before. And we're all so hip and cool and bored that the only way to make this stuff palatable is to mock it right out of the gate. Put out crap with "Crap!" stamped on it. Wink at the world—hey, everybody's in on the joke, we all know what's going on. We get all those in-jokes, all those little digs and pop-culture references. My Spanky-sense is tingling! Luke, I am your father-figure! Scotty, beat me up!

It's all shit. Literally. The baby boomer culture ate all this stuff, digested it, and then crapped it all out again. We're wallowing in the excrement of the last generation, and none of us cares.

And then there's what I call the New Irony. Take an idea so bad, so tasteless, so kitschy, that it gets on the air through the shock value alone. Right off the bat the intelligentsia love it, because it's so over-the-top it's brilliant satire. It's parody, it pokes fun at sacred cows through extreme exaggeration.

Problem is, *half of fucking America doesn't get the joke.*

Oh sure, they laugh along with everyone else—but for completely different reasons. *All in the Family* wasn't a huge hit because people hated Archie Bunker's racism—it was because they *loved* him for it.

He said all those things everyone was thinking, but listen—there's a laugh track! It's okay that he's a bigot, because it's *funny!*

Liberals patted themselves on the back. Conservatives just grinned. It's all just a joke. We're just kidding. Laughter's always a *good* thing, right?

Hogan's Heroes taught us that Nazis are bumbling clowns. *M*A*S*H* gave us that wonderful combination of surgery, promiscuity, alcoholism and war. Women are emotional airheads, men are sex-obsessed pigs, everyone in power is a corrupt imbecile—media shoves those ideas down people's throats twenty-four-seven, and it doesn't matter if you laugh *at* it or *with* it because it's *always there.* From the time your parents plunked you down in front of *Sesame Street* to when you fell asleep watching *Saturday Night Live,* it was always there.

When I was in school, there was a kid named Darryl. Darryl's idea of a good time was to make fun of my sister, who was born mentally handicapped and with epilepsy. She died when she was six.

At the height of his wit, Darryl would suggest an incestuous relationship between us. But that's okay, because *everyone laughed.*

Right?

Jack's quest had led him to the ultimate answer. Not just who had killed his family, but why.

Transformation.

The Patron had done it to change him, mold him into something more than he had been. He had plunged Jack's soul into fire, burning away all that he loved, then hammered what was left into something harder, sharper, stronger.

No. Jack himself had done the last part—and what had emerged was not the artist the Patron had hoped for. Jack was a weapon now. A tool of destruction, not creation.

One that would destroy its own creator.

He explored the website carefully, deactivating all the hidden erase codes Djinn-X had warned him about. When he was done, he had full access to all Djinn-X's data—but just as his prisoner had said, the webmaster knew no more about the rest of the Pack than what they had posted themselves. Even among themselves they were careful . . . but still, they were willing to reveal much to their own.

The identity of Deathkiss might still be useful, but the creator of The Pack would have more influence— and it had to be utterly convincing.

He would have to *become* Djinn-X.

In art school Jack had always been an excellent mimic, able to reproduce another artist's style with ease—not just duplicating technique, but the artist's approach to his subject. It was closer to acting than drawing, being able to dive into somebody else's point of view and see through their eyes—but Jack had never dove into waters quite this deep.

Or this dark.

WHY I KILL

An Essay by Djinn-X

Okay, all you profilers and serial-killer groupies— assuming you're reading this after I'm long dead or in prison—here it is: the One Big Question that always gets asked and never seems to produce a decent response. Well, I don't know about anybody else's answer, but here's mine:

Physics.

Everybody gets angry. Anger gets compared to fire a lot, but it behaves more like water. It flows from person to person, and it always moves downhill. Owner to manager to employee to temp. It's like a big drainage system, and the lower you are on the chart the more anger flows down to you. And it works that way right across the board, from the financial to the political to the personal. The lower you are, the more anger you get dumped on your head—and just like water, it accumulates. Once the vessel's full, it starts to pressurize.

You apply enough pressure to a liquid—*any* liquid—it'll transform. Become a solid. When that happens to anger, it becomes something else: hate. Hate is slower, colder, denser. Hate is geologic. When I hear about ethnic feuds going back centuries, it doesn't surprise me at all. Hate's the emotional equivalent of fucking bedrock.

So what happens when you get a demographic like the baby boomers? Well, let's break it down. Millions of soldiers come home after fighting WW II. After four years they're considerably horny, and start fucking their brains out. Umpteen million kids are born as a result. They grow up as happy little youngsters in the fifties, and then POW! they hit puberty in the sixties. They spend the next decade having sex, listening to bad music and taking drugs. This fries their brains so badly they spend the seventies doing harder drugs and listening to worse music. In the eighties they decide to settle down, sell out, and become yuppies. By the nineties they're all having midlife crises and whining about how great the sixties were. It makes them bitter, because they know how badly they fucked up. They didn't change the world, *and they know it.*

Funny thing about self-loathing. It's the most deceptive of emotions, one that deliberately disguises itself. Someone who hates himself can rarely admit it because that leaves him with only two choices: self-destruction or change.

If there's a monster in your mirror, you can't look him in the eye and stay sane.

So the self-hater lies to himself. Every disillusioned, pissed-off baby boomer out there is looking for someone else to blame for how fucked-up the world is—anybody but themselves, of course. Is it any wonder we're a nation of lawyers?

So some corporate jerkoff sues a different corporate jerkoff who yells at his secretary, and she gives the guy at the Starbucks counter a hard time, and he goes out after work and gets drunk and punches me in the nose.

And I don't hate the guy that punched me. He's just a conduit that anger flows through. No, I savor that anger. I add it to all the rage inside me, and let it build. Let the pressure change it into hate. And when that hate has coalesced into a hard little bullet, I go out looking for a corporate jerk off . . . and I give it back to him.

Because it's really his in the first place, isn't it?

• • •

Jack had converted the basement of the bungalow into his interrogation room, using plywood, foam insulation and sheets of black polyurethane to turn it into a sealed, soundproof cube. Nikki rarely went down there, but now she stood at the base of the stairs, in front of the locked door.

Jack was upstairs, reviewing Djinn-X's files. Usually at this point in the process, Nikki would be doing verification—checking dump sites or the killer's house for evidence. Jack wouldn't send her out until he was sure his subject wasn't trying to set a trap or simply stalling for time.

This time, though, was different—Jack was doing all the checking via computer. But that wasn't the only thing.

She unlocked the door and opened it.

Djinn-X was chained, naked, to a chrome-frame kitchen chair Jack had bolted to the floor. His wrists were manacled to a chain around his waist, his ankles to the chair itself. A child's rubber ball with a rope punched through its middle functioned as a gag. The only light came from the open door; Djinn-X's head jerked up as Nikki entered, his lidless eyes twitching as he tried to blink. Dried blood streaked his face like rust-colored mascara. He grunted frantically.

Nikki stepped inside. She turned on the lamp on the small table, then shut the door.

"So," she said. "You kill boomers. That's *fucked up,* you know?"

She sat down in the chair the Closer usually occupied.

"I mean, much as I hate the assholes we usually burn, at least I understand them. They get off on hurting women, it's that simple. Most people like it a little rough now and then, but these guys are wired wrong—they have to take it too far. That's sick, but I get it. You, though—you kill people because they're a certain age? Maybe you're just nuts. . . ."

"Nnnn! Nnnn!"

"Yeah, yeah. Like I want to hear some fucked-up explanation about how aliens or Satan or your dead grandmother told you to do it. I don't really care, okay? You did it, you told Jack where and how and when, and once we check a few things we'll put you out of your fucking misery."

His eyes were two bloodshot, quivering orbs. She looked away, then fumbled at her purse.

"All right, all right, just a second . . . here." She pulled a bottle of Visine out of her purse.

"Tilt your head back . . . okay." She put a few drops into each of his eyes. He grunted gratefully.

"Look, I want to ask you something," Nikki said. "I'm not as good at that as Jack, but if you give me a straight answer, maybe I can do something for you. Send a last message to someone, maybe. Interested?"

He nodded.

"Yeah, like you'd say no. You better not lie to me, motherfucker." She stood up, walked behind him and undid the gag.

He spat out the ball. "What if I do?" Djinn-X said. "What are you gonna do—*hurt* me?"

"I won't do a thing. I'll just tell Jack."

He gave a weak little snort. "I don't think so. Only reason you're asking me and not him is you don't want him to know. And I don't know if I can betray my old buddy Jack like that. . . ."

He started laughing, a choking, high-pitched kind of laughter on the edge of tears. It took all Nikki's self-control not to scream at him to shut up.

After a minute he wound down to little gasps. "Sorry. Sorry," he managed. "Go ahead. Ask your question."

She stared at him for a second. "When Jack was . . . interrogating you. How was it affecting *him?*"

He met her gaze unflinchingly. A grin slowly surfaced on his face. "I see. What you really mean is, did he *like* it?"

Nikki studied him impassively. She said nothing.

"You need to know just how far gone he is, don't you? Whether or not you can still trust him. Man-oh-*man*. I can see how that might be kinda important to you. . . ."

"Don't fuck with me—"

"'Cause what if he turns out to be one of the bad guys, right? Maybe he's 'wired wrong' too? Or maybe its just that *all* men are like that, deep down. Maybe you'll wake up one night and find out you can't move your arms or legs and there's a bright light in your eyes and now it's *your* turn to answer questions—"

"I said *don't fuck with me!*" She slapped him across the face, hard. He gave a loud whoop and started laughing, harder than before. She glared at him, then reached over and picked up a ball-peen hammer from Jack's table of instruments.

She smashed it into his knee, hard. His laugh turned into a scream.

Her head was pounding. Her hands were shaking so hard she dropped the hammer. She leaned against the wall dizzily, afraid she might pass out.

Djinn-X sobbed in pain. Nikki took deep breaths and tried to get herself under control.

"Not as easy as it looks, is it?" Djinn-X managed.

"Shut up."

"I could tell you what you're afraid to hear. I could tell you that he loves it, that he had a huge hard-on the whole time he was pulling my eyelids off. I could tell you that and you'd believe it . . . but I'm not going to. *Fuck*, that hurts."

Djinn-X took a long, shaky breath. "The truth is— it's killing him."

Nikki closed her eyes. She focused on two things: Djinn-X's voice, and what her gut told her about what he was saying.

"He's *empty* inside, girl. All the torture, all the terrible things he does—that's just his fucking *job*. It doesn't bother him at all. He's like somebody running a concentration camp—here comes another truckload of victims, into the gas chamber, is it time for a coffee break yet? People can get used to anything—after a while, even torture is routine. Fuck, I swear I caught him *yawning* once."

"No," she whispered.

"But even Nazis have lives, right? Hobbies. Families. But not the Closer . . . this is all he's got, isn't it? All he does, all he *is*. That's how he caught me, how he caught all of us. He's pure fucking predator."

"He's a *man*—"

"He's a *cannibal*. He's eating his own because there's a big black void inside him he's trying to fill and never will. Sooner or later he's going to figure that out, and then he's going to implode. And you're gonna be standing right at ground zero, sweetheart."

"Maybe," Nikki said. "But at least I'll be standing. You're never getting up from that chair."

"Yeah," he said. "I know. Now, while we're both being so fucking honest, are you gonna deliver my last message or not?"

"Tell me."

She listened to what he had to say. She thought about it for a long, silent moment.

"Okay," she finally said. "If that's what you really want."

On the table beside the Closer's instruments, a pen lay on top of a yellow legal pad. Nikki glanced down at Jack's notes. They were in his usual neat handwriting, but there was something different at the bottom of the page.

It was a doodle. A martini glass, with an eyeball instead of an olive, skewered on a little sword. There was something shriveled and reddish brown stuck to the drawing, positioned along the top of the eyeball.

Something with black, curly eyelashes jutting up from it . . .

A Guide to Tracking and Killing the Hippie in His Natural Habitat

By Djinn-X, Esquire

Ah, the wily Hippie! Where once teeming herds thundered majestically across our fruited plains, their locks flowing freely in the patchouli-scented air, there is now a landscape littered with strip malls and skinheads. The Hippie is now only found in isolated game reserves in Oregon and California, where it is protected by local zoning ordinances.

Fortunately, there is still a way to obtain the

magnificent tie-dyed pelt of one of these creatures. Many species of Hippie are migratory, and often congregate in large groups called Festivals. By studying the location and frequency of these Festivals, a hunter can easily find a large herd that will stay in one place for an entire weekend.

A) SPECIES

The Hippie is, by and large, a peaceful herbivore. Their senses are usually dulled by the consumption of marijuana, and the fiery political convictions of their youth invariably dim into a pacifist, nonconfrontational acceptance of the universe. Most species are more to be pitied than feared, with several notable exceptions:

1. *The Junkie.* Any Hippie who wasn't killed off by the eighties or his own addictions is dangerous indeed. Subgroups include the Speed-Freak, the Cokehead and the Acid-Casualty. The first two tend to be aggressive and violent, while the last is unpredictable in the extreme. Cross-breeding between these species and Bikers are commonplace. While their position outside the mainstream of society can make them seem an attractive target, their paranoia and tendency to own guns makes them tricky to bag safely.

2. *The Back-to-Earther.* Often similar in appearance to Bikers, this species favors rawhide over leather and tends to be tough and self-reliant. They live in the

wild, and usually shun civilization. Some band together in tribes known as Communes. Years of hard physical labor make them physically strong, and some even shun drugs. This species has sharp instincts, and are hard to fool. Fortunately, many remain deliberately ignorant of advances in technology, which can be used to your advantage.

3. *The Vietnam Vet.* Many of these turned Hippie after their military service. Potentially mean, weapons-proficient and savvy, their mental and emotional instability can produce nasty surprises.

However, the mortality rate among Junkies and the antisocial nature of Back-to-Earthers mean you're unlikely to run into either unless you deliberately seek them out. Likewise, the number of Vietnam vets turned Hippie continue to shrink every year (and as a rarer breed, some consider them more valuable).

More common types (and much easier to take down) are:

4. *The Deadhead.* Even though Jerry Garcia's heart exploded, this species is still widespread. They can be readily found at Rainbow Gatherings and Phish concerts.

5. *The Flower Child.* Usually attracted by the lifestyle or the philosophy, many young women turn Hippie every year. While this

is good news for the overall health of the herd, many consider these to be mere imitators and not true Hippies at all. Still, there's nothing like the sight of a long-haired, eighteen-year-old Hippie chick, stoned out of her mind and dancing naked around a campfire. Until, of course, you hang her with her own intestines.

6. *The New Ager.* Despite their claim to be something "new," they dress like Hippies, they act like Hippies and they smell like Hippies—although they lean more toward incense and sage than B.O. New Agers embody the flakiest "spiritual" ideas of the Hippies, which can range from reincarnation to alien abductions. Naïve and gullible, they're among the easiest to isolate and kill.

B) TRAPS AND LURES

As in hunting most game, one of the paramount principles is to lure the prey into a controlled environment to minimize the chance of interruption and maximize a leisurely enjoyment of the kill—both before and after the fact. The Hippie mindset and the terrain they choose to occupy are, fortunately, ideal for this.

The simplest and surest incentive is drugs. Few true Hippies can resist the call of the little plastic Baggie, and it offers the perfect excuse to get your prey alone. Pot is easy to obtain, even if you have little or no street experience, and you don't even have to smoke yourself—with a little practice it's easy to feign taking a puff from a pipe or doobie, and after a few hits it's unlikely your target will notice anyway.

The method of ingestion makes it hard to effectively add a knockout drug to marijuana, but it is useful as a "gateway" drug—one of the common side-effects is dry mouth, and a casually offered bottle of water will rarely be turned down or questioned. Always make sure you familiarize yourself with side-effects and onset times before using chemical methods, though—nothing can ruin a good time like the prey wandering back to the party and *then* passing out, or worse, choking on their own vomit while you're in the bathroom.

If you feel uncomfortable using drugs as bait, there's always protective coloration. A wig, a beard, some sunglasses and a tie-dyed T-shirt—not only will you fit in, you've got a handy disguise as well.

Then, of course, there's always sex—but be careful. Hippies are promiscuous and notoriously lax about hygiene. No prey is worth getting a disease over.

Probably the best lure to use on a Hippie is their own psychology. Remember, Hippies want to Make the World a Better Place; if you tell them you need help, you'll probably get it. Ted Bundy got a lot of mileage out of the old fake arm-in-a-cast bit, and I'm sure it'd still work on any Hippie today. However, be wary of getting too much help—Hippies tend to live and travel in groups, so it's essential to cut one out of the herd before going after it.

As far as traps go, think mobile. Hippies made the van popular, so it's fitting it gets used against them. As long as you're meticulous about cleanup, a van makes the perfect Killing Floor on wheels, letting you go where the action is and then move to a more secluded location. Hippies are also one of the few groups stupid enough to still hitchhike, so you never can tell when an opportunity might come up. Afterward, body disposal is as easy as taking a drive in the country-side.

If you're worried about being pulled over and searched, or having that old assault charge come up when the cops run your license plate, you might want to consider a tent. Hippies love the great outdoors, and placing your camp a five-minute hike away from an outdoor festival can ensure you plenty of prey to pick from and all the privacy you need. Cleanup is also simplified—the entire crime scene can be bundled up and dis-posed of. Ah, there's nothing like the smell of fresh blood and pine needles!

There was more, much more. Jack shook his head and got up to get more coffee.

Djinn-X had contributed a lot to the Stalking Ground—weapons lists, methods of body disposal, even historical research on other killers—but he de-voted the most space to essays. Topics ranged from the ethics of killing children to the pros and cons of matricide. While the essays were the least useful in terms of hard data, Jack read them all first. They were good for learning Djinn-X's politics, his prejudices, his sense of humor. Even hints of his history came out—his father's army career, places he lived in as a boy. By the time Jack read the last of them, he thought he knew his subject—no, his "prey"—quite well.

Jack leaned against the kitchen counter and rubbed his temples. The laptop sat on the table in a pool of light thrown off by a desk lamp, but the rest of the room was dark. He hadn't slept in over thirty hours; once he started an interrogation, he didn't quit until he was done. This was by far the most information he'd had to digest, though, even more than the oil-rig worker in Calgary had given up—he'd babbled non-stop until his voice was no more than a croak, realizing that when he stopped talking he stopped living. When all he had left to offer was whispered gibberish, Jack cut his throat.

But even then, all Jack had to do was verify a few key facts, and turn the rest over to the police. Djinn-X's information had to be understood . . . *absorbed*. He'd never had to do that before.

It was easier than he'd expected.

He poured himself a cup of coffee and sat back down. Normally Jack took cream and sugar, but now he was drinking it black—Djinn-X's preference.

He took a long, bitter sip, then closed his eyes. Thought about a generation stealing his birthright. Thought about his bastard of a father. Thought about a lifetime filled with frustration and disappointment and rage.

He opened his eyes. Reached out and tapped a key.
A menu scrolled down: KILLS.

"All right," Jack whispered. "Let's fucking *rock*. . . ."

KILL #1: Let's Make a Deal

"Ah, I see you're looking at the Lexus. Sweet ride."

"Yeah, I guess. Kinda pricey, though."

"Sticker shock, huh? Well, that's just a starting
point. Actually, I was just coming out here to mark
this puppy down. Here—that seem a little more reasonable?"

"Well, yeah—"

"Whoops! Made a mistake. Actually, this should be
a seven. Better?"

"Sure."

"Get in, see how it feels. Check out the stereo. Nice
sound, huh? Kleghoffer speakers. CD player, even
satellite radio—why listen to all that drivetime crap,
right? Pick a station that gives you what you want and
listen to that. Right?"

"Sure."

"Sure, of course. Here, take the keys, start it up.
Vortech engine. Sounds good, but it drives like a fish and
couldn't pass a tricycle—ha, ha, just kidding. There's
only one way to see how she performs, and that's to take
her for a spin. C'mon, just around the block."

"Uh, okay."

"Great! Just turn left, that'll take us toward the
freeway—may as well open her up, right? Don't
worry, the gas is on us, ha ha. Listen, I can really offer
you a great deal on this car. Don't be fooled by the

price, it's actually a lot cheaper than you think. Our financing department can work with anyone, any situation. They can have you cruising around in this for what you spend on lattes. And a car like this, it's actually an investment, right? It's an investment in your image, in your lifestyle. Just hang a right up here."

"I'm a little lost now."

"Don't worry, you're in good hands—what am I gonna do, kill you? Ha ha. This road's in terrible condition, which is why I always take people up here. See, with the suspension system this car has, you hardly feel a bump. It's got Positrack stabilizers, complete BS frame, and Thisisallcrap struts."

"What?"

"That's not all. There's also the whole Ima braking system: Imajerk pads, Imaliar rims, Imawasteofspace axles. All standard, always included."

"I'm not sure I heard you right—"

"Sorry, didn't mean to get all technical on you. Occupational hazard with salesmen—it's how we deal with insecurity, right? We try to impress people with all these facts and figures. Comes off a little intimidating sometimes, I know. I just want to establish my credibility with you—I'm not just some guy in a suit pretending to work at the dealership, right? Ha ha."

"Not a lot of businesses around here."

"No, just warehouses and trucking companies, mainly. Still, there's quite a bit of green space, isn't there? I guess it's because we're right on the edge of the city. Say, pull over for a second, will you? There's something I want to show you."

"I really have to be getting back—"

"It'll just take a second. Right here's fine. Okay, now just push that button there, that pops the trunk. Great. You can leave it running, just don't lock the keys in it. C'mon back here."

"What did you want to—Jesus! What the *fuck!*"

"Ha! Ah, you should see the look on your face. . . . I'm just messing with you. Pretty nice meat cleaver, huh? Solingen steel, just like the rest of the set. We're throwing one of these in with every Lexus this week. Leather case, hand-stitching, seventy-two pieces. All top-of-the-line, every kind you can think of. Look at these Yora blades: Yorajoke paring knife, Yorafool fileting knife, Yoratotalloser butcher knife. You hear what I'm saying?"

"I—I think so."

"Good, good. There's also the Fuckyoumakemesick steak knives, the Whatareyouwaitingfor bread-and-butter knives, the serrated Killmeyoufuckingpussy. . . ."

"Okay. Okay, enough with the hard sell. You got me. Can I see that one, please?"

"Sure. That's—uff. What? Oh *Christ*—"

Salesmen. They'll talk themselves into a fucking grave.

If the proceeding was a little unclear at times, I apologize—but if you think *you* were confused, imagine how I felt.

It's called the aura phase. It's the first of seven that psychologists say serial killers go through. (Though I gotta say, I ran through the next four pretty fucking quick: trolling, seduction, capture, and the kill. Totemizing and depression cap off the list.) The aura phase is typically characterized by vivid fantasies and sometimes hallucinations; in my case, I heard the asshole practically begging me to kill him.

So I did.

I used a butcher knife, and went straight for the throat. Thrust, not slash. The blade went through the windpipe no problem, but I felt it glance off the spine before it came out the other side. The cutting edge was pointed outward, and the edge was so fucking sharp it sheared right through the rest of the neck when I yanked it back. The blood looked like a special effect—it sprayed everywhere. The guy spun around, tried to run, and fell over after two steps. It looked fucking comical.

Of course, I had quite the head of steam built up by that point. One thrust just wasn't gonna do it, y'know? So I went over to where he lay and worked out for a while. Nothing fancy, just slamming that big, heavy blade down over and over and over again. *Thunk, thunk, thunk.* It reminded me of baseball, somehow— you know that feeling when you swing and really connect with the ball? Like something gets transferred at the point of impact, from you to it, and then that ball is *gone.* Flying away, getting smaller and smaller and you hope it never comes back.

Deeply satisfying.

"How's it going?" Nikki asked.

Jack looked up from the screen. "Satisfactory," he said. "I'm checking his list of dump sites now. Up for a trip to California?"

"Depends. I could use the sunshine, but—I don't know, Jack. He could be jerking us around, stalling for time. For all we know he hunts in Ohio."

"I don't think so." Jack stood up and stretched. "He gave me a phone number with a California area code, and it's his voice on the answering machine."

"You didn't call from here, did you?" She regretted it as soon as she said it; Jack was too smart to do anything that could be traced.

"No, I drove to a pay phone a few miles away. While you were downstairs."

Nikki crossed to the refrigerator, opened it and peered inside. "Oh," she said.

"He say anything interesting?" Jack asked.

"No, just the usual bullshit—threats, bribes, pleading. You know."

"He could still be lying."

"Well of *course* he's lying, I'm not stu—oh." She shook her head. "You meant about the dump sites."

"Yeah. Give us the right area, wrong details. Buy him a few more hours."

"Either way, I guess we have to check it out. I'll go." She took a long-necked beer out of the fridge and closed the door. "Once I'm there, he won't dick us around long."

"No. I don't think he will."

She twisted off the cap and tossed it clattering into the sink. "So," she said. "Is it just me, or is this one . . . different?"

He eyed her warily. "In what way?"

"His targets, for one thing. He kill any women?"

"One. A stockbroker."

"Well, that's what I mean." She took a long, thoughtful swallow of beer. "A stockbroker. I don't know, maybe I'm just being a bitch, but I find it hard to give a fuck about a stockbroker. Girls working the street I can identify with—someone working Wall Street, not so much." She frowned, then smiled. "Funny, huh? Most people would feel the opposite way."

"We're not most people."

"Yeah, no shit. It's not just his targets, it's why he's going after them. Almost like it's—I don't know, political or something."

"It doesn't matter. Everybody kills for the same reason."

"Yeah?"

"They kill because they're killers. Whatever their stated reasons, they're just rationalizing to let them do what they want. It doesn't matter if it's sex, or money, or revenge. Someone wants to take up murder as a hobby, they'll find a reason."

"Even us?" she asked softly.

"Like I said—it doesn't matter." Jack turned back to the laptop. "Results do. They end people, we end them. We give the families of their victims some answers. Nothing else is important."

"Yeah," she said. "Nothing else. I'm gonna go pack."

She put her half-finished beer down on the countertop and strode out of the kitchen.

Jack returned to work.

Jack went downstairs. He unlocked the door to the interrogation room, stepped inside and turned on the light. He left the door open.

Djinn-X looked up. "What do you want now?" he snarled.

"There are some things I don't understand."

"I don't believe you. You understand, you just don't want to admit it."

"No." Jack pulled up a chair and sat down. "The lawyer you killed. I don't get it."

"Jefferson? What's to get? He worked in tax law. He specialized in making sure multinational corporations gave up as little of their huge profits as possible. He was a scumbag with the morals of an eel and I killed him."

Jack leaned forward intently. "No, it's *how* you did it. You beat him to death with a golf club."

"So?"

"So you killed him at his house. He was a hunter. He had game trophies mounted over the fireplace, twelve-point bucks and bighorn sheep and cougar heads. Right?"

Djinn-X nodded. "Yeah, I remember. Place looked like a fucking taxidermist's."

"Well, don't you think it would have made more of a statement if you'd decapitated him and stuck *his* head up there?"

"Hmmm. I never thought of that."

"Here, let me show you something." Jack reached out and freed Djinn-X's ankles and hands. "It'll just take a moment."

There was a door in the far wall, a plain white rectangle with a small sign on it that read *Studio*. Jack opened it and walked through. Djinn-X followed him.

On the other side, a flower garden. Sunflowers and rosebushes and hollyhocks taller than Jack bloomed in a vast, tangled sprawl, but all the plants were covered in a thick layer of dust as gray as the sky overhead.

"Looks like the day after fucking Pompeii in here," Djinn-X said.

"Look," Jack said. There was a stone fireplace in the middle of the garden, with a crackling blaze going. A naked man stood in front of it, his face a featureless blank.

"See, this is how I would have done it," Jack said. He used the hunting knife in his hand to make a long, vertical slit down the naked man's chest, then made two more cuts along the length of his arms and legs. He handed the knife to Djinn-X, then quickly stripped the skin from the man's flesh. He was careful to keep it in one piece.

"See?" Jack said. He lay the skin down in front of the fireplace.

"Bare skin rug," Djinn-X said. "Now, why didn't I see that? Jack, you're a fucking natural."

"No, I'm just doing my job," Jack said. "That's all."

"Hey, what's that?" Djinn-X pointed down at Jack's feet. The plant growing there was unlike any Jack had seen before; knee-high, it had a thick, central stalk with a cauliflower-like growth at the top, surrounded by a collar of wide, flat leaves. A thick network of red veins webbed the stalk, leaves, and the silvery gray central growth— which, Jack realized, wasn't a cauliflower at all.

It was a brain.

"That wasn't there before," Jack said. "I didn't plant that."

"Well, it didn't just fucking appear out of nowhere," Djinn-X said. "Looks a little dry, though. Here, lemme help."

He held a hand over the plant. Blood dripped down his arm and off his wrist.

"No, don't do that," Jack said. "Don't feed it."

"Sorry, Jack," Djinn-X said. "Gotta take care of The

Pack, right? And hey, this is my job now. Fertilizer."

The red veins wrapped around the plant were pulsing, twitching . . . and then they pulled free, rising up like a nest of red snakes, writhing and flexing and getting longer. They formed an intricate, rippling network in front of Jack's eyes, branching from artery to vein to capillary, a crimson mesh growing ever finer as it expanded to fill his vision, his whole world. . . .

It was terrifying. It was beautiful. It was—

The phone rang.

Jack jerked awake, fumbled for the handset. "Hello?"

"Jack. It's Nikki. Everything checks out."

"Everything?"

"Yeah. I'll be back tomorrow—just have a last errand to run."

"Okay." He hung up.

He shook his head, trying to clear it. He couldn't get rid of that last image of an endless, scarlet mesh.

He had a cup of coffee, and then went downstairs.

The black cube of the interrogation chamber was just as he'd left it. There was no white door marked *Studio*. Djinn-X was still securely chained to his chair.

"You told the truth," Jack said.

"I—I could use some water," Djinn-X croaked.

"I didn't."

"What?"

"I lied. I'm not going to release your methods on the net. I *am* going to pose as you in the Stalking Ground. You'll never be known as anyone but another psycho who got caught. And I'll make sure every member of your 'family' knows you were the one who gave them up."

Djinn-X started to cry.

"Seduction isn't a word most people associate with serial killers, but that's exactly the process, isn't it?" Jack asked. He picked up the ball-peen hammer, hefted it with both hands. "You gain your victim's trust first. They have to feel safe before they'll make themselves vulnerable. That's part of the thrill, right? That moment when you yank the rug out of from under them and drop them into Hell."

"Their fault. It's all *their* fucking fault—"

"You know that horrible, sick feeling you have right now, in the pit of your stomach?" Jack said. "That's what every victim of a serial killer feels. Betrayal."

He put down the hammer and picked up a meat cleaver. "It's the last thing they feel."

"No. No, please, there's something I didn't tell you—"

"And it's the last thing *you're* going to feel. . . ."

Nikki used Djinn-X's keys to get into his place. She'd been there once already, to check some of the information he'd given and pack up his computer equipment in two large suitcases. She'd taken them back to her motel and called Jack from a pay phone.

Now she was back. To keep a promise.

The place wasn't much, just a studio apartment in a concrete-block high-rise. The walls were bare and white, the carpet a stained beige. A tiny balcony looked across at another high-rise.

She pulled the drapes closed, then took a can of black spray paint out of her purse. She shook it methodically for a full minute, looking around. The room held a ratty pull-out couch, a high-end mountain bike in immaculate condition, a dresser, a couple of bookshelves and a desk with the monitor and printer she hadn't bothered taking.

She sighed and got to work.

When she was done, she dropped the now-empty can back in her purse. FUCK YOU was now stenciled everywhere: the walls, the monitor, the rows of books. She'd sprayed it on the ceiling, the floor, the drapes, over the appliances and across the bed. The same message screamed from every surface, over and over.

"You wanted it, you got it," Nikki said. "And fuck you, too."

CHAPTER SEVEN

Parker Stoltz's day got off to a good start. The song playing when his clock radio went off at 5:55 was "ABC" by the Jackson Five, so he watched the local ABC news affiliate that morning. The weather was overcast but not raining, with patches of low-lying fog—not unusual for Portland at this time of year. The traffic report said volume was steady with no major problems.

He had a shower and then examined himself critically in the bathroom mirror, looking for changes. The five moles on his pale skin—three on his back, one on his thigh and one on his neck—remained the same. The bald spot in the middle of his lank brown hair seemed no larger. His face—slightly bug-eyed, crooked nose, froggy mouth—showed no new wrinkles or blemishes. His stoop-shouldered, small-chested frame looked a little out of alignment; he reminded himself to book a chiropractic appointment.

He did nick himself shaving, but he made four small horizontal cuts just below his right nipple to balance things out, and managed to cover them with only one Band-Aid.

Breakfast, as always, was orange juice, coffee, an egg, one slice of toast and five pieces of bacon. He was done by 6:45, leaving him plenty of time to run through his checklist.

He turned the lights on in the garage, fluorescents gleaming off the freshly waxed white of his 1995 Taurus. He started with the tires, making sure each one was at exactly fifty-five pounds of pressure. He made sure all the lights and switches were functioning properly, and that the radio was properly tuned. He made sure the locks still worked.

Then it was time to leave.

Everything was fine at first. He made his way from the quiet, tree-lined streets of his neighborhood to the freeway on-ramp without incident. He merged quickly and cleanly into the flow of traffic. He drove the speed limit, as always, and avoided the passing lane.

The trouble began with the pickup. It was an old blue Ford, rusty and belching smoke, loaded down with landscaping equipment. It was going at least six miles under the speed limit, and it was right in front of him. He signaled for a lane change, but the traffic suddenly closed up on his right. No one was willing to let him in.

He shook his head and changed his signal from right to left. He would have to use the passing lane.

He shoulder-checked, looked in both the rear-view and side mirror, and accelerated smoothly into the lane. He passed the blue Ford, being driven by a man in his sixties wearing a greasy-looking baseball cap. Stoltz gave the man a cold stare but was ignored.

Once he was past the truck he slowed and signalled to return to his lane, but a yellow Beetle was already doing the same from the far right. He slowed further, intending to slip into the rapidly widening gap between the pickup and the Beetle.

And then the silver SUV appeared.

It roared up behind him in the passing lane, doing eighty easily. It decelerated abruptly, stopping only inches from his rear bumper. The massive chrome grille looked like the bars of a cage in his rearview mirror.

Before Stoltz could even react, the driver of the SUV had flicked on his high beams. Halogen brilliance flared in the rearview, blinding him for a second. He reached up quickly and flipped the mirror to night vision, but the glare was still painful.

The driver laid on the horn. Stoltz gritted his teeth and sped up, but the SUV stayed on his tail. The driver honked again, a long, mindless bleat of anger.

He looked for an opening, but an endless line of cars stretched out beside him, practically bumper-to-bumper. He was going seventy now, and the SUV was still there. He couldn't change lanes now even if there was an opening: he was going too fast.

A vision flashed into his mind, so intense it was overpowering. Losing control of the car, the rear wheels drifting to the right as the front went to the left, landscape rotating around him as the car went sideways and then the sudden shock as the tires dug in and it flipped, spinning around and around and crashing onto its roof and the agonized rending of metal and bone. He could smell the burst fuel line, hear the sirens as they came to cut his body out of the wreckage. . . .

The blare of the horn snapped him back to reality. He slowed down, forcing himself to ignore the frenzied honking he got in response, matched the flow of the lane beside him and turned on his signal light. A pretty, freckled girl driving a Ram truck waved him in; he nodded and waved back in thanks.

Simple courtesy, he thought as he changed lanes. *Why is that such a rare commodity?*

The driver of the SUV made a point of leaning over and giving him the finger as he blew past. The man was in his thirties, wearing a gray suit with a yellow tie, his face red and contorted in anger.

Stoltz met the man's glare with a slight smile. Once the vehicle was past, he noted the licence plate number and wrote it down on a pad mounted on the dash.

Stoltz's job wasn't terribly exciting, but it did have its advantages. He worked at the Department of Motor Vehicles.

Most of his time was spent in his cubicle, doing data entry. That was fine with Stoltz; the less he had to deal with the public the better. Most of his coworkers were reasonably polite—at least to him—and data never argued. It simply was what it was.

His cubicle was neat but sparse. A framed landscape of Mt. Fuji, done in the Japanese style, hung on one wall; everything else was work-related. A black coffee mug sat on a cork coaster on his desk beside a neat pile of papers.

Any DMV record he cared to look up was his to access, but he always took special care to hide his tracks when indulging his private hobby. He used his supervisor's password to get into the system, and routed all his requests through one of the terminals at the front counter—none of his actions would show up on his own computer.

The registered owner of the SUV was one Peter New. His driver's license listed his address as 6090 West Summervale Street; he weighed two hundred pounds, had green eyes and black hair and needed corrective lenses to drive. Stoltz guessed he had been wearing contacts.

Not that it would matter.

The next morning Stoltz spotted the same SUV on the freeway. This time, he followed it to the parking lot of a Denny's, and pulled in across the street.

He went inside and spotted New at the counter. He sat down on the stool beside him.

"Hi," Stoltz said pleasantly. "Remember me?"

New looked up. "No," he said. "Should I?"

"That depends on whether you're as stupid as you are rude," Stoltz said.

"Excuse me?"

"I'll have a coffee, please," Stoltz said to the waitress. She nodded and put down a cup and saucer.

"You drive like young people fuck," Stoltz said, turning back to New. "Too fast and too frantic. Personally, I don't care if you wrap yourself around a lamppost, but I'd rather you didn't take someone else with you."

"Wait a minute. I remember you," New said. The confusion on his face was replaced with recognition. "You were the jerk driving slow in the fast lane—"

"And you were the jerk with his dick on the gas pedal," Stoltz said. He added a teaspoon of sugar to his coffee and stirred it slowly. "Although I guess that big SUV is *all* dick, isn't it? Right down to the prick behind the wheel."

"That's right, pal," New said. "And I'll fuck up anything that gets in my way—including you. Got me?" He poked Stoltz in the shoulder, hard.

"Oops," Stoltz said. "Careful. I might spill—"

He tossed the coffee in New's face.

"—my coffee," he finished calmly.

New screamed. He lurched backward off the stool, clawing at his scalded face—

No. That wasn't quite right. Back up.

"That's right, pal. And I'll fuck up anything that gets in my way," New said. "Including you."

Stoltz put down his coffee and stood up. "I don't think so. You can buy a four-wheeled, chrome-plated penis substitute, but you can't buy the balls to go with it."

New snarled and lunged from his seat, throwing a wild punch at Stoltz's head. Stoltz dodged it easily. He retaliated with a quick jab to the man's midsection, doubling him over, then smashed his knee into the man's face, knocking him up and back with blood fountaining from his nose—

No. Too messy. Besides, who knows what he might have? Safety first.

—retaliated with an elbow to New's windpipe, sending the man staggering backward, choking and sputtering. A lightning-fast spin-kick slammed Stoltz's foot into New's jaw and dropped him unconscious to the floor.

A girl sitting alone at a nearby booth stood up. She

was pretty, with a spray of freckles across her face. "That was amazing," she said. "That guy totally deserved it. I saw the way he drove."

Stoltz smiled at her. "Well, people should think more about the consequences of their actions," he said. "Driving is a privilege, not a right."

"Can I buy you a cup of coffee?" she asked with a grin.

"Sure—but let's go someplace else," he replied. "This place has trash all over the floor. . . ."

Yes. Yes, much better.

He came back to himself slowly, hands poised over his keyboard. His screen was filled with the number five, typed over and over while he fantasized.

Except—it wasn't *really* a fantasy, was it? No. It was more of a . . . romantic exaggeration. The process would differ, but the end result would be the same.

For Mr. New, anyway.

Jack dumped Djinn-X's body into the Green River. He removed the hands first.

Usually Jack wanted his targets to be quickly found and identified—this time was different. He needed Djinn-X's death to remain a secret, at least from the other members of The Pack. That meant that all the information Jack had on Djinn-X's murders also had to be kept secret, at least for now.

For the first time since he'd become the Closer, Jack felt no sense of finality when he disposed of a killer's body. The families of Djinn-X's victims would sleep no easier tonight; their questions would remain unanswered for another day. For them, in a very real sense, the person who took away their loved ones was still loose in the world.

For three consecutive days, Stoltz got up an hour early—at 4:44, to be precise—and switched the plates on his Taurus with another set before driving to the suburb where Peter New lived. Stoltz parked across the street and studied New's routine.

New was married, but had no children. His wife, a plump blonde, left for work twenty minutes before he did. By the time her car—a red Toyota Supra—was at the end of the block, the automatic door on their two-car garage was only half shut. There was a three-foot gap between the garage and the six-foot fence that bordered their property that seemed ideal, and no one else on the block seemed to be pulling out of their driveway at the same time New's wife left.

On the fourth day, Stoltz parked in the alley behind the News' house. He wore a black trenchcoat and carried a black umbrella, opened and angled slightly forward and down to hide his face. He walked briskly to the end of the alley, up the block and down the street to the News' house. He stopped, pretended to check his watch and glanced around. Nobody in sight.

He closed his umbrella and walked up the News' driveway, then around the corner of the garage. There was nothing there but the fence, a stack of lumber, and the side of the building. He leaned against the wall and took long, deep breaths. His heart was pounding; it was beginning.

When New's wife left ten minutes later, he waited until her car was out of sight, then darted around the corner. He easily ducked under the closing garage door.

The SUV hulked beside him, pale silver in the early morning glow of the garage's single window. Stoltz regarded it as he slipped on a pair of surgical gloves; it reminded him of a sleeping dinosaur, some huge carnivore hunkered down for the night before another day of roaring through the blacktop jungle, terrorizing anything in its way. It was tempting to think about emasculating that power, slashing the tires and pouring sugar in the gas tank—but that would be blaming the body.

Simpler and more elegant to kill the brain.

He dropped the umbrella and took the pistol out of the pocket of his trenchcoat. The gun looked rather ridiculous at the moment, because it had a potato securely duct-taped over the end of the barrel. He'd read about the trick on Djinn-X's website; it made for a cheap and disposable silencer. It wasn't entirely quiet, but it muffled a gunshot enough that it would probably be mistaken for a backfire or firecracker. He also put on a pair of safety goggles—the potato could be rather messy.

Of course, it was only good for one shot. Stoltz liked that; it increased the level of risk, added to the challenge. Otherwise, it would be too easy.

He tried the door between the garage and the house—unlocked. He opened it and stepped inside.

He crept down the hall. Ugly orange carpet. White walls. Door on the right, closed. Noise ahead to the left.

End of the hall. Stairs on the right, living room ahead.

He peered around the corner to the left. Peter New was seated at the kitchen table, reading the paper and eating a bowl of cereal. His back was to Stoltz, but it looked like he was wearing the same suit as he had on the day they met.

There was a sliding glass door on the far wall. If New looked up, he would probably see Stoltz's reflection in it.

He stepped around the corner. New didn't look up. He raised the gun to the back of Stoltz's neck.

"Driving is a privilege," Road Rage whispered, and pulled the trigger.

It didn't take Jack and Nikki long to get set up in Portland.

Another run-down house in a run-down neighborhood. Another landlord who took cash and didn't ask questions. Another trip to the Home Depot to buy plywood, foam insulation and a roll of black plastic.

Dealing with an internet provider was a little trickier, but Nikki had a credit card under another name she used when she had to. She kept the account scrupulously up to date.

Jack set up the computer equipment in one of the bedrooms; he'd picked up a secondhand monitor and printer from a pawnshop downtown. It was strange, he reflected as he attached cables to the back of the tower. In a sense, this *was* the Stalking Ground. This chunk of plastic and metal was their tribal lodge, the place they met to trade methods and secrets and boast of their kills. It was a place they drew strength and comfort from. Jack had a sudden urge to smash the tower into a million pieces, sentence all of them back to the lonely hells they came from.

But he knew he couldn't do that. No, he would have to walk into that lodge himself—as their leader.

DJINN-X: I gotta say, RR—that's some great shit you pulled the other day.
ROAD RAGE: Thank you.
DJINN-X: And that picture you posted, of the guy sitting in his SUV with his driver's license nailed to his forehead—classic! That should have been on the front page of the newspaper!
ROAD RAGE: Yes, it did show a great deal of style, didn't it? I was tempted to mail a copy to the media, but of course they'd never run it—though they did publish my manifesto.
DJINN-X: Is it hard to drive a nail into a guy's skull?
ROAD RAGE: Not as hard as you'd think. I'd prefer a nail gun, but the logistics of hauling an air compressor around make that unworkable.
DJINN-X: Yeah, I'll bet.
GOURMET: I have a suggestion. Cordless technology has dramatically improved in the last decade. I find the Black and Decker MT1203K-2 Multi-Tool to be extremely powerful and efficient. I use the jigsaw attachment to remove the top of the cranium, but there's no reason you couldn't drill a hole of the right diameter just as easily.
ROAD RAGE: Hmmm. Sounds a little messy.
DJINN-X: Not to mention unsatisfying. I mean, driving a nail into a guy's skull—WHACK! WHACK! WHACK!—that's gotta be gratifying. Even a nail gun has that solid, *thunk! thunk!* feel to it. But a drill—that's kinda sterile.

GOURMET: Efficiency has its own beauty.
ROAD RAGE: True. And ultimately, the message is more important than the medium. . . .

A Few Simple Rules

By "Road Rage"

Power corrupts.

In today's world, more and more power is concentrated in the hands of the individual. The only hope for primitive man to kill something as large as a woolly mammoth was to band together in a group; today, any cretin with an automatic weapon could destroy an entire herd.

But this isn't an essay on gun control. It's about a far more dangerous and pervasive weapon: the automobile.

Driving a car is having two thousand pounds of armored beast under your total control. A twitch of the wheel can wipe out a life, and let you be a hundred miles away from the crime an hour later. And how is this power restricted?

It's not.

Society lets us drive cars before we can vote, have sex, drink alcohol, or join the armed forces. Our culture glorifies reckless driving in video games, movies, television. Driving infractions usually garner only fines, which are often simply ignored.

This is unacceptable.

Vehicles are weapons; and an armed society *must* be a polite society. Anything else leads to chaos.

The problem lies in the interaction between man and machine. A vehicle is not simply a method of transportation; it functions more as an actual extension of ourselves. It encases us like our skin, gives us information like our senses, moves us back or forward like our muscles. It eats, it needs a place to live, it has a voice. A man driving a car is not like a man on horseback; he's more like a centaur. A blend of both, a mesh of metal and meat—a cyborg.

But a poorly designed one. One can imagine a herd of centaurs moving from place to place over well-established trails, the individuals moving at a gallop sticking to one trail, those moving at a trot to another; one can imagine a code of conduct, a certain caution around smaller and younger centaurs, a certain respect for the older ones. These are the simple rules that evolve in a civilized society with a large population.

But take those same creatures and cover them in armor that cuts them off from contact with each other. Increase their speed so that the slightest contact between them could cause both parties to go wildly out of control. Take away their language, so that the only method of communication left between them is the most basic of hand gestures, blinking lights and a horn. Cram them onto highways and try to make them act not like living creatures but parts of a machine: stop, go, turn left, turn right.

This system encourages the worst behaviors of man and machine. The creature that evolves is frustrated and overstressed, in control of tremendous power but forbidden to use it. Insulated from his fellow creatures but forced into close proximity with them, a herd of angry, armored beings thunders forward every day. It's no wonder some of them go rogue.

And for the good of the herd, the rogues must be removed. Permanently.

From the Portland *Oregonian*, January 14:

RULES REDUCE RAGE

Are drivers in the Portland area becoming more polite—or just more afraid?

Whatever the reason, the number of reported violent incidents between drivers has dropped in the last two months by approximately thirty percent—ever since the publishing of the so-called "Road Rage Manifesto" by the *Oregonian*. Originally thought to be a hoax, the Manifesto was printed at the request of the police after certain details in the letter were verified. "Our primary concern is in saving lives," Chief Berenson said. "We saw nothing wrong in the letter being published—all it does is endorse common sense. If it had been inappropriate in some way our response would have been different. And so far, he's kept his word—there haven't been any more killings since it was printed."

At least not until yesterday, when Peter New was discovered behind the wheel of his 1998 Ford Explorer. Evidence at the scene, a police spokesperson said, confirmed it was the work of the same killer who'd struck five times before. Despite the falling number of con-

frontations between drivers, it seems local residents
are still not living up to his standards.

Although the *Oregonian* does not endorse his methods, we are reprinting his demands in the interest of
public safety:

1. ALWAYS signal lane changes.
2. If another driver is signaling to enter
   your lane, let them in.
3. Never tailgate.
4. Refrain from obscenities directed at
   other drivers, verbal or otherwise.
5. Slow down when you see a yellow light.

Five simple rules—hardly worth dying for.

DJINN-X: You disrespect a man's wheels, you
disrespect the man.
*ROAD RAGE: Exactly. In many ways, your vehicle is
you.*
DJINN-X: I remember the first car I ever owned—a
'77 Rabbit. Not very powerful, but it got me around.
Did great on gas, easy to park. I can still spot one
from a mile away.
*ROAD RAGE: Mine was a 1965 Chevy Malibu.
Two-door, black. Six-cylinder engine, three-speed
transmission.*
DJINN-X: Nice car. I could never afford anything
like that.
*ROAD RAGE: The type of car you drive isn't important.
It's how you conduct yourself behind the wheel.*
DJINN-X: Yeah, I get that—but to people like us,
vehicle type is definitely a consideration. I mean, not

so much for you or me, 'cause we generally do our kills onsite—but what about someone like the Gourmet? He's got to get his dinner back to the kitchen.

ROAD RAGE: *I suppose. But wouldn't anything with a trunk do?*

DJINN-X: Not necessarily. Putting someone in a trunk means you risk being seen. Better to get them inside on their own, then you can control the situation. You don't even need a lot of room—Ted Bundy used to do his kills in a Volkswagen Bug. Me, I prefer something with a little more room—I got an old white panel truck I picked up for cheap. White panel trucks are like fucking ghosts in any city, man—there's so many nobody even sees them. Lots of room inside, easy to swamp out with a garden hose.

ROAD RAGE: *I know what you mean. I drive a late-model white car myself—a Taurus, actually— largely because it fits in so well. Did you know that, statistically, white is the most common color among mid-size cars between five and ten years old?*

DJINN-X: Yeah, it does seem they're everywhere you look. But most people never actually *recognize* what they're fucking looking at, do they? I mean, when I pick out a sheep, I study them—but they *never* see me. I'm just another fucking bike courier, in their office to pick up or drop off more bullshit paperwork. As far as they're concerned, I'm nonexistent.

ROAD RAGE: *No. You're* invisible. *That's completely different—it gives you power. It lets you move among them unseen.*

DJINN-X: I guess.

ROAD RAGE: Don't you know how strong that makes you? How exceptional? You, me, all the members of The Pack—we're a breed apart. It's true that others—coworkers, women, our families— don't truly see us, but it's because we're above them, not below. We do what they can only dream about.

DJINN-X: But we can't fucking *tell* them. Man, some days all I want to do is scream into the next bland face I see, "I could kill you without a second *thought,* motherfucker!" How do you deal?

ROAD RAGE: I find certain rituals help. I take a small object from my victim, something innocuous but personal, say, a key chain—and keep it in my pocket. When things get stressful, I just put my hand in my pocket. It reconnects me to the act; it reminds me of who I really am, not the person others think me to be.

DJINN-X: Yeah, but a trophy-buzz just gets me all pumped up, man. I'm more likely to just do the fucker than calm down.

ROAD RAGE: You have to learn to focus. Channel your anger. Kill them in your mind, where there are no consequences.

DJINN-X: And that works for you?

ROAD RAGE: Let me tell you a story. The last time I struck, I was late for work. I had gone straight from the kill to the office; I'm sure there were still traces of gunpowder on my hands.

My supervisor reprimanded me. Despite the fact that he's a career civil servant with no interest in his job beyond one day collecting his pension, he still thought he could criticize me. I was still "pumped

*up" from the kill; I felt like pulling the gun out of my
pocket and shooting him on the spot.*

*But I didn't. Instead, I made him beg for mercy.
I paraded him around the office and then out to
the front counter to tell everyone what a pathetic
excuse for a man he was. And then I blew his
brains out.*

But only in my imagination.

DJINN-X: Well, I guess if you can show that kind of
self-control right after a kill, I can, too. Thanks for
the insight.

*ROAD RAGE: Any time. Remember—The Pack Hunts
Together.*

Jack surfed the web, hit news sites and searched
archives. He read everything he could find on Road
Rage's crimes.

Police seemed to think he was an opportunistic
killer—that he cruised around until a driver did something to anger him, then followed that person to their
home. He didn't kill them right away, though, waiting
one or more days until the time was right. The media
had identified the stretch of freeway most of his victims had frequented, but thousands of cars used it
every day.

Jack knew the authorities must have decoy cars on
the road, trying to lure the murderer into a trap—but
he also thought he knew why the strategy wouldn't
work.

Road Rage's online remarks indicated he was a civil
servant. He could be using a government database to
look up his victims' license plates, might even work

for the DMV itself. He didn't have to follow his victims home; he could drop in on them any time he liked. Jack knew the police must have already considered the same theory—so Road Rage was obviously smart enough to use the system without being detected, or he'd already have been caught.

But Jack had information the police didn't.

Road Rage had referred to a "front counter." That suggested an agency that dealt with large numbers of people every day: Immigration, Social Security, the DMV. He could even work for the police in some capacity, though Jack doubted he was a cop.

Jack called up a map of the Portland area. There were government offices everywhere, of course—but if he encountered his victims on the freeway, he probably lived at one end of his trail and worked at the other. Road Rage was meticulous, methodical; Jack thought he probably drove the same route every day.

His first car had been a '65 Malibu. First cars were usually hand-me-downs from parents or cheap pieces of junk; the Malibu would seem to fit the former. Assuming his parents gave him a ten-year-old car when he was sixteen, that would put Road Rage in his mid-forties.

A middle-aged civil servant, driving to and from work every day during rush hour in his white, late-model Taurus. Jack sighed and rubbed his temples.

It wasn't enough; he needed more.

"The Pack hunts together," he muttered. He didn't know why. "The Pack, The Pack . . ."

He closed his eyes. Saw them, suddenly, as an actual pack of wolves. Road Rage was a sleek, white wolf with blazing red eyes; the Gourmet was a hulking gray beast with enormous, slavering jaws; the Patron was simply a black silhouette. Even Djinn-X was there, a four-legged ghost whose skeleton shone right through its skin.

And lurking at the edge of The Pack was Deathkiss. The new one. Tested, but not yet trusted.

Slowly, Jack smiled.

DJINN-X: We got trouble.

GOURMET: How so?

DJINN-X: You may have noticed Deathkiss hasn't logged on in a few days. That's because I've restricted his access while I checked a few things out—namely, that he may be a fake.

ROAD RAGE: I thought our verification system made that impossible.

DJINN-X: It does. Deathkiss was the real deal—or at least he was until the Closer got to him.

PATRON: Stanley Dupreiss.

Jack stopped, stared at the screen. The Patron hadn't logged on since the exchange where Jack had posed as Dupreiss—at least not while Jack was online.

DJINN-X: Yeah. I didn't put it together until I started comparing Deathkiss's kills with Dupreiss's victims. The media is saying the Closer did Dupreiss, even though Deathkiss has been active since Dupreiss's death. That means only one thing.

GOURMET: The Closer is posing as Deathkiss.

ROAD RAGE: He must have gotten the information from Dupreiss before he killed him.

DJINN-X: But he doesn't know that we know. This is the perfect opportunity to get rid of the son of a bitch.

PATRON: Indeed. Do you have a plan?

DJINN-X: Yeah. We whack the motherfucker.

ROAD RAGE: Easier said than done.

GOURMET: Anonymity is our cornerstone. He knows that. Suggesting a physical meeting will look suspicious.

PATRON: Not if the bait is irresistible.

DJINN-X: And that would be?

PATRON: All of us. All together in one location.

ROAD RAGE: Giving him the opportunity to eliminate the entire Pack in one blow. I doubt he could resist—but what if he does something crude? Using a bomb, for instance?

PATRON: He won't. I'd like you all to look at something.

A picture downloaded. It was one of the photos of Djinn-X Jack had taken during his interrogation.

He knew. The Patron knew that Djinn-X was dead. In a second he was going to reveal it to the entire Pack. . . .

Jack grabbed blindly for the power cord. He could still shut down the whole system, blame it on a power surge—

Too late.

PATRON: Deathkiss sent me this. I believe it is actually Deathkiss himself—and that the wounds you see are the Closer's work.

Jack froze.

PATRON: We had a most interesting conversation. I believe the Closer does more than simply kill our kind—he tortures them. Not simply for pleasure, but for information.

Jack swallowed, then forced himself to type a reply.

DJINN-X: Then he'd never just try to wipe us

out all at once. He'll do the same thing we do—
try to get us somewhere he can control the
situation.

PATRON: Then we must offer him such a place.

GOURMET: Yes. And make sure he doesn't leave it alive.

DJINN-X: We can't risk the entire Pack. We should
only send one of us to take him out, just in case.

*ROAD RAGE: Well, it can't be Djinn-X—as webmaster,
you know too much that could be potentially damaging.*

**GOURMET: Agreed. Let me do it—I'd love to sample his
gray cells.**

PATRON: I have no problem with that.

Jack frowned. He'd scanned the Gourmet's section,
but he was still largely an unknown.

DJINN-X: Hang on. Maybe we should figure out
how we're gonna trap him before we decide who
should make the kill.

ROAD RAGE: I have an idea. A competition.

GOURMET: Explain.

*ROAD RAGE: All members of The Pack attend a
large public event. Nobody can identify anybody
else. We establish rules and objectives concerning
prey, methods of killing and body disposal. Most
importantly, we provide a space the Closer thinks
he can control, one where he believes he can lie in
wait and take us out one by one.*

PATRON: A hunt. Where the prey is hunting the
hunters, who are in turn hunting him. Elegant.

DJINN-X: I like it. And I've got just the thing for a
killing floor—a big white panel truck. I don't know
about driving it all the way out to Nevada, though.

*ROAD RAGE: Not a problem. I can obtain access to
one easily enough here—and I don't think our newest*

member will object to driving from Seattle to Portland, do you?
GOURMET: Unlikely. Congratulations, Road Rage—you would seem to be the logical choice.
ROAD RAGE: Thank you. I'll do my best.

They chose the Rose Quarter Memorial Coliseum as the hunting ground.

The Gourmet devised most of the rules. Jack wasn't sure if he was the smartest member of the Pack, but he certainly portrayed himself as such—despite the fact that the hunt was simply a ruse, the guidelines were well thought out.

They titled the competition, "Anyone *you* can kill . . . I can kill *better.*"

It was to take place next weekend, during a Home and Garden show. The place would be swarming with thousands of people, but security would be restricted to rent-a-cops; no actual police presence was expected.

Jack went out there the next afternoon to look around. He wandered down halls, poked his head in empty meeting rooms, rode escalators up and down.

He paid special attention to back areas. Jack had worked part-time in a hotel while he attended art school, and he knew as long as he looked like he belonged no one would question him. He took along a sealed cardboard box as a prop, and tried to look bored.

He scoped out the kitchens, the staff rooms and the storage areas. He noted the location of freight elevators, stairwells and administrative offices. No one bothered him.

He saved the loading dock and parking area for

last. They were usually monitored, both by cameras and security guards. He didn't linger.

When he was done, he went shopping.

The hunt was planned for Sunday; Stoltz rented a white panel truck Saturday morning, then spent the early afternoon at the Home and Garden show. It would have made an interesting place for an actual hunt, he thought as he wandered between the displays. He eyed a large, bearded man in a denim jacket inspecting a kitchen suite, and entertained a brief fantasy about the man stealing his parking spot. It ended with him following the man into the bathroom and shooting him on the toilet—*a crudely fitting end for such a crude human being,* he thought with satisfaction.

The Home and Garden show itself even provided him with the supplies he required. He purchased six large garbage bins—the plastic kind with a wheeled base—some rope and a heavy tarp. The bins were ostensibly for the victims of the contest, but only two would actually be used; one to hold the Closer's body, and one to conceal his killer. The other four he dropped off at prearranged spots around the arena, in areas they wouldn't seem out of place, then parked the truck in a lot across the street so he wouldn't have far to move it in the morning.

Of course, there was always fine-tuning to be done. First, he strung the tarp inside, dividing the truck into a back section and a front, then secured the bins behind the tarp. Anyone entering the truck from the rear would see only the tarp; enticing them to step behind it would be easier than slamming the heavy rear door down.

He encountered a problem with the dimensions of the bin itself, so he walked back to the Home and Garden show and bought a few more things: a cordless tool with a serrated blade, four small plastic clamps and a hose.

Fortunately the bins were squared-off, not round, and butted up against one another nicely. He cut away most of the sidewalls of two of them, leaving only a thin lip running down each side. He used the plastic clamps to attach the lips together; from outside the bins would look like they were just standing side by side, but in fact they were now one, roomier unit. Stoltz could sit quite comfortably with his legs stretched out; it would be serviceable.

There. He was almost ready. He would stop at a grocery store and pick up some produce, and make himself another silencer tonight. In the morning he would add the rental truck to the many other white rental trucks in the Coliseum parking lot, and add a few final touches.

And then he would wait.

ANYONE YOU CAN KILL . . .

The rules are simple.

The Hunt begins at noon on Sunday. Method of termination must be personal—no poison, bombs or arson. Anyone is fair game, but different prey have different point values.

Body Disposal Units—plastic wheeled bins—have been placed in various areas. Click on the link below for a complete floor plan. These units are for your convenience; their use is not mandatory. However, in order to fairly judge the competition, all bodies must be transported to the central dump area to be counted. It doesn't matter if the prey is alive when it gets there—as long as it doesn't leave that way.

Using the dump area—a white panel truck—as a kill site is perfectly acceptable. You must call 555-6661 from a local phone after 11:45 A.M. to find out the license plate number and which parking lot the truck is in. Its rear access door will be locked from the outside; the combination is 12-17-64. The front doors will be open to provide alternative access, but the engine will be disabled to prevent theft. It's unlikely anyone will steal the contents of the BDUs, but providing additional proof of a kill through visual documentation is encouraged.

Points are as follows:
> White Adult Male—75
> White Adult Female—100
> Adolescent Male—50
> Adolescent Female—75
> Minority Female (any age)—150
> Minority Male (any age)—125
> Prepubescent Male—100
> Prepubescent Female—150
> Security Guard—50

This point system is based on the assumption that the harder it is to isolate the prey, the more they're worth. Members of another race and sex are ranked highest, as are children. Security guards and male teenagers are worth the least, as both tend to be overconfident and curious.

The Hunt ends at six P.M., when the Home and Garden show closes. A final body count will be tallied and posted by our onsite representative.

Good luck, and good hunting.

Something wasn't right.

Jack knew it even before he and Nikki pulled into the parking lot of the Coliseum in their van at 11:30 A.M. He had helped plan the entire setup, had even been the one to suggest the last-minute phone ID of the truck. Road Rage would be recording a message in another few minutes, but he wouldn't have to leave the truck to do it—he'd probably use his cell. Which meant there was no way Jack could find out which one of the dozens of white rental trucks was his, not right now—he'd have to wait and check the message, just like Deathkiss was supposed to do.

But something wasn't right.

"Where you think it'll be?" Nikki said. "Close to a loading dock to make it seem believable?" She wore dark sunglasses, a gray skater's toque and a black track suit; she looked nothing like she did on the street.

"I don't think so. More likely someplace low-traffic to cut down on potential witnesses."

"Which will work for us, too. Road Rage's the only Pack member even in town, and he should be sealed up in a big garbage bin right about now."

"Yeah. But—" Jack shook his head. "I don't know. My gut's trying to tell me something."

"If we're gonna change the plan, we gotta do it now," Nikki said. "They're gonna expect the Closer to show up about two minutes after he finds out where the truck is so he doesn't miss anyone. If you don't, double-R is gonna know something's wrong."

"The plan is fine. It's something else."

"It's different from the others, Jack. This guy knows you're coming. And he's not going to dick around with trying to take you alive, either—he'll just put a bullet in you."

"I'm not afraid," Jack said softly. "Maybe I should be. . . ."

"We can still call it off. Always trust your gut, you know that."

"There's too much at stake. If I take him out, they'll think the Closer is gone for good. If they let down their guard—just a little—it'll give me the opening I need."

"Yeah, and then you'll have *another* identity to juggle," Nikki pointed out. "Deathkiss'll be gone, but you'll have to pose as Road Rage *and* Djinn-X from now on. Which means a lot more chances for *you* to screw up, too."

"I can handle it."

"Yeah, well . . . I'll be there to watch your back, okay?"

Jack nodded, but his eyes were distant.

"Kinda weird, huh?" Nikki asked. "You being the target, me being the muscle. I get a catchy nickname, too?"

"Sure. How about . . . Captain Hooker?"

She stared at him in surprise, then laughed. "Okay, who are you and what have you done with Jack?"

"Sorry. I—just nerves, I guess. Trying to loosen up."

"No, no, it was funny. Just not what I expect from you."

"Maybe that's my problem," Jack said. "I keep trying to expect the unexpected."

"You're used to being in control. The capture, the interrogation—you hold all the cards. You can't think like that now. On the street, it's all about reflexes and instincts. React to what's happening, not what you think should or could be. Listen to your gut."

"I'll try. You ready?"

"Let's do it."

There was something Stoltz hadn't mentioned to the rest of The Pack.

He knew the folly of relying on others. The only thing people could be trusted to do was break the rules—it was just human nature. So despite the fact that he felt closer to The Pack than he ever had to his family, he'd kept certain preparations of his own secret.

He checked his watch—11:50. Five minutes ago he'd left a message on a voice-mail account The Pack had set up specifically for the occasion, revealing the plate number of the truck and which lot it was parked in.

Once he got there, though, the Closer was in for a surprise. . . .

• • •

Jack wheeled the garbage bin down the ramp of the loading dock. He'd picked it up right where the map had said it would be, beside a booth selling garden gnomes. People had been using it—it was half-filled with empty soda cans and crumpled sales brochures— but nobody said a word when he took it away.

Jack himself was wearing a pair of dirty orange coveralls, work boots and a baseball cap. He'd used Nikki's cell phone to call the number he was supposed to, and now he knew where the truck was: in the northwest corner of the parking lot on the south side of the building.

There it was, parked between a hedge and another truck. Jack looked around carefully; no one under the truck or in the cab. A chrome combination lock secured the rear door, just as it was supposed to. A sliding ramp was built into the base of the truck, and Jack pulled it out before he undid the lock.

The door ratcheted upward noisily when Jack yanked on it. He could only see half the interior—a blue tarp hung from the ceiling midway down the box.

He wheeled the garbage bin around and started pushing it up the ramp.

Sweat oozed down Jack's neck. Any second now, bullets would come ripping through that tarp. . . .

He reached the top of the ramp. Parked the bin against the wall. Drew the gun from the pocket of his coveralls.

Slowly, he reached forward and grabbed the edge of the tarp. He pulled it aside.

Two garbage bins identical to his were roped against the wall.

He lifted the lid of the first.

• • •

Stoltz had read about infrared imaging systems and
high-tech devices that let you see right through
walls—and who knew what the Closer had at his disposal? The mannequin he'd put inside the garbage
bins may not have been very flexible—the knees
didn't even bend—but the hooded jumpsuit he'd
dressed it in, made out of two electric blankets, would
ensure it had the right silhouette and heat signature.

Of course, he felt a bit silly now. Unless the bin the
Closer had just rolled inside was loaded with sophisti-
cated equipment, Stoltz's precautions had been completely unnecessary. . . .

Stoltz eased up the trunk lid of the car where he'd
hidden and climbed out. He'd parked directly opposite
the dump site; only a few feet separated him from the
open back of the truck. He slipped his safety goggles
down over his eyes. Gun in hand, he crept up the
ramp.

"Don't move," Jack said. The figure inside the bin was
wearing some kind of hood—Jack couldn't see his
face. "Raise your hands, slowly."

No response. Was it Road Rage—or a body?

"Stand up!" Jack snapped.

The figure didn't twitch. Jack grabbed the hood and
yanked it back.

"Dummy," Jack whispered.

He whirled around. The tarp had fallen back into
place when he'd stepped past it.

He aimed at its center. Felt the truck shift ever so
slightly as weight was added to it.

• • •

Road Rage pointed his gun with its home-made silencer at the tarp. The Closer should be standing right about there. . . .

"Ahem."

He looked down. The lid of the bin the Closer had brought with him was ajar, and the muzzle of a gun poked out. Behind it was a pair of very blue, very cold eyes.

"The fuck is that—a potato?" Nikki said.

INTERLUDE

Dear Electra:

You'll never believe it. Today I got to drive!

And before you ask—yes, it was Uncle Rick who let me. When the weather's bad, he drives a car instead of his motorcycle. His car is pretty old and beat-up—it's a junky-looking Toyota from twenty years ago—but it gets him around. I was with him today, "just hanging out," as he says, and he asked if I wanted to go for a drive out to Cloverdale to get some art supplies. Now, with Uncle Rick, "art supplies" could be anything from a stuffed moose to funhouse mirrors, so of course I said yes.

He seemed a little down when he picked me up. Turns out he had a fight with his girlfriend last night—I didn't even know he had one! She's some waitress he's been seeing for the last month, apparently. He said the fight was because he was spending too much time on his art. I told him, "If she doesn't understand how important your art is to you, she doesn't deserve to be with you." I think that cheered him up.

The shopping part was pretty cool—he was picking up an old saddle he saw in the Buy and Sell. We went to this funky old farmhouse in the middle of nowhere, and bought it from this guy who looked like he was around a hundred and fifty. He had crazy white hair like a mad scientist, and said "Praise Jesus!" about every three sentences. He hauled the saddle out of this barn almost as old as he was; there weren't any horses or cattle living in the place, just some chickens. The barn was really cool—it was all gray and weather-beaten, and sunlight shone through about a zillion gaps in the walls. It reminded me of Uncle Rick's loft.

At first I didn't get why Uncle Rick wanted the saddle. The thing was really beat up—the leather was cracked and stained and the pommel was broken. There was no way you could ever use it again. He gave the guy fifty bucks, and put it in the trunk.

"You're awfully quiet," Uncle Rick said on the ride back.

"Thinking about the saddle," I said. "I think I get it."

"Enlighten me," Uncle Rick said. He likes to say that.

"Well, at first I thought it was just a piece of junk. Old things can be cool—but it's not just old, it's broken. But then I started thinking about the barn."

"Yeah? What about it?" He gave me this little smile that told me I was on the right track.

"Well, the barn is broken, too. It's barely standing. I'm sure the roof leaks in a million places."

"But?"

"But the barn is cool. I really liked it. And I think I figured out why."

"Don't keep me in suspense."

"Because it's barely standing—but it is standing."

Uncle Rick's smile got bigger. Sigh. "Bingo," he said.

"It's like the building has gone through all this stuff, and it's managed to survive. It's still there. Kind of like that old guy, too, I guess."

"That's right. And all that history—everything they went through—is still there, too. It's an artist's job to see that, and try to bring it out in the light where everyone else can see it."

"Really? I thought an artist's job was to 'create his own language and teach it to others.'"

"You're a brat. And if you're gonna quote me to me, try not to make me sound so pompous."

"Or what?"

"Or I won't teach you how to drive."

Okay, I'm gonna stop writing down actual dialogue now, 'cause there was much girlish squealing. Followed by teasing, mock threats, begging, and finally blood oaths to not tell my parents.

We went down this side road with no traffic, and then he pulled over. We switched places. I thought it was going to be easy, Electra, but I was in for a surprise. See, Uncle Rick drives a standard—for those of you who are uninformed, that means there's a whole other pedal *you have to operate called the* clutch.

The Clutch of Death, I call it. I swear, who designed something *like that? "Y'know, Al, there just aren't enough pedals in this thing. We should add another one, right there."*

"Good idea, Ralph. That whole left foot just isn't being properly exercised. Let's add a spring to it, too."

"Right. Can't make it too simple, though."

"No, of course not. Let's hook it up so you have to let it out while you press down on the gas. That should confuse everyone."

"Not good enough, Al. Let's make the whole

thing stall if you don't do it right, and throw in a gearshift."

"Brilliant, Ralph."

The first ten times I tried to do it, the whole car lurched and died. Fortunately, Uncle Rick is both smart and patient—know what he said before we started, Electra?

I DO NOT CURRENTLY POSSESS THAT INFORMATION.

He said, "The first ten times you try to do this, the whole car is going to lurch and die." That's what he said.

HOW PERCEPTIVE.

I know. But I finally got the hang of it, Electra. I really did! I actually learned how to shift and everything. Okay, I only got as far as second gear, but that's still pretty good.

I'M SURE MACHINES EVERYWHERE ARE IMPRESSED.

Probably not. But I don't care.

Uncle Rick was.

CHAPTER EIGHT

The woman in the bin stood up. Stoltz fired.

The potato exploded like a bomb, chunks spraying everywhere. Stoltz was ready for it, not even flinching as a piece ricocheted off his goggles. His shot went through the tarp, and he could tell from the sound on the other side he'd scored a hit.

The woman had jerked backward when the potato blew up. Off balance, she knocked over the bin with her still in it.

Stoltz stepped on her outstretched arm, pinning her wrist beneath his foot. She still had the gun, but she couldn't aim it. Coolly, he pointed his own weapon at her. "Please," he said. "Relax your grip. It's over. . . ."

Over.

Over.

". . . roll him over." *Woman's voice. What?*

"Can't believe he fainted." *Who's that? Is that—no. Oh, no. No no no—*

"—no chance at all, my dear," Stoltz said. "You have no idea who you're dealing with."

Tied and helpless, all the woman could do was snarl at him. "Just wait until the Closer gets through with you," she hissed.

"Ah, but it's he who is through," Stoltz said. He pulled aside the tarp, revealing a handsome, muscular man with a blond crewcut and a bullet hole in the center of his forehead. "A pity he wasn't quite as quick a shot as he should—"

"—should be no problem, unless he throws up."

Can't move. Can't see. Gagged. They're lifting me up. Moving me where?

Someplace private.

"No one will disturb us here," he said. She was lovely, even with bits of potato stuck to her face.

"I'm so glad you killed him," she said. "He made me do those things. I never wanted to be with him." She slipped both straps of the evening gown off her shoulders and let it drop to the floor. Her breasts had five nipples.

Floor lurching, bumping. In a vehicle.

"It's just the tide," he whispered in her ear as they danced on the deck of the ship. "The lift and fall of the waves. Nothing to worry about."

She held him tighter and whispered back. "How long to get his password?"

"What?"

"Depends. If he goes catatonic, never."

No. No. Nononononononononono . . .

"I know who you are."

"Please. Please don't hurt me."

"I know who you are."

"I *don't* know who you are. I don't want to, okay? Just let me go."

"I have some questions."

"I'll tell you anything you want to know, just don't hurt me, okay? Please—"

"What's your password to the Stalking Ground?"

"The what? I don't know what you're talking— AAAAAAAH!"

"I know you don't want to betray them. But it's too late for that."

"Oh fuck. Oh fuck. My girlfriend wrote down your license plate, she'll call the cops, don't do this. C'mon, I'll give you a nice blow job, you can do anything you want, just please don't kill me. I'm only twenty, oh Jesus—"

"Your name is Djinn-X. You are the webmaster. I'm going to do terrible, terrible things to you. Would you like a little glimpse into the future? Here, look at this picture."

"Oh God. That's not real, that's not real—"

"Not real? It's a masterpiece, my dear girl. And I'm going to do to you exactly what he did to this poor fellow. It might seem a little derivative—but then, he's the artist, not I. I'm just his Patron. . . ."

"I know who you are."

Stoltz opened his eyes. He was tied to a chair in the center of a room with walls made of slick black plastic. The only other furniture was a table with a lamp and a laptop. A man stood there, his face hidden by shadow.

He shut his eyes. *The dungeon was made of damp, cold stone, but he would find a way to escape. They didn't know about the five blasting caps hidden in his—*

A hand cracked across his face. His eyes snapped open.

"No. I'm not going to let you do that," the Closer said. "This is reality. This is not going to go away. If you shut your eyes again, I'll remove one of them."

"What—what do you want?" Stoltz managed.

"Your password to the Stalking Ground."

"It's Stoltz007," he blurted out. "Please. It's Stoltz007."

The Closer stared at him for a second without a word. "I almost believe you," he said. "But I know you must have programmed in an erase sequence. I have to assume that was it."

Stoltz swallowed. A pit opened up in his stomach, a vast yawning well dropping away to infinity. He realized, with a pure and sudden clarity, the immense mistake he had just made.

"The erase code is Blofeld2," he said. "But you don't believe me, of course. And there's only one way you'll know for sure."

"Actually, there are two. I can gamble, and try what you just told me—or I can be sure beforehand."

"Yes," Stoltz said. "I understand."

"Now," the Closer said. "Let's start at the beginning. . . ."

ROAD RAGE: *Gentlemen, a celebration is in order. The deed is done.*

GOURMET: **Were there any problems?**

ROAD RAGE: *None to speak of. The trap worked perfectly. He showed up precisely at noon, and was dead before 12:01. The expression on his face*

*when he opened the bin lid to find me inside was
priceless; I wish I'd thought to rig a camera to
capture it.*

PATRON: You don't have pictures?

*ROAD RAGE: Of course I have pictures—but only
of his corpse. And I'm afraid you'll have to wait to
admire them, as my scanner is being repaired.*

GOURMET: Tell us about him.

*ROAD RAGE: He had no ID on him, so I can't give
you a name. Caucasian, scrawny build, mid-forties.
Brown hair, somewhat froggy-looking face.
Unremarkable, really.*

PATRON: A shame you couldn't have done to him
what he did to us. There was much The Pack could
have learned.

*ROAD RAGE: I'm afraid that sort of thing really isn't
my style. He was a worthy opponent—he deserved
a swift death.*

GOURMET: He's been neutralized. That's all that matters.

PATRON: Absolutely. This is a tremendous victory
for the entire Pack—well done, Road Rage.

GOURMET: Yes. Excellent work.

ROAD RAGE: Not at all. Glad to be of service.

PATRON: I'm sure Djinn-X would offer his
congratulations as well. Odd that he isn't online—
I assumed he'd be as eager as the rest of us for
results.

*ROAD RAGE: Yes, that is strange. Perhaps he's
occupied with work.*

"I told you I was telling the truth," Stoltz whimpered.
"I told you. I told you."

It was bound to happen sooner or later, Jack thought. *A killer with no resistance at all. One so terrified of pain he surrenders everything he knows immediately.*

The horrible thing was, it made no difference.

Jack couldn't trust his answers. No matter how much Stoltz pleaded and sobbed and screamed, Jack had to be sure. Predators like him were masters of deception, their lives—sometimes their entire personalities—an elaborate falsehood. Even if he told the truth nine times in a row, there was no guarantee the tenth wasn't a lie. And if he thought Jack felt sorry for him, even for a second, he would try to twist that to his advantage.

Still, the interrogation wasn't long. All but one of Stoltz's kills were public knowledge; what he mainly supplied Jack with were the details of what had angered him in the first place. It was a sad list of petty annoyances, ranging from people cursing at him to someone who failed to signal a lane change.

"And the prostitute you killed for your initiation?" Jack asked. "What driving infraction did she commit?"

"I'm sorry for that one, I really am," Stoltz sobbed. "But it was the only way. The only way they'd let me join."

"Why did you? None of them kill for the same reasons you do. Why would you *want* to be a member of The Pack?"

Stoltz's sobbing slowed and stopped. Jack let him catch his breath.

"When you were younger, did you know what you wanted to do with your life?" Stoltz managed.

Jack thought back to the first time he'd made something he thought of as art. "Yes," he answered.

"Well, I never did. I never had any specific plan or purpose. That's what most people are like, you know."

Jack said nothing.

"My job, my life—it just sort of *happened* to me. And I realized one day that I was insignificant, that nothing I did really mattered. That I would never accomplish anything important. It felt like dying, to realize that."

"So others died instead."

"It wasn't supposed to be like that! The first one, I was just going to scare him. Give him a good talking to. But—but he *laughed* at me."

"So you killed him. And to show your remorse, you nailed his driver's license to his forehead."

"He didn't deserve that license! I had to show people *why* he'd been killed, don't you see? There had to be a *point.* I couldn't have people thinking I was just some random *criminal.*"

"Ah. Of course not. You were *special,* weren't you?"

Stoltz looked up. For the first time, there was something besides fear in his voice. "I was *never* anything special," he said. "Just another face in the crowd. But when I started my work, all that changed. I made a *difference.* I made the world a *better place.*"

"And the other members of The Pack? Do they make the world a better place?"

"They—they're my friends. I don't have many friends."

"So you just ignore the fact that they murder people?"

"Friendship is a contract," Stoltz said stiffly. "You agree to ignore the other person's faults, and they agree to ignore yours. Friends don't judge each other."

"No, you just judge strangers—and then kill them. You really think what those six people did was so bad that eliminating them would change anything?"

"But it did. Not because they were gone, but because everyone knew *why*. And people's behavior *changed*."

"Yes," Jack said softly. "Yes, it did. But not in the way you wanted. You didn't make anyone more polite—you just made them *afraid*. There's nothing noble or enlightening about that."

Jack leaned forward, his face intent. "You want to know where you had the biggest effect? On the families of your victims. Innocents. Do a father's bad driving habits mean his children should suffer, too? Or his wife?"

"I—I didn't mean—"

"You didn't *care* about the victims you left behind. The survivors. *But I do*." Suddenly, there was a thin steel rod in Jack's hand. A car antenna.

"There are three stages victim-survivors usually go through," Jack said. "The first one is *impact*."

He whipped the antenna across Stoltz's face. Stoltz screamed.

"A victim in this stage is in shock. He may be unable to concentrate, or feel distanced from his own emotions. He may experience despair, horror, or denial."

He struck again, a vicious backhand across Stoltz's forehead. Stoltz cried out, "Don't!"

"The next stage is *recoil*. The victim feels many things—anger, depression, rejection, guilt. And, of course, loss—loss of identity, loss of self-respect, loss of control. Unpredictable mood *swings*—"

Another strike.

And another.

And another.

"Oh God, please don't, why are you doing this *why*—"

"Finally, there's *resolution*. The victim assimilates

his pain. He accepts that it will never, ever go away—that it is *part* of him, now. It's a weight he must carry for the rest of his life. The weight never decreases, but the muscles that support it can grow stronger."

"What do you want? I told you everything, please don't hurt me anymore—"

"No two victim-survivors are the same. Each person experiences the three stages differently. But there is one constant each and every one shares—do you know what that is?"

"No. No. Please, I don't know—"

"They want to know about the end. No matter how horrific, how wrenching, they need to know how the person they loved so much died. They need *details*. They need them so they can re-create the last moments of that person's life in their head, because it's the only substitute they'll ever have for what they truly want—to be there. To say good-bye."

Jack paused, looked down at the antenna in his hand. Blood on chrome glinted a deep ruby in the glare from the lamp, sliding down the silver rod in discrete droplets.

"I can't give them that. But I *can* give them the details. I can give them facts, if not understanding."

"Please," Stoltz moaned. "I've told you everything, *everything*—"

Jack put down the antenna. He picked up a length of cord and wrapped one end around his fist, then did the same with the other end. He pulled the garrote taut between his hands.

"I know," he said.

•　•　•

Nikki sat in the back booth of the coffee shop and studied the objects in front of her.

There were six of them lined up on the table. She'd taken them out of a small plastic Baggie, using a napkin to make sure she didn't actually come into physical contact with them. She knew they'd be exhaustively analyzed by the police.

Trophy collection was common among serial killers. If they kept body parts of their victims, Jack left those for the police—but sometimes, what was taken was small and easily missed. In that case, he sent Nikki to get them, labeled each item and left them with the body. At first Nikki thought it was too big a risk to take for something so inconsequential, but she quickly changed her mind. Keeping a trophy might not seem like much compared to rape and murder, but the violation was an intimate one—stealing a tiny bit of someone's life to help you relive their murder. If the object was innocuous enough, the killer might even be able to hang on to it after being arrested; she wondered how many murderers in prison carried a good-luck charm.

The first item was a small plastic tag shaped like a number one. Printed on it were the words, You're Number 1 with Us! and the logo of a car dealership.

The second was a small, brightly colored plastic frog. Nikki looked at it for a second, then took a pair of red gloves out of her purse and pulled them on. They were Italian leather, smooth and thin and form-fitting. She had to push her charm bracelet up her arm to get the right one all the way on, though the loop of chain wouldn't go too far; it was made of tempered steel, welded on, and had very little give.

She picked up the frog and looked closely at it. It

was bright orange and blue; Nikki wondered if there actually was a frog like this, or if the original owner had painted it for their own reasons.

She put it down and picked up the third object, a Pez dispenser with a Batman head on it. She popped a little candy tablet into her hand, then put it in her mouth. Cherry. She briefly worried that Stoltz might have done something crazy like coating the candy with cyanide—Jack said he seemed to have some kind of secret agent fixation—but nothing happened.

The fourth was a piece of a jigsaw puzzle, heavily laminated. A metal grommet was punched into the corner of the plastic, probably to attach it to a key chain. There was no telling what the larger picture had been of; it was simply a splash of color and a few lines. Again, Nikki didn't know if the puzzle piece had been laminated by Stoltz or his victim. Either way, it would have been done to make the piece last, so the owner could reach into his pocket and touch the smooth plastic next to his keys, a reminder of—what? A puzzle solved—or a life ended?

Maybe there wasn't any difference.

The fifth was a Smurf, a little figure made of blue plastic. It was heavily scuffed, the painted eyes scratched and faded; someone had been carrying it around for a very long time. A gift from a child?

The last item was a small aluminum plate, embossed with a serial number and the words City of Portland. A dog tag.

She squinted at it, turned it over. On the back was engraved the word Rosie.

She tried to imagine Stoltz carrying the tag around with him, fondling it in moments of stress. Reliving his crime, fantasizing about the next one. But she didn't have Jack's gift of seeing things from the killer's perspective—all she kept coming up with were images of dogs. Big ones, small ones, barking and jumping and running around. She wondered what kind of dog Rosie had been, and how long ago she had died.

She ran a finger over the dense cluster of charms on her bracelet, hearing their familiar rattle against each other. She had every type imaginable, hearts and Goddess figures and shamrocks and skulls. Some had been gifts, others she'd bought herself. When people asked about them, she just shrugged and said she was superstitious.

In the end, she gathered up the objects, placed them back in their bag, and left.

Better to leave the questions to Jack.

Before disposing of Stoltz's body, Jack took pictures.

The Stalking Ground worked on a barter system, information for information. If Jack wanted details that could lead him to other members of The Pack, he would have to pay for them—and there was only one kind of acceptable currency.

He took lots of close-ups.

He was good with a camera, had even done some professional work before deciding to concentrate on sculpture. He'd always preferred shooting static objects to people or landscapes—he liked being able to control the lighting, angle, and background without any distracting variables like movement. And an object always had a story to tell; you just had to find the right way to reveal it.

Stoltz's body was a documentary of pain. Abrasions, burns, cuts . . . each one a milestone of destruction. Not of Stoltz's will—his own fear had destroyed that almost immediately.

It was a record of erosion. Jack's erosion.

The more questions he asked, the more certain he was that Stoltz was telling the truth.

But he hadn't stopped.

He told himself it was because he had to be sure. It could have all been an act. All it would take was one lie to trip him up and reveal his secret to The Pack.

But Stoltz's body told a different story.

Jack remembered every step, the significance of each wound. It was a landscape of loss, a ruined fortress of secrets that he roamed at will. He remembered how he felt at every stage . . . and at a certain point, he'd simply stopped feeling guilty.

He was still taking pictures when Nikki came downstairs.

"You're gonna what?" Nikki said.

Jack studied the edge of a hacksaw. "I'm going to courier Stoltz's brain to the Gourmet."

"The Gourmet? *Fuck* the Gourmet—let's go after the goddamn *Patron!*"

Nikki paced back and forth in the chamber. Road Rage's body, its face bloated and purple, was still tied to the chair.

"I don't know how to get to him yet," Jack said. "The Gourmet has very specific tastes. He won't pass up the chance to consume the brain of the Closer."

"I'm starting to think the brain of the Closer has *already* been fucking consumed, Jack. You wanna warm up with *this* loser—" she said, gesturing at the body in the chair, "—fine, I get that. But we're talking about the fucker that killed your *family.*"

"Yes," Jack said quietly. "And now I'm killing his—"

She stopped and stared at him incredulously. "Is that what this is about? You think killing off The Pack is gonna make the Patron *suffer?* That is complete *bull-shit,* Jack, and you know it. First, the whole happy-family-of-serial-killers was Djinn-X's thing, and he's gone off to that big Kurt Cobain concert in the sky. Second—Jesus, Jack, the Patron doesn't care about *anyone.* He goes through body parts the way a writer goes through paper. He's the biggest fucking monster we've found—and I'm starting to think he's got bigger balls than *you* do."

"This isn't a contest. It's a process of elimination."

"I don't know about that, Jack. Maybe when it was just us hunting them, that was true. But now, they *know.* They tried to fucking *assassinate* you—"

"And they think they succeeded." Jack started un-doing the nut that secured the hacksaw blade. "But we did. One less of them."

"Right. So they're weaker, we're stronger. And right now, they're probably even feeling a little cocky. Over-confident. But it won't last, Jack—we gotta go after them *now.*"

He detached the blade, selected one with larger teeth. "We are. I just want to make sure we do it right—"

"Right? *Right?*" She laughed. "Jack, you got a copy of *Hunting Serial Killers for Dummies* you haven't told me about? 'Cause I kinda thought we were making this up as we went along."

He aligned the blade, tightened the holding nut.

"Nikki, you know how the process works. It takes patience."

"It's different now, Jack. Can't you see that? We're not doing the bait-and-switch thing anymore—we're going *after* the motherfuckers. *And they know it.*"

"I told you, they think I'm dead—"

"And how long before they figure out that isn't true? You really think you can fool these guys forever?"

Jack put down the hacksaw and looked at her levelly. "Not forever. Just long enough."

Nikki shook her head. "I don't know, Jack. I can't tell if you're just so focused you can't change your plan—or maybe you don't *want* to go after the Patron."

"You think I'm afraid?"

"Nothing wrong with being afraid, Jack. I just wonder what you're afraid *of.*"

The laptop chimed.

"Incoming message," Jack said. "Someone wants to talk to Djinn-X."

"Go ahead, chat with your pals," Nikki said. "Just don't forget who you're supposed to *be.*"

She stalked out of the chamber.

PATRON: Where have you been, dear boy? We've missed you.
DJINN-X: Ah, some asshole stole my bike. I've been dealing with insurance and cops and shit.
PATRON: I understand. Quite the frustrating experience, isn't it—having something important taken away from you?
DJINN-X: Yeah, well, if I ever find the shithead, I'll make him pay.

PATRON: I hate to sound cynical, but—that's highly unlikely, isn't it? Some things, once gone, are gone forever. Better to move on.

DJINN-X: What the fuck are you talking about?

PATRON: Well, that's your own philosophy, isn't it? The person who stole your bike wasn't responsible— there's a whole chain of blame leading upward, isn't there?

DJINN-X: Yeah, yeah. You're right. Guess I need to put a few rounds into some corporate dickwad to make me feel better.

PATRON: Well, I have something that may change your mood: a sound file. I'm sending it now.

Jack frowned. He'd almost slipped up with that last exchange. The conversation with Nikki had upset him more than he'd thought—he'd have to be more careful.

He adjusted the volume control on the laptop's speakers, and activated the file. The first voice he heard sounded like a young woman's; the second was electronically disguised. Obviously, the Patron was taking no chances . . . but when Jack heard his first words, his heart froze.

Patron: I know who you are.

Woman: Please. Please don't hurt me.

Patron: I know who you are.

Woman: I *don't* know who you are. I don't want to, okay? Just let me go.

Patron: I have some questions.

Woman: I'll tell you anything you want to know, just don't hurt me, okay? Please—

Patron: What's your password to the Stalking Ground?

Pure, paranoid fear paralyzed him. He was suddenly sure that disguised voice was his, that the Patron had somehow recorded one of his interrogations and was playing it back to him in the moment before he burst through the door and ended Jack's life—

Woman: The what? I don't know what you're talking—AAAAAAAH!

The woman's scream jolted him, sent his pulse racing. He gasped.

Patron: I know you don't want to betray them. But it's too late for that.

Woman: Oh fuck. Oh fuck. My girlfriend wrote down your license plate, she'll call the cops, don't do this. C'mon, I'll give you a nice blow job, you can do anything you want, just please don't kill me. I'm only twenty, oh Jesus—

Patron: Your name is Djinn-X. You are the webmaster—

The file ended.

Jack forced himself to look down at the next message.

PATRON: But that's not really true, is it . . . Closer.

DJINN-X: You're outta your fucking mind.

PATRON: Perhaps. But I'm not wrong. Police fished a body out of the Green River yesterday—one with the hands missing. I presume that's the real Djinn-X, and you removed the hands to impede identification. For shame, Closer—what about all his poor victims? Aren't you denying them their *closure?*

DJINN-X: Okay, I'll play. Let's say I *am* the fucking Closer. That would mean he got me as well as Deathkiss—oh, and Road Rage, too, since his claim of killing the motherfucker must be a lie. So who's left—the Gourmet? Or have I managed to nail him, too?

PATRON: I don't believe the Gourmet has been compromised yet. The rest of your assessment is correct.

DJINN-X: That's it, man. The Pack is based on trust. I won't have you spreading this poisonous bullshit to the other members, telling them I'm the enemy. I'm cutting off your access—something, by the way, the Closer *couldn't* do, because there's no way I'd ever give up the fucking access codes.

PATRON: I expected you'd do as much. Of course, if I truly wanted to expose you to The Pack, I'd have already posted a message to the General Discussion group—which I haven't.

I don't care if you restrict my access. You're the one I want to talk to.

DJINN-X: What makes you think I have any interest in listening to your paranoid ravings?

PATRON: The real Djinn-X wouldn't. To try to convince me you're him, you're going to end this conversation quite soon. But before you do, let me send you something you should appreciate: an answer.

Another file began downloading. It was much larger than the last one.

PATRON: The question being asked is: how *did* the Closer get those access codes? I've tried to reproduce the process as best I could, though of course there was a certain amount of guesswork involved. Still, I have to thank you for creating such an entertaining blueprint to follow; I did, of course, have to supply my own raw material.

DJINN-X: You think I'm gonna just shut up and go away? Wrong. No matter how misguided you are, you're still a member of The Pack. I won't—I *can't* let you think this way. The trust we all share is the most important thing in the world to me, man. One way or another, I'm gonna convince you of that.

No reply.

It seemed to take forever for the file to finish loading. Jack couldn't keep his eyes off the icon that told him how far along the file was; the Stalking Ground used a little guillotine. It chopped off tiny cartoon heads which then fell into a basket, over and over.

Chop. Chop. Chop.

Finally, it was done. Jack swallowed, then opened the file.

It was a recorded video feed. A young woman was tied to a chair. In the background, black plastic gleamed wetly. It was identical to Jack's interrogation chamber.

The voice was the same heavily filtered one on the first recording.

Patron: Tell me about your first victim.

Woman: I don't know what you mean, I don't—what?

Another figure entered the frame. It was cloaked in a hooded plastic rain slicker, the same shiny black as the walls. The Patron. Keeping his back to the camera, he reached out with black-gloved hands and wrapped something around the woman's forehead, just above her eyebrows: a thin strand of wire.

Jack knew what was coming. "No," he whispered.

The figure held up a thin gray rod, about eight inches long, the bottom two inches or so bare wire. A sparkler, the kind you put on a birthday cake. He slid the gray end under the wire wrapped around the woman's head, then fixed the other to her cheek with a piece of duct tape. The sparkler was now a vertical bar across her right eye.

"What are you *doing?*" the woman moaned.

"This will burn slowly, but very hot," the Patron said. "If you tell me what I want to know, I'll put it out before it reaches your eye."

"I told you, *I don't know anything—*"

The Patron grabbed the woman by her hair to keep her head still, and lit the sparkler.

"WHAT IS THAT? WHAT IS IT? OH GOD OH GOD OH GOD," the woman screamed. Her head thrashed around violently. Sparks flew everywhere and shadows did a violent, jerky dance on the black walls. "GET IT OFF I'LL TELL I'LL TELL I'LL TELL YOU ANYTHING—"

When it reached her eye, she stopped trying to talk and just screamed.

Just like Djinn-X had.

Jack remembered. The sparks, the jumping shadows. The smell of magnesium and charred flesh and burning hair.

The sparkler was done. The woman made a high, keening noise of pure agony.

"Say 'Thank you, Closer,' " the Patron said. " 'For the inspiration.' "

"Th-thank you, Closer," the woman sobbed. "For the in-inspiration . . ."

The file lasted another two hours.

CHAPTER NINE

Sergei Yanovitch tended to his menagerie.

They were housed in a quonset that used to store farm machinery; he'd walled off the back third into two separate rooms, but the rest of the building was one big, echoey space, easily twice as large as the trailer Sergei himself lived in. The trailer sat at the front of the property, a hilly piece of desert with only sagebrush and rattlesnakes for neighbors, while the quonset was farther back. This time of year, the temperature dipped below freezing at night; he made sure the fuel tanks for the heaters were full, then starting dishing out supper.

First was the octopus tank. He had a couple of nice specimens, the largest a good twenty pounds or more. Their food went into glass jars with the lids screwed on; the ones who figured out how to open them would eat.

Next were the dogs. He had two Standard poodles and a black-and-white Border collie—the collie had a pedigree from two World Champion herders. The poodles' background wasn't quite as distinguished, but they were a good breed. The collie yapped happily to see him, and he let it out to blow off some steam. He exercised it every day, but the dog was never satisfied—it would take up all his attention if he let it. It followed him from cage to cage, watching him alertly.

He'd obtained the chimpanzee from a private owner in L.A. who'd gotten bored with the novelty—not surprising when you considered the chimp liked to throw feces when she was angry. She was quiet today, staying in the corner of her cage when he slid in a plate of fruits and vegetables.

Last was the elephant. He was an elderly male, content to spend most of his time munching on hay and spraying himself with water. Sergei stopped and stared up at him in admiration. He identified with the old bull more than any of the other animals, with his power and strength; his weight bench was placed so he could watch the elephant while he worked out. Sergei himself stood only five foot six, but his muscular frame bulked out at close to two hundred pounds. The white T-shirts he wore to display his build—and his habit of keeping his scalp smooth and hairless—had earned him the nickname of Mr. Clean at the bar where he worked as a bouncer. The job didn't pay much, but shrewd investing in the stock market had earned him a substantial trust fund. The income from that paid for the animals, both purchase and upkeep.

Chores done, he locked up the quonset. He let the Border collie stay out with him, which drove it almost frantic with happy barking. He silenced it with a hand command—the dog knew almost thirty, and could easily have learned more if he'd taken the time to teach it.

He returned to his trailer, the dog trotting along at

his side. The trailer wasn't much, but it was sufficient for his needs: a bedroom, a kitchen, a bathroom, and a living room. Every wall of the living room was taken up by floor-to-ceiling bookshelves, with the exception of the desk that held his computer. There was no television or stereo.

He gestured to the dog. The collie ran to the fridge, grabbed the short rope tied to the handle and tugged the door open. He stuck his head inside and came out with a can of beer held in his jaws. He nosed the door shut and then ran up to Sergei and dropped the beer gently into his waiting hand.

"Good dog," Sergei said absently. He popped the beer open and sat down in front of the computer.

He spent some time surfing around doing research on large freshwater tanks—he was thinking about adding an otter pen—then checked his email. He had a number of accounts, under various names.

The Japanese import company he dealt with had a new catalogue out. He skimmed through it quickly, but there was little to interest him. A bankrupt zoo in Romania had a bear he was considering, but the price seemed excessive. He answered some correspondence from the Tropical Bird Appreciation Society.

There was one email that made him smile. "Well," he said to the dog, "this calls for a celebration, don't you think?" The dog panted enthusiastically.

He finished his beer and logged off, then went outside. He paused to admire the sunset; the hills looked like they were glowing red-hot, as if the sun were some giant molten coin sinking into the hump of a mountain-sized piggy bank.

He unlocked the back door of the quonset and motioned the dog inside, into his workshop. Tools hung in neat array along one wall, while a table held more delicate electronic gear. There was a drill press in one corner and a table saw in another. Bins held wood, iron rods and sheet metal, while shelves were filled with model paints, clay and various glues.

He crossed the room to another door, also locked. He opened it and again motioned the dog inside; this time, the collie hesitated at the entrance. Sergei gestured again, impatiently, and the dog lowered its head and went in.

A thick-legged wooden table stood in the center of the room. A wave of his hand and the dog leapt gracefully onto the table.

Sergei put one arm around the dog's neck. With the other, he thrust an icepick into the dog's heart. The collie yelped, then went limp.

Humming softly to himself, Sergei wiped clean the icepick and replaced it in the rack he'd taken it from. He picked up the electric shears, plugged them in and began to remove the collie's fur.

A few chops with some mushroom sauce, the Gourmet thought to himself. *Yes. Just the thing to celebrate the death of the Closer . . .*

NAME: The Gourmet.
HUNTING GROUND: Nevada.
PERSONAL BELIEFS: The soul is located in the pineal gland.

The pineal gland is located in the center of the human brain, at the top of the spinal column and between the two lobes. It is the most ancient part of the organ. All higher animals that demonstrate intelligence possess a similar gland, regardless of their morphology: dolphins, octopi, pigs, parrots.

The energy located in this gland is what elevates these creatures above their fellow beasts. It would be unscientific to speculate on the specific origins or properties of this gland—it may be the source of the Divine Spark of life itself, or perhaps merely a focal point for naturally occurring energies of the space/time continuum.

In any case, these energies can be transferred. While direct consumption of the gland itself produces the best results, energy from the gland does permeate the entire organic structure of the animal that contains it. The most marked effect of consuming the gland is an increase in intelligence; the degree of effect is directly proportionate to the intelligence of the animal. As well, the proximity of the gland to the rest of the body regulates the amount of energy the flesh absorbs. The brain itself is the most enriched, followed by the eyes, jowls and tongue.

These principles hold true for humans, with an even more pronounced difference between individuals. Those of subpar intelligence generate no more energy than a clever pig, whereas someone of advanced intellect will produce a cornucopia of brilliance.

I believe this is simply a natural facet of evolution. Discovering this effect requires intelligence; utilizing it means outsmarting intelligent prey. Once the first two steps have been taken, the corresponding rise in IQ allows you to go after those at the very top of the intellectual food chain, and by doing so raise yourself above even them. Survival of the brightest.

Even primitive peoples stumbled across this secret. Tribes in Papua, New Guinea believed that eating the flesh of a warrior imparted to you his strength and courage. Many cultures regard the brain as a culinary delicacy, perhaps recognizing its power subliminally.

The process is not without its dangers. Encephalitis can be transmitted through brain tissue. However, this is largely a disease of bovine origin; it makes sense that consuming the brain of such a mindless creature would naturally have dire consequences.

• • •

Jack forced himself to watch the entire file.

Underlying the horror was an eerie sense of *déjà vu;* the Patron had not only duplicated many of the things Jack had done to Djinn-X, he came very close to reproducing the order as well.

And he never stopped asking questions.

Patron: Where did you bury the bodies?
Woman: What do you want me to say? What?
Patron: Where did you bury the bodies?
Woman: In—in the ground? Is that right?
Patron: Where in the ground?
Woman: My—my backyard. I buried them in my backyard?

Patron: You're lying.
Woman: NNNNNAAAAAA!

The answers, of course, didn't matter. That was the worst part, knowing that no matter what she said, the Patron would continue.

That, and knowing what was coming next.

He watched the woman slowly go insane. In the beginning, she seemed convinced that if she just said the right thing, found the answer her tormentor was looking for, he would stop.

Jack knew that wasn't true. The point of the questions was that they couldn't be answered.

As the interrogation went on and on, her hope died. Her eyes began to dull. She stopped pleading and simply sobbed.

And screamed.

• • •

When preparing brains, it's best to first boil them in
salted water and then store them in the same
liquid they were cooked in; this gives them a
firm texture that is much easier to work with.
Remember to remove the membrane when done.

Here is one of my favorite recipes:

Peppered Brains

1 brain, precooked
¼ cup pickled jalapeño peppers
1 tablespoon diced green pepper
¼ cup sliced onion

1 tablespoon flour
2 tablespoons butter
1 cup beef broth
1 egg yolk, beaten
8 oz. can whole tomatoes
1 tablespoon capers
2 garlic cloves, minced
1 tablespoon lemon juice
½ teaspoon salt

1. Cut the brain into thin slices.

2. Mix the butter, flour, onions, and garlic
   in a hot frying pan until the butter melts.

3. Add the brains. Sauté until golden brown.

4. Add the beef broth and egg yolk. Stir briskly.

5. Add the peppers, tomatoes, lemon juice
   and salt.

6. Reduce heat and cook for another ten
   minutes.

Best served fresh. For a garnish, unconventional
though it may sound, I recommend a sprinkling of
Pop Rocks. The fizzing crackle as they go off is like
neurons sparking in your mouth. It's as if you're
tasting thought itself.

• • •

Jack limited the Patron's access to the Stalking
Ground. He could send messages to Jack himself, but
no one else. Unless the Patron was communicating

with the Gourmet in some other way—highly unlikely—that would buy Jack some time.

The thing was, he didn't know what he should do.

If the Patron truly knew he was posing as Djinn-X
and Road Rage, there was no way Jack could lure him
into a trap. The only upside was that while Jack didn't
know where the Patron was, neither did the Patron
know where the Closer was. Stalemate.

Should he tell Nikki?

Once, he wouldn't have even asked the question.
Nikki was his partner, the only other human being on
the planet who understood his mission. He trusted her
with his life.

But did she trust him with hers?

He was no longer sure. The only room in Jack's life
for questions were the ones he asked himself, and
Nikki's sudden attack of doubt was a factor he didn't
want to deal with. But he couldn't have one of the few
reliable things in his existence suddenly turn into an
unknown, either. If Nikki found out their cover with
the Patron was blown—exactly as she'd warned—
would her confidence in Jack vanish completely?

Would she walk away? Could she?

Yes. If her gut told her to.

He wasn't sure what his own gut said. Seeing that
innocent woman tortured by the Patron had brought
the guilt and horror he kept suppressed surging up like
bile. That he could fight; he had an endless supply of
cold rage as a defense. But the questions the Patron
had posed to the woman were disturbing for an entirely different reason.

They were close—far *too* close—to what Jack had
actually asked.

Some of it was simple extrapolation—how many have you killed? Where are the bodies buried?—but it went beyond that. How they were asked, which act went with which question, even the actual phrasing.

The Patron understood how Jack's mind worked.

No, Jack thought. *He understands how the Closer's mind works. That's not hard—the Closer is a relatively simple construct. He doesn't understand how my mind works, because he doesn't know who I am. He doesn't know what my resources are. He doesn't know what I'm willing to do to get him.*

If he was going to catch the Patron, Jack had to be more than just the Closer.

He had to be The Pack.

Djinn-X's fierceness. Road Rage's meticulous planning. The Gourmet's hunger. Even Deathkiss's obsession was a source of energy to draw upon. Jack would consume it all.

He knew what he had to do, now. The Gourmet had to be eliminated, before the Patron found a way to warn him. The Patron would be left without allies, and he would know it. It would give Jack—it would give The Pack—the advantage they needed to bring him down.

Nikki wouldn't understand. She'd fight him, argue that the Patron was the more important target. There was only one way he could see to circumvent that— even if it meant risking her walking away.

He logged on to the Stalking Ground.

CLOSER: Hello, Patron.
PATRON: Hello, Closer. Decided to come clean?

CLOSER: Maybe. Maybe I'm still Djinn-X and I thought this would be a fun way to fuck with your head.

PATRON: That's the spirit. But Djinn-X held me in far too much esteem to ever do that—the boy looked upon me as a role model, I think. Perhaps even a father figure. That, combined with his trust issues, means he would never indulge in such a game. Try again.

CLOSER: All right. You're next.

PATRON: Ah—*very* effective. Short, brutal, to the point. If I believed you, I'd be quite concerned.

CLOSER: I have no reason to lie.

PATRON: You have no reason to be honest, either. People fail to realize not everyone defaults to the truth.

CLOSER: I do. Truth means everything to me.

PATRON: No. Asking questions means everything to you. The answers, as you have found out, are not always what you want them to be. . . .

"You did *what?*" Nikki said. She and Jack were walking in a park close to their house. It was dark and quiet, no one else around.

"I told the Patron I was the Closer."

"Why the *fuck* would you do that?"

"Because he already knew," Jack said patiently. "If I'd kept up the pretense, he'd have lost interest and stopped talking to me. This way, he maintains contact."

"And he can't talk to the Gourmet?" Nikki stopped and glared at him.

"Not through the Stalking Ground. But he knows

the general area the Gourmet lives in—he might find another way."

"So now we can't go after *either* of them? Fucking *Christ*, Jack—"

"The Patron will require more time and planning—but we can get the Gourmet now, if we move quickly."

"Yeah? How?" She jabbed him accusingly in the chest with a long, red-nailed finger.

"By using our brains," Jack said. "More specifically, by using Road Rage's . . ."

ROAD RAGE: I have something for you.
GOURMET: Go ahead.
ROAD RAGE: Precisely. The head being the Closer's—and you being where it should go.
GOURMET: What do you want for it?
ROAD RAGE: Seven body locations.
GOURMET: Normally I would bargain. But the head of the Closer is worth at least that much—not to mention the risks you took in getting it. Seven bodies is an agreeable price. What storage method are you using?
ROAD RAGE: Refrigeration, but not freezing. It would be best if I sent it soon, I think.
GOURMET: Indeed. What method did you have in mind?
ROAD RAGE: Courier would be fastest. You would have to arrange a delivery point, of course.
GOURMET: Yes. That shouldn't be difficult.
DJINN-X: If I might make a suggestion, guys? Use the method I do for the hands. Mail it to a P.O. box, and make sure the mailbox is in the downtown of a major city. Have a bike courier pick it up at rush hour—*nobody* can track those fuckers through

heavy downtown traffic. Specify when the package gets picked up and when it has to be delivered, so he'll be in a hurry. Pick a big office building with underground parking for the drop, and wait for the courier in the lobby. Get on the elevator with him and accept the delivery. Get off the elevator on a different floor, take another down to the parking lot, and leave. Look out for surveillance devices—fucking cameras are everywhere now, including elevators. If you can, change your appearance in a washroom right after the drop.

GOURMET: I'll consider your ideas and post instructions within six hours. My final precautions will be my own.

ROAD RAGE: Of course.

• • •

Methodology of Pursuit and Capture

The most important aspect of hunting intelligent prey is knowledge of your subject. Observe his or her behavior over an extended period of time. Familiarize yourself with their habits, routines, likes, and dislikes. Keeping a journal is extremely helpful, but a code should be used in case of discovery.

I recommend the birdwatching technique, substituting ornithology terms for key words: "nest" for apartment, "feeding ground" for restaurant, "mating ritual" for dating behavior, etcetera. This also provides a convenient excuse for the use of binoculars, cameras, and surveillance in general.

Trash and recycling bins are also a gold mine of information on your subject. Credit card, social insurance and even driver's license numbers can be obtained this way, as well as details like dietary and shopping habits.

To truly understand your subject, two methods are invaluable: firsthand observation of the subject in a social setting, and an analysis of their living space. Both of these are not without risk, but patience, planning, and caution will always produce results.

Beyond these broad strokes, each subject is different. I vary my technique accordingly, and therefore cannot list any generalized "hunting tips." Instead, I offer a specific case study, that may or may not be useful to the reader.

Case Study 32: Ulysses

"Ulysses" is a fifty-one-year-old university professor. He holds degrees in English Literature and Philosophy. He is married, with two grown children. He is president of his local Mensa chapter, with a listed IQ of 141. He has a fondness for Rocky Road ice cream.

This much was determined by casual observation. More detailed investigation reveals that Ulysses also has a fascination with medieval armor, and in fact owns several authentic pieces.

This suggested a possible approach. After doing some research, I constructed a full-face helmet (or "helm") from sheet metal, and contacted the professor via email. Posing as an English major and fan of Renaissance fairs, I asked him if he would evaluate my work for its historical accuracy, and offered him a "knighthood" in a historical-recreation organization I claimed to belong to.

Despite the fact that I was a complete stranger, his vanity wouldn't let him refuse. He agreed to meet me on campus, in a spot I chose for its seclusion.

When we met, it took little encouragement for him to try the helm on. I had lined the headpiece with heavy plastic, with a folded hem around the rim of the opening. Threaded through the hem was a long, industrial-strength band of plastic, sometimes called a "zap-strap." The tail end of the band is fed through a hole at the head, forming a loop. A one-way set of teeth embedded into the band allows it to be tightened but not loosened. This is essentially the same technology used by the police for their "disposable" handcuffs.

Once he was wearing the helm, it was easy to pull on the band, tightening it around his neck. The helm itself kept him from tearing a hole in the plastic manually. Blinded, and with his air supply cut off, it was a simple matter to subdue him. Death occurred within minutes through lack of oxygen.

I found this method to be particularly satisfying, as it combined aspects of both old and new technology.

• • •

Jack and Nikki drove from the courier office straight to the airport. Jack wanted to be on the ground in Nevada and ready by the time the head itself arrived the next day.

He'd embedded a GPS tracking unit inside the

skull. The Gourmet's inclinations meant he'd probably discover the unit almost immediately, so they'd have to move fast.

It was too dangerous to try to bring firearms with them, but Jack thought the stun gun would be all right if they put it in with their regular baggage. He kept the laptop and the GPS tracker with him.

Nikki hardly spoke to him during the flight.

They flew into Reno, rented a car and a motel room. Jack set up the laptop. The equipment that hosted the Stalking Ground was still back in Portland, but he could access it easily from almost anywhere.

He logged on while Nikki went out to pick up some supplies, intending to study the Gourmet's postings.

The Patron was waiting to talk to him.

PATRON: And how is your plan to bag the Gourmet coming along?

CLOSER: I'm not coming after him. I'm coming after you.

PATRON: I don't think you are. Would you like to know why?

CLOSER: All right.

PATRON: It doesn't fit your arc. Serial killers escalate, as I'm sure you're aware. The Gourmet, while dangerous, isn't really on my level. You're going to have to eliminate him first, because you're saving your greatest challenge for last.

CLOSER: You're certainly impressed with yourself. Sadly, my opinion of you isn't nearly as high.

PATRON: Perhaps I can raise it. How's the weather in Nevada?

Jack stopped. He stared at the screen for a moment.
CLOSER: Sunny, I assume. Why don't you check the
Weather Channel?
PATRON: Do you know how easy it would be for me
to alert the Gourmet? You must have realized an epi-
curean of his tastes would be a regular visitor to
other websites. Here are the top candidates:

A list of twenty names scrolled down, with titles
ranging from *Le Meilleur Cervelle* to Bizarre Recipes.

PATRON: A properly worded posting on any of these
would get his attention. Something like this, perhaps:

FAUX CLOSER BRAINS

A Recipe for Disaster

Take 1 Gullible Gourmet

Add 1 Head of Irresistible Bait

Mix with a dash of Subterfuge

Finish with Murder

Serves the General Public.

PATRON: What do you think?

Jack's mouth was dry. "Fuck," he said softly.

CLOSER: I think you haven't posted that message on any of those sites. If you had, you'd have told me to go look for myself.

PATRON: Which would have wasted your valuable time and mine. Very good. But here's the far more important question, Closer: why haven't I?

CLOSER: I don't know.

PATRON: It's quite simple. *The Gourmet doesn't exist.*

Jack frowned. "What?" he muttered.

CLOSER: I don't follow.

PATRON: But you do, Closer. You're following in my footsteps. Do you think you're the only killer with more than one online persona?

CLOSER: *You're* the Gourmet?

GOURMET: That's right, Closer. Come and get me.

It's not true, Jack thought.

But it could be.

It made sense. Another persona to deflect blame onto, another voice added to yours on the Stalking Ground. An insurance policy. All it would take is another dead hooker's hand to establish your credibility.

But why tell him? Arrogance? *I know you're coming and I don't care.* Or fear? *I'm ready for you so you better stay away.*

Neither made sense. The Patron was too smart to give away such an advantage, and too confident to try scare tactics. More importantly, he *knew* the Closer would never give up.

He checked the websites the Patron had listed—no message to the Gourmet. He did a search for key phrases like *brain recipes* and pulled up a dozen more sites; nothing on them, either.

All he'd done was waste time.

Maybe that was the point. Not to stop him—just to make him hesitate. To make things *harder*.

Was the Patron's claim true? No way to tell. But Jack knew one thing for sure.

It was a challenge.

"Hey," Nikki said. "I got it."

She closed the motel room door, then pulled a pistol out of one pocket of her overcoat, two boxes of ammo out of the other. The gun was a blocky automatic, black with a brown grip. "Cost me five hundred and a blow job—old Mob guy I used to do. They may not run this town anymore, but they're still around." She tossed it on the bed Jack lay on, his hands behind his head.

He reached over, picked up the weapon. Examined it carefully. "Good. Hand me those bullets."

She brought over a box, gave it to him. "Yeah, well, I've been doing some thinking . . . Jack, what are you gonna do after we take down the Patron?" Nikki sat down on the edge of the other bed.

Jack didn't answer.

"Jack?" Nikki said gently. "What are you gonna *do?*"

"Keep going." He opened the box of ammunition.

"Yeah? For how long?"

"Until I can't," Jack said. "You know that."

"I know. We made a pact, right? We keep going as long as we can. But Jack—I'm getting a little worried."

"About what?" He started loading bullets into the

magazine. Clicking them into place one by one, feeling the push of the spring against his fingers.

"About everything you're not talking about."

"It's . . ." Jack closed his eyes. "It's not a problem."

"Look, Jack, I don't know how to say this, but—I don't know if you *want* to catch the Patron."

Jack opened his eyes and turned his head. "What?"

"He's the reason you're doing all this, Jack. He's what made you. What's gonna happen when you finally take him out?"

"I don't know," Jack said quietly.

"Maybe he should be the last, Jack. Maybe after him, it wouldn't be smart to keep going."

"This isn't about revenge, Nikki. You know that."

"No. It's about closure. And when we get the Patron, you'll have yours."

"And what about you, Nikki? What about all your friends on the street, and their families? What about *their* closure?" He slammed the full magazine into the pistol.

She stood up, walked over to the small table and poured a shot of vodka into a water glass. "We can't help those people if we're dead."

"We have to try. *I* have to try."

She slammed her drink down on the table and turned. "Goddammit, this isn't about me quitting. *This is about you looking for a way to kill yourself.*"

He met her eyes levelly. "I see."

She laughed once and picked up her drink. "Sure. You're the Closer, you're cool and in control. You're going to capture and question the fucker who murdered your family and left their corpses for you to find, and it's not going to affect you a bit. *Are you out of your fucking mind?"* She was yelling now, waving the glass around—a drop of vodka splashed against Jack's cheek, making him flinch. "No, of course not! You're too fucking *focused* for that. Well, maybe it's time the Closer asked *himself* some questions."

He got up off the bed. "I don't have time for this."

"What's going to happen when you have the Patron in that chair, Jack?" she demanded. "What's it going to do to you when he describes exactly what he did to your parents? To your wife? To your *kid?*"

Jack went to the closet and took his jacket off a hanger. He slipped the gun into his pocket. "I'm going out. I'll be back in a few hours."

She grabbed his arm, forced him to turn and look at her. "I *count* on you, Jack," she said. "I put my life in your fucking hands every night. I never felt unsafe before, you know that? Never."

"Maybe you should have," Jack said.

He pulled away from her arm, opened the door and left.

INTERLUDE

Dear Electra:

Today I got a huge surprise.

It turns out . . . I'm an alien! My real parents are from Alpha Centauri, and they had me raised here to protect me from an evil Galactic Empire! So, I'm not even related to Uncle Rick—technically, I'm not related to anyone on the planet!

Not buying that one, huh?

Okay, so I'm not an alien. But I could be adopted, right? That's possible. It would even explain why I feel like I don't fit in—maybe it even explains why I like Uncle Rick so much in the first place.

It would be weird to find that out, though. Kind of like losing your whole family all at once. And then you'd have to do the looking-for-your-real-family thing, which would be cool but scary—you know, you hope they'll turn out to be rich and famous, but you're afraid they'll be a bunch of psychopathic hillbillies. And if they were, you'd start to wonder how that was going to affect you—were you going to go crazy at some point? Start drinking moonshine and shooting at squirrels?

Or maybe I'm already crazy. Do crazy people know they're crazy? I asked Jessica at school and she said that if you think you're crazy, it proves you're not. That sounded pretty dumb to me, but I didn't tell her that.

I think if you're completely insane, you proba-bly wouldn't even understand the question. If

*you're just a little bit nuts, it's like having the be-
ginnings of a cold—you know it's there, but you
can try to fight it off. Of course, with a cold you
can take Vitamin C and drink lots of fluids and
stay in bed—what do you do if you start losing
your mind? And with a cold, all you have to worry
about is being sick for a week—if you go insane,
anything could happen. You could go to school
wearing nothing but a bucket on your head. You
could eat bugs. You could grab a butcher knife and
kill your best friend.*

*And right at the start, there would be a point
where you knew something bad was happening to
you, but you wouldn't be able to stop it.*

*Let's change the subject, okay, Electra? (She said
to her imaginary electronic friend.)*

*Back to the surprise. The reason I was thinking
about the whole adoption thing is that it's my birthday. Fifteen, thanks for asking. I didn't have a big
party or anything, just a few friends came over and
we hung out. My mom gave me an ice cream cake
she got at Dairy Queen, and I got a new mountain
bike, which was pretty cool.*

*I was kind of bummed that Uncle Rick wasn't
there, though. He told me he was going to come for
supper, and I have to admit I was pretty disappointed when he didn't show.*

*Then at around seven, the doorbell rang. My dad
told me I should get it.*

*And when I opened the door, Uncle Rick was
there with my present.*

*It was a puppy, Electra. The cutest, wiggliest,
lickingest puppy you ever saw, with a big red bow*

around his neck. Uncle Rick just grinned, handed him to me and said, "Happy Birthday."

"Oh!" I said. "But, but—" and then Rufus was licking my face. I knew his name was Rufus right away—don't ask me how.

"Don't worry, I talked it over with your mom and dad," Uncle Rick said. "They think you're old enough to handle the responsibility."

Okay, this is kind of embarrassing, Electra, but I started crying. I'd wanted a dog for so long, you know? And I didn't think I'd ever get one.

"Uh, just one thing," Uncle Rick whispered. "Your parents think he's a cocker spaniel/beagle mix—actually, he's a Rottweiler/shepherd." Uncle Rick knows I like big dogs.

"Aren't they going to find out?" I whispered back.

"Sure, once he gets older—but by then he'll be part of the family."

So I spent the evening playing with Rufus and cleaning up dog pee and hanging out with Uncle Rick, and it was probably my best birthday ever. And after Uncle Rick had left, I asked my mom how he'd convinced her to let me have a dog—I'd been trying since I was eight.

"He reminded me what it was like to be a teenager," my mom said. "How sometimes the loneliness is the worst thing. How a little bit of unconditional love from something that's yours can make a big, big difference." She'd had a few glasses of wine, and got a little teary-eyed, and that set me off, and I gave her a big, drippy hug and ran up to my room with Rufus. And now I'm talking to you.

Happy birthday to me, Electra.

CHAPTER TEN

Jack walked through downtown Reno.

He felt like a modern-day Alice, having stepped through a TV screen instead of a mirror. Everything was the colorful brightness of television, illuminated by rippling street signs a hundred feet high. People packed the sidewalks, laughing and drinking and smoking, like extras waiting for the next scene.

He moved through them silently, studying faces, trying to figure out which ones were predators, which ones prey. Wondering if it mattered.

He didn't know why he hadn't told Nikki about the Patron's claim of being the Gourmet. He should have—if nothing else, it would have brought her on board, made her see that the Gourmet had to be next.

But he hadn't. He'd kept it from her deliberately. Because he was . . . angry?

Yes.

He found himself entering a casino, into the windowless gleam and flash of another world. The smell of American tobacco hung in the freon-cooled air, darker and more aromatic than Canadian cigarettes. The continuous, rolling chime of hundreds of slot machines sang mindlessly, hypnotically in his ears.

He'd never been angry at Nikki before. He hadn't been angry in a long time; there wasn't room for it inside him. The rage he felt every day was a vast, cold thing, heavy and hard and inevitable. Anger was a dim, guttering candle next to it.

Nikki was questioning him. Questioning *him*.

It wasn't as if they hadn't disagreed before. They had. But they'd both always had the same objective— to refine their methods, to make themselves better. Now . . . now Nikki was asking whether or not they should be doing this at all.

There was something else nagging at him, a very odd feeling just below the surface. He couldn't put his finger on what it was, but it felt familiar, somehow.

He found himself at the bar, and ordered a dark rum, neat. He hadn't had a drink in a long time either, not even beer, but it felt like he needed *something*.

The drink came. He took a sip, felt it warm his throat. It didn't taste quite right for some reason; it should be sweeter.

He suddenly realized what felt so familiar.

The last woman he'd argued with had been his wife.

A deep, aching sadness opened inside him like a gaping mouth. He took another long, shaky gulp, and suddenly he could taste eggnog beneath the rum.

He didn't try to hold it in, but he wept as quietly as he could. Just another victim on a barstool in Reno, crying over everything he'd lost.

"Hey, man, you all right?"

"Yeah. Yeah, I'm fine." Jack blew his nose on a bar napkin. He didn't feel embarrassed—embarrassment seemed like such an *insignificant* emotion at the moment.

"Lady Luck not on your side tonight, huh?" The man with the Yankees baseball cap was sitting two stools away, drinking a beer.

"Ladies in general don't seem to be on my side," Jack said.

"Yeah, I know what that's like," Baseball Cap said. "Don't get me wrong, I like 'em just fine—they just don't seem to return the favor."

Jack signaled the woman behind the bar and asked for a Coke; alcohol now seemed like a very bad idea.

"So, she break your heart or your balls?" Baseball Cap asked.

"Some of each, I guess," Jack answered. "Two different women."

"Well, *that's* a game plan for pain," Baseball Cap said. "I'm Dwight, by the way."

"Todd," Jack said.

"Yeah, they sure know how to getcha, don't they? Comin' and goin'. Say they want one thing, and then complain when you give it to 'em. You know what they *really* want?"

"No idea."

"Mind readers. Forget about what they say, they want you to know what they're thinking. I'll bet the Amazing Kreskin has the happiest goddamn wife on the planet."

"Telepathy. Yeah," Jack said. "That would solve a lot of problems."

"That, and a rewind button. How many times you

said something you wish you could take back? I know I have."

"We already have a rewind button," Jack said. "It's called memory."

Dwight laughed. "Yeah, guess so. Too bad you can't *edit* it, too. Right? Go back to the master tape and remix it. Add some new tracks, erase all that bad shit you don't want."

"I'd kill for an erase button," Jack said. He changed his mind about the Coke and waved the barkeep over. "I'll have a beer," Jack said. "Something dark."

"But you know what?" Dwight asked. "Sometimes you get a second chance. Not a rewind, exactly, more like an overdub. That's what I got."

Dwight caught Jack's flat look and grinned. "Don't worry, I'm not gonna get all religious on you. I'm talking about a second chance at success. A shot at fame. See, I'm in a band—well, I was in a band. Called ourself Tunguska—I was lead vocal. We started right here in Reno, did all right doing covers in clubs.

"Then we met this guy named Montrose. He had some money and wanted to break into the entertainment biz. He was pretty smart, so we took him on as manager. He fronted us enough to do a decent demo disc, even got us some airplay on local radio. Next thing you know, we got an offer for a recording contract from EMI."

Dwight shook his head. "And that's where it all went into the shitter, man. This Montrose, he'd gotten us to sign contracts. And he was a *lawyer,* man—those contracts were air-fucking-tight. And when he and I stopped getting along, he invoked this clause that let him fire anyone he thought was 'detrimental to the future of the enterprise.' Makes me sound like a fucking *Star Trek* villain, don't it?"

Jack smiled. It felt strange.

"So we got into this massive four-way fight—me, the band, Montrose, and EMI. And you know what? The band stuck by me. Montrose wouldn't give an inch, EMI didn't seem to care, I didn't know *what* the fuck to do—but the band wouldn't let me quit. Said they'd play in fucking airport lounges for the next ten years before they'd leave me behind."

"That's—that's pretty fucking cool," Jack admitted. He had a sudden flash of Djinn-X onstage, screaming his anger into a microphone.

"Yeah. We're pretty tight. And that thing they said about airport lounges—they weren't kidding. They're on a tour in the Philippines right now, doing cheesy dance music in every Holiday Inn big enough to have a nightclub."

"So why are you here?"

"TCOB, my friend—Taking Care of Business. I been working on the legal angle, and I finally got that lawyer fuck right where I want him. Turns out he was shuffling funds around in a way he wasn't supposed to, and I can prove it. I showed him the proof, and he agreed to let us out of the contract. I'm flying down to Manila tonight to tell the guys, show 'em the release papers. Man, is *that* gonna be a party."

"So loyalty pays off," Jack said. "That's great. *Fucking* great. I mean that."

"Yeah, sometimes the good guys win, right?" Dwight took a last swallow and put down his empty beer. "And hey, I gotta get going if I'm gonna catch my flight. Nice talkin' to you, Todd—hang in there with the ladies, huh?"

"Sure," Jack said. "Congratulations."

Dwight grinned, slipped off his barstool and was gone.

"Sometimes the good guys win," Jack muttered. "Nice to know . . ."

"Hey," the bartender said. "I think your friend left something behind."

A white square lay on the barstool Dwight had just vacated. A folded envelope. Jack picked it up, opened it.

Inside was an airline ticket: one-way to Manila, leaving in seventy-five minutes. Plus a stub for a rental car—and what looked like a bunch of contracts.

"Fuck," Jack said.

Jack left a message with the bartender and caught a cab to the airport.

He didn't know exactly why. Dwight would catch another flight, his good news would wait another day. He could have left the envelope with the bartender, let her handle it. And why should Jack give a flying fuck, anyway?

Because those were probably the only copies that Dwight had, and there were no addresses on any of them, and bartenders lost things.

And goddammit, sometimes the good guys were supposed to fucking *win*.

"Yeah, right," Jack said to himself, staring out the window of the cab. He had another flash of Djinn-X singing onstage—but now, he saw the rest of The Pack as the band. Road Rage sitting primly behind the drums, rapping out a carefully regulated beat. The Gourmet and the Patron, hooded figures in black plastic slickers, playing guitar and bass. Blood dripping off their instruments . . .

He was walking up to the ticket counter when his cell phone rang. He'd left the number with the bartender in case Dwight called—and sure enough, it was him.

"Hello?"

"Hey, Todd! I hear I left a little something behind!"

"Yeah, you did. Where are you?"

"I'm just pulling into the airport. Gotta drop off the rental, but I think you got the stub, too."

"Yeah, it's right here."

"Hey, I really appreciate this, man. Can you meet me in the Avis parking lot? I really need that stub."

"Uh, sure. At the entrance?"

"I'll flash my lights, just come on over." Dwight hung up.

The Avis lot was across from the main terminal, on the main level of a parking garage. There was a fair bit of foot traffic, but it thinned out as Jack got farther away from the terminal.

Lights flashed in the back corner of the lot as he walked in. Dwight got out of a large Buick and waved as Jack approached.

"Hey! If it isn't the Good Samaritan!" Dwight called out.

"I prefer Boy Scout," Jack said. "Why'd you park so far from the front?"

"Just pulled into the first spot I saw," Dwight said. He moved to the rear of the car and opened the trunk. "Hate to impose again, but can you give me a hand getting this out?"

"I don't think so," Jack said. "Be a little too easy to put me in that trunk, then, wouldn't it?"

"Huh?"

"Come on. You think I'm that stupid? Think again." Jack took his hand out of his pocket. The gun Nikki had picked up for him when they hit town had been expensive, but sometimes insurance was. "Keep your hands away from your body. You're very convincing, you know that? That whole story you spun. Almost believable."

"Look, man, I don't know what you're on, but I don't want any trouble. Take my wallet, take the car, just don't freak out."

"Play it to the end, huh? Okay. Plenty of time for truth later. There always is."

Dwight looked terrified. "Oh, man. You're fucking crazy, aren't you. Oh fuck, oh shit."

"Step back, against that wall. Get down on your knees." Jack moved closer, looked into the trunk. One large suitcase, one smaller one. Nothing else. "Empty your pockets. Slowly."

Dwight pulled out a wallet, a key chain, a packet of gum. Jack patted him down to make sure that was all there was.

No weapons. No restraint devices. No drugs.

ID in the wallet said he was Dwight Holcomb from Oklahoma. Mastercard, gas card, video rental card.

"Where's your driver's license?"

"DUI," Dwight said. "Don't drive much anymore, that's why I got the rental, I had to have a friend rent it for me—"

Jack opened the smaller of the two suitcases. Clothes, shoes, a toiletry kit. Two porn magazines. He rifled through the toiletry kit, but the most dangerous thing in it was a pair of nail clippers.

He tried to open the larger suitcase, but it was locked.

"The key's on the chain," Dwight said. His voice trembled. "It's the little one."

Sure. Dwight was going to wait until he was distracted, then pull out his key chain and unlock the suitcase so he could pull out—what? Another porn mag? Even if he had a shotgun in there, it didn't make any sense that it wasn't immediately accessible. Not if this was supposed to be a trap.

Nothing. There was nothing.

I'm losing it. Nikki was right, I don't know what I'm doing. How could the Patron even find me, let alone stroll into the same bar? This is just paranoia, complete paranoia. I have to get back in the game.

"Uh—look, I'm sorry," Jack said. "This was all just a misunderstanding. I made a mistake."

"That's—that's okay," Dwight said. "Can I stand up?"

"Yeah, sure, of course." Jack slipped the gun back into his pocket. "I'm really sorry. It's hard to explain—"

"You don't have to explain anything," Dwight said. "Everybody's got weird shit going on, right?" He crammed stuff back into the small suitcase, shut it, picked it up and started backing away from Jack. "I gotta go. I gotta go."

"Hang on," Jack said. "Don't forget this—" He reached into the trunk and grabbed the handle of the large suitcase. He pulled—

Blank.

On the ground. Hand stuck to something—

Blank.

Stun gun I've been hit with a stun gun—

Blank.

Hands cuffed. Chemical smell. Darkness.

Dwight closed the trunk, got back into the car and drove away.

"Do you know who I am?"

Jack opened his eyes blearily. His stomach lurched, and he thought he might throw up. All he could see was a bright circle of light.

"No," he croaked.

"Sure you do." Dwight's voice. "Just like I know who you are."

He couldn't move. His arms and legs were spread-eagled. Tied to a bed?

No. A table.

"I'm your replacement," Dwight said. "I'm going to be you."

"You wouldn't want to," Jack said.

"Well, in the short term, that's true," Dwight said with a chuckle. "Right now, I definitely wouldn't want to be you. But it's not something you'll have to worry about for long."

"Why would you want to be me?" Jack asked. He squinted into the light. "Killing innocent people not enough, anymore?"

His own words seemed strangely familiar to Jack, and then he remembered: Djinn-X had said almost the exact thing at one point: *Killing sluts not good enough any more, huh?—you had to go after one of your* own. *One of your own . . .*

"Oh, I don't mean that *literally,*" Dwight said. His voice was much more self-assured than it had been in the bar, and had lost that Midwest twang. Jack wondered if he could do other accents, as well. "Some of the targets you go after have a certain attraction, of course, but mostly I just want your access. Access is power, you know."

"The Stalking Ground," Jack said.

"Of course. It's a very useful tool, and I think I could make much better use of it than you. I'm rather—*inventive.*"

"How'd you find me?" Jack asked. He was starting to be able to make out dim shapes beyond the light. Things hanging on the walls.

"I've been trying to trace the website's physical location for some time. Impossible, as you know. But luck occurs when preparation meets opportunity—recently you started to access the site from remote locations, and you weren't quite as thorough in your precautions. You should be ashamed—no one could ever find *me* through *my* remote connection. But I traced *you* right to the motel room you're staying in. I watched. I followed. I dangled the bait."

Jack could make out Dwight's form, moving around behind the light. Heard a sound he couldn't quite identify—metal on metal.

"Bait you couldn't resist, could you? A sweet story about tribal loyalty, spiced up with a Big Bad Lawyer as villain. The perfect lure, even for someone as cynical and paranoid as yourself."

Dwight's face was suddenly inches from his own. He'd taken off the Yankees cap, and his bald head gleamed in the lamp's glare. "Djinn-X, the webmaster," Dwight said softly. "Well, you're in my web, now."

Jack met his eyes. "Go fuck yourself, Gourmet," he said.

"You know, I never did understand your obsession with trust," Dwight said. "A pack isn't based on loyalty, it's based on *strength*. The leader of the pack is always the strongest, the fiercest."

He pulled back, becoming only a silhouette once again. "The *smartest.*"

"And you think you're smarter than I am?"

"Of course. I've proved it, haven't I? I found you, I maneuvered you, I caught you."

"Should have looked in that fucking suitcase, huh?"

"It still would have taken you out—it was rigged with a hundred-thousand candlepower flashbulb and a capsicum grenade. Less noise than a firecracker, but you would have been blinded and choking in a fog of pepper spray within seconds. Of course, the handle trigger is much more elegant; it's wired to a taser capacitor that pulses every two seconds. I add a little superglue at the last moment to keep the target from disengaging—if you'd have checked under the back wheel you would have found the tube."

"Guess you're just two jumps ahead of me," Jack said.

"More than that. I know why you're here."

"I don't think you do."

"The Closer, of course. You intend to hijack the delivery. Consume his power yourself."

Jack said nothing.

"You see? You can't outsmart me. I've eaten the brains of people brighter than you for breakfast."

"Right," Jack said. "You know exactly what's going on, all right. I suppose you've figured out the access codes to the Stalking Ground all by yourself, too?"

The Gourmet sighed. "Sadly, no. But we have almost six hours until I have to pick up the Closer's head—I think I'll have the codes by then, don't you?"

The light shut off. Overhead fluorescents hummed to life. Blinking back spots, Jack took in his surroundings.

He was in a kitchen. Spotless white tile walls, racks of gleaming stainless steel pots and utensils. Two-tiered oven, large double sink, metal door to what had to be a walk-in freezer. And sitting on a counter a few feet away, an industrial meat-slicer, circular blade still flecked with blood.

"Interrogation isn't really my specialty," the Gourmet said. Jack saw what he held and realized what had made that sound he heard earlier: a pair of butcher's shears, the kind used to cut through bone.

"But I'm a fast learner. . . ."

Seven A.M.

Jack still hadn't returned. Nikki didn't know what she should do.

The delivery was scheduled for nine, on the nose. The handoff would take place in an elevator, just like Jack had suggested. The Gourmet would be alert for anyone following him, but he shouldn't find the GPS unit until he actually cut into the head itself. He'd wait until he was someplace secure before doing that—more than likely, the same place he usually cut up brains.

But there was no telling how soon he'd do that. They had to track and corner him as soon as possible, which meant her and Jack in a vehicle a block away from the drop site no later than 8:45. So where the hell was he?

She pulled out the GPS tracker and checked it. Looked like the package was at the airport; it'd be moving downtown soon enough. She poured herself another cup from the motel coffeemaker and peered out between the drapes again. She hadn't slept all night—she kept thinking Jack would walk through the door any minute.

But he hadn't.

She tried his cell phone again. She'd been getting a no-carrier signal for the last two hours—he'd either turned it off, his batteries were dead, or he was out of range.

Something was wrong, she was sure of it. No matter what he was going through, Jack wouldn't just walk away. Maybe he was in jail, or the hospital. Maybe he'd been mugged—Reno wasn't quite as family-friendly as Vegas yet.

Which was why Nikki had gotten two guns, not one.

She hadn't told Jack because he wouldn't have approved. They avoided guns whenever possible; killing the target would defeat the purpose of capture. Tasers, Mace, pepper spray, anything nonlethal was how Jack preferred to work. The fact that he'd asked Nikki to procure firearms at all showed how off his game he was . . . so the second gun was Nikki's insurance.

And it looked like she was going to need it.

"Fuck it," she said. She could do the tail without Jack. Once she had the Gourmet's location nailed down, she'd play it by ear.

She put the gun in her jacket, grabbed the GPS tracker and left.

• • •

One hour in.

"Give me the access codes," the Gourmet said.

"Go fuck yourself," Jack hissed through clenched teeth.

He was terrified his cell phone would ring. It was the disposable kind you bought in airports, with a preset number of usable minutes. It only worked in the area you bought it in, was made out of cheap materials and wouldn't operate at all under some conditions—even the charge from the stun gun's capacitor might have disabled it.

None of that mattered, though—because if Nikki called, the Gourmet would know Jack had a partner. If he'd been watching the motel he might already know; the only thing that gave Jack any hope at all was the fact that the Gourmet hadn't brought it up yet. If Jack had been doing the interrogation, he would have crushed that hope right off.

But then, Jack was much more experienced.

"You *will* tell me," the Gourmet said. He'd used the butcher's shears to cut the clothes off Jack's body, though he'd left his underwear on. When he was done, he'd put down the shears and picked up a wooden mallet, the kind used to tenderize meat.

He'd started on Jack's arms.

Jack couldn't move either of them now, but he was pretty sure no bones had broken. Jack thought the Gourmet was holding back, but that might have been because Jack was seeing everything through a haze of endorphins.

"Fucking *pussy*," Jack said hoarsely. His voice was

nearly gone; he'd yelled his lungs out while the Gourmet worked him over. Jack had noticed that the screamers seem to last longer, as if they were somehow riding the pain instead of fighting it. "That the best you can do? You don't *deserve* to lead The Pack."

"If you tell me now, I'll let you go," the Gourmet said. "Just like one wolf exposing his throat to another, submitting to his authority. I'll let you slink away into the night."

Jack grinned through bloody lips. "You've got to be fucking kidding. You don't know the first thing about torture, do you?"

"Oh, I'm just getting started."

"You've *already* fucked *that* up, Magoo. The beginning is *important;* it establishes the entire fucking *relationship.*"

"Oh? How so?"

"You know the expression, to 'give someone the third degree'? Know what it's from?"

"Third-degree burns, I assume. Which reminds me . . ." The Gourmet walked past the head of the table, moved to where Jack couldn't see him.

"No, asshole. That's what everyone thinks, but they're wrong. It's from the Inquisition. There were three degrees of torture—the first one was just showing the subject the instruments. Letting their imagination do the work, you know? But you rushed it."

"And the second?"

"Asking the questions. Giving the subject a chance to confess. You couldn't wait, though—just jumped right to number three. Hey, I don't much give a fuck about tradition, but only an *amateur* shows that kind of impatience."

"Maybe. But I do learn from my mistakes."

"Well, at the rate you're making them, you should be a genius pretty fucking soon. Oh, no, wait—you have to chow down on somebody *else's* brainpan for that, right?"

"At least I adhere to my principles. That prostitute I saw going into your room—she wasn't exactly a baby boomer, was she?"

Jack snorted. "Fuck you. I'm in a different town, I set up another sheep for the next initiate. See, it looks like The Pack is going to need some *fresh blood* pretty soon."

"Your bravado is transparent. There's no point in stalling."

"Right. Because as soon as I give up those codes, you're *not* going to turn my frontal lobes into a casserole."

"I was thinking more of barbecue. . . ."

Jack could suddenly smell hot metal. The Gourmet returned to Jack's line of sight. The tool he held was a simple loop of metal attached to a black handle with a cord trailing from it. Thin wisps of gray smoke were beginning to rise from the metal.

"This is used to light charcoal," the Gourmet said. "Not as common as they once were, with so many people using gas grills."

The metal was beginning to glow red hot. "Still," the Gourmet said, "it's a useful instrument. As I'm sure you'll agree . . ."

Three hours in.

"You know why this is happening to you?" the Gourmet asked.

"Because I deserve it," Jack mumbled.

"No," the Gourmet said patiently. "Because I want it to. My will is supreme. Your will is nothing."

"I *am* nothing," Jack managed. "Djinn-X . . . is nothing. Heh."

"That's right. Djinn-X is nothing."

"Just a shell," Jack whispered. "Can't hide behind it anymore."

"No. You can't."

"Good," Jack rasped. "I'm the one who should suffer. Me. *Me.*"

The Gourmet frowned. "Explain."

Jack raised his eyes. There was no defiance in them.

"Make me," he said.

Five hours in.

"I may have made a mistake," the Gourmet said. "Your endurance is impressive, but it shows little intelligence. Eating you would be a step down."

Jack didn't answer. He had passed out.

"Ah well," the Gourmet said. "I suppose we can continue this later. It's almost time to get ready for the delivery, anyway." He turned out the lights and locked the door behind him.

Jack came back to consciousness in the dark, burns on his torso screaming at him to wake up. His head swam and his body ached, but he knew where he was.

"Nikki," he whispered. The Gourmet still didn't know about her; she was his last hope. His last chance.

All he could do was make sure he was ready.

• • •

"I'm gonna fucking kill him," Nikki said. She wasn't sure if she was talking about the Gourmet or Jack.

She was driving down a two-lane highway through the desert, through a landscape dotted with low, yellow-brown hills and dusty clumps of scrub. The smell of sage underlined the car's air-conditioning. She hadn't been there for the actual hand-off—Jack was supposed to have done that—but if everything had gone as planned, the Gourmet was no more than a mile ahead of her. The GPS signal was supposedly good for up to forty, so unless he jumped in an airplane she should be all right.

Except she didn't know what had happened to Jack.

What if the Patron had somehow gotten him? She didn't know how that was possible, but her gut kept telling her it was. But then, her gut told her a lot of things about the Patron—and for once in her life, she was trying not to listen.

The Patron terrified her.

Out of all the monsters they'd hunted, she knew he was the worst. Any of the postings Jack had shown her had sent gooseflesh rippling down her back. Nikki had faced evil in more than one guise, from explosive craziness to cold, methodical sadism . . . but the Patron was something else entirely. She had no doubt he was both highly intelligent and clinically insane, but what bothered her the most was his *imagination*. His ability to take something sweet and pervert it, twist it through horror and so far beyond it took on a kind of striking surreality all its own—one that was somehow more sickening than the act itself. Like two mirrors facing each other, one beauty and one horror, with his victims

throwing endless reflections back and forth between
them . . .

He wasn't just a monster. He was *alien,* something
as far beyond murder as a computer was beyond an
abacus; she was afraid of him in the same way some
people were afraid of spiders. She would die rather
than fall into his hands.

Unless, of course, someone else killed her first.

She had to consider the possibility she was heading
into a trap. Jack gone, the Patron claiming he knew
Djinn-X was dead—things were spinning out of control. Maybe it was time to just leave, stay on this highway and keep driving. Hit Vegas, or maybe California.
She still had a few good years left in her. . . .

Sure. Wind up just another old hooker, turning
cracked and brown under the West Coast sun. Live in
a run-down motel and crack a beer first thing in the
morning to make the day go by faster. The days, the
weeks, the empty months and years.

The GPS showed a change in direction: her target
had turned onto a side road. She spotted it a minute
later by the dusty cloud still hanging in the air, kicked
up by the Gourmet's tires.

She slowed to make the corner, but never gave the
highway a second glance.

The road led to a mobile home in the middle of
nowhere. Nikki pulled off onto the shoulder as soon as
she spotted the place; fortunately, the rise of a low hill
blocked her from sight.

She got out of the car, taking a pair of binoculars
with her. A lizard scurried away and into the meager

shadow of a clump of sagebrush. The sun was still low, but the heat was starting to climb.

She crouched down and peered over the crest of the hill. A few hundred yards away, a white trailer sat at the end of the road. A black Jeep was parked in the front; to the rear, the rounded bulk of a quonset jutted like a barrel on its side, half-submerged in a flat and sandy ocean. Other than the slowly settling dust, she could see no movement at all.

"Okay, fuckwit, which building are you in? Eeny meenie, miney moe . . ."

Time to make a decision.

"Damn you, Jack," she muttered. "If I wait, he's gonna find that tracking unit and rabbit. If I go in alone . . ."

She could what? Die? Wind up an entrée for a psychopath?

"Least I don't have to worry about funeral expenses," Nikki said. "And who knows, maybe I'll wind up giving the fucker heartburn."

She went back to the car and got her pack. She left the car where it was and struck out deeper into the desert, keeping the hill between her and the buildings. When she was a hundred yards out, she started angling to the side, staying low and behind the sage.

The Gourmet could hardly wait.

It had gone perfectly. The courier delivering the package had been more than happy to give it to him in the elevator; no more than a business card had been necessary for ID. He had driven straight home, considering recipes all the way. Perhaps he would pickle the tongue. . . .

Once he got in, he took the package straight to the workshop. With Djinn-X captive in the next room, he hardly thought he had anything to worry about—but still, there was no excuse for sloppy security.

His metal detector was an old model, a disc the size of a dinner plate mounted at the bottom of a five-foot handle. He put the package on the floor and passed the disc over it—to his surprise, something registered immediately.

Fillings? Or something more dangerous?

He moved the box immediately to his workbench. He wasn't terribly worried about explosives—anything traveling on an airplane would already have been checked for chemical traces. But that still left many, many possibilities.

He was excited, rather than afraid. He'd laid and sprung many traps, and no one ever suspected a thing until the very last second. He'd often wondered what would happen if the roles were reversed; now was his chance to find out. Was he clever enough to figure out the package's secret without it destroying him?

He considered options. He believed in the inviolability of the Stalking Ground; the system was a good one, and he didn't think the authorities could crack it. Even if one of The Pack were caught, it was in their own best interests to keep the website a secret.

So the surprise was courtesy of a member of The Pack. Road Rage had no motive that he could see—but maybe the motive wasn't his. If Djinn-X had detected his attempts to track the location of the Stalking Ground, perhaps this was the webmaster's try at a preemptive strike. He could have offered Road Rage some sort of deal to take him out.

But Djinn-X would want to recover the head himself, without destroying it. Which meant . . .

A tracking device.

He got a box cutter, and slit open the top of the package.

Nikki approached the quonset from the rear. There were no windows that she could see, but there was a door. As she got closer, she could smell animal manure, though she didn't hear anything that sounded like livestock.

Gun out, she cautiously tried the doorknob. Locked.

She thought for a second, then crept around the side of the building. When she got to the corner, she peered around the edge toward the trailer. It had windows, but shades blocked the two she could see.

The front of the quonset had two doors, a big double-sided one in the center and a regular-sized one next to it. She took a deep breath, then moved cautiously toward the smaller door. She tried very hard to keep her feet from crunching on the gravel underfoot.

The door was unlocked.

She pushed it open.

Inside the box was a plastic bag, sealed with a strip of tape. The Gourmet examined it from the top carefully, then slit the box down the sides. There were no wires he could see.

Inside the bag was a human head. He studied it without touching it, looking into the glazed, bulging eyes. "Hello, Closer," the Gourmet said.

When he was satisfied there was nothing attached to the outside of the bag, he opened it. The head was still fresh, so the only odor was a slight coppery smell. He lifted it by the hair out of the bag and onto a plastic sheet on the table. He picked up the metal detector and waved it over both the remains of the box and the head; as he'd suspected, the metal was in the head itself.

He pried open the mouth—nothing obvious there. But when he upended it and used a penlight to peer down the stump of the neck, he spotted a slit in the upper palate.

He reached in and poked a finger into the slit. Where he should have felt the soft resilence of brain tissue, there was something hard and angular.

He withdrew his hand and considered.

Abruptly, the perfect solution came to him. A wide smile on his face, he picked up the head and took it into the kitchen.

"Well, fuck me with a wire hairbrush," Nikki said under her breath.

The inside of the quonset looked like one of those roadside zoos, the kind where you paid five bucks to see a cage full of sleeping snakes and an old, toothless alligator. A large tank—five hundred gallons, easy—against one wall contained dozens of octopi. Empty jars and lids littered the bottom. Nikki had always thought of the creatures as being gray or pinkish, but these specimens rippled with bands of color, from a deep blue to an orangey green. Many were attached to the glass by suckered tentacles, while others pulsed through the water, disembodied lungs trailing ropy guts.

A face stared out at her from behind a metal mesh. For one queasy second she thought it was a child, dressed in black and somehow disfigured; then her perception adjusted and she recognized it as a chimpanzee. It gazed at her silently with sad brown eyes, its wrinkled fingers hooked around the wires of its cage.

And of course, there was the elephant.

It was blithely stuffing hay into its mouth, and hardly spared her a glance. It wasn't in any sort of pen—only a thin cord attached to one of its hind legs tethered it to the wall, a cord that looked barely strong enough to restrain a large dog.

She had only a moment to take it all in—and then the two poodles in the large pen beside the chimp started barking.

The Gourmet flicked on the fluorescents. "Look what just arrived!" he said cheerfully, dangling the severed head by its stringy brown hair.

Jack blinked, tried to focus. "No, thanks," he managed. "I had Italian for lunch."

"Oh, you're not going to dine. You're going to be the *sous* chef—that means you help prepare the ingredients." He placed the head squarely on Jack's crotch, so the dead eyes seemed to be looking down the length of Jack's body disapprovingly.

The Gourmet rummaged in a drawer, brought out an old revolver. "Genuine six-shooter," he said, holding it up for Jack to see. "Old, but perfectly functional." With his other hand, he took a long, thin filleting knife from a rack.

He put the gun to Jack's head—then cut the ropes binding his wrists.

The Gourmet stepped back, returned the knife to its slot while keeping the gun trained on his prisoner. Not that Jack was in any shape to jump him—his arms were all but useless.

"Sit up," the Gourmet said.

"I can't," Jack replied. "You tenderized my arms, remember?"

His captor leaned forward, grabbed Jack by the hair and pulled him upright. Jack tried to support himself with his arms, but they wouldn't take his weight; when the Gourmet released him, he crashed back onto the table, crying out as pain lanced from his wrists to his shoulders.

The Gourmet tried again, yanking Jack toward him at the same time, so that his behind scooted forward and his legs bent at the knees. By leaning forward Jack was able to keep his balance, but the head rolled off his groin and landed between his spread thighs. It stared blankly up at him as if to say, "Hey—you're the one that chopped me up in the first place." Jack's arms flopped limply at his sides, screaming sacks of dead, useless muscle.

"Now," the Gourmet said, taking a step backward, "I think there's a prize hidden in this particular container. I'd like you to pull it out."

"All right," Jack said. He didn't see any reason to resist.

It took an agonizing effort to move his arms at all, but his hands still worked. He managed to fumble the head around so it wasn't looking at him anymore.

"Is this a twist-off, or do I need an opener?" he asked.

"Go in through the neck. There's a slit in the back of the throat—it's behind that."

Of course there is, Jack thought. *I put it in there myself. Too bad I didn't put a .38 in there while I was at it.*

He was about to reach inside—when suddenly, dogs started barking.

Nikki froze—then darted inside and pulled the door shut behind her.

She looked around wildly. If he came out of the trailer to check on the noise, she should have a place to hide—and then she noticed the door in the far wall, beyond what looked like exercise equipment. What if he came out of there?

There was a pile of bales in the far corner, next to the elephant. She ran without thinking, ducked down behind them. The elephant favored her with a bemused glance.

She heard the door in the back open.

The fuck am I thinking? I know he's the Gourmet. I should just stick my gun in his face and wrap him up for Jack.

Except this one wasn't going to faint the way Road Rage did, was he? No. Somehow, she didn't think that a guy who kept a bull elephant in a shed behind his house would be intimidated by a woman with a pistol. She might have to just shoot him—and she knew, with a cold certainty, that she could.

But what if it *wasn't* the Gourmet? What if he'd used a go-between, or it was some half-bright local he'd hired to feed his fucking menagerie?

She heard footsteps.

• • •

The Gourmet glanced sharply at the door, then back at Jack. "Of course," he said. "You're working with Road Rage, aren't you? That would be him, now."

Jack knew better, knew who it had to be. "You fucking moron," he said, forcing a laugh. "Think you've got everything under control? That's not Road Rage—*I'm* Road Rage. You've been torturing the *wrong guy*—Christ, you haven't even figured out that Djinn-X is a *woman.*"

That got his attention. Good—if he thought Nikki held the keys to the Stalking Ground, he'd think twice before killing her. Jack continued, "And she didn't come alone, either. See, we all talked it over, and we realized something—namely, that you're a fucking *loon.* And since we never got to have our little hunt, we thought it might be fun to do the real thing."

He fixed the Gourmet with his eyes, tried to project a savage glee. "You poor asshole—*the Patron's out there.*"

The Gourmet swallowed.

"Then I don't need *you* anymore, do I?" he asked.

He raised the revolver and shot Jack in the head.

Was that Jack's voice?

She barely had time to finish the thought before the sharp *crack!* of a gunshot made her jump. Before she knew what she was doing, she was sprinting around the elephant and for the back of the quonset. That's where the shot had come from—where Jack's voice had come from. Jack's voice, saying something about the Patron.

She stopped herself just short of the door. The dogs were barking crazily now, yelping at the top of their poodle lungs. The elephant raised his trunk and trumpeted. The chimp, completely unmoved, continued to stare at her with mournful eyes. It seemed resolved to whatever fate had in store.

She had to think. Think like Jack.

No. Think like the Gourmet. . . .

Fortunately, it wasn't *Jack's* head.

By the time the Gourmet finished his statement, Jack knew what he was going to do. Gambling that the Gourmet's habits would make him go for a body shot, he raised Road Rage's head to chest level.

Impact slammed the head against him, knocked him flat on his back on the table. The sudden movement of his arms was excruciating; he wanted to scream, but the breath had been knocked out of him.

He wondered how much of the damage the skull had absorbed.

He wondered how long he had to live.

The Gourmet didn't waste time putting a second bullet into his captive; he moved quickly and quietly from the kitchen to the workshop, frightened yet exhilarated. *The Patron? Here?*

Djinn-X may have been the Stalking Ground's creator, but the Patron was its undisputed champion. The Gourmet knew he'd have to eat him eventually, but . . .

He wasn't sure he was ready. This was the *Patron,* for Christ's sake. His elaborate scenarios, his attention to detail, his knack for eliciting horror—all inhumanly perfect. If he and Djinn-X had pooled their talents, his chances for survival were minimal.

Except—they were on *his* turf. *His* stalking ground.

Smiling, he opened the electrical panel on the wall of the workshop and flipped three of the switches— the ones marked in red.

Too late, Nikki remembered how much the Gourmet liked traps.

A loud *chonk!* from the front of the quonset caught her attention. A steel bar had swung down and locked into place, blocking the door she'd come through. The overheads shut off, and a bank of colored spotlights behind the octopus tank flared to life and began to flash. The room flickered blue, red, green.

And the sound began. A rhythmic, bass pulsing, so deep Nikki felt it in her bones. Speakers, mounted somewhere above her.

"Hello." The disembodied voice issued from the same speakers. "Are you aware that elephants can converse across many miles?"

Abruptly, the chimpanzee began to scream. It was a crazed, wild sound, both heartbreaking and terrifying at the same time. The chimp began to throw itself around its cage, slamming into the wire mesh with no apparent regard for its own safety.

"They use ultra-low frequency waves, undetectable to the human ear. The French have experimented with the same type of waves on human beings, and discovered they can produce a wide range of effects: disorientation, nausea, extreme anxiety."

Nikki's heart pounded. The bass pulse got quieter and deeper at the same time—it felt like she was hearing it with her whole body, not just her ears. Her stomach lurched in panic and her head ached.

"Pachyderms are much more sensitive to these waves, of course. I've done a few experiments of my own. At a certain level of intensity, they become quite agitated. I imagine it's like having the whole universe screaming in your brain. . . ."

The elephant bellowed, much louder than before. There was an audible *click* and Nikki saw the cuff around its leg fall off. It shambled toward her, madness in its eyes.

Nikki did the only thing she could think of. She shot the octopus tank.

The front exploded outward in a wave of water, tentacles and shattered glass. She was already sprinting— not away from the elephant, but toward it. She cut to the side, ducked as it swung the wrinkled gray club of its trunk at her, went into a shoulder-roll and came out of it in a desperate, full-length leap.

She landed sprawled on top of the pile of bales at the same moment the wave of water sloshed against them. Against them, and past—to the cuff lying on the floor, the one that had restrained the elephant.

The cuff attached to the wall with the thin, insulated cord.

For a second, she thought she had guessed wrong. The elephant had turned, a corrugated cable of muscle was reaching for her neck—and then there was a sharp crackle, followed an instant later by a deafening bellow of pain. The colored spots died, as did the speakers.

The sound of the elephant collapsing in the dark was like someone dropping a waterbed from a two-story window. She'd been right—the cuff had been electrical, had shorted in the water. The jolt had been enough to knock the pachyderm for a loop, but she could tell from its ragged breathing it was still alive. The chimp had stopped its screaming, the dogs their barking; she hoped she hadn't killed them, but at least they wouldn't be dinner for a sociopath. She could hear octopi flopping wetly on the floor.

She stepped down cautiously from the bales, hoping that the power wouldn't suddenly come back on. Cool water soaked through her shoes. She kept as far away from the wheeze of the elephant as she could, and began once again to make her way through the darkness toward the back of the quonset.

She was in the middle of the room when she heard the door open.

The Gourmet heard the shot, the surging splash, the elephant's roar and collapse and the dark silence that followed. He knew what must have happened: overloaded by fear, about to be trampled, the intruder had shot at the elephant and missed, hitting the tank. A single shot meant the elephant must have dispatched him immediately afterward. The water had then shorted out the electrical systems, incapacitating the animals and causing the collapse of the elephant.

Well. He'd have to work quickly to get the necessary organs into storage.

He quickly located a flashlight in the darkness, though he didn't turn it on. Opening the door, he ducked through quickly, staying low. He had the revolver in one hand and the flashlight in the other. He really didn't think there was anyone left alive in the room—if there had been more than one person, there would have been more than one shot—but he liked to be thorough.

He crouched in the dark, listening.

Nikki stayed perfectly still. She brought her gun up and trained it on where she thought the Gourmet would be. She waited.

Abruptly, the lights came on.

Nikki had enough time to see one thing—*that's not Jack*—and then she fired.

Bullets slammed into the Gourmet's body. He staggered back, dropping the revolver and the flashlight. The last rational thought he had was *why are the lights on?* and then he died.

Jack appeared in the doorway. He met Nikki's eyes.

"You killed him," Jack said. "Fuck."

And then he collapsed.

Jack came to on a couch. He looked around; he seemed to be in a mobile home. "Nikki?" he croaked.

She came in from the kitchen holding a glass of water. She tried to give it to him, but Jack couldn't seem to raise his arm. She held it to his lips and he drank.

"Jack," she said. "What the hell happened?"

"Got sloppy. Gourmet traced my remote access to the motel, staked it out. Followed me."

"Yeah? How'd he miss me?"

"Didn't. Assumed you were just a hooker I was going to do—thought I was Djinn-X."

"A real genius. Sure did a number on you, though."

Jack glanced down at the mottled green, purple and yellow of his arms; they looked like the skin of something from another planet. "Yeah. I'd have a bullet hole in my chest to go with them if the GPS unit hadn't caught the slug. Lucky he didn't stick around for a second shot."

"Well, I'd be elephant toe-jam right now if I hadn't shorted out Jumbo's electric leash." She described how she'd managed to incapacitate the elephant. "I guessed he had it wired up to give the beast a jolt if it tried to break free—otherwise, there was no way that cord could be strong enough."

"You guessed wrong."

"Sorry?"

"Baby elephants are restrained with a thick chain— they soon learn they can't break it. As they get older, the thick chain is replaced by a thinner one, and eventually by a rope. The elephant is conditioned to think it can't break free—so it doesn't. Only the lock was electric, so he could release it remotely."

"Huh. Well, what the fuck do I know about elephants? I've never even seen *Dumbo*, for Christ's sake. . . ."

Jack struggled to his feet, wincing in pain. "Come on. Let's get out of here."

"You expecting friends of his to show up?"

"No. I doubt if the Gourmet had any." Jack edged past Nikki, headed for the door.

"But—shouldn't we go through his stuff while we're here? Check for notes, trophies—"

"There's no point. We're done."

"Jesus, Jack, you sound like you're giving up."

"Giving up?" He turned back and faced her. "There's nothing *to* give up. We *lost*. Don't you get it? All we can do now is screw up evidence—there's nothing we can accomplish now that a forensics team can't do better. I'll send the Gourmet's files from the Stalking Ground to the police, and hope he was arrogant enough to be honest. If not, we'll never know. You understand? *We'll never know.*"

"What was I supposed to do, Jack? Let the asshole shoot me?"

"No. You were supposed to do your job."

"Yeah? Kinda hard to do when your partner disappears in the middle of the fucking night."

"I wouldn't have gone anywhere if you hadn't jumped down my throat—"

"You were fucking up! *Somebody* had to tell you, and it wasn't gonna be one of our targets, was it?"

"My targets," Jack said, "tell me everything I need."

It hurt like hell, but Jack forced himself to grab the knob and open the door. He walked out into the pitiless Nevada sunshine, and told himself he was lucky to be alive.

He almost believed it.

They erased as much of their presence as they could, though they didn't re-enter the menagerie. Nikki could hear the elephant moving around, and she didn't think he was happy. They broke down the back door instead, and retrieved the remains of the GPS unit. "So what about Road Rage's head?" Nikki asked. "Or what's left of it . . ."

"Leave it," Jack said. "We get rid of the packaging, the authorities will think he was just another victim."

"Once this hits the papers—with the fucking elephant and all—the Patron's gonna figure out what happened," Nikki said.

"Yeah. The Stalking Ground is just him and me, now. . . ."

They drove back to Reno in Nikki's rental. They didn't talk much. When they got to the motel room, Jack took four painkillers and slumped onto one of the beds, exhausted. He was asleep in seconds.

When he woke up, Nikki was gone.

Dear Jack:

I saved your life, you asshole.

Not that you haven't saved mine—but at least I say thanks when you stop some maniac from gutting me like a fish. I do the same for you, and I get the feeling you're disappointed.

I can't do this anymore, Jack.

I still believe in what we do. I do. Other people would say we're crazy and doomed and sooner or later, we're going to get caught. I don't give a shit. I know we made a difference, that we've saved lives and helped people in pain get on with living.

This is hard for me to say, Jack. I'm quitting because I've lost faith in you.

You're looking to fail. I've seen that look in the eyes of other people on the street, and they've just stopped believing in anything but death. They know it's coming and they wish it would get here just a little bit faster.

I don't want to die. For a long time I didn't know what I wanted—maybe I still don't—but I don't want that. I've tried talking to you, but you don't hear me. I don't think this will change your mind, either.

I'm sorry, Jack. I hope you can at least admit what you're doing to yourself, if not to me. Do what you have to, I'm not going to judge. I wish you luck.

Nikki

PART THREE:

Critical Response

There thou mayest wings display and altars raise,
And torture one poor word ten thousand ways.

—John Dryden, *The Maiden Queen*

CHAPTER ELEVEN

Charlie Holloway stood on the roof of his gallery and looked up. It was late afternoon in October, almost five o'clock or so, and the gray Vancouver sky was punctuated with thousands of dashes of black. Crows, flying southeast to rookeries in Burnaby, just like they did every day at this time. Charlie knew a flock of crows was called a murder, but what would you call this? A massacre? A holocaust?

He watched for another few minutes as the last stragglers swooped past, trying to beat the sinking sun, then climbed back down the fire escape and into the alley. His assistant, Falmi, leaned next to the open back door, smoking a clove cigarette. He looked even more Gothic than usual; his spiky black hair was stiffened with some arcane styling product, every inch of exposed skin was dead-white, his nose and eyebrows and lower lip all sported silver rings or studs. His pants were made of skin-tight black latex, his shirt a mesh of some bright orange industrial plastic. Silver barbells pierced his nipples, stretched the gaunt scarceness of his belly button. His boots were high-heeled, black, and laced to the knee. He sported a new tattoo on his right arm, a naked woman draped over a grinning, fanged skull.

"You know, you can see the crows from here," Falmi said in his high-pitched voice.

"Yes, but you can't see them filling the whole sky," Charlie said. "Expanse, vista, that's what I like."

"Expense, Visa, *that's* what you like," Falmi said. He dropped the clove cigarette to the ground and crushed it out delicately with one thick-soled boot.

Charlie chuckled. Falmi knew one of the reasons Charlie kept him around was the image he projected, and his sardonic attitude was part of that. "Everything ready?" Charlie asked as they went inside.

"Caterers are just finishing up," Falmi said. "We're good to go."

Charlie bustled around, checking on last-minute details. He expected a good turnout for this opening, lots of media, and he wanted to make sure everyone was fed and happy.

There was a rap at the front door. "We're not open yet," Charlie said, strolling up to the glass. The man outside looked unkempt, with bleary eyes and a week's worth of beard. Probably a transient, hoping to scarf some free appetizers and a glass of wine—

And then Charlie recognized him.

"Oh my God," Charlie said. "Jack?" He quickly unlocked the door and opened it.

"Hi, Charlie," Jack said. "Got a few minutes for an old client?"

"Of course, of course," Charlie said. "We're having an opening in an hour or so, but I'm free until then."

Jack stepped inside. Charlie thought he looked terrible, but didn't say so. He knew what Jack had been through. "Haven't heard from you in a while," Charlie said. "How have things been going?"

"Not so good, actually. I've been kind of . . . adrift."

Charlie nodded. "Ah. Why don't we sit down, have a glass of wine, catch up? Falmi has everthing under control."

Jack glanced over at Charlie's assistant, who returned his look with a smile that bordered on a sneer. "Sure," Jack said. "That sounds good."

Charlie led him into the gallery. A buffet table along one wall was laid out with finger foods: smoked oysters, paté, deep-fried East Indian *pakora*. Charlie grabbed a bottle of red wine and two glasses from the bar as they passed it and nodded at the bartender. "Open another one and let it breathe, Paulo," Charlie said. "This one's ours."

Charlie strode to the back of the gallery and sat at one tip of a crescent moon-shaped divan richly upholstered in dark green velvet. Jack sat at the other. A small table with an etched-steel star for a top stood between them; Charlie put the glasses down and poured.

"You've done some redecorating," Jack said.

"Business is good," Charlie replied. "The artist we're showing right now, he's local, but I think he'll do well."

Jack glanced around, nodded. Tried to smile, but it was like a swimmer fighting an undertow; it hovered at his mouth and then sank beneath the surface, too exhausted to reach his eyes.

"And you?" Charlie said gently. "What have you been up to?"

Jack stared at him. Opened his mouth, closed it again. Looked down at his hands in his lap. "I've been doing research."

Charlie smiled. That was an old joke between him and Jack—Jack always claimed that since every part of life informed art, an artist should be able to basically write off everything as a research expense. "Keeping receipts, I hope?"

"Uh . . . yeah." The question seemed to confound him, as if small talk was a separate language he no longer understood. He looked at Charlie blankly.

Charlie sipped his wine. "What did you want to talk to me about?"

"Nothing, really. I just—" He stopped.

"Just what, Jack?"

"I just wanted to . . . reconnect." Jack took a gulp of his own wine. "You know?" There was a note of pleading under the feigned casualness of the question.

"Sure, Jack. You know you're welcome here anytime. And I don't mean to pry, but—"

Jack held up a hand. "Please, Charlie. No questions, not yet. I've had enough questions for a while. . ."

It was an odd comment, but Charlie let it pass. He noticed Falmi trying to get his attention with an arched eyebrow and sheer force of will. "Just a second—I think my young protégé is feeling a little insecure." He put his wineglass down and got up. "I'll be right back."

"Sure," Jack said.

He sounded anything but.

• • •

Nikki wasn't sure why she went back to Vancouver. October on the Canadian West Coast was cold and rainy; she should have just stayed in Nevada, or gone to California.

Maybe that's why she picked Van. She wasn't in a sunshine kind of mood.

She found a decent place in Kitsilano, only a few blocks from the beach. It wasn't as big or new as her last place in the city, but she didn't have the same kind of budget, either. She didn't know if she was going to go back to hooking, and if she wasn't, she'd have to get used to a different lifestyle—to a whole different life.

That was fine with her. The last two and a half years with Jack had changed her; all the activities she once used to fill her spare time seemed like pointless distractions now. She bought a futon and some kitchen stuff, but didn't bother with a TV or stereo.

So what was she going to do?

She went for long runs on the beach and thought about it. She ran at first light when the beach was deserted, ran with the rain and the cold wind off the ocean lashing her face, ran until her lungs ached and her feet were raw. She tried not to think about anything at all while she ran, but sometimes she couldn't help it; Sally and Janet and all the other victims she'd known would rise into her thoughts one by one, like flotsam washing up on the shore. She'd think about all the girls she and Jack had saved, the ones they'd never get to meet, and wonder if it made any difference . . . or if those girls were doomed anyway, destined to die of suicide or an overdose. To float out to sea alone and unmourned with the tide.

She didn't have any answers. She kept running.

• • •

Charlie disappeared into a back room with Falmi. Jack sat and drank his wine, and when his glass was empty he poured himself another. His arms were still sore, but in the few weeks since he'd returned from Nevada the bruises had begun to fade.

He didn't know if coming to the opening was a good idea or not. He knew why he was here—he just wasn't sure if what he was trying to do was possible. His previous, mundane existence seemed like a dream to him now, something that had happened to another person in another reality. Wife, child, career; just shiny surfaces that had been scraped away to reveal the cold, black iron beneath. Trying to get that life back seemed as pointless as throwing rocks at a thunderstorm.

But parts of that life were still around, still alive; parts like Charlie. He was one of those rare people who really listened when you talked—Jack had always admired how grounded he seemed, how aware of the world around him. Jack supposed it was why he was such a good agent.

When Nikki had left him, Jack hadn't known what to do. He found himself at the airport with no clear destination in mind; he'd finally decided to go back to Portland, but only to pack up the computer equipment. Nikki's stuff was already gone.

And then he found himself returning to Vancouver.

He hadn't been back since his first interrogation, his first kill. He'd long ago sold the house, moved out of his studio; the only thing left for him there were memories.

That was why he'd come. He needed to find out if he was still human, and memories were the most human thing he had left.

He stood up after a bit and wandered around the gallery, looking at the pieces. The artist's name was Ranjit Thiarra, and he worked in a number of mediums; photo-collage, sculpture, oils. His work tended toward the ethereal, juxtaposed images of angels and eclipses against backdrops of highly polished metal or exotic wood. Pretty, but to Jack they seemed as shallow and safe as a child's wading pool.

He hadn't logged on to the Stalking Ground since the shootout in Nevada. He was sure there would be some taunt from the Patron, some insinuation that it had all been Jack's fault. He knew the Patron's claim that the Gourmet had been a second identity was false; for all his boasting, the Gourmet simply hadn't been smart enough to be the Patron.

Only the Patron was left in The Pack. He wouldn't be drawn into a trap—and without Nikki, Jack couldn't hunt at all. If he was ever going to walk away, now would be the time.

As long as there was somewhere to go.

He studied a deep blue glazed bowl, inlaid with photographs of tropical fish and lightning. Ran a finger lightly over the smooth, curving surface, tried to imagine what Thiarra had felt when he made it. Was it a reminder of a vacation in the tropics? Azure ocean, glittering schools of fish, a sudden squall cracking open the sky?

Charlie bustled up behind him. "Sorry, Jack—last minute details, you know how it is. I'm going to open up now, but you're welcome to stick around. I'd like to talk more."

"Thanks," Jack said. "I think I will."

People began to trickle in. Jack noticed that people

on their own tended to arrive first; he supposed it was because they had no other place to be. Then came the couples, and finally groups of three or more, clusters of friends who had probably met for drinks or dinner beforehand. The usual opening types were all there: the immaculately dressed older man with the silver hair, examining the art with great care; the stern-looking, square-bodied women wearing denim and leather; the bright-eyed boys and girls barely out of their teens, sporting outrageous hair and clothing.

It was all familiar. Jack remembered the last opening he'd had, Janine keeping everyone's wineglass filled, Jack circling the room nervously and trying to be charming. It had been just like this, this swirl of color and voices and music; soft jazz playing on a boombox in the corner while people laughed and talked and traded opinions, sipping wine and taking bites of sushi.

It was all so *normal*.

He got himself another glass of wine and made a circuit of the room. There were a few people he knew, none well; he smiled and nodded and kept moving.

He was studying a painting when he heard Falmi's voice beside him. "Do anything for you?"

He glanced over at the Goth. Falmi had been with Charlie for years, but he and Jack had never particularly gotten along. He suspected that was just part of Falmi's personality—he wore his cynicism like a designer suit, showing it off whenever possible.

"I'm fine, thanks," Jack said.

Falmi sighed. "I meant the *painting*. Does it *do* anything for you?"

Jack considered the canvas in question. It was a painting of a statue—except, when Jack looked closer, he saw that it was a photo of a painting of a statue, the statue being Rodin's The Thinker. "I'm not sure," he said.

"Well, it does for me," Falmi said. "But nothing a good laxative couldn't fix."

"It seems . . . detached," Jack said. "So many layers between the original and the viewer."

"Exactly," Falmi said grudgingly. "Layers of merchandising. A copy of a copy of a copy—even the statue itself is a fake." He pointed to the base of the statue, where Jack could make out the words Made in China in tiny letters. "It's just a cheap plaster knock-off, the kind you buy in a tacky tourist shop."

"Maybe that's the point—what we're supposed to think about."

"Right. Making the observer the fifth 'thinker' in the series. How clever." Falmi tapped the small label to the right of the display; sure enough, its title was, The Fifth Thinker. "Too bad it doesn't give us anything to think about, other than how clever the artist is."

"It's about disconnection," Jack said. "Cognitive dissonance. What happens when you overthink something, overanalyze it. It loses its meaning."

"Maybe that's why I dislike it so much," Falmi said. "Too cerebral."

"Yeah. The original had power, depth, intensity. You felt it," Jack said. "In your gut."

"Well, all this makes me feel is the urgent need for another drink. Excuse me." Falmi marched away.

Jack continued to stare at the photograph. He had the overwhelming desire to reach out and touch it, reach through it, past all the imitations and to the heart of the real thing.

To feel the passion he knew was there, under the cold, hard stone.

In the end, it was a combination of restlessness and curiosity that drove Nikki back to the street. She felt like she needed to prove something, even if she wasn't sure what that was.

Nothing much had changed. New faces, of course, but that was a constant. She checked out the scene carefully, quickly learned who claimed what territory, and went to work.

The first night she was a little nervous, which was strange; this was undoubtedly the safest sex she'd had in the last two years. For the most part, things went smoothly . . . except for the gentleman who seemed to be reaching for something beside his seat while she blew him. He suddenly found the business end of a .38 inches away from his nose—until she saw he was only groping for the recline lever.

And then, three days after she'd returned, she got a call on her cell from Richard.

"Remember me?" he asked. She didn't, at first; it had been two and half years ago, and he'd never registered that strongly on her radar to begin with. Just another creep—but he'd been the creep that somehow pushed her over the line.

"Yeah, I remember you," she said. "How'd you get this number?"

"I know all sorts of thing about you, Nikki. Welcome back."

"I'm still not interested, Richard. I don't work for pimps."

"Please, Nikki—I'm not a pimp. I own an escort agency, very high-class. Very exclusive clientele. Wouldn't you rather have a steady flow of generous, affluent businessmen than the trash you meet on the street?"

"I've worked for agencies before—didn't like it. I have this problem following the rules of people I don't respect."

"But Nikki—you don't even know me. And surely you'd rather take a cab to a five-star hotel than walk in the rain to some hourly fleabag off the Stroll?"

"I like the rain. Clears my head."

"Look, I'm not trying to talk you into a free mattress dance. I just want you and me to sit down and discuss this, face-to-face. A job interview, okay? I'll tell you about the setup, give you a few references. You can think it over."

She hesitated. Normally she avoided agencies, mostly because she liked her independence. But they did provide stability and a certain amount of safety . . . and maybe that's what she needed right now.

"All right, I'll listen to what you have to say," she said.

"Excellent! Why don't we meet at my favorite restaurant, say tomorrow around two? I'll give you the address. . . ."

"Well, Jack?" Charlie asked. "How are you doing?"

"Better," Jack said.

They were sitting on lawn chairs on the roof. The opening was done, the appetizers consumed, the wine and beer drunk. The artist had sold several pieces; everyone was happy. Falmi was downstairs, cleaning up.

"Better than when you got here, or better in general?" Charlie asked.

"Both. It's been a long time since I even set foot in a gallery," Jack said. He stared up at the overcast sky. "Feels good. Comfortable."

"Of course it does. You put a scientist in a lab, an actor on a stage, a singer behind a mike. That's where they belong."

"You missed 'jockey in a stable,'" Jack said. "You know, to fully round out that 'get back on the horse' metaphor you're leading up to."

"Okay, so subtlety isn't one of my strong points," Charlie said. "Feel like a cigar?"

"Why not?" Jack said. Tobacco wasn't really one of his vices, but he indulged now and then. Charlie pulled out two *cubanos* and handed one to Jack. The rich, earthy aroma tickled his nose even before it was lit.

Charlie reached into his jacket, took out a small cigar lighter, snapped it to life. The blue hiss of the flame drew Jack's eye, called up images he didn't want to recall. He forced himself to lean forward and let Charlie give him a light.

There. Sharp, fragrant smoke. Burning leaves, not burning flesh.

"So . . ." Charlie began. "You want to tell me what you've been up to these last few years, or is that still a big secret?"

Jack shrugged. "Nothing much, really. Did a little traveling in the Northwest. Got into martial arts for a while to clear my head. Spent a lot of time reading."

"Sounds restful. Make any new friends?"

Jack hesitated. "One."

"Female?"

"Yeah. But it wasn't what you think."

"Since when do you know what I think? What, my mind's in the gutter all the time? This female, I'm sure she's like a sister to you. No, a mother—a *grand*-mother. She's like sixty years old, kindly, wrinkled face, boobs that hang down to her knees—"

"Okay, okay. She's in her thirties. Attractive, unattached, straight. All right?"

Charlie exhaled slowly, squinted at Jack. "But?"

"Let's just say Nikki's a career woman."

"Ah. How'd you meet her?"

"We worked together." Too late, Jack realized he should have said something else.

"Oh? Doing what?"

Jack took a long, careful drag on his cigar, took the time to think. "She handled some investments for me, but they didn't work out. I haven't talked to her in a few weeks." He said it flatly, and Charlie took the hint.

"Well, as long as she isn't trying to sell your art," Charlie said. He leaned back and blew a series of small, whirling smoke rings.

"I'm not sure what my art is, anymore," Jack said.

"That's okay. Art changes. You know, for years I tried to come up with a definition of art, one that would fit every style, every medium, and here's what I came up with: art is subjective. That's it. You don't even need an artist; you just need someone to *perceive* something as art in order for it to *be* art."

"So the creator is incidental?"

"He can be. Look, let's say you go down to the ocean, there's a beautiful sunset, a particular play of light on the water. Did you create that? No. You take a picture of it, are you an artist? Yes. So what if you just look at it, you don't take a picture; you memorize that scene, but you're the only one who ever sees it. Was art created? I think so. The scene was there, someone experienced it, it affected them."

"You put it that way," Jack mused, *"everything* is art. All experience. All pain."

"All *perception,"* Charlie said. "Art isn't a thing—it's a *sense."*

Jack thought about the things he'd done in the last three years. About his own, gradual shift in perception, his way of looking at what he did. "So something you never thought of as art," Jack said slowly, "could *become* art. Without ever really changing."

"Sure. Main difference between an artist and an audience is that the artist perceives the art *first*, then tries to convey his perception to others. In my humble opinion."

"I always thought art was about communication," Jack said. He studied the glowing tip of his cigar. "Using specific methods for relaying specific messages. The last few years, my view of that has kind of turned upside down. Now . . . now it's about using specific methods to *get* specific messages."

"I'm not sure I follow you."

Jack shrugged. "I don't know if I can explain. My point is . . ."

He trailed off. What was his point, exactly? That he thought he was starting to enjoy torturing people—not because he was causing pain, but because it was a form of self-expression?

"My point," Jack continued, "is that I'm starting to think about art again."

Charlie glanced at him, couldn't keep the beam off his face. "That's terrific, Jack! Only—" He leaned forward, the smile vanishing. "Only, you feel bad about it. I can tell. And I know why."

"I doubt that," Jack said.

"It's guilt. I've seen it before. Something bad happens to an artist, his first impulse is to express that feeling through his art. Only, his art is how he makes his living—so, by extension, he's profiting from his own misery. He even blames himself, thinks he somehow caused this so that he could make money."

Charlie clasped his hands together, the cigar sticking up between his fingers like the chimney on a church. "It's a loop, Jack, and it's one you can't let yourself get caught in. Every artist in this situation needs to be told this, so I'm the one who's gonna tell you: *it wasn't your fault*. And just as importantly, expressing your grief and loss and rage through your art isn't wrong, it isn't disrespectful to the memory of Janine or Sam or your folks. They'd *want* you to do this, Jack; they'd want you to let go of all that poison in your heart. Let it out, let it go, move on. You feel bad about making money off it, donate the profits to charity. Hell, don't even show your efforts to another living soul. But *do the work*."

Jack sighed. "Do the work."

"Yeah. I know it's hard, but—what else are you gonna do? It's who you are, Jack. It's *what* you are. You know, some people, they go their whole lives without knowing what they're supposed to do; they get up, they go to work, they come home. You've got more than that. You've got a purpose, a passion. You try and bury that, it'll come out one way or another."

"Yeah," Jack said. "One way or another. . . ."

• • •

The restaurant Richard chose for their meeting was called DV8. It was a small, hip place, more bar than bistro, only a block off the Stroll. He was waiting for her at a table upstairs, wearing a green silk suit and drinking an oversize martini with four olives in it.

"Hello, Nikki," he said as she sat down. He was just as unattractive as she remembered, with a pushed-in looking face and tiny eyes that reminded her of one of those yappy little dogs. His hair was spiked up with gel, and she could smell his cologne before she ever got to the table.

"Richard," she said with a professional smile.

"Would you like a drink?"

"Scotch and water." He signaled the waiter and made a point of ordering their best single malt.

"How'd you know I was back in town?" Nikki asked.

"Oh, I have a lot of contacts," Richard said breezily. "One of them gave me your cell number. Don't ask who, though—confidentiality is something I take very seriously."

"Just not mine."

"Well, that would change if you came to work for me. I meant what I said about our clientele; they're very affluent, very private. Very careful. I like you, I think you'd be quite popular, but that doesn't mean I don't have to check you out first."

"You seem to know a lot already."

"Not as much as you might think. For instance— what have you been doing since you left town?"

"Same thing I did when I was here—just different cities."

"Ah. Which ones?"

"Let's see . . . Des Moines, Calgary, Seattle. Portland for a little while."

He'd taken out a pad of paper and was making notes. "Uh-huh. Work for anyone there?"

"No. Strictly independent."

"Any arrests?"

"No."

"Can you give me some dates? Just roughly."

She felt a spark of irritation, but fought it down; it was a fair question. She gave him an approximation of the times she'd spent in various cities for the last two years. Her drink arrived and she accepted it gratefully.

"You know why I like coming here?" he asked her abruptly.

"The abundance of olives?"

He laughed. "No. It's the art." He pointed at the nearest wall, where a huge painting hung. The canvas was black velvet, like the cheesy ones you could buy in Mexico, but rather than depicting a matador, sad clown or doe-eyed child, the subject was a soulful-looking Captain Kirk. "It's always changing, too. Lots of local artists display and sell their stuff here."

"Yeah, it's a real cultural nexus. Now, *I've* got a few questions for *you*."

"Ask me anything."

"Who's backing you? A Triad?"

"No, no—nothing like that. No Tongs, no Triads. I'm just a successful local businessman."

"Right. Who's working for you—anyone I might know?"

"Perhaps. I've prepared a list of a few of my girls; you can call them yourself and ask. I'm sure they'll have nothing but good things to say." He pulled a folded piece of paper out of his pocket and gave it to her. She opened it up, scanned it. The letterhead at the top read *Exquisite Ecstasy Escorts,* with a dozen or so first names and phone numbers underneath it. A few looked familiar, but you could throw a used condom anywhere on the Stroll and hit a hooker called Jennifer or Brandy.

She asked him about rates and rules—both seemed acceptable. He said he retained a lawyer in case of trouble, though they hadn't any yet. Everything was done on an out-call basis; the girls never came into the office itself. They used a credit card system, which would show up on their clients' bills as "shipping expenses." Cash tips belonged to the girls.

It seemed reasonable. Richard was well-spoken and polite. And yet . . .

She told him she'd consider it and get back to him. He smiled and shook her hand when she got up to leave.

So why did she feel something wasn't right?

Afterward, Jack walked home.

"Home" was a third-floor walk-up on Commercial Drive. The neighborhood was low-rent but funky, frequently doubling for New York in locally-shot films or TV shows. A light rain was falling, the kind of sporadic, almost-mist that longtime Vancouverites wouldn't even acknowledge with an umbrella.

He walked past pool halls, bodegas, closed shops advertising hemp-weave clothing and African art. The damp air carried invitations of many kinds: fresh-ground coffee beans from the late-night cafés, cheese and pepperoni from the pizza-slice joints, laughter and samba rhythms from a Latin restaurant. He realized, abruptly, that he'd chosen this part of town for more than just the affordability; he'd chosen it because it was *alive*, ripe with people and food and activity. With potential.

Not that it didn't have its dark side. A homeless man with a scraggly beard wandered past, a stained blanket wrapped around his shoulders. His eyes were vacant, his cracked lips moving silently as he communed with something only he could see. Jack wondered if Charlie would consider the man's perceptions art.

Neon painted wet blacktop. Electric trains, powered by railed lightning, rumbled their faint and polite thunder in the distance. His muscles felt loose and purposeless, his head pleasantly buzzed by the wine.

He wondered what Nikki was doing right now.

He could probably track her down, if he tried. He had a few phone numbers in various cities, names of people she knew. People she'd asked him to contact if anything ever happened to her. "You do it for strangers, you can do it for me," she'd told him. "Let people know how I died. *Why* I died. What we do is the only goddamn thing I ever accomplished that has any meaning, and I don't want it to end with me in some unmarked fucking grave."

Then she'd added, "You sell the movie rights, get Cameron Diaz to play me."

He walked past an Ethiopian restaurant, a South American bookstore, an Italian deli with giant jars of olives and loops of sausage in the window. Lots of different cultures on the Drive. A skatepunk with a stubbly head, studded leather jacket and baggy pants ratcheted past him on his board, lit cigarette in his mouth and a pit-bull loping beside him. Jack wondered if either of them hated baby boomers.

The stairwell of his apartment building smelled like the ghosts of smoked joints and fried onions, but Jack didn't mind; it was better than Pine-Sol and bleach. He could hear televisions and radios murmuring faintly behind closed doors as he climbed the stairs.

His own place was small, but it looked out over the Drive itself. He tossed his jacket on the worn couch, the only piece of furniture other than the foam pad he slept on in the bedroom, and stood by the window looking out for a minute.

Then he went to the stack of boxes along one wall, and started unpacking computer equipment.

When she got home, she started calling numbers on the list Richard had given her.

The first one was out of order. So was the second. The third had never heard of the name she asked for.

She tried the number for the agency itself, and got a funeral home. She crumpled up the list and threw it in the garbage.

Why? He hadn't tried for a free fuck, and he must have known she'd check the numbers. Obviously, he hadn't cared—which meant he'd already gotten what he wanted. But all she'd given him was a little history—places she'd been over the last two years.

Places that she'd been with Jack.

•   •   •

Once again, the Stalking Ground was online.

There were no new messages, of course. The Patron was the only member of The Pack left alive, and he couldn't contact the site unless it was connected. Now that it was, the site itself would automatically email the members and advise them of its new location.

Jack thought about sending the Patron a message. Just to see if there was a response—maybe he'd been wrong, maybe the Gourmet and the Patron had been one and the same.

While he was thinking about it, a message arrived.

Apparently, the Patron had been thinking about him, too.

PATRON: Hello, Closer. Congratulations on taking out the Gourmet.

CLOSER: What color is the sky?

PATRON: Ah. Very clever. Want to make sure you're not being taunted by an electronic ghost, hmm?

The sky is as blue as the depths of your soul. Satisfied? Or would you like me to talk about my mother?

CLOSER: It's just you and me now. No more distractions, no more posing. I caught the other members of The Pack. I killed them. And I'm going to do the same to you.

PATRON: I believe you may. But let's not get rid of the Stalking Ground just yet; it does provide us with a handy forum to explore our views, and there's still a lot we have to discuss.

CLOSER: If you think you can track me through the site, you're wrong. The Gourmet came close, but I learn from my mistakes.

PATRON: I don't. I simply don't make them.
CLOSER: Don't you? I know you, now. I know who
you target, I know what you're trying to accomplish,
I know you like to strike around holidays. All your
killings involve elaborate scenarios—and the more
details there are, the more that can go wrong.
    I only have one thing to do—catch you.
PATRON: Don't worry. You'll soon have plenty of
other things to think about. Pleasant dreams.
The Patron logged off.

Jack stared at the screen for a while. Then he went
to bed.

He was awakened the next morning by a knock on his
door.

He went from a muzzy, half-asleep state to wide, pan-
icked alertness. He scrambled up from his foam mattress,
dug into a half-opened box and came up with a pistol.
Staying in the bedroom, he called out, "Who's there?"

"Federal Express."

"Right," he muttered. Who even knew where he
was staying? "Who's it from?" he called out.

"Can you open the door, sir?" The voice sounded
young, male, bored. Of course.

"Tell me who the fucking package is from!" he
yelled.

"Okay, okay . . . it says, 'Charlie Holloway.'"

Suddenly feeling like an idiot, Jack stuck the gun
back in the box and padded to the front door in his box-
ers. Peering through the peephole, he saw a twenty-
something male in a Fed-Ex uniform, holding a box and
an electronic clipboard. Jack opened the door.

"Jack Salter? Sign here."

"Sure. Uh—sorry about that."

"No problem." The delivery guy gave him the box, took back his clipboard and left without another word.

Jack closed the door. "Charlie, I could kill you," he muttered, then grinned despite himself. He put the box down on the kitchen counter, then rummaged around until he found a knife. He slit open the box and opened it.

The first thing he saw was a plain sheet of white paper. He picked it up, unfolded it.

It read: *A little something from a Close Friend.* There was no signature.

He reached in, pulled out a smaller box. It was rectangular, wrapped in brightly-colored paper with little spaceships and a sprinkling of stars on it. It looked strangely familiar.

There was a tag on it, a tag with a little drawing of a reindeer on it. The tag read: To Sam, From Santa. It was in Jack's own handwriting.

The box started shaking. No, it wasn't the box, it was his hands. And those weren't stars at all; they were spatters. . . .

The last time he'd seen this box was under his own Christmas tree, three years ago.

The Patron knew Jack was the Closer.

The Patron was Charlie Holloway.

INTERLUDE

Dear Electra:

I feel terrible. And the reason I feel terrible is awfully complicated, so be patient and I'll explain.

Uncle Rick came over for supper. I could tell right away that something wasn't right—he gets this look in his eyes when he's upset, and it's there even if he's smiling and laughing and pretending everything's fine. So after we'd eaten and Mom and Dad were in the other room, I asked him point-blank what was wrong. I know it was nosy, but that's just the way I am. Here's a condensed version of the conversation that followed:

Me: So, what's wrong?

Uncle Rick: What? Wrong? Don't be silly. Ha, Ha. How's school?

Me: Fine. So—what's wrong?

Uncle Rick: Nothing, nothing, couldn't be happier. Ha ha ha. How's the dog?

Me: Fine. Sooooo . . . what's wrong?

Uncle Rick: Not a thing and besides you wouldn't care anyway. Ha.

Me: Uncle Rick. WHAT. IS. WRONG.

Uncle Rick: My girlfriend dumped me. Wah!

Okay, okay, he didn't cry. But Electra . . . he looked so hurt. Like Rufus when I tell him he's bad. Except Uncle Rick wasn't bad, his girlfriend was. I mean, how could she not see how great he is? She must be a complete moron, and I said so. I don't think it helped.

And I felt terrible for Uncle Rick, I really did. But . . . I was also kinda glad. And being glad about him being sad made me feel terrible all over again, in a different way.

I wish I could make him feel better. I wish Uncle Rick and I could be together.

But that's not ever going to happen, Electra. He's just my Uncle Rick, and anything else just wouldn't work. I'm not crazy (even though I talk to you like you were real); I know it would be wrong and weird and illegal. I'm sure it would creep him out if he ever found out how I feel—if the situation was the other way around, it would creep me out. "What's that, my young nephew Rick? You want to jump Aunt Fiona's bones? That's just grand. Shall I call the police now, or wait until afterward?"

Yup. Definitely creepy.

But I do love him. In a nonhormonal way, I mean. I want him to be happy.

When I told him that—the happy part, I mean—he just shrugged and said, "At least the experience will inform my art." I thought that was a strange way to put it: informing your art. Like you go through something horrible and painful, and then a statue walks up and hands you a questionnaire to fill out.

YOU DON'T NEED A STATUE, FIONA. YOU HAVE ME.

That's right, I do. Thank you, Electra.

And good night.

CHAPTER TWELVE

The voice on the other end of the line sounded confused but sincere. "I don't know what you're talking about, Jack," Charlie said. "I didn't send you any package."

Jack held the phone in one hand, the Christmas present in the other. He put the present down, picked up the Fed-Ex package and examined the shipping label. His address was printed in block letters, done with a felt-tip marker. Nothing like Charlie's handwriting—nothing like anyone's in particular.

"Sorry," Jack said. His head was pounding from the wine he'd drunk the night before. "I think someone's playing a joke on me. Never mind."

"So—what'd they send you? Dog poop? Gay porn?"

"If I told you," Jack said, "I'd be delivering the punchline."

"Well, then *don't* tell me, the joke'll be on them, right?"

"Right," Jack said. "I'll talk to you later." He hung up.

He sat down and stared at the brightly wrapped box. It seemed unreal, as if it had suddenly dropped in from another dimension. It had a horrific kind of gravity, drawing his eye to it no matter where in the room he was.

He forced himself to think.

He knows I'm the Closer. He knows who my agent is, where I'm living. Of course he does—he killed my family, he was in my house, he knows all kinds of things about me. He even alluded to me when I was posing as Deathkiss—I was the one with "the greatest potential." The one he still had high hopes for . . .

Or maybe the Patron was simply making an educated guess. Gambling that Jack and the Closer were one and the same, hoping that the package would make him do something crazy.

Like killing Charlie.

He thought for a long time about what to do next, and then he logged on to the Stalking Ground.

A message was waiting.

Patron: Dear Jack—by now you'll have received my little gift. Not much, really, but it's the thought that counts. I was hoping to keep it as a souvenir—you know how we collectors are—but I really think you should have it. If the wrapping looks familiar, it's because I believe in recycling; the original package contained a small plastic "action figure" of some sort, but you'll get a much bigger kick out of its current contents.

Oh, and now that we're on a first-name basis, please—call me Pat.

Jack looked up from the keyboard, over at the box. He swallowed. Somehow, he hadn't considered that there might be something else in the box. Something other than the brightly colored toy he'd bought for his son.

It didn't matter. It was just more mind games, more distraction. He didn't have time for that now. He had to focus.

He had to be the Closer.

CLOSER: I think you're slipping, Patron. Whatever package you're talking about didn't reach me, nor is my name Jack. You obviously have no idea who or where I am. That's good.

A reply came back almost immediately.

Patron: My apologies for any confusion. Identity is such a tricky thing over the net, isn't it? As is truth. Anyone can claim—or deny—anything. I suppose there's only one way to truly be sure.

I'll just have to kill Jack.

CLOSER: I doubt that. It doesn't fit your profile. You won't kill out of simple expediency.

PATRON: Ah, but necessity *is* the mother of invention—don't forget, all the members of The Pack had to kill a prostitute in the first place, even yours truly. She was a lovely little Asian thing, Vietnamese I believe—I was most grateful to Djinn-X for his discerning taste, even though the kill itself wasn't terribly exceptional. Still, one does what one has to. . . .

Not that it matters in this case—dear Jack is an artist, which places him squarely in my purview. Normally I wouldn't dream of ending the career of such a promising candidate, but Jack has been something of a disappointment, so far. Hasn't produced anything in ages. I'd almost forgotten about him. . . .

CLOSER: Perhaps you're going after him because you're afraid of going after me.
PATRON: Are you offering me a choice? Because I'll gladly switch targets.
CLOSER: You know I can't do that.
PATRON: And after I kill Jack, I'll know even more.

The first thing Jack did was close the curtains.

And then he sat and stared at the present. At the past. And tried to think about the future.

Would the Patron try to kill him? He obviously knew where Jack was staying, might even be watching him right now. Jack could simply leave town—but that would tell the Patron he'd been right.

Did it matter?

Anonymity was the factor that leveled the playing field. Being identified meant becoming a target. But what was identity, anyway: a name, an address, a social circle? Each one was a ring around a bull's eye, a boundary defining that person in the center. The more rings you could get rid of, the harder you were to pin down.

Right now, Jack Salter was little more than a convenient label. No family, no partner, no permanent residence, no job. Who cared if the Patron knew his name? There was nothing in his life he couldn't walk away from in the next hour without ever looking back.

Except, maybe, what was inside that present.

He picked it up at last and began to open it. He peeled the taped paper away from itself slowly, not out of caution but respect. He had an idea of what it must contain.

There were no wires, no explosives. There were two items, carefully wrapped in white tissue paper, dried and delicate but perfectly preserved. They looked like little bird's claws, the fingers curled into tiny, wizened fists. He could see where Sam had bitten his nails.

Jack broke down and began to cry, holding his son's hands in his.

It didn't take long to pack. Jack saved the computer equipment for last, and checked the Stalking Ground a last time. As he expected, a message was waiting—but it was addressed to Djinn-X.

And it wasn't from the Patron.

Dear Djinn-X:

I want to join your group. I undrstand you dont want any wannabes and are being careffl about the law. **I am not a cop.** I have killed three people so far, all bitches. I can proove this. I have done all your tests and ansered all your questions. I beleave the Pack is real and I want In. Let me know what you want me to do and I will do it.

Red Ed

PS please forgive the bad spelling I am not dum but I have trouble with words.

Jack frowned. A newcomer? He supposed it was possible; the test sites that Djinn-X had set up were probably still active, still attracting the same mix of freaks and law enforcement. Red Ed could be either. He could even be the Patron in another guise.

Or he could be for real.

He typed out a reply, telling Red Ed he would be in touch but was in the process of moving the Stalking Ground. He couldn't ignore another killer—he just couldn't. He wondered how old the "bitches" had been.

When he was done, he disconnected all the equipment and packed it up, then took one last look around the apartment. He hadn't been there long enough for it to feel like home, but it was the first place he'd lived in for any length of time that didn't have a blacked-out room in its basement. Jack took a deep breath through his nose, smelled just the faintest whiff of curry from one of his neighbors. A sad smile crossed his face.

The Closer started moving things down to his van.

Jack was very, very careful.

He checked the van for bugs. He took the freeway out of Vancouver and made sure he wasn't followed. He found a run-down little place in Surrey and rented it, made arrangements for utilities, and paid a visit to the local hardware store. It was slightly more difficult without Nikki to provide that extra buffer between himself and the rest of the world, but he managed. It wasn't all that hard to travel through the modern world like a phantom, not as long as people still took cash. Money that folded had a short memory.

And then he shut out his surroundings. Shut out sounds, smells, memories, anything but the screen in front of him. It was time to go back to work.

He looked through Djinn-X's files on recruiting, studied his notes on past applicants and reasons they didn't make the cut. The final initiation had only been

offered to a few, and Djinn-X had exhaustively analyzed those that hadn't passed, looking for hidden
clues that might have revealed their insincerity beforehand.

What it always came down to was evidence. The
test that Djinn-X had come up with was simple and
foolproof . . . and Jack couldn't use it. He would have
to devise something else.

DJINN-X: Tell me about your first kill.
RED ED: It was a hitchhiker. I picked her up on the hiway outside
of town on a friday night and I was already Pissed off. My boss
hates me and I hate her but I cant afford to quit. This woman was
blond like my boss and I was thinking about how much I hate all
those Bitches so after driving for a while I stopped and pretended
somthing was wrong with the car. I asked her to help when I
was looking under the hood and when she did I slammed the
hood shut on her head. She started Screaming and it sounded all
weerd and echoed under the hood. She couldnt get out and her
one arm was trapped but she was kicking like crazy. I couldn't let
go of the hood or she would have got away so I stabbed her with a
screwdriver I had with me. I stabbed her in the side over and over
and she took a long time to go. I put the body in my trunk and
had to piss on the side of the car to wash off the blood so I wouldnt
get pulld over.
DJINN-X: What did you do with the body?
RED ED: I buried it in a field. I cant say exacly where but I could
show you.
DJINN-X: That's not how we do things. It's too
dangerous to meet face-to-face. You'll have to
send me proof.
RED ED: Ok. What do you want?

DJINN-X: Pictures. And a hand from the corpse.
RED ED: I gess I can dig her up and do that. Ok. Just tell me
where to send them.
DJINN-X: I'll get back to you with a drop point.

Jack wasn't sure what he should do. Red Ed sounded
genuine . . . but that meant nothing. And anyone
could dig up a grave, take a few pictures, chop a hand
off a corpse. He needed to be sure.

When in doubt, turn to the experts. Jack went back
to the Stalking Ground.

He reviewed firsthand accounts of execution and
body disposal. He compiled a list of last words, read
descriptions of the death rattle. He looked at downloaded photos and video. He studied methods, details,
commonalities. He tried to put together, in his head, a
comprehensive overview of the act of murder . . . then
compared it to his own experience.

While he was still assimilating, the Patron contacted
him.

PATRON: Hello, Jack. A shame you bolted like
that—I wasn't really going to kill you, you know.
You're my greatest success.
CLOSER: Why is that?
PATRON: Because of all of the artists I've influenced,
you're the only one to follow in my footsteps. You and
I work in the same medium: pain.
CLOSER: To very different ends.
PATRON: I disagree. We both create suffering in
order to reveal truth. Your technique is simply less

refined than mine . . . you're too focused on specifics, on control. My methods allow for free will. I let my subjects express themselves however they want. You're a craftsman, but you could be so much more.

CLOSER: My goal is to end pain, not increase it.

PATRON: I'm sure you believe that. But that's simply not the way things work . . . everyone has a dark side, Jack. We keep it suppressed through a process of indoctrination, a set of civilized rules of behavior. Once you break those rules, that dark side begins to emerge—and the process always accelerates. A good profiler like yourself knows this; you've seen it time and time again. Do you think you're somehow immune to the process? That your own taste for torture hasn't been increasing? If you value honesty so much, be honest with yourself.

CLOSER: I will if you will.

PATRON: Certainly. What would you like to know? My name, address, a convenient time to stop by?

CLOSER: Tell me about Sam.

PATRON: Jack. You surprise me. All that coyness and denial, gone in an instant. Not that I ever had any doubts.

CLOSER: The question proves my identity, and therefore my honesty. Answer it.

PATRON: Are you sure you want to venture into that territory, Jack? After all, you said your goal is to end pain, not increase it.

CLOSER: You don't understand me or my goals. Nothing you can say about my son can hurt me or him any further.

PATRON: I know, I know—you simply want *closure*.

But Jack—if I give you that, it destroys that
wonderful creative tension that drives you. I'm
sorry, but I just can't do that. If you want answers,
you'll have to come and get them. . . .

However, you were honest with me, so I'm going
to be honest with you: I don't intend to kill you, Jack.

I have much bigger plans.

There were other problems.

Djinn-X had a built-in system for mail drops; he
could simply route them through the courier business
he worked for and pretend to deliver them to a ficti-
tious address. Jack would have to arrange an actual location—and even if he used the intercept method he'd
suggested to the Gourmet, there was still a chance he
could be set up.

He finally hit on something he thought might work.
It would take some scouting and was a little risky, but
he thought he could pull it off.

It would have been easier if Nikki were still around.

The restaurant was called Bon's Off Broadway, a small
but busy restaurant on Vancouver's east side. The waitress behind the cash register looked up as the front
door opened, and saw a delivery driver in a brown uniform, carrying a padded envelope under one arm.

"Delivery for—actually, it just says, 'owner,' " the
driver said.

"Just a second," the waitress, Julia, said. "Bon?"

Bon, a Chinese man with a broad, smiling face, hurried up. "Yes? What's going on?"

"Delivery," Julia said. She was a tall brunette, with spiky black hair and a mermaid tattoo on her arm. "Expecting something?"

"No, I'm not expecting anything," Bon said. "What is it?"

"Beats me," the driver said. "Sign here and you can find out."

Bon scrawled his signature while Julia examined the envelope. "Says it's from Idaho," she said.

"Idaho? I don't know anyone in Idaho," Bon said. The driver was already gone.

Bon shrugged, then looked at the shipping label. "Well, it's the right address," he said. "From someplace called 'FX Labs.' Let's see what it is."

He ripped open the envelope. There were two things inside: a videotape, and a sealed plastic Baggie. Clearly visible within was a human hand.

"Gross!" Julia said, laughing. "You got a new special on the menu?"

"I know what this is," Bon said, shaking his head and grinning. "It's those guys from that movie. They said they were going to make me famous!" Vancouver hosted so many film productions it was known as Hollywood North; people in the industry often found themselves sitting in one of Bon's booths or on one of his many mismatched chairs. Movie posters and memorabilia covered the walls.

"Is there a note?" Julia asked.

"No." Bon frowned, then slipped the Baggie underneath the counter so customers wouldn't see it. "Just a joke, I'm sure. . . ."

They went back to work. About an hour and a half later, a man in a suit entered through the back door that led to the parking lot. He walked up to Bon and said, "Uh, excuse me? Can I ask you a question?"

"Sure, what can I do for you?" Bon beamed at him; he treated all his customers like they were regulars.

"I was just wondering if a package might have been delivered here by mistake."

Bon squinted at him, grinned. "Depends. What was in it?"

"Well—a fake hand. And some pictures."

Bon laughed, clapped the man on the back. "Aha! So you're the one! We were wondering what the heck that was all about!"

The man smiled sheepishly. He was in his thirties, clean-shaven, tie loosened around his collar. "Yeah, sorry about that. It's from a special-effects place in the States, they're doing a little work for us. TV pilot."

"Sure, sure. No problem. I'll go get it." Bon led the man to the counter, pulled out the bag and video. "No pictures, though—just this tape."

"Oh, right, that makes sense. They were going to send me some stills, but I guess they went ahead with the footage instead. Thanks."

"No problem!"

The man left the way he'd arrived, through the back.

Jack had arrived early, checked for possible surveillance. There didn't seem to be any. He parked across the street, watched the delivery happen through the glass front door, and studied the customers coming and going for ninety minutes. If the place was being watched by the police, he couldn't tell.

Finally, he'd gone in and gotten the package. Nobody swooped in to arrest him. He hadn't expected a videotape; the first thing he'd done when he got back in the van was crack it open with a pair of pliers. There was no tracking device he could see, nor was anything hidden in the flesh of the hand. He drove back to Surrey, stopping along the way to pick up a secondhand VCR and TV at a pawnshop.

Once home, he hooked up the TV equipment and repaired the casing of the video with some duct tape. When he was satisfied that it would run, he slipped it in and hit Play.

Black screen. Words in red appeared: *Ad mala patrat haec sunt atra theatra parata.* Apparently Red Ed was trying to make up for his lack of eloquence online by impressing Djinn-X with his knowledge of Latin.

A shot of a young woman, naked, tied with her hands over her head in what looked like a barn. Light was provided by a single bare bulb hanging from an extension cord. Another figure entered the frame, dressed in white painter's overalls, rubber boots, workman's gloves and a green rubber mask. The mask featured a wide-open mouth crammed with white fangs and a foot-long tongue that hung down to mid-chest like an obscene pink tie. The eyes were insectile, bulging orbs made of some holographic material that rippled with rainbow color.

The masked man advanced on the woman. He had a hedge trimmer in his gloved hands.

The tape ran just over an hour. There was no sound. The camera, obviously on a tripod, never moved. There was only one, continuous shot, though sometimes the masked man moved behind the camera to change the focus. The footage was graphic and bloody and didn't stop with the woman's death.

When he was done, the masked man held up a sign, obviously prepared beforehand: HOPE I PASSED THE AUDITION. The tape ended.

Jack rewound it and watched it again.

CHAPTER THIRTEEN

He'd killed her.

Jack watched the tape over and over, compulsively. There was no denying it. It was there, it was real, it had happened. He watched the masked man reach into the woman's belly and pull out handfuls of her guts while she screamed and writhed. It might be possible to fake something like that, but it would have taken an expert, a large budget and weeks of prep time. No, there was no doubt in his mind.

He'd killed her.

If the masked man had raped her, he'd done it off camera. His intention here was simply to cause massive bodily harm, and to prolong it as long as he could. He showed little restraint.

He'd killed her.

Jack studied her face. She was gagged throughout, but her eyes were painfully expressive. She didn't look like a prostitute to him; more like a college student.

He'd killed her.

Red Ed had been trying to impress him. If he'd

phrased things differently, been more specific in his instructions, maybe the woman would still be alive. But she wasn't.

Jack was responsible.

He'd killed her.

The next message Jack got wasn't from Red Ed, or the Patron. It was from Nikki.

Dear Jack:

I hope this gets to you. I don't know if you even check this account anymore, but we said we'd use it if we ever got separated and needed to find each other.

Something weird just happened to me, and I think it might be connected to you. Maybe I'm being paranoid, but I figure I should let you know.

He read about Richard, and his interest in which cities Nikki had been in and when. The description she gave wasn't anyone Jack recognized.

Anyway, I'm taking some time off. I have a little money saved up—I hope you're doing all right for cash. If you need some, please let me know.

I'm still pissed at you, Jack, but not because of the job. I'm still 100% behind you on that. I just think that sometimes you get so focused, you can't see the whole picture. You have these blind spots, and it makes me crazy that you won't listen to me when I try to point them out. I'm not trying to get in your way, I'm just trying to help. You taught me that the best way to go into a dangerous situation is to be as prepared as you can, to do lots of research beforehand. How can you make good decisions when you don't have all the information?

I don't want you to self-destruct. The letter I left you was kind of harsh, but it was honest. And just in case kicking your ass doesn't work, I thought I'd try something else.

I know you remember Luis, our first job. But do you remember Stacy Lombardo?

Well, I got in touch with her mother. Here's a message from her to you.

Dear J.:

Your friend would only give me one letter when I asked for your name, which only makes sense. I want to tell you, though, that I will never, ever, tell anyone (especially the police) even that detail. Your friend showed tremendous courage in taking the risk of contacting me, even on the internet. By the details she shared, I know she and you are genuine and not hoaxes.

I just wanted to say: THANK YOU. Knowing how and why my daughter died, as horrible as it was, means more than I can say. You asked all the questions that I never got to, and you made sure you got honest answers. I am not a vengeful person, but I believe Luis Chavez got what he deserved.

Your friend says that lately you seem to be having problems. I am truly sorry to hear that. I'm sure the price you pay for what you do is high. I can't say that I understand what you are going through, because what you do is something few people could. Your friend says that you do not enjoy inflicting pain and only do so because you have to. I believe that, because only someone of honor would put themselves in the position you have. You risk your life, your freedom and maybe even your soul, and nobody even knows who you are.

I just wanted you to know you make a difference. My

*daughter and my family are at peace, now. You gave us that,
and we are eternally grateful. You are a good man. Please, be
careful and take care of yourself. What you do is important.*
> *God Bless You,*
> *Emily Lombardo*

Jack looked up, his eyes stinging. "You're welcome,"
he said softly.

DJINN-X: Congratulations—you're in. The video in
particular was very convincing.
RED ED: Thanks. I know you said to send pictures but I thought
the video would be better. She was a hore I picked up in the city.
In case you can't tell, the hand isnt from her its from the one I told
you about.
DJINN-X: I noticed that. Can I ask why?
RED ED: The body kind of fell apart when I dug it up and I
didnt think it looked very real. Plus this way I have prooved
two kills not one.
DJINN-X: I hate to break it to you, but you haven't
proved as much as you think. The hand could have
come from any grave. The video was convincing, but
how do I know when it was done? Maybe you killed
someone ten years ago and haven't done anything
since.
     I hope I'm not coming across too harshly. You
have to understand how careful we have to be,
for your protection as well as ours. If I truly didn't
think you are what you claim, I wouldn't be talking
to you.
RED ED: Thats okay. I should have thought of that and used a

newspaper with the date or somthing. I could do another one.
DJINN-X: All right, but this time let me have some
input. Let's do this right, so I can introduce you
properly to the rest of the Pack.
RED ED: Okay.

Three days later, Jack found himself in a motel room
in Idaho.

Red Ed operated out of Coeur d'Alene, but he liked
to make his kills in more remote areas; there were
plenty just outside the city, where mountains and
dense forest dominated.

Jack had decided to go with a modified version of
Djinn-X's initiation. He told Red Ed that he'd lifted
the prints of a local hooker, and that he expected her
hand to be delivered the same way the last had been.

From his motel room, Jack dialed numbers at random with a tape recorder in his hand. When he got an
appropriate answering machine (Hi! This is Naomi—
call me back, I'd love to hear from you!) he recorded it.
He set up a cell phone account in Coeur d'Alene under
the name Main Street Escorts, and sent the number to
Red Ed along with a made-up description of Naomi.

Then he sat back and waited.

"Hello, Main Street Escorts."

"Hi. Uh, I'm interested in one of your girls."

"Sure. What are you looking for?"

"Uh, I had this one girl recommended to me? By a
friend?"

"What's her name?"

"Naomi."

"Okay, yeah, Naomi's working tonight. Are you in a hotel or a private home?"

"A hotel. The Broadmoor Arms."

"Room number?"

"417. Uh, when do you think she'll get here?"

"Probably about half an hour, unless she's with a client. I can give you her cell number if you want, or I can call her myself."

"You can give me the number."

"Okay. If she doesn't answer, just leave a message with the hotel name and room number. She won't be longer than an hour."

Jack gave him the number and then hung up.

Red Ed sounded younger than he'd expected.

It went smoothly, so smoothly he should have known something was wrong from the start.

The Broadmoor Arms was an old hotel, a four-story brownstone built in the twenties. It had lost any tourist appeal it had long ago, and now functioned chiefly as a way station for people on a downward spiral toward no home at all. The desk clerk was a young black man with a face so pitted with acne he looked like he'd lost an argument with a hornet's nest. He asked if Jack wanted the room by the hour, the day, or the week, and put him on the fourth floor as he requested.

There was no porter, so Jack had to haul his luggage upstairs by himself. He only had one suitcase, but it was almost the size of a small trunk. Jack made sure that when he carried it, he didn't give away how light it was.

Jack was in 402. He put his case in his room, examined the door. It had a cheap chain lock and no peephole. He nodded, left his door open, and walked down the hall to 417. He drew his gun. With his other hand, he tapped on the door with his fingernails, just hard enough to be heard.

"Hello?" The voice on the other side sounded hesitant.

"Police. Open up," Jack snapped.

The door was open no more than a quarter-inch when Jack slammed into it with his shoulder. The chain broke and the person inside was knocked backward; Jack stepped in and closed the door behind him.

The boy sprawled on the floor looked no more than seventeen. His body was chunky, his face square. He had glasses with thick black frames and long, greasy-looking dark hair. He wore jeans, sneakers, and a black T-shirt with a Metallica logo on the front. He looked terrified.

"Don't, don't shoot," he gasped. "I give up, okay? I surrender."

"Lie on your stomach with your hands behind you," Jack said. He pulled a pair of handcuffs out.

"Hello, Red Ed."

"Wha-whass happenin'?" The voice was thick and slurred.

"You're my prisoner. I gave you a drug to make you easier to transport."

"I can't. Move."

"That's because you're restrained," Jack said patiently. "Listen carefully. What do you hear?"

"Hissing. I hear hissing."

"That's the Coleman lantern. Anything else?"

". . . no."

"That's right. No cars, no people. That's because we're in a U-Haul trailer in the middle of nowhere. A trailer I outfitted just for you."

"Who . . . who are you?"

"I'm the Closer, Ed. Or maybe I should call you Mark? Mark Reilly Anderson, of 109 West Florence Street, Coeur d'Alene, according to your driver's license."

"I'm a fake," Mark whispered. "I'm a fake, oh God, I didn't kill anyone."

"I don't believe you, Mark. I think you're young and stupid and inexperienced, but I don't think you're innocent. That videotape was very convincing."

"The Closer. The Closer. Oh fuck, oh fuck." Mark started crying. "Please, please, that wasn't me, I stole the hand from a funeral home, I didn't make that tape—"

"Then who did?"

"Furious George. I met him online, we both hang out at the same site, massmurder.org—"

"Right. You didn't kill anyone. A complete stranger did, someone you've never met. And they decided to send a tape to you."

"It's true, it's true, I wouldn't have even *known* about The Pack if George hadn't told me—"

"That's a clumsy lie, Mark. See, everything The Pack knows, I know. And I've never heard of Furious George. But I *have* heard of Red Ed . . . and I think Red Ed's heard of me. Haven't you?"

"I know who you are," Mark sobbed. "I know what you do. Everybody on the site does."

"Good. Then you know we have a very long night ahead of us. . . ."

After the first hour, Jack realized how much he needed Nikki.

"This is how it works," Jack said. "You may think I've done horrible things to you, but I've barely even started. We're at the point now where you're going to be tempted to lie to me, to tell me what you think I want to hear, just to get me to stop. That's a very bad idea. It wastes my time and makes my job harder. So. Do you see this?"

"Oh God. Oh fucking Jesus—"

"If you lie to me, I'm going to use this on your genitals. So no matter how bad you want to tell me something that isn't true, remember—I'm going to find out, sooner or later. And this—"

"Aaah!"

"—will be waiting."

The problem was, without Nikki he couldn't do verification. Fear, no matter how intense, would only work to a point—pain would eventually trump Mark's responses, make him say anything for even a temporary respite.

It didn't matter, though. That would only be a problem if Mark were innocent. . . .

"NNNNNNGGH! ALL RIGHT! I DID IT, I FUCKING DID IT!"

"Who was it?"

"A girl, I don't know her name, she wasn't a hitchhiker like I said, she, she, was just this girl I met in a bar—"

"Where?"

"Am—Amsterdam. I went there with some friends last year and we did lots of drugs and there, there was this girl, we went into this alley to do some crank and I—I wanted to kiss her but she just laughed at me so I stabbed her. I lifted her right up off the ground and her shoes fell off when she went limp—"

"Mark. I'm not stupid. You think I don't watch movies? What is that from, *Friday the Thirteenth?*"

"*Halloween II,*" Mark whispered.

"Right. And Amsterdam is kind of hard to check, right? Except I don't think you've ever been off the continent, Mark. I doubt if you've ever been outside the good ol' U.S. of A."

"Please. Please don't use that thing on me—"

"This isn't a movie, Mark. It's not a videogame or a Stephen King paperback or a TV show. *This is real.*"

"GAAAAHH!"

"You fuck. You miserable *fuck.* I don't have *time* for this. *Stop lying to me!*"

"I won't. I won't," Mark whimpered.

"Ah, *shit.*" Jack dropped the pliers on the table with a clatter. He leaned against the cool metal of the wall, feeling sweat trickle down between his shoulder blades. "Do you even know what real life *is?*" he demanded. "It's not body counts and hacksaws and bleach. It's not about immersing yourself in blood and horror, about being *proud* because you came up with a new way to make someone scream. That's death, it's *just death.*"

"It's still better than my life. . . ." Mark whispered.

Jack shook his head. "No. *I don't accept that.*" He

picked up the pliers again, then threw them convulsively against the wall. He slammed open the back door of the U-Haul and stalked out.

He was parked in a little clearing just off an old logging road. A crescent moon gave off enough light to show the bulk of mountains rising all around, but the forest itself was a dark, rustling mystery.

He went for a walk.

He didn't have a flashlight, so he stuck to the road. It was possible, though highly unlikely, that a vehicle might discover Mark in the U-Haul, but right now he didn't care. He was so tired of being in control . . . he wanted to just let go. He wanted to chop Mark into a hundred pieces while both of them screamed.

"Why don't you?" a voice whispered in his ear. It was so sudden and so real that he stopped dead, his heart hammering.

"You know you can. No one can stop you. And it would feel so *good*, wouldn't it?" The voice sounded weirdly distorted—just like the audio file Jack had downloaded.

It was the voice of the Patron.

"No, no, *no*," Jack said. "No fucking voices in my head. I'm still in control, I *am*."

"Remember your methodology, Jack. Aura phase. The first symptom a serial killer develops when his subconscious is amping up for a kill. Characterized by heightened sensory input and vivid hallucinations . . ."

The smell of the woods seemed suddenly overpowering, moss and wet pine and decaying logs. Hypnagogic patterns danced in the darkness around him, his brain painting random psychedelia on the night. Jack closed his eyes, but that only made it worse; the patterns were inside his eyelids, crimson swirls and slashes and grids that bulged and shrank with the rhythm of his own pulse.

"You're not real," Jack gasped.

"Sure I am, Jack. I'm as real as Son of Sam's dog." The voice laughed, a horrible electronic barking. "And I'm here for the same reason—not just to tell you it's okay to kill, but *why*."

"What?"

"At what point would you say a group becomes a subculture?" the voice asked.

"I don't know. I don't care."

"I think you do . . . there are things all subcultures share, Jack. First and most obviously, a common bond. Model railroaders, *Star Trek* fans, gun collectors, whatever . . . but that's not enough. Lots of people like to eat French fries, but that doesn't mean they have a newsletter, does it? Open your eyes."

Jack did. A figure stood on the road in front of him, barely visible in the dark.

"Which brings me to the second factor, communication," the voice said. The figure took a step toward him. Jack still couldn't make out its face. "Members of a subculture always organize around shared information. This leads to their own language—a specialized lexicon will always evolve within a subculture that deals specifically with their area of interest."

The figure took another step, and now Jack recognized him: Djinn-X. Dressed in the same bloodstained clothes Jack had executed him in.

"Yeah," Djinn-X said. "Pick out a sheep, *do* her, use a Bundymobile as a BDU. Keep the nipples for a little trophy buzz later."

"Fuck off," Jack said. His voice was hardly more than a croak.

"Uh-huh," the Patron's voice continued. The figure faded back into an indistinct blur. "Next is congregation. The members of the subculture gather to celebrate their subculture in specific, ritualized ways. These gatherings are often geared toward increasing the size of the group, as well as letting members hook up with each other in various ways."

The figure stepped forward again. This time it was Road Rage. "A membership drive? Excellent idea. I'm more than willing to help organize. Perhaps we could combine it with some sort of fund-raising effort. . . ."

"That's—that's not a good idea—"

Road Rage stepped back into the darkness. "Organization, communication, congregation," the Patron said. "The subculture has evolved a brain, a tongue, and a means of reproduction. But it's not complete until it has a *soul*—something that not only manifests its values but transcends them."

The figure stepped forward again—but this time, it wasn't someone Jack had killed.

It was Jack himself.

"It's not a culture," he said, "until it has its own art. . . ."

Two hours later, Jack returned.

He closed the door of the U-Haul behind him, and sat down opposite Mark. The boy's face was covered in mosquito bites, and four or five were still feeding.

Jack stared at the boy for a long time before speaking.

"You know what you are?" Jack said at last. "You're

a product of your culture. To you, violence and entertainment are the same thing. Right?"

"Yeah, right. You're right." He sounded desperately eager to agree.

"That's the easy answer. In my experience, easy answers are usually bullshit." Jack leaned forward intently. "Millions of other people are exposed to exactly the same thing you are, and they don't bring handcuffs and a butcher knife to a rendezvous with an escort."

"I—I wasn't really going to do it."

Jack picked up a bottle of water from the table and took a long drink. "Maybe not. The important thing is, you had the choice—so let's forget all that bullshit about you being some kind of robot programmed by horror novels and slasher flicks. Just because you belong to a subculture doesn't make you its slave."

Jack put down the bottle, picked up a box cutter. Studied its edge. "What it does mean," Jack said softly, "is that when you join a subculture, you agree to an unspoken contract. A contract to abide by the rules of that subculture—to not only enjoy its fruits, but endure its penalties. And sometimes, a subculture will demand a sacrifice from one of its members. . . ."

Mark swallowed.

At the end of eight hours he was sure of two things: first, that Mark simply wasn't strong enough to lie to him.

And second, Mark hadn't killed anyone.

He was a wannabe, a kid who surfed the net for Nazi porn and true-gore sites. He had an unhealthy obsession with serial killers, and might very well grow up to be one . . . but if he actually planned to use the knife Jack found in his suitcase, it would have been his first time.

And Jack had tortured him.

The tape was still real, Jack was sure. But Mark hadn't made it—"Furious George" had. A real serial killer who was apparently smart enough to send in a decoy first. If Mark had been accepted into The Pack, Furious George would have been the next to apply . . . and now Jack had to start all over again.

Except . . . he didn't know what to do about Mark.

If Jack let him go, he might go to the police. He'd seen Jack's face, he knew about the Stalking Ground, and he could warn Furious George.

Jack couldn't afford any of that.

"Mark."

"What? What? I've told you everything I know—"

"Not quite. Tell me *why*. Tell me how you could become so obsessed with something like this."

Mark laughed weakly. "I don't know. It's just—it's not like anything else, you know? It's *real*. It's like, everybody *wants* to do this stuff, but nobody ever does."

"Except for The Pack. They were the real thing . . . and you wanted to be a part of that."

"Not anymore. Not anymore—"

"Remember what I said about subcultures? That's what The Pack was turning into—a serial killer culture. The internet is the perfect spawning place; it's like a conceptual rain forest. They had their common bond, their own words—trophy buzz, sheep, BDUs—

and a place to come together and share information. They even had art—photos, videos, sound-files."

"Had?"

"Yeah. Had. What they have now . . . is me. See, one of the things that tend to evolve in rainforests is specialized predators, ones with highly developed camouflage abilities. Did you know there's a white praying mantis that looks just like an orchid?"

"No. No, I didn't."

"Talking to you has made me realize how important the Stalking Ground is. I was going to just destroy it . . . but if I did, another one would inevitably evolve. One that would attract people just like you."

"But—but I haven't *killed anybody*—"

"I know," Jack said. "But if you had joined The Pack, you would have. And with their help, you would have killed many, many more. That's why I have to keep the Stalking Ground open. That's why I can't stop. I have to stay in control."

"I—I get that."

"Do you? I want to be very clear on one thing, Mark. I don't do this as an excuse to kill people. I do it to *prevent* killing, and to bring some peace to the families of murder victims."

"So you—you don't want to kill me?"

"No. I don't. Killing is the ultimate control, the ultimate power . . . but the thing about power is, sometimes it can get out of hand. You have to be careful." Jack stood up.

"I know. I know. You're right."

"Real power isn't controlling other people's lives, Mark. It's controlling your own. You have to be very clear on the consequences of your actions." Jack walked behind the boy. He put one hand on his shoulder.

"I will be, I swear I will be—"

"We all have choices. Choices we'll have to live with. And sometimes . . . sometimes those choices are very hard to make."

"I can do it, I can do the right thing—"

"I'm not talking about your choices, Mark. I'm talking about my own."

Jack reached around, and cut his throat.

He could have turned into the real thing.

"Sure," Jack whispered. "Or he could have outgrown it. Found another outlet instead of murder."

Like you did?

"I never wanted to be a killer. Just an artist."

You seem to have combined the two rather nicely, though, haven't you? Just look at the pattern that blood spatter formed. You can't take your eyes off it. Looks sort of like a lion. Or it could, with a little work . . .

"I had to do it. I had to."

So you can't make choices anymore? If that's true, you're just a machine. A killing machine.

"No. I'm still a man. I am."

Right. So what was all that crap about subcultures and art? You know what that sounded like? Like one of those bullshit "mission statements" artists put beside pieces to justify them. And that's just what you were doing, weren't you? Justifying yourself? Sure, you added all that rationalization at the end about how you couldn't afford to have the kid tip anyone off . . . but that's not what you were really thinking. You were thinking the kid should be grateful *you were the one that killed him—that it was like a musician getting to jam with the Rolling Stones, or a sports fan getting to pitch to Babe Ruth. Lucky, lucky him* . . .

"It doesn't matter," Jack said wearily. "What happens to *me* doesn't matter. . . ."

Because it's already too late.

Quietly, methodically, he started cleaning up the mess.

Like he'd done so many times before.

When it was done and the body had been dumped, when an anonymous call had been made to the police and Jack had returned to his motel room, he checked the Stalking Ground for messages. He wasn't surprised to see there was one from the Patron.

PATRON: "Dark theaters are suitable for dark deeds."

"No," Jack muttered. "No, it couldn't be."

PATRON: That's the translation of the quote at the beginning of the film, Jack. Considering your penchant for black plastic and pain, I thought you'd appreciate it.
CLOSER: I shouldn't be surprised, should I.
PATRON: Not really. Though I imagine Red Ed certainly was. . . . How young was he, Jack? From the conversations we had I would guess under twenty. Certainly the youngest person you've ever killed, hmm?
CLOSER: I asked him a number of things, but his birthday didn't come up. A lot of other interesting details did, though.

PATRON: If you're trying to rattle me, you're taking the wrong approach. Ed can't tell what he doesn't know . . . and he knows very little about "Furious George."

CLOSER: But I do. I know you killed the woman in that video.

PATRON: Of course I did. Because Red Ed has never killed anyone. And I suspect that after *you're* through with him, Jack, he never will. Technically, that makes him the first innocent you've done—how's that make you feel?

CLOSER: Smarter than you. "Red Ed" is in his forties. He's killed six women in Idaho over the last four years. . . . And you know what else? He can spell just fine. As a matter of fact, he's something of a computer whiz. He can do things even I didn't know were possible.

PATRON: Jack, Jack—that's a clumsy lie. You know what I think? I think you suspected I was behind it all along. It really wasn't that hard to figure out . . . but you didn't *want* to figure it out. Did you, Jack? You wanted an excuse to express some of the frustration that's been building up in you since we started having these little chats. But it proved a poor substitute, I'm sure. I'm sorry, Jack—I simply don't believe you.

CLOSER: You will.

For the first time, Jack signed off first. He glowered at the screen for a moment, then slammed his fist into the wall.

"Mother*fucker*," he hissed.

INTERLUDE

Fiona Stedman did a little pirouette and smiled impishly. "Well, Uncle Rick?" she asked. "What do you think?"

Rick Stedman studied his niece carefully. She wore an outfit she'd made herself, a full-length gown of black gauze with flowing, harem-style sleeves, the pattern embossed with tiny silver moons. A full moon pendant hung around her neck, and a tiara of stars perched on her head. A pair of sandals with elaborate black strapping wrapped around her calves finished it off.

"I think you're going to break some hearts," Rick said with a chuckle.

"Oh? You gonna give me lessons?" she shot back.

"Me? I wouldn't know the first thing about that," he deadpanned. He took a sip of his coffee and absently petted Rufus, who wriggled in glee and did his best to lick the skin off his hand.

"That's not what I hear," Fiona said. She threw herself down on the couch beside him. Rufus lunged for her lap, but Rick held him back.

"Hold it, fur-monster," he said. "I think she'll throttle you if you mess up her outfit."

"Mom says you're dating some blonde now," Fiona said. "What happened to Sophia? Or did she just dye her hair?"

"Uh, Sophia and me are just friends now," Rick said. "But yes, I do have a new girlfriend. Her name's Amber."

"Girlfriend? Girlfriend? That's the first time I've heard you use that word since The Evil One broke up with you."

Rick sighed. *"Her name was Karen. You're allowed to say it."*

"Well, she'll always be The Evil One as far as I'm concerned. So tell me about Amber."

"She's twenty-five, she's going to school and majoring in English, she plays a mean game of backgammon. And she's very cute."

"Sounds acceptable . . . any long-range plans?"

"You know, the usual—marriage, three kids, world domination. Science experiments in the garage, fleeing to a country without extradition."

"Right. I'm sure you'll be very happy in Lower Botswana."

"Actually," Rick said hesitantly, *"We are thinking about traveling. Maybe Asia, in the summer."*

"This *summer?"*

"I know, it's kinda soon—but I really like her. I'll bring her over, you'll see."

Fiona narrowed her eyes, then smiled. *"Okay. As long as she gets the Fiona stamp of approval."*

"How about you? How's your love life?"

She groaned and threw herself back on the couch. *"Don't ask. I'm so desperate for a date I'm starting to make up stalkers. The other day I managed to convince myself I was being followed."*

Rick frowned. *"What happened?"*

"Oh, don't look so worried. It was just a car looking for an address or something, driving slow. You know what my imagination is like."

"Yeah. It runs in the family, remember? Which

reminds me . . . I came over to show you something."

Fiona bounded up, her eyes bright. "What? Did you finish your costume? Finally?"

"Well, I don't know about finished—"

Fiona rolled her eyes. "Artists. 'You never finish anything—'"

"'—you abandon it.' *Yeah, I know. But it's close enough to show off."*

"Aha!" she crowed. "I knew what had to be in that big clanky duffel bag! Let me see!"

"Oh, no," he said. "You're gonna get the full effect. Wait here, I'm gonna go put it on. It may take me a few minutes."

"Hurry up!"

Fiona sat back down and tucked her legs up underneath herself. Rufus jumped up beside her, but he lay down when she told him to. "Well, Rufus?" she said to him. "What do you think it'll be? Something cool, for sure . . ."

Rufus panted eagerly. She scratched behind his ears and waited.

When her uncle walked through the door, she whispered, "Wow."

What he wore was clearly modeled on a Roman centurion's outfit, with an armored breastplate, short toga and crested helmet, but he'd used unusual materials. The breastplate was made of panels of stained glass, the pattern a radiating sun in the middle of the chest. The toga was made of the same kind of gauzy material Fiona had used but in a deep blue, emblazoned with miniature suns. The helmet was copper, with a sculpted face mask and a mohawklike crest of bright scarlet and yellow feathers

*carefully placed to simulate flames. Black leather
gauntlets and knee-high boots both sported burnished copper panels.*

"Here's to the Sun God, he's such a fun God, Ra!
Ra! Ra!" Rick said, his voice muffled by the mask.

Fiona sprang off the couch and hugged him.
Rufus started to bark.

"It's going to be the best Halloween ever," Fiona
said.

CHAPTER FOURTEEN

PATRON: Tomorrow's Halloween, Jack.
I haven't done one on Halloween yet. It seems a
bit obvious, don't you think? Too on-the-nose, too
Hollywood. Halloween is already about death, so
using my skills to link the day and the deed seems
redundant.

But therein lies the challenge.

Halloween is about *mocking* death. About
dressing it up in silly clothes, smothering it with
children and candy. About pretend scares, so we
can laugh after we shriek; about peering cautiously
into the Abyss before spitting into it. In that sense,
it's as innocent a holiday as any, perhaps more so.

And of course, Halloween is about masks.

Masks to hide behind, masks to reveal. Masks to
express our true selves. More art goes into this
celebration than any other, I think. How much
creativity goes into Easter or July the Fourth or
Saint Patrick's Day? They're about tradition and the
repeating of ritual behavior more than anything . . .

but few people wear the same Halloween costume two years in a row.

We've worn our own share of masks, haven't we, Jack? Djinn-X, Road Rage, Deathkiss, Furious George. Mr. Liebenstraum.

But the masks we wear now, of the Patron and the Closer, those are the Yin and Yang masks of our true faces. We both destroy in order to create. I created you . . . and so you must destroy me. Perfect symmetry.

But Jack, this dance is not quite done. As your progenitor, I have certain responsibilities, certain duties. I have wisdom and experience I must pass on to you. Don't worry, it won't be painful; quite the opposite. You've gone through the pain already, it's a part of you forever. It makes you strong. You simply need to learn to direct it properly . . . not that you haven't done admirably so far.

The only thing holding you back is that most useless of emotions, guilt. You've come so far, Jack; you're almost there. You don't need to feel bad about doing what you're so good at. Let go and a whole world will open up to you. A wonderful, creative world.

Perhaps hearing about my next project might inspire you. I'm rather proud of the concept myself, but I'm sure you could add so much more.

The artist in question is primarily a sculptor, though he works in a variety of materials. His work is good, his technique excellent, but he lacks that depth of feeling a real visionary needs. I think I know how to provide it.

He has a young niece. They visit often, and I

believe she has something of a schoolgirl crush on him. Here's what I'm considering: tie her naked to a bed, and tape firecrackers all over her body. Inspired, of course, by that brilliant gag you pulled with the sparkler. Placed strategically, I imagine you could selectively destroy quite a bit of the human body before causing death. Urban renewal on a physiological level— "This nipple to be demolished. Coming soon: a bloody, charred crater."

And of course, there's the smell. The scent of exploded firecrackers is a constant in the weeks before and after the end of October, and it's a smell that lingers; in a closed room, it should be quite pungent. Add a few decorations—a carved pumpkin, some cut-out ghosts and skeletons—and a CD playing that perennial favorite, "The Monster Mash." *Voilà!*

Still, it's a bit of a departure from my earlier work. I prefer a quick, clean kill, with the majority of the creative process being expressed after; my work is more postmortem than postmodern. The firecrackers will be unavoidably loud, messy, and unpredictable. In order to mount a successful piece, I believe a test run is called for.

How about I use Nikki?

It couldn't be. There was no way.

Jack paced back and forth in his motel room. He had the gun in one hand, and he kept reflexively thumbing the safety off and on.

"How? How?" he mumbled. He caught a glimpse of himself in the bathroom mirror as he stalked past the doorway; unshaven, no shirt, eyes bloodshot. He looked liked he belonged under a bridge with a bottle in his hand. He shook the gun at the image and demanded, "How? How, goddammit? How does he *know*?"

The wild man in the mirror had no answers.

Nikki hadn't worked since her "interview" with Richard. She *had* gone to the Stroll and asked a few questions of her own, but none of the girls had seen or talked to him. It seemed that she was the only one he was interested in.

Jack hadn't responded to the email she'd sent him, but that could mean anything. He might not have checked the account, or maybe he'd decided she was better off without him; she could see Jack doing that.

She didn't feel safe on the street anymore. It was time to move on, find another city; she should already be gone, but she wasn't sure where to go. One thing she did know: it wouldn't be to any of the cities she'd mentioned to Richard.

She ran in the evenings now, her biological clock swinging back to her natural rhythm as a night person. She wasn't sure what the dawn runs had been all about—something to do with fresh starts and isolation, she supposed. It had been what she needed to do, she'd done it, and now it was over. Running at dusk— the parks and paths filled with strolling couples, dog-walkers, other joggers—was what seemed natural now.

It was almost full dark by the time she got in, out of breath and sweaty. She unlocked the door to her suite, went straight to the fridge and got herself a beer.

The first thing she noticed was that the papers on her kitchen table had been moved.

It was a small thing, but Jack had trained Nikki to notice small things. Someone had been in her place.

She froze, put down her beer, and listened.

Nothing.

She always ran with the .38 in a fanny pack. She took it out now, took the safety off, and moved quickly and quietly from room to room. She searched the closets, the bathroom, beneath the bed. She was alone.

There were other traces that someone had been there—things ever so slightly askew or misplaced. When she returned to the living room, she checked the door and found scratches around the lock.

She frowned, picked up her beer and took a long swallow. Nothing had been taken—even the scratches might be old. Was she just being paranoid?

She searched the place again, looking for a reason. When she was done, she was even less sure than before; maybe she was jumping at ghosts. She sighed, sat down, and finished her beer.

Definitely time to move on, she thought. *This place is making me squirrelly.*

She thought about having another beer, but when she got up to get one, she felt suddenly dizzy. She sat back down.

Whoa. Maybe I need to have something to eat, instead. . . .

Too late, she realized her mistake. She grabbed for the phone, but her arms seemed a million miles long.

Everything went away.

CLOSER: Go ahead and boast. You have no idea what you're really dealing with.

You don't impress me, Patron. You're like all the rest of them, a pathetic loser who tells himself he's special because he does ugly things and no one can find him. That's a good description of *all* vermin, don't you think? I imagine rats and cockroaches and maggots think much the same thing as they wallow in filth: all this richness, just for me. I'm *special*.

You're a fake.

You don't understand what real torment is. A few eviscerations, a hanging or two, cutting some throats . . . gory, but over in moments. Do you know what it's like to torture someone for twelve hours straight? To have them piss and shit themselves in terror and pain? To have grown men beg and plead and cry for their lives as you make them suffer?

I do. And I'm very, very good at it.

You boast about creating artists because you have no talent yourself. You brag about murder because you don't have the balls to do what I do. Anyone can prey on the innocent; they make easy targets. Me, I hunt predators—and I always get what I go after.

You won't go after Nikki. I'm telling you this because you already know I'm going to catch you; you practically said so in your last message.

Well, here's a very simple promise from me: anything you do to her, I'll do to you.

A reply came back almost immediately:

PATRON: Harsh words, Jack—but heartfelt, I can tell.

Still, there's a certain desperation in them, isn't there? I hold all the cards here. I mean, you've even provided me with the means for a quick and merciful death from you—all I have to do is kill Nikki in the same manner. If, of course, you're a man of your word.

Sadly, though, that's not going to happen. Nikki's death will be long, agonizing, and worst of all—a complete mystery. You'll never find out exactly what happened to her, Jack. She'll simply vanish, another hooker swallowed by the street, and her body will never be found. I'll never tell . . . unless you make me.

There is an alternative, though, one that could save Nikki a great deal of suffering.

You could kill her yourself.

It's the only way to protect her, Jack. You didn't think I knew she even existed, but I know much, much more. I know where she is right now . . . and it's not with you.

You don't need her, Jack. You know that. The reason I kill the people close to artists isn't just about the fire of inspiration—it's about the fire of cleansing, of purity. A corpse focuses; a live person distracts.

Do what you have to.

"He's trying to make me rabbit," Jack muttered. "Make me panic, lose my head. Have to stay calm. Have to stay *focused.*"

He couldn't lead the Patron to her. Just because the Patron knew about Nikki didn't mean he knew where she was. But he knew a lot, that much was obvious. He knew about Jack, he knew about Nikki—

He had to find her. He just wasn't sure why.

"Oh no," Jack whispered. Suddenly, he understood. Mentioning Nikki was just a distraction. The Patron wanted to eliminate any humanizing influences from Jack's life, true—but there was a much more obvious target.

"The smell of firecrackers in October," Jack murmured. "You don't get that in the U.S., not until July. . . . Vancouver. He's in Vancouver."

A target the Patron had already revealed he knew about. Charlie.

Nikki opened her eyes. She wasn't sure where she was, or what had happened, but she knew it wasn't good. Her head was muzzy, her vision blurred. Drugged. She'd been drugged.

She was lying on a cot. Wrists and ankles tied to the frame. Overhead, cracked plaster and black Rorschach blots of mildew. She turned her head to one side, and that was enough to make her dizzy and nauseous. She fought it down.

Small room, bare wooden walls, exposed pipes. Looked abandoned, industrial. Against the far wall, another cot, with another person tied to it. Male, white, forties, dressed in white pants and a blue silk shirt. Bloodstained white bandage wrapped around his left hand. Gucci loafers. He wasn't moving, but she could hear him breathing. Unconscious?

Her head was starting to clear. She did a quick mental inventory of herself: she was in her underwear. All limbs accounted for. Earrings were gone, but her charm bracelet wasn't. No shoes.

The man on the other cot stirred, moaned.

"Hey," Nikki hissed. "You awake?"

The man tried to move, discovered he couldn't. His eyes struggled open. "Whuh?" he said.

"Keep it down," Nikki said in a low voice. "You all right?"

The man turned his head toward hers. He had a round, fleshy face with a bulbous nose, and he looked terrified. "What—who—who are you?" he croaked.

"My name's Nikki," she said. "Who the fuck are *you*?"

The man's face, already pasty, had blanched even whiter at her name. "Oh no," he said. "I'm sorry, he made me tell him, I—*he cut off my fingers!*" The man started to cry.

Nikki glanced at the man's bandaged hand. For a fleeting second, she thought he was talking about Jack . . . but she knew who it had to be. "Shit," she cursed softly. "C'mon, man, get it together. What's your name?"

"Charlie. Charlie Holloway . . ."

Charlie and Nikki were the only two people in the world Jack cared about. He left a hurried email to Nikki, then tried to call Charlie. He got only an answering machine, and hung up.

He paid for a week's rent in advance, and caught the next flight back to Vancouver; he took the laptop with him, but left the Stalking Ground equipment behind. He tried Charlie's number several times, from the airport and the plane, but nobody picked up.

He wondered if Charlie's voice on the machine was the last time he'd ever hear it.

He took a cab from the airport to Charlie's gallery. The gallery was dark and locked. He banged on the door—no answer.

He went around to the back. The fire escape in the alley was down; Jack looked around, saw no one watching, and climbed up. He tried a window on the second floor—it looked like it was painted shut.

He had no time to be subtle. He smashed the glass with his elbow.

No alarms went off, at least not ones he could hear. He kicked the shards hanging from the frame inside, and climbed in after them. He was in a hallway, with doors on either side and one at the end marked *Office*. He headed for it.

The door was open. Inside, a desk cluttered with papers and stacks of magazines. A couple of plush upholstered chairs along one wall. Three filing cabinets along another, and a separate desk with a computer on it.

There was blood on the keyboard. It was spattered across it in a wide arc, like someone with a nosebleed had done a pirouette.

He was too late.

"Listen to me, Charlie," Nikki said. She kept her voice quiet but forceful. "If we're gonna get out of this alive, we have to stay sharp. Focused. You with me?"

"Yes. *Yes*," Charlie said. "He's—he's insane. He's the one who killed Jack's family."

"I know," Nikki said grimly. "He calls himself the Patron. You and me are next on his list, and it's *not* gonna be pleasant. How tight are your ropes?"

"Uh—pretty tight."

"Well, see if you can loosen them. Never know if you don't try. I'm gonna do the same."

"All right. How—how did he get you?"

"Dosed me. I had a beer from my own fridge . . . that's the last thing I remember." Nikki tugged at the ropes, wished she'd been conscious when she was tied up—she could have tensed her muscles, given herself a little slack. "What about you?"

"It—what happened to me, it sounds crazy. I still don't believe it. I was working in my office, when suddenly he was just standing there. I didn't hear him come in or anything, it was like he just materialized. He was wearing this black cloak, and I couldn't see his face. He pointed his hand at me, and suddenly—I couldn't move."

"That's a new one," Nikki muttered.

"He tied me to my chair, and took out a pair of pruning shears . . ." Charlie's voice broke. After a moment, he went on. "And when he talked, his voice was all distorted. Inhuman."

"Voicebox modulator," Nikki said. "He's afraid you'll recognize his voice. Might be someone you know—or not. Could be he's just being really careful."

"He asked about you. About Jack. I didn't know much . . . but I told him. I told him everything I knew. I'm sorry." Charlie's voice was hardly more than a whisper.

"It's okay," Nikki said. "Everybody has a breaking point. Any luck with the ropes?"

"I—I think I can slide them along the bedframe."

"Good. Try and find an edge, a corner, anything you can rub them over."

"There's something sticking out—I think it's a screw or a bolt."

Nikki wasn't having any luck herself—the Patron had been more thorough with her. "Okay, rub the ropes over the screw," she said. "It might take a while, but don't give up. Keep at it."

"Okay, yes, I will. Oh, *Christ,* my hand hurts."

"You don't get us free before the Patron comes back," Nikki said, "and you might look back on that amount of pain with fond memories. . . ."

Jack prowled through Charlie's place, searching. He wasn't sure for what . . . but his gut told him he was missing something.

The building wasn't just Charlie's gallery, it was also his home; he used the upstairs rooms as his living space. Jack roamed from room to room, looking for anything that might tell him about where the Patron had taken its owner.

When he finally stumbled across it, he couldn't believe his eyes.

One of the rooms was a spare bedroom; Jack had crashed there once after a particularly late after-opening party. When Jack first stuck his head in, he thought Charlie had turned it into storage—paintings were hung on every available inch of wall space. But then he noticed the bed was still in the corner, and a small dresser and wardrobe had been added.

The painting over the bed was of a man lying in a twisted heap on the ground. Leering, demonic angels and a sharp-fanged God loomed over him.

"Salvatore Torigno," Jack whispered.

It was the same picture the Patron had downloaded to the Stalking Ground, back when Jack was posing as Deathkiss.

• • •

"The rope is fraying," Charlie said. "Oh God, I think this is going to work."

"Keep going," Nikki urged.

"It's coming apart! Almost—there!" Charlie pulled his wrists free with one convulsive yank. He sat up and fumbled at the cords binding his feet.

"Hurry!"

A second later, Charlie was standing over her. His eyes looked glazed.

"Don't just stand there, untie me!" Nikki hissed.

Charlie looked down at her. He didn't say a word.

Jack looked around the room slowly.

Every painting spoke of death and despair. Screaming faces and ripped flesh seemed to be the dominant theme. It was a room full of windows into Hell.

Jack walked over to the wardrobe and opened it. He already knew what he was going to find.

Shiny black latex, oiled leather, and chrome chains gleamed from the dozen or so outfits that neatly hung there. Apparently, the bedroom was no longer spare.

"Falmi," Jack breathed.

Outside, he could hear the pop and snap of firecrackers. Halloween had begun.

CHAPTER FIFTEEN

Charlie swayed, shook his head. "Sorry," he mumbled, "Still dizzy." He bent down and started working on Nikki's restraints. In a minute he had her free.

She stood and tried to rub circulation back into her wrists. The wooden floor was cold and rough under her bare feet. "Okay, Charlie. Try to find something we can use as a weapon."

They searched the room, came up with a length of rusty pipe. Nikki hung on to it—Charlie didn't look like he'd be much use in a fight. She tried the door, and it swung open without resistance.

"Come on," she said.

"Wait," Charlie whispered. "He didn't drug me until after he tied me to the bed—I remember the way out."

"Then lead the way. . . ."

They crept out into one end of a dark, dusty hall. Pigeon droppings crusted the floor, and the dim yellow glow of a streetlight through a dirty window to their left provided the barest illumination. They went the only way available, to their right.

• • •

Jack searched the rest of the room. There was a trunk under the bed; it was locked, but he found a hammer downstairs and smashed it open.

It was full of photographs. The ones on top were of Jack's family . . . and the rest were just as horrifying. The trunk also contained a semiautomatic pistol, five pairs of handcuffs, and a cell phone.

Jack heard the lock on the front door *chunk* open.

He picked up the gun, checked to make sure it was loaded and the safety was off. He could hear someone moving around downstairs; he slipped out of the room and positioned himself next to the stairs.

A minute later, Falmi's skeletal frame shambled up the steps. Jack waited until Falmi had one foot in the hallway, then poked the gun into the dead-white side of his neck.

"Hello, Falmi," Jack said. "I've got a few questions to ask you."

It got darker as they moved away from the window, until Charlie was a barely discernible blur in front of her. There didn't seem to be any other doors in the hall. She stepped on something sharp—broken glass, most likely—and winced but didn't cry out. Her stomach churned, nauseous with the aftereffects of the drug and adrenaline.

"There's a staircase here, going down," Charlie whispered. "Careful."

The stairs creaked and complained under their weight; to Nikki it sounded as loud as gunshots. She thought about booby traps, swallowed, and kept going.

The stairs went down to a landing, then angled to the left. Once around the corner, there was light once more, halogen glare filtering through some kind of grate high in the wall. It was enough to show that the stairwell ended in a door.

"Don't let it be locked, don't let it be locked," Charlie murmured, and pulled on the handle.

"You're out of your fucking mind," Falmi said. His voice trembled, ever so slightly.

Jack had him cuffed to the chair in the office. He studied the Goth intently, not saying a word. Not moving, not blinking. Thinking.

"I don't know what this is about, okay?" Falmi said. "Just *talk* to me, all right?"

"Where is he?" Jack asked calmly.

"Who, Charlie? He said he had an interview—"

"Stop it. You know you can't lie to me—not for long."

"I'm not lying!" Falmi sounded close to tears. "He had an interview with some new artist he's interested in, some guy named Stedman—"

"An artist with a young niece, right? An artist that needs a little push . . . is that where you just came from?"

"I don't know what you're *talking* about—"

"Ssssh." Jack held a finger to his lips. "I understand. After all the buildup, you need to *see*, firsthand. To experience the end result of your 'art.' To find out just what you've changed me into . . ."

He stared into Falmi's eyes. "All right," Jack said softly. "I'll give you what you want. And you'll tell me what I want to hear."

He didn't have his equipment with him, but Jack was sure he could make do.

The door swung open.

Revealing a solid brick wall, blocking the entrance.

"What the *fuck?*" Nikki said. She stepped forward, put her hand flat against it. The bricks were cool, pitted, the mortar holding them in place crumbly with age. They looked like they'd been there for decades.

"No," Charlie said. His voice was loud and echoey in the stairwell. "No, that's impossible. This is the way we came—it's the *only* way, goddammit. It's not fucking *possible.*"

Nikki pushed on the wall, tried to find some kind of secret door. Nothing.

"He's not human. He's not human. That's how he paralyzed me, that's how he did this, he's some kind of fucking *demon*—"

Charlie's voice was getting high and panicky. Nikki whirled and said "Shut up!" but the snarl she tried to put into her voice sounded shaky, scared.

And then she saw the look on Charlie's face.

He was grinning.

"Oh, I'm sorry, Nikki," Charlie said, chuckling. "I just couldn't resist. I suppose I'm something of a trickster at heart—and after all, it *is* Halloween." In the dim light, a pistol glinted in his right hand.

"I've never done this to someone I know," Jack said.

He'd wheeled the office chair into the kitchen. He

turned the front element of the stove on to high. "But then, I don't really know you at all, do I?"

"Jack, I know we've never been close, but *Jesus Christ*—"

Jack opened the silverware drawer, rummaged inside. He selected a large, serrated knife, and a pair of metal tongs.

"Pretend I don't know what's going on," Falmi said. *"Please,* Jack."

"You should concentrate less on ignorance and more on bargaining," Jack said. He wedged the blade of the knife between the coils of the element. "Because this session is going to have to be more . . . *condensed* than usual. This location isn't secure or soundproof, so I'm going to have to improvise."

"Bargaining? What the fuck do you *want?*"

"The truth."

"Look, the truth is that I'm scared *shitless*, okay? Can't you *see* that?"

Jack looked at Falmi expressionlessly. "I saw the paintings in your room. Quite the collection."

"Those? Those are Charlie's, he just stores them there, he knows I like that kind of stuff—"

"And the trunk under your bed?"

"What? I don't *have* a trunk under my bed, just some old art supplies—"

Jack placed a pen and a pad of paper on the edge of the kitchen table, within reach of Falmi's cuffed hand. "One hand. One eye. One ear," Jack said. "That's all I require you to have. Everything else I can subtract . . ."

He grabbed Falmi's lower lip, yanked downward to make him open his mouth. He reached inside with the tongs, clamped onto the tip of his tongue. Stretched it out between his teeth while Falmi's eyes bulged in terror. *"You killed my family,"* Jack hissed.

The serrated knife on the stove was glowing red-hot down its length, white where the blade pressed against the element. Jack pulled it free with his other hand.

"I don't want you choking on your own blood," Jack said. "The heat *should* cauterize the stump . . ."

Falmi scrabbled for the pen, began to write frantically.

Jack looked down, read what Falmi had scrawled. *Warehouse.*

Jack released Falmi's tongue. "Paintings," Falmi gasped. "Charlie's got lots more. Paintings, art, sculpture. Took me there once. Called it his legacy. Maybe that's where he is now, I don't know—"

"How do I know it's not *your* warehouse?"

"I—I don't know."

"You're his assistant. You're in the perfect position to frame him. Plant evidence, register things in his name."

"But I haven't!"

Jack stared at him. "No, you haven't. . . you kept the paintings and the trunk in your own room."

"I don't *own* a fucking trunk!"

"Perception," Jack murmured. "Art isn't an object. It's a sense . . ."

A sense to be manipulated.

"You know that moment when you're studying a piece, and suddenly you get it?" he asked Falmi. "I think I just did."

He turned off the stove, put the knife in the sink and ran some water. Steam hissed into the air.

"Tell me what you know about this new artist," Jack said.

• • •

"I may be gone for a while," Charlie said. He'd returned Nikki to her room; this time he'd used handcuffs to secure her to the bed and gagged her before wheeling in an oxygen tank on a dolly. "I have some trick-or-treating to do, as well as a costume to pick up. But don't worry—I'll be back before this runs out." The hose from the tank was attached to a military-style gas mask; Charlie slipped it over Nikki's head, then securely strapped it in place. He fiddled with a small device attached to the tank and adjusted the flow.

All Nikki could do was glare.

"Oh, come on," Charlie said with a chuckle. He took out a prefilled syringe and uncapped the needle. "Don't you want to be immortalized? That's what art is really all about, you know—ego. Artists are all desperate to be remembered. Of course, you're *not* an artist, are you?" He stuck the needle in her neck and pressed the plunger. "You're just a whore . . ."

He turned out the lights when he left, leaving her alone in the dark. Sinking into a deeper blackness.

INTERLUDE

"The Parade of Lost Souls," Fiona breathed.

She'd read about it for years, even did a report on the Mexican Day of the Dead festival it was based on, but she'd never been allowed to go before. Now, it swirled past her in all its dark, heady glory. Stilt-walkers dressed as gigantic skeletons strode past, holding aloft blazing torches; devils capered and danced to the insistent pulse of hand-beaten drums; lanterns of colored paper shaped like stars, ships, birds, beasts, and a hundred other forms were lofted high on poles; neon glow-ropes outlined elaborate costumes or spun past threaded through the spokes of bikes. The air smelled of burning kerosene and damp vegetation.

It was all wonderful, but ... where was Uncle Rick?

He was supposed to pick her up at her house and drive her to his studio, where they were going to get ready. But when she'd gotten home from school there'd been a message that he'd had a sudden emergency and was going to be late. They'd arranged to meet at a corner down on the Drive, in-stead. She didn't mind taking the bus—her costume was easier to travel in than Uncle Rick's—but she was a little nervous about being alone, especially without her cell phone. She was still annoyed some-one had stolen it two days ago.

And then a car pulled up, and somebody leaned over and waved at her. It looked like Uncle Rick, al-

ready in costume—she caught a flash of copper. She reached for the door.

Abruptly, someone pushed past her. A man, wearing a black leather trenchcoat, someone she didn't recognize. He opened the door, got in and slammed it shut.

"Hey!" she said. The car pulled away from the curb, leaving her standing there. She caught only a glimpse of the back of the driver's head . . . but she was suddenly sure it wasn't her uncle at all. It wasn't even his car.

"Weird," she muttered. She must have made a mistake.

CHAPTER SIXTEEN

"You're not going to shoot me, Jack." Charlie's voice behind the mask was muffled, but confident.

Jack kept the gun leveled at Charlie's belly. "If I have to, I will. Keep driving."

"Can I take the headgear off?"

"Go ahead."

Charlie pulled the helmet off at a red light. "Ah, that's better," he said, smiling. "Face-to-face at last."

"You fucking bastard," Jack said.

"I know questions are really *your* forte," Charlie said, "but I have a few of my own. How'd you find me?"

"Falmi helped me track down Stedman. You'd already decoyed him away from his niece, but I convinced him to tell me where they were supposed to be meeting."

"How? Pull a few teeth?"

"No. I told him I'd found a cell phone in the back of my cab and his number was the first one in the directory."

"And he told you his niece's cell phone had recently been stolen. How did you know?"

"I found the cell phone you stashed under the bed to incriminate Falmi."

"So Stedman gave you a description and told you where she'd be, so you could return her phone. Smart." Charlie nodded. "I have to say, this is both a relief and a disappointment. I mean, I've really enjoyed our interaction online and I'm sorry it's over, but it's also great to be able to talk honestly—"

Jack hit him in the mouth with the gun. Charlie's head snapped back; the car swerved abruptly to the right, and then Charlie regained control. He glanced at Jack, and grinned. Blood trickled from the corner of his mouth. He spat a tooth onto the dashboard.

"Heh. Guess I should have expected that," he said.

"You're going to be a long time dying," Jack said.

"Before you hit me again, you should know—I have Nikki."

"Prove it."

"Five foot six in her bare feet, bright blue eyes, nice tan, and a charm bracelet she's *very* attached to; I couldn't get it off. I'll bet every one of those charms reminds her of a different dead friend . . . that's how you persuaded her to join you, isn't it?"

"Tell me how you found her."

"You really *are* brilliant, Jack. Your secret weapon? A hooker! All those people who thought the Closer had to be a cop, using inside information to nail serial killers . . . and it turns out his information is a lot more 'inside' than anybody thought." Charlie laughed out loud, exposing bloodstained teeth. "I mean, come on! It's like Batman pimping Robin! 'Let's go, Boy Wonder—and don't forget the Bat-Condoms!'"

"Tell me where she is."

"She's tied up, with a limited oxygen supply," Charlie said. "About an hour's worth. Think you can break me in an hour, Jack?"

"No."

"Good answer! You played a nice end-game, Jack, but I've been playing this game longer than you. . . . I knew you two must have had a little spat after doing the Gourmet. That didn't go quite as planned, did it? Police reports were sketchy, but they made it sound more like a home invasion gone wrong than an interrogation."

"I cut her loose. I can always find another whore."

"*Excellent,* Jack. Always negotiate from a position of strength . . . and knowledge is strength. You want to know how I found her? Easy. I never really *lost* her. Nikki Jasper. Thirty-four. Born in Toronto, birthday is April 11. I hired a private detective to keep tabs on you three years ago, Jack—ugly little fellow, but very efficient. After you recruited Nikki, I had her checked out quite thoroughly. See, I always had high hopes for you, Jack. I kept an eye on you . . . right from the beginning."

"You knew I was the Closer. All along."

"Of course. This whole dance was choreographed, Jack. I could've stopped you at any time . . . but why should I? Do you realize how singular you and I are? There is no one—*no one*—in the world who has accomplished what you and I have. We belong to the realm of *legend* . . . and when you and your sidekick split up, I knew Vancouver was the place she'd probably run back to. Just like you did. Despite what you say, the two of you must have quite the bond. Guess the only tie stronger than sex is death. Isn't it, Jack?"

"Where are we going?" They'd been driving for a few minutes now; Charlie had taken them north, toward the industrial docks on the other side of Hastings.

"I want to show you something. Don't worry, Nikki's nearby. You might even save her life . . . if you'll listen to me for a few minutes more."

Charlie pulled the car into a gravel parking lot beside a two-story warehouse. A faded, barely legible sign over the door read Kim Luc Imports.

Charlie turned off the motor. "Come on in, Jack. Not too many people have seen this." He got out of the car. Jack followed, keeping the gun on him. Charlie hardly seemed to notice it was there.

Charlie unlocked the front door and they went inside. The interior of the warehouse wasn't what Jack expected; the ceiling was no higher than an ordinary room, but a long hallway extended all the way to the back of the building, at least a hundred feet. Doorways were spaced evenly along its length on either side. Overhead spotlights sprang to life as Charlie flicked a switch.

"This is my real gallery, Jack," Charlie said. "Everything in here, I'm directly responsible for. None of it would exist without me. I want you to consider that before you do anything else." For the first time Jack got a good look at the outfit Charlie was wearing: a breastplate made of stained glass in a solar design, a blue toga emblazoned with suns, and boots and gauntlets made of leather and polished copper. He looked like a modern-day incarnation of Nero, an emperor of madness and flames.

Jack raised the gun. "Ten minutes. After that, you

take me to Nikki—or I'll burn everything in this place, piece by piece, and make you watch."

Charlie's grin vanished. He nodded. "Fair enough. This way . . ."

Everything in the first room was made of light.

At least, that was how it seemed to Jack. The artist had used various sources of light—neon, bulbs, ultraviolet, even monitors—then redirected them with mirrors, magnifiers, colored filters. Specific images were heightened or reflected, multiplied or distorted. A chandelier hung from the ceiling, shards of mirror suspended from electroluminescent wires of vivid scarlet. In the center of the chandelier, a nude figurine of glass, a woman with her arms over her head. The base of the figurine held a bulb that simulated a candle flame; the light seemed to fill the figure to bursting. Every line of her body was underscored in brilliance, from the muscled tautness of her calves to the elegant curves between hip and breast. The shards surrounding her revolved slowly: one side was a true mirror, while the other was some kind of foil, ever so slightly crinkled, reflecting an image warped and jagged. The shards were hung so thickly it was impossible to see the entire figure at once—glimpses of beauty were all you could catch, interspersed with bits of unpredictable, distorted sharpness.

The piece was simply labeled *Memory*. It was the most beautiful thing Jack had ever seen.

There were others, too: a cluster of words made from blue neon, interlinked in such a way that they merged into a complex maze at their center—Jack could make out *Skin*, *Sweet* and *Loss*. There were images projected onto twisting screens of silk, mosaics made of stained glass, even a hologram suspended in a teardrop-shaped container of liquid. The same woman appeared in almost every piece.

"You killed her," Jack said.

"And he immortalized her," Charlie replied. "In beauty and wonder, and awe. You can't deny it, Jack . . . there is *genius* here. I know you see it. *And I created it.*"

"It's too high a price."

"Is it? Come on, Jack—you went to art school, you know how many artists had horrible, screwed-up lives. True talent thrives under that kind of pressure. All I'm doing is replacing the chaos of natural disasters with directed ones. . . ."

"I understand the process. What I don't understand is what you want from *me*," Jack snarled. "I'm not going to create anything like this, Charlie. I create *suffering,* I create *horror.* I'm not your greatest success, I'm your biggest failure."

"Not true," Charlie said softly. He put a hand up to the chandelier, set it spinning with a gentle push. "All the artists who are represented here have one thing in common: their art is reactive. They're responding to what I did to them, to their lives. But you—you did something else. You made a choice, turned your pain inward instead of outward. You chose transformation over expression."

"I know what I did."

"But you don't understand the implications. Expression is basically selfish—but what *you* did was not. You gave up your humanity, Jack. You chose to become a monster, for the sake of the greater good. *Just like me.*"

"What?" Jack whispered.

Charlie spread his arms, indicated the art around him. "Right now, the value of all this is going up and up," Charlie said. "And when it gets high enough, I'm going to sell. Send it out into the world. And long after those people I killed are forgotten, all this will live on. It will inspire, it will uplift, it will bring joy. In the end, I'll have made the world a better place. . . ."

"And you'll be rich."

"Yes. And you'll be dead or in jail . . . unless you join me."

Jack just stared at him.

"We deserve to be rewarded, Jack. Both of us. We do important work, and we do it isolated and unthanked. That's why I joined the Stalking Ground in the first place—I wanted to find someone I could share this with. Someone who might understand. All I found were lunatics and rapists—until you."

"What do you *want* from me? Congratulations? Absolution? *What?*" Jack shouted.

"I want a partnership, Jack," Charlie said. "You and me. You keep the Stalking Ground going, and I keep doing what I do. I'm a much better partner than Nikki could ever be . . . because I can do things she'd never dare. With my credibility on your side, we can *triple* the size of the Stalking Ground—you'll have your pick of victims. We can go *global*, Jack. Think of all the killers you can end—"

"Anyone but you," Jack said. "I can kill anyone but you."

"Yes." Charlie met Jack's eyes. "We've been friends a long time, Jack. Right now, you might think you don't really know me—but you do. You know what matters to me. I really think we could make this *work* . . . as long as we maintain the balance of power. I'm going to take something out now; don't be alarmed." From the folds of his toga, Charlie pulled out a small black unit that looked like a remote control. He held it up for Jack to see. "This is a little extra insurance, Jack. I press this button, Nikki's air supply gets cut off. She'll asphyxiate in around two minutes. I'll make you a deal, though—I'll trade this for your gun."

Jack thought about it. "Deal."

He held out the gun, still pointed at Charlie's head. He reached for the remote—and at the last second, hit the cartridge release. The magazine dropped to the floor as Charlie took the gun and Jack snatched the remote.

Charlie laughed. He tucked the gun into his belt as Jack kicked the magazine into a corner. "Nicely done. Now that we're on a more even footing, I want you to give serious consideration to my offer. And if you accept—Nikki goes free."

Jack backed away. His head throbbed. It was insane . . . but then, so was everything else about his life. He'd already traded away so much—was this any different? Nikki could be safe. And no matter what he did, his family would still be dead. . . .

"Time's almost up, Jack," Charlie said. "There's one last thing you should know." Charlie hesitated, then said, "They didn't suffer."

"They. You mean—"

"Your family. I killed them, but everything else was done postmortem. I can even prove it—look." Charlie pointed at the corner.

Jack turned. A Polaroid was pinned to the wall. He swallowed, and took a step closer.

Details came into focus. It was a picture of Janine, Sam and his parents. They were lined up in the living room, in front of the Christmas tree; his father looked angry, the rest of them looked terrified.

"This doesn't prove anything," Jack said. He turned back—

Charlie was gone.

He'd been standing next to a full-length mirror that had been used as a canvas—and, Jack saw when he looked closer, to disguise a door. It was ajar now; Jack reached out and pulled it open. The room beyond was dark.

An overhead spotlight snapped on.

A monstrous figure reached for Jack with huge, missshapen hands, its mouth stretched open in a silent scream of rage. Jack shouted, backpedaled, lost his footing. He crashed to the floor, trying to cushion his fall with one arm and fend off the attack with the other—

An attack that never came.

Heart hammering, Jack looked around. The room was full of statues, most of them life-size. Their faces radiated intense emotions: fear, grief, rage. All of them were reaching forward, straining for something just out of their grasp. He got to his feet.

Charlie was nowhere to be seen—but there was another door at the end of the room.

Jack made his way through the gallery slowly, alert for traps. Halfway across the room, he heard Charlie's voice—from a speaker mounted near the ceiling.

"The artist's name is René Deslane," Charlie said. He sounded slightly out of breath. "Wonderful *yearning* quality to his work, isn't there?"

Jack didn't bother answering. He kept moving faster now.

"You don't really want a gallery tour, do you, Jack? That's all right. The work speaks for itself."

The next room was hung with paintings, floor to ceiling canvases. Lots of black, lots of red—that was all that registered as Jack broke into a run. There were two doors, one leading out to the hall and one connecting to the next room. Another speaker was on the ceiling. Jack kept going in a straight line, trusting his instincts.

"Nikki's running out of air, Jack. You know what I think you should do? Just press the button on the remote. She's been drugged, so she'll suffocate without even waking up. No more pain for her, Jack—don't you think that's the greatest gift you could give her? No more back alley blow jobs, no more living in fear of dying horribly or spending the rest of her life in prison. You wouldn't even have to watch. Press the button, Jack . . ."

Through another door. Framed black-and-white photographs, a wall-size collage blurred past.

"You can't even turn me in to the police, Jack. I rented this warehouse in Falmi's name, told him it was a tax dodge. I made sure he was working, alone, every murder I committed; I've gotten his prints on weapons, planted all sorts of evidence. I've had a long time to think this through, Jack. I'm what the textbooks call an *organized* killer."

He stopped. The door leading to the next room was closed; all the others had been ajar. Jack whirled, dashed for the one leading to the hall, instead. It was closed, too, but unlocked. He yanked it open.

The corridor was dark and empty . . . but at its end, on the other side, a thin crack of light shone from the bottom of a door frame.

Jack crept quietly down the hall. He could still hear Charlie's voice, coming from the galleries. He wondered how many of them there were, how many rooms stocked with distilled torment and destroyed lives.

He reached the door. Stopped, with his hand hovering above the doorknob.

Abruptly, he took several steps backward, and wrenched open the door he had just passed.

Charlie stood with a double-barreled shotgun aimed directly at the wall. A hole had been knocked through it, with some sort of cloth covering it up on the other side. The only light in the room spilled from the face of an ancient amplifier on a table. A cord led from it to the microphone in Charlie's hand.

As Jack leaped for him, Charlie whirled and fired.

The impact caught Jack high on the left side, spinning his body but not stopping him. Pain seared all the way down his arm and into his shoulder. He slammed into Charlie at an awkward angle, knocking him back and into the wall.

Jack hit him as hard as he could with a right, snapping Charlie's head to the side. He grappled for the shotgun with his left, but his arm was starting to go numb.

Charlie brought his knee up into Jack's belly, doubling him over. Jack had a grip on the barrel of the shotgun with his left hand, and managed to keep it pointed away from him. He clawed at Charlie's face with his free hand, trying for his eyes. Charlie threw

an elbow into Jack's face, smashing his nose in a deto-
nation of pain. His vision blurred, but he hung on to
the barrel grimly. Charlie yanked on the gun, bringing
it between them, pointed at the ceiling.

Jack grabbed for the trigger guard with his right
hand. With the last of his strength, he pushed the barrel forward and the stock back.

The gun went off under Charlie's chin.

Jack staggered back, tripped over his own feet and
crashed to the ground. Charlie fell backward, knocking over the table with the PA system. He sprawled to
the floor, blood seeping from his throat.

Jack gasped for breath. He felt light-headed, dizzy.
He wondered how badly he was hurt.

"You're—not dying, Jack," a voice said wetly.

Charlie lifted his head from the floor. His neck was
covered in blood, but there was no gaping wound. "My
own—invention," Charlie managed. His voice sounded
like he was drowning. "Chloral hydrate crystals instead
of—buckshot. Fast-acting . . . knockout. Guess the first
to wake . . . is the one that wins."

Everything was going gray. He could barely hear
Charlie's final words.

"Either way . . . Nikki dies . . ."

The last thing Jack heard were sirens, getting closer.

The first thing he saw when he opened his eyes was
green.

He blinked a few times until his eyes focused. It
was a drab, industrial green. It surrounded him on
all sides. He tried to raise his hand, and it moved

only a few inches before it stopped with an audible clink.

The green was curtains, drawn around his bed. A bed with chrome handrails, that he was handcuffed to. He was in a hospital.

Slowly, Charlie Holloway smiled.

The police must have responded to the gunshots. They'd found him and Jack. Both of them were now in custody . . . but Charlie wouldn't be for long. Even if they found Nikki's body in the hidden room upstairs, he could still pin it on Falmi.

He heard footsteps. The curtain was drawn aside.

The walls of his room were made of shiny, black plastic.

"Hello, Patron," Nikki said. "How did you enjoy *my* little mind-fuck? See, us whores know a few things about tricks, *too.*"

Charlie gaped at her.

"For instance," Nikki said, "this." She held up her wrist with the charm bracelet dangling from it. "You were so sure this was a bunch of sentimental shit you never took a second look at it. Otherwise, you might of noticed one of these charms is a handcuff key . . . works on most models, too, at least the cheapass ones. You hadn't shot me full of dope, I would have been outta there thirty seconds after you closed the door. 'Course, once I woke up, it took me a few minutes to find the real exit—and guess who I found taking a nap downstairs?"

"You—you *bitch*—" Charlie rasped. His throat ached.

"Save your voice," Nikki said. "You're gonna need it."

She pulled the curtain the rest of the way aside.

Jack stood beside a long table. Various instruments gleamed under the glare of a single lamp.

"He's all yours," Nikki said.

Jack reached down and pressed the Record button on a small tape recorder. His face was expressionless.

"Let's go back to the beginning," the Closer said.

EPILOGUE

Dear Electra:

This was one of the strangest Halloweens ever.

Don't get me wrong, I had lots of fun. Uncle Rick was late, but we still managed to catch the parade. What really sucked, though, is that someone broke into his car and stole his costume. Jerks. And somebody found my cell phone and was supposed to return it, but they never showed.

Uncle Rick still dressed up, though—he grabbed some old stuff from his studio and made this kind of werewolf/astronaut thing on the fly. It looked weird but it "worked as a concept," as Uncle Rick said. And it still kind of went with my Moon Goddess costume, though it wasn't as cool as his Sun God. Sigh.

Still, it was a blast. There were people spinning fire around on chains and a big metal dragon on wheels and thousands of people. The streets the parade went down were decorated too, with jack-o'-lanterns and spiderwebs and torches. I think what I liked best, though, were the shrines in the park. They were all dedicated to different people or groups or even things—the only thing they had in common was, well, death. There was a shrine for pets that had passed on, and another to people who had died of AIDS. There was even one for murder victims. You could light a candle, or incense, and put something personal on a little altar. People left pictures, toys, flowers, clothes—all kinds of stuff. I even saw an electric mixer. I guess almost anything can remind you of someone if you miss them enough.

And then, of course, the very next day IT happened.

Christmas.

I don't know why I should be surprised, Electra. I mean, it happens every year—the day after Halloween, Santa and company hit town like a convention of drunk reindeer salesmen. Sometimes it even starts before October 31, which as far as I'm concerned is a hanging offence.

Uncle Rick agrees with me—which is why he and his new girlfriend are taking off. They're going to travel around the Pacific Rim for two months, and they're not coming home until the last Frosty the Snowman has been put back into cold storage. They're gonna just bypass the whole commercialized holiday thing: no carols, no Santas, no Christmas trees or lights or decorations.

I tell you, Electra: some people just don't know how lucky they are.

Not sure what to read next?

**Visit Pocket Books online at
www.SimonSays.com**

Reading suggestions for
you and your reading group
New release news
Author appearances
Online chats with your favorite writers
Special offers
And much, much more!

POCKET BOOKS
A Division of Simon & Schuster
A VIACOM COMPANY

POCKET STAR BOOKS
A Division of Simon & Schuster
A VIACOM COMPANY